MW01004488

BISON FRONTIERS OF IMAGINATION

Master of Adventure

The Worlds of Edgar Rice Burroughs

Richard A. Lupoff

WITH AN INTRODUCTION TO THE BISON BOOKS EDITION BY THE AUTHOR

FOREWORD BY MICHAEL MOORCOCK

PREFACE BY HENRY HARDY HEINS

WITH AN ESSAY BY PHILLIP R. BURGER

University of Nebraska Press
Lincoln and London

Library of Congress Cataloging-in-Publication
Data
Lupoff, Richard A., 1935–
[Edgar Rice Burroughs]
Master of adventure: the worlds of Edgar
Rice Burroughs / by Richard A. Lupoff;
with an introduction to the Bison Books
edition by the author, foreword by Michael
Moorcock, with an essay by Phillip R. Burger.
p. cm.—(Bison frontiers of imagination)
Originally published: Edgar Rice Burroughs.
New York: Canaveral Press, 1965.
Includes bibliographical references and index.
ISBN 0-8032-8030-0 (pbk.: alk. paper)
1. Burroughs, Edgar Rice, 1875–1950.
2. Authors, American—20th century—Biog-
raphy. 3. Adventure stories, American—
History and criticism. 4. Fantasy fiction,
American—History and criticism. 5. Tarzan
(Fictitious character) I. Title. II. Series.
PS3503.U687Z77 2005
813'.52—dc22 2004024160

For Pat

Contents

List of Illustrations

The four drawings (which includes the cover) by Al Williamson and Reed Crandall were created especially for the first edition of this book. The drawings by Crandall alone and those by Frank Frazetta were commissioned for Canaveral Press editions of Burroughs novels that in the end never appeared.

MICHAEL MOORCOCK

Foreword

It's probably fair to say that I owe my career to Edgar Rice Burroughs. From the age of fourteen I produced an ERB fanzine, *Burroughsiana*, before I really knew what fanzines were. Through it I discovered the world of science-fiction fandom and began to exchange letters with Richard Lupoff!

When I was sixteen I interviewed the editor of *Tarzan Adventures* in London. He didn't much like my interview, but his assistant liked it a lot. Before I knew it I was writing a series of articles about Burroughs for that magazine. *Tarzan Adventures* published reprints of the Sunday newspaper strips as well as original text features and fiction. Soon the assistant editor, the new editor, had commissioned a serial, an ERB pastiche, for *Tarzan Adventures*. This was *Sojan the Swordsman*, my first fantasy hero. The new editor offered me the job of assistant. My career in journalism and fiction had begun.

In the late 1950s, by the time I was seventeen, I was editing the magazine and filling it with all kinds of Burroughs-derived science fiction and fantasy as well as more features about Edgar Rice Burroughs himself. By the 1960s, when my magazine *New Worlds* needed financing, I wrote a series of Burroughs-type novels to support it (more of this later). My last close association with Burroughs was writing *The Land that Time Forgot* for Amicus Films in the early 1970s. As Lupoff does, I regard that novel as probably Burroughs' finest, with an intriguing idea that puts it firmly in the realm of science fiction, even though the form of the story is more of a fantasy adventure. I worked with Jim Cawthorn, a long-time friend and Burroughs illustrator, who had also drawn strips and written stories for *Tarzan Adventures*. Cawthorn broke the book down into scenes. I then did the finished script, turning the stereotypical German U-boat commander into, I hope, a subtler character who became the intellectual "voice" for the story's fascinating central idea, which Lupoff describes in detail here.

Cawthorn and I also wrote an outline for the sequel, *The People that Time Forgot*, but after seeing the final shots of the first film, we pulled out from any further involvement. We had hoped to bring "authentic" Burroughs to the screen. We didn't want any part of producing further bastardizations.

We had been attracted to doing the film for the same reasons Richard Lupoff liked the book—it is perhaps one of the two best science fiction ideas Burroughs ever had. In the hands of its producer, John Dark, *The Land that Time Forgot* (with Doug McClure and Susan Penhaligan) rather obscured its central idea and came dangerously close to being just another dinosaur picture with a volcanic explosion as the cliched denouement, robbing the movie of much of its special atmosphere, although some, I think, was retained.

The same company corrupted Burroughs' novel *At The Earth's Core*, another of his best works, but luckily box office receipts began to drop, as they deserved to, so that the producers gave up any further attempts to bastardize the work of a writer who, for all his faults of repetition and sometimes hasty writing, deserved far better treatment. What was more, as I understood it, Edgar Rice Burroughs, Inc., the company which looks after Burroughs copyrights, couldn't stand the bastardization any better than we could. Aside from some decent versions of Tarzan made in recent years, ours was more or less the last attempt to make a movie worthy of Burroughs' originals. He has never been well served by movies, which, considering that he lived within driving distance of most of the Hollywood studios, has always seem ironic to me.

It makes me wonder whether, for instance, John Carter's Martian adventures will ever successfully be brought to the screen. I would love to see the moody landscapes of the Red Planet populated with baroquely armored Tharks and their noble human foes, the ancient towers of gorgeous Helium rising into the thin air, the horrors of the River Iss, the lazy curve of fliers as they stream across the skies beneath the twin moons of Mars. It would need the same sort of loving attention as that which brought *Lord of the Rings* to the screen, but it would definitely beat anything *Star Wars* has yet been able to offer. If they ever do decide to make the movies, I hope the writers, director, and producers will read Lupoff's excellent account of the stories and their merits before they begin.

Lupoff has an intelligent, sensitive taste for the virtues of Burroughs' books. Not only can he explain the merits of Burroughs' best work, he can say what's wrong with the fiction that doesn't measure up to the best.

I was surprised to learn from this book how poorly served American readers were with Burroughs during the years I was most enjoying him.

Unlike American readers of the 1950s I had plenty of Burroughs available to me in the United Kingdom. The Methuen hardbacks with their wonderful J. Allen St. John dust wrappers were still cramming our library shelves while the Pinnacle paperbacks could be bought at any bookstore or railway newsstand. Not only the Tarzan stories, but the Martian, Venusian, Pellucidarian, and other novels could be found everywhere. It was even possible to get relatively obscure titles, such as *The Outlaw of Torn* and, as I recall, *The Bandit of Hell's Bend*, *The Eternal Lover*, and *Apache Devil*. Why this should have been so, I have no idea, except that perhaps Burroughs' popularity remained high in Britain, where we did not have quite so many rival fantasy publications in the years immediately following the Second World War.

The paperback covers weren't always the best, but I spent many a summer vacation acquiring and reading most of what ERB had published in book form before his death. When I bought secondhand hardbacks I could even write to Methuen and ask for fresh jackets, which they were happy to send entirely free of charge! A different and happier era!

Contrary to George Orwell's predictions about the bad influence of popular fiction on young minds, I did not grow up to become a fascist, racist, or casual killer of beasts and men from reading Burroughs. Indeed I somehow managed to be a left winger, a committed antiracist, and a preserver of animal life firmly opposed to the death penalty! If I now blanch at some of the disgusting racial language which so infects Burroughs' work, as it does that of John Buchan, Edgar Wallace, Ernest Hemingway, and a mass of lesser writers, I can always listen to the BBC serialization of, say, *Tarzan of the Apes*, which was cleansed of its racist comments and stereotypes yet lost none of the pace and pleasure of the original. A talking book can get rid of a multitude of sins.

Burroughs was indeed a master tale-spinner. The serial devices he used keep readers turning pages as fast as you would in Dickens. His influence on the likes of Robert E. Howard, Leigh Brackett, Philip Farmer, and Fritz Leiber continues to be felt in the work of writers *they* influenced. He is without doubt a key figure in the history of science fiction, fantasy, and adventure fiction.

In the mid-1960s, as I said, I paid direct homage to Burroughs. Writing as Edward Powys Bradbury I produced, in nine days, three books still in print as *Kane of Old Mars*. In them I tried to make my hero behave not like John Carter of Mars but according to Burroughs' stated moral views. Rather than respond violently to aggression, as they usually do in his books, I have my heroes and heroines incline, as much as they can, to negotiate their way out of trouble. I never read the Kane books myself (I sent them directly to the publisher as I finished them), but the act of writing them at such speed had induced in me a kind of trance-state, where I began to understand Burroughs as a true visionary!

I eventually calmed down and my mind readjusted to the business of real life, but I never entirely lost a sense of the genuine quality of that rather crude genius whose books were not always served by the best prose.

Burroughs' vision of Mars has lasted almost as long as Dickens' vision of London. The place has become a character. It is so pervasive it has continued through the work of Leigh Brackett, Ray Bradbury, and P. K. Dick, and even to the sophisticated stories of J. G. Ballard. Burroughs' Mars, all scientific and historical evidence aside, *is* Mars. The collective unconscious being the powerful thing it is, my guess is that by the time we get a proper chance to explore the Red Planet we'll find the wondrous city of Helium, various tribes of four-armed Tharks riding their *thoats*, and somewhere we'll interrupt a pair of red-skinned men sitting outside an atmosphere plant profoundly engaged in a game of *jetan* (Martian chess).

As Lupoff so convincingly tells us here, Burroughs was more than a popular writer. With Tarzan's fantastic Africa, John Carter's ancient Mars, and David Innes' hidden world of Pellucidar, he created an enduring and powerful mythology.

Constantly reprinted, forever being rediscovered, Burroughs, for all his extraordinary visionary gifts, continued to think of himself throughout his own life as "a normal bean." Sometimes he seemed almost ashamed of his original imagination and tended to minimize his gifts.

But along with Lupoff and millions of readers I believe that Burroughs was a master, an original. As you will discover when you read this study (which I found as absorbing as one of Burroughs' own books), the creator of Tarzan may have written a few too many sequels, but the core of his work remains powerful and influential. Lupoff's study is a fascinating account of a seminal American writer, as influential in his own way as James Fenimore Cooper or Mark Twain. He is a writer whose best work is quite as readable now as on the day it was published almost a century ago. Few more respected writers have lasted as well. I suspect few writers today will continue to be as successful as Edgar Rice Burroughs, Master of Adventure. He deserves this book. I am glad Richard Lupoff has revised and reprinted it. I hope you'll find it as illuminating as I do.

RICHARD A. LUPOFF

Introduction to the Bison Books Edition: Nineteen Sixty Five and All That

Nineteen sixty-five.

Nineteen sixty-five. It's hard to believe that I wrote this book that long ago, but the calendar doesn't lie and I cannot get it to change its story.

Lyndon Johnson was President of the United States, the Cold War was in full sway, and the reported joke du jour in Vienna went something like this:

Q: What's the difference between an optimist and a pessimist?
A: An optimist is studying Russian and a pessimist is studying Chinese.

There were three television networks in 1965 and most of us got our daily ration of news in thirty-minute doses from our preferred choice—ABC, NBC, or CBS—each evening. They frightened us with footage of Nikita Khrushchev pounding his shoe on his desk at the UN or of Mao Tse-tung (now rendered Mao Zedong) waving to masses of cheering blue-clad Chinese who responded by brandishing copies of Chairman Mao's infamous Little Red Book.

The Golden Age of radio had ended with the cancellation of the last great dramatic and variety shows. The day of the disc jockey had dawned and that of the blustering talk-show host lay shrouded in the seemingly distant future. Television was the king of media. Computers were gigantic and slightly threatening machines that whirred and buzzed in their air-conditioned temples. The idea that little devices more powerful than a Univac II or an IBM 709 would someday reside in millions of homes sounded like a technophile's science fiction pipe dream. The idea of a computer you could slip into your briefcase or even your pocket would have seemed laughable.

Cell phones, VCRs, CDs, DVDs, MP3 players and iPods, digital cameras, the Hubble Telescope, spaceships, men on the moon, robots on Mars, and athletes racking up amazing statistics through the miracle of anabolic steroids were simply not part of anyone's everyday world.

Everything is changed now. The Cold War is over. The Soviet Union has "devolved" into its constituent republics, each of them now independent. The nation we once called—and feared as—"Red China" has turned into our capitalist trading partner and potential rival in a new space race. New York's Twin Towers are but a terrifying memory, and radical Islamic terrorism has replaced former national rivalries as the center of world attention and source of our most dire fears.

Nineteen sixty-five seems, in the words of the song, "long ago and far away."

The great Burroughs revival of the 1960s was well under way. It was neither the first nor the last upswing in that writer's popularity. But it was the most vigorous and exciting, and I had the good luck to be part of it.

Master of Adventure: The Worlds of Edgar Rice Burroughs (originally published as *Edgar Rice Burroughs: Master of Adventure*) was written almost by accident. I was working as an editor at Canaveral Press in New York at the time. All right, as *the* editor—Canaveral was a small company. In addition to our other projects, I was asked to assemble several volumes of Edgar Rice Burroughs' stories. Some of these materials had been previously published only in magazines, while several manuscripts had never been published at all.

In fact this proved a more demanding but also a more congenial and rewarding task than simply supervising the reissue of older Burroughs books, long out of print and heavily in demand by collectors and new readers. The Burroughs "firsts" that Canaveral Press published under my watch included *Savage Pellucidar, Tarzan and the Madman, Tarzan and the Castaways, John Carter of Mars*, and *Tales of Three Planets*.

A problem arose regarding the last-named volume. Paperback reprint rights to the Canaveral "firsts" had been divided between Ballantine Books and Ace Books. Ballantine got the Tarzan and Martian series; Ace got Burroughs' Venus and Pellucidar series; other titles were distributed between the two publishers.

My own duties, in addition to working on the books themselves, included trying to keep Ian Ballantine of Ballantine Books and Donald Wollheim of Ace Books happy. It helped that I was on friendly terms with both men. It did *not* help that there was, to put it very mildly, serious antipathy between them. The ill will was of long standing. It had reached white heat over the copyright dispute and the publication of rival editions of J. R. R. Tolkien's *Lord of the Rings* by their respective firms.

Certainly I didn't want to exacerbate their mutual ill will by creating a new topic of contention between them—especially as I stood to find myself squarely in the middle!

The original plan at Canaveral Press had been to include stories set on Earth, Venus, and Jupiter in *Tales of Three Planets*. Alas, this would have created a major problem over the paperback rights to the book since the "Jupiter" story was actually part of Burroughs' Martian series. In order to prevent a new outbreak of hostilities, I agreed to transfer "Skeleton Men of Jupiter" to another volume. This eventually appeared as *John Carter of Mars*, along with the dubious novelette "John Carter and the Giant of Mars," which was actually written by Burroughs' son John Coleman Burroughs. The addition of Burroughs' two opening novelettes to his abortive Poloda series brought *Tales of Three Planets* back to proper length and content. With the addition of a superb dust jacket designed by Roy Krenkel and some lovely interior artwork, the result was one of Canaveral Press' most attractive and successful books.

But what about *John Carter of Mars*? With only two novelettes to fill it out, the book was distinctly on the skimpy side. The solution, proposed by Jack Biblo, one of Canaveral Press' co-owners, was simple enough. "Write an introduction," he directed me.

"But this book is much too short," I protested.

"Write a *long* introduction," Jack replied.

So, home I went. I revved up my cast-iron IBM Selectric typewriter and set to work.

In due course I returned to the offices of Canaveral Press, manuscript in hand. My opus was called "Edgar Rice Burroughs: Science Fiction Writer." I offered it to Mr. Biblo.

He accepted the package, riffled the pages, and gazed at me quizzically. "What's this?"

"It's the introduction you asked for. To fill out *John Carter of Mars*."

"But look at the size of this!"

"You said to make it long."

"I didn't mean *that* long!"

This exchange would call for a rim-shot, if not a brass fanfare, had it not . actually happened.

"Go home and write another introduction for the book," Jack told me. "Shorter than this one."

Crestfallen, I reached for my manuscript. But Biblo hung onto it. "I want to read this," he said.

The next time we assembled at Canaveral's modest offices, I turned in my much shorter introduction for *John Carter of Mars*. It was accepted without dispute. But Jack Biblo told me, "If you can expand the longer version to include all of Burroughs' works and keep up the quality of the version I just read, Canaveral Press will publish the book."

What a thrill! I'd been an aspiring author from childhood and had worked as a newspaper and broadcast journalist, but the longest pieces I'd ever published were a few magazine articles. Now I was faced with the chance to get my first book into print. So once more it was a matter of hauling out old novels and collections and pulp magazines, reference books, notepads, and finally my trusty Selectric. I didn't keep records of how long it took me to write the book, but it was a marathon. Of course I had to keep up with my other duties at Canaveral Press, try not to neglect my family too badly, and put in hours at a second job to help make ends meet. (Canaveral Press was a wonderful place to work, but the pay was very poor.)

Even so, in due course the book was finished and delivered to Jack Biblo, his associate and partner Jack Tannen, and their longtime friend and schmoozing buddy David Garfinkel. From the day the manuscript was completed to the day I held my first copy of the book, I was as impatient as a kid counting the days 'til Santa's visit.

Finally the book was published. Reviews were favorable, sales were good, and paperback rights were snapped up by—surprise!—Ace Books. The Ace paperback went through three editions. *Master of Adventure* became a minor classic in its own right, referred to in critical volumes as the definitive work on its subject. But after the third Ace edition, the book went out of print, and this new edition, published by the University of Nebraska Press, will be the first in more than thirty years.

Naturally I was pleased when Gary Dunham of the University of Nebraska Press inquired about reprinting the book. I had a tussle to get the rights back from Ace. Not because that publisher felt any great interest in reissuing their own version, but because Ace had long since been swallowed up into a globe-spanning media conglomerate. Trying to find anybody who knew anything or could do anything about a copyright that was thirty-odd years old was a task as daunting as David Innes' conquest of the Mahar horde!

But then a tougher problem presented itself. In the years since the last Ace printing of *Master of Adventure* my own career has moved away from the Burroughs realm and into other areas of cultural history (e.g., *All in Color for a Dime*, *The Comic-Book Book*, *Writer at Large*, and *The Great American Paperback*) as well as something like fifty novels of my own in such fields as science fiction, mystery, and horror tales. In some circles I seem to have become something of a cultural icon myself. To be candid, I'm not entirely comfortable with lionization, but I guess the status of icon is better than that of fossil.

In 1994 when I attended a Burroughs conference at the University of Louisville, I was accosted by a series of Burroughs scholars, collectors, and fans. Most of them wanted me to autograph their copies of *Master of Adventure*. There were some gorgeous, mint-condition copies of the Canaveral Press hardcover edition as well as the various Ace versions. Bibliographers wanted me to establish priority of editions of Canaveral books by Burroughs himself.

"I've seen copies of *Tales of Three Planets* in light blue, dark blue, tan, and green cloth. What was the sequence of issue?"

Alas, I could offer no help. Canaveral Press had been a low-budget operation, so its subcontractors missed no opportunity to cut corners on production costs. When a Canaveral book arrived at the bindery, the binders would use "roll ends" of binding cloth. Thus the same true first edition might appear in as many as five different "states" depending on how much binding cloth was available of any given color.

The only book that I was sure of was *John Carter of Mars*. There was a single first printing, but initially only half the copies were bound. The title stamping on the binding cloth was erroneous—it read *John Carter and the Giant of Mars*. When the rest of the copies were bound the stamping was corrected. So in terms of first edition and "first state" collecting, the "wrong" *John Carter* is the right one to have and the "right" *John Carter* is the wrong one!

In the summer of 2004 I learned of still another version of *John Carter of Mars*, this one bound in green cloth with gold stamping. This state of the book—apparently it is a third state of the first edition rather than another edition—is a complete mystery to me. I'm sure that Burroughs collectors and bibliographers will delight in trying to unravel this arcanum for years to come.

More than once at Louisville I was startled to be asked, "Mr. Lupoff, did you ever write anything else after *Master of Adventure*?"

My questioners seemed startled to learn that I had written a great many books, most of them fiction, plus an assortment of magazine pieces, screenplays, and broadcast scripts. In the years since then the number of books has surpassed fifty, many of them translated into languages ranging from Japanese to Russian to Greek.

But what about this new edition of *Master of Adventure*? To be honest, I have not kept up with the Burroughs field very well, and I did not feel qualified to do the work on the book necessary to bring it up to date. One option would have been to reprint the first edition, unaltered, as a kind of literary fossil. But I think a revised edition, including information on events in the Burroughs field through the early years of the twenty-first century, would be preferable.

Enter Phillip Burger, Burroughs scholar *extraordinaire* and a writer of no mean talent himself. Mr. Burger has gone through the texts of all prior editions, updating information where appropriate. He has also furnished a new chapter for this new edition, detailing events in the Burroughs field in recent decades. He has my admiration and gratitude for his outstanding work.

Michael Moorcock, another Burroughs pioneer and one of the major literary talents of his generation, has added a lovely foreword detailing his own involvement with Burroughs in comics, in novelistic pastiche, and in motion pictures. I'm delighted to have his contribution as part of this book.

And yet I must add another small personal note before I end this little essay. In the year 2003 I was hospitalized for a lengthy period. I tried to spend my time productively, catching up on my reading and writing (courtesy of a laptop computer—how different from 1965!). The hours eventually did drag; there was a TV set in my room and I found myself channel-surfing.

To my surprise I stumbled across a new series of Disney Tarzan cartoons, and to my utter delight I realized that they were produced with taste, care, and a degree of respect for the Burroughs originals. Best of all, there was a high fantasy content in the cartoons.

It had always been my chief complaint about Tarzan movies that they were reduced to simplistic jungle adventures. The great appeal of the Burroughs books had been the author's vivid and creative powers of imagination. Lost races, exotic species, strange powers, magical potions, miniature cities, ancient colonies of Rome or of Atlantis surviving in the depths of the African jungle. These provided the immense charm of the Tarzan books, at least for me, and at least after the Ape Man's identity and personality were forged in the earliest volumes.

But the typical Hollywood product for too many years seemed to miss the point. Or maybe it was a budget problem. Fantastic sets are expensive; stock footage of stampeding antelope is cheap. Talented actors can prove budget-busters; trained chimps are available by the hour, day, or week.

But a cartoonist is restricted only by the limits of imagination. You can draw a towering, shimmering, fantasy city as easily as you can draw a village of straw huts in the jungle. And the people behind these cartoons were taking full advantage of the freedom their medium offers. The cartoons were a pleasure, and a revelation, to me.

Eventually I was able to return home and resume my normal life, thanks to the support of my family and friends and to the almost miraculous skill of my surgeon. Imagine in 1965 sending miniaturized instruments down the patient's gullet, along with a fiber-optic light source and a tiny television camera, and performing surgery via a video monitor and a set of electronic controls!

When I got home I was greeted by the news of a new live-action Tarzan series on television. I watched it. The scripts were adequate, the cast was talented, and the production was admirable. But the scene had been shifted to New York City, and Burroughs' brightly colored and vividly painted fantasy world had been reduced to the dark and dirty mean streets of today's urban jungle.

Comparing the surprisingly enjoyable animated version with the regrettably unsuccessful live-action series, one can only conclude that the world (or worlds) of Burroughs without the glowing colors and brilliantly imagined images are quite pointless. This is, of course, not surprising. *Noir* imagery and *noir* themes are readily available in the works of Dashiell Hammett, Raymond Chandler, and literally hundreds of their disciples. And more power to them! But to draw the value of Burroughs' works, one must remain true to the always imaginative, often playful spirit of the originals.

What next? Well for starters a series of feature-length films based on Burroughs' Barsoomian novels, starting obviously with *A Princess of Mars*, has been the subject of rumor, Hollywood trial balloons, story-boarding, fantasy-casting, and deal-making literally for decades. It now appears that such a film may actually be on the brink of becoming reality.

The exploration of Mars by robotic "rovers" has rekindled interest in that planet and has reignited the debate over whether Mars once possessed a thicker atmosphere, flowing water, and a warmer climate than it now has— in short, all the conditions necessary for the development of life. Wouldn't it be astonishing if it turned out that a very "Barsoom-like" environment did exist on Mars at one time! What if John Carter's strange journey to the Red Planet involved travel into a distant past as well as through space? Given this new fillip the wild fantasies of Burroughs' imaginings suddenly attain a degree of plausibility.

Even in 1965, when the first edition of *Master of Adventure* was published, the question had arisen as to whether Burroughs' writing would survive the test of time. In the early years of the twenty-first century, we are beginning to see the leading writers of pulp in fuller perspective. In the realm of the fantastic, three writers have had the greatest and most enduring impact on the world of popular culture. These are Robert E. Howard, H. P. Lovecraft, and Edgar Rice Burroughs. It is probably no coincidence that Lovecraft was a reader and admirer of Burroughs while Howard, in turn, was heavily influenced by Lovecraft. The works of all three remain in print. Each of them has a sizable and enduring following, and each of them has become the subject of increasing academic and critical interest.

A generational change is also taking place. In the Burroughs community, the most obvious change has been the passing of Burroughs' three children. Younger members of the family continue to participate, but Burroughs' works have already become part of our general culture. In itself, this is a sign of the enduring significance of those works. The community of Burroughs fans and scholars has also suffered major losses with the deaths of Vernell Coriell, a pioneer Burroughs fan publisher; Sam Moskowitz, another early supporter and commentator on Burroughs; and Henry Hardy Heins, Burroughs' great bibliographer. And David G. Van Arnam died suddenly while working on a new edition of *The Reader's Guide to Barsoom and Amtor.*

The four major publishers responsible for the 1960's Burroughs revival have all passed away. Jack Biblo and Jack Tannen have died and with them Canaveral Press. Donald Wollheim is deceased. Ace Books has all but disappeared into a massive media conglomerate. Wollheim's longtime rival, Ian Ballantine, is also deceased and Ballantine Books, like its rival Ace, has long since been absorbed into a huge conglomerate.

At the same time younger and newer enthusiasts have taken up the preservation and perpetuation of the Burroughs legend in the mass media, in the fan community, and in the academic world. George McWhorter at the University of Louisville has created a major Burroughs archive at that university's library and has taken on the chore of reviving the publications suspended after the death of Vernell Coriell. My good friend Phillip Burger, whose contribution to the present book has been truly immeasurable, has become a leading Burroughs scholar. And Gary Dunham, of the University of Nebraska Press, has spearheaded the publication and republication of historically important and long out-of-print volumes by and about Burroughs and other pioneers in the field of fantastic literature.

It is clear now that Burroughs and his creations are an enduring part of our collective culture. Whatever happens today or tomorrow or in the decades to come, it is more than likely that the preservation—and when necessary the *restoration*—of the kind of wondrous worlds that Edgar Rice Burroughs and his colleagues created, will win the admiration and the loyalty of whole new generations of readers and viewers.

HENRY HARDY HEINS[1]

Preface

"I am sorry that I have not led a more exciting existence, so that I might offer a more interesting biographical sketch; but I am one of those fellows who has few adventures and always gets to the fire after it is out.

"I was born in Peking at the time that my father was military advisor to the Empress of China and lived there, in the Forbidden City, until I was ten years old. An intimate knowledge of the Chinese language acquired during these years has often stood me in good stead since, especially in prosecuting two of my favorite studies, Chinese philosophy and Chinese ceramics."

With these eyebrow-raising words, the son of a Chicago distiller once began a short, and purportedly autobiographical, manuscript which he appropriately entitled: *Edgar Rice Burroughs, Fiction Writer.*

The elder Mr. Burroughs did his distilling not in the liquor industry but in the manufacture of batteries, and it is reasonable to assume that his imperial military contacts with Peking were somewhat less than few. His son, the "fiction writer" responsible for that delicious cock-and-bull story, was a man who enjoyed life to the fullest, and who loved to regale his friends and readers with the fruits of a sense of humor paralleling that of Irvin S. Cobb or even Mark Twain.[2]

I never met Edgar Rice Burroughs, and yet I feel that I have known him all my life. Perhaps—although I doubt it—it could have something to do with the fact that our family lines brushed together in Sudbury, Massachusetts

---

1. Henry Hardy Heins, LHD, passed away on October 1, 2003, at the age of seventy-nine. His contributions to Burroughs scholarship, most notably the *Golden Anniversary Bibliography*, were of immeasurable value and importance. The *Bibliography*, both in its original editions and in facsimile reprints, remains a seminal work. A Lutheran minister, a scholar, and a historian, Heins was the author of works ranging from the evolution and comparative texts of Christian hymns, to volumes on banking law, philately, and the Canadian railway system. He was truly a Renaissance man, and those who knew him personally were privileged to do so.

2. Originally appeared in Bob Wagner's *Script* magazine. Reprinted in Irwin Porges, *Edgar Rice Burroughs: The Man Who Created Tarzan* (Provo UT: Brigham Young University Press, 1975).

three centuries ago, when his ancestors and mine both settled down in the same village as early American colonists. But even if we had both lived together in some fancied previous incarnation, it would only have been as in-laws. Nevertheless, in Burroughs I feel a kindred spirit.

The world may think me in a strange position, as a churchman, to be writing these words of intimate appreciation about someone who did not have any great enthusiasm himself for organized religion. But ERB respected those who tried to live sincerely according to their beliefs, while reserving his contempt for lives ruled by sham and hypocrisy. And, although my own gospel is squarely centered in the Church of Jesus Christ, I make no apologies for having allowed myself to be influenced from afar by the contagious charm of the master story-teller. And actually, when it comes right down to the core of the matter, the barbed shafts which he occasionally hurled in his books at the followers of established religion are virtually identical with the indictments that I and my fellow pastors must sometimes preach to our own congregations; the necessity, for instance, of having a faith that is more than mere outward form.

I learned to read in kindergarten days by sitting on my father's lap and watching the "bugs" on the page from which he would be reading to me the comics. This was just about the time when the Tarzan comics first appeared (1929), so perhaps it would not be stretching the truth too far to say that Tarzan may have helped teach me to read. In any case, I know that I had progressed on my own to the regular Tarzan *books* before I was very far advanced in the elementary grades. And then there came the unforgettable day when I discovered the first three Mars novels in an upstairs bookcase at my Aunt Martha's. Another whole new world of reading pleasure thus opened up, but the same author was responsible. I can truthfully say that there are only two sets of books which I read in my childhood and which I still read and enjoy today, over thirty years later. There are the *Holy Bible* and the Lutheran *Service Book* on the one hand, and the works of Edgar Rice Burroughs on the other.

I don't mean to give the impression that I read nothing else now, but it is simply that all other boyhood favorites have long since been tossed out, both physically and mentally. Those proliferous series—*The Bobbsey Twins*, *Bomba the Jungle Boy*, *Tom Swift*, *Jerry Todd* and *Poppy Ott*—they and many others all had their day, but the attempt to read them again as an adult is painful; the mature mind rejects them.

Not so with Burroughs. Twenty-five or thirty years ago I was reading his books for the sheer enjoyment of thrilling adventure in exotic locales. Now at the age of forty I am reading them for the enjoyment of Edgar Rice Burroughs as a humorist and satirist of no mean distinction, sometimes marvelling at the subtle points that escaped my notice as a boy—but, in all truth, I'm still enjoying them as fascinating adventures, too! And I have also recently found myself with my emotions so captured as to reach the last page of such novels as *The Son of Tarzan* and *Apache Devil* with actually a glistening eye. That, to my mind, takes *writing*.

(Perhaps you'll say it also takes a sentimental fool for a reader, but I give full credit to the literary power of an underrated author.)

ERB knew the difference between right and wrong, and he spun his yarns so that there was never any doubt in his reader's mind either. His heroes and villains, together with the characteristics of each, were painted in unmistakable terms of black and white. And he was always scrupulous to keep his stories *clean*, even though they might also include violent battles and the spilling of countless buckets of blood. This is why it seems downright foolishness to me, to hear of anyone alleging that Burroughs' works are unfit for children. Actually, taken in *toto*, they depict most clearly the relative merits of Good and Evil, along with an exaltation of the simple virtues such as honesty, kindness, and family devotion—with the opposing vices often played up in order to intensify the contrast. (The distortion of the movies has given many the false impression that Tarzan and Jane were not married, but ERB wrote them into wedlock in 1913—at the end of *The Return of Tarzan*—long before the first jungle picture was ever filmed.)

Burroughs was a family man himself before he ever started to write. His children were climbing over his lap while he was turning out his earlier tales of Tarzan, John Carter and the rest. He was writing for an adult audience, but at the same time he could not help but have the children very much in mind. And so he created characters that were larger than life, yet still completely believable. His Tarzan and John Carter, for instance, were mature men, even supermen. Without being dull, they exemplified noble and chivalrous ideals to a lofty degree. But they were also completely human, and the reader of any age has no trouble in identifying himself with them.

Burroughs later wrote that he hoped his readers would not take his stories too seriously. This unusual admonition was occasioned by the fact that many people were refusing to believe that they were reading fiction. He had such an uncanny skill at creating an aura of reality on the printed page, and drawing the reader right into the thick of even the most implausible situations, that it has always called for somewhat of a conscious mental effort *not* to take him seriously. The whole matter reached the point in the presidential election year of 1932, when depression-weary Americans were groping for a new leader, that one of the country's popular magazines devoted its entire editorial page to a halfway serious review of the new phenomenon, under the banner headline, "Tarzan for President"![3]

Let me conclude these already-overlong personal reflections by stating that I can have naught but respect and gratitude for Edgar Rice Burroughs. He wrote for the escapist enjoyment of countless thousands of adult readers like himself, but he also helped to mold *my* mind as a *boy* so that I grew with an appreciation of the finer traits of manhood and true nobility, as set forth in the little-short-of-real people whom he created. Life is not, as Burroughs over-simplified it, an existence in which one can always clearly distinguish between right and wrong. But when fundamental decisions must be made, the teachings of God's Word would certainly not be vitiated should one also happen to have a background in the works of ERB. (There may be challenges to this statement, reflecting specific instances in a few places, but I am referring to the over-all impact of his writings as a whole.)

In what was undoubtedly one of the first articles about Burroughs ever published, Norma Bright Carson, editor of the John Wanamaker *Books News Monthly*, wrote in August 1918:

> To every man his calling. There are those to whom God has given the power to instruct and lead their fellow men, and there are others endowed with a no less important ability—the ability to entertain— and to give to the world clean, strong, virile stories—stories that grip the boy and the boy's father, and his mother and his sisters and his aunts, and such is the ability that God has given so bounteously to Edgar Rice Burroughs.

The writer did not dwell continuously on this high level; she also sketched a few of Burroughs' other characteristics in the same article:

> . . . But his hands! The Lord never intended those hands to wield anything lighter than a sledge, or play upon a more delicate instrument than an anvil—that the four-pound aluminum typewriter he uses in his work can withstand them is always a source of wonder to me.

* * * *

3. *The Blue Book Magazine*, July 1932.

Next to Mr. Burroughs' devotion to his family comes his love of motoring. Rain or shine, summer or winter, you may see him every afternoon with his family upon the Chicago boulevards or far out on some delightful country road beyond the city's limit. He loves the country, too, and the great outdoors, and every sport and game that needs the open for its playing. Yet in few such sports does he excel. In football and horsemanship he climbed close to the top, yet his tennis is about the funniest thing I ever saw, and his golf is absolutely pathetic . . .

The latter comment is echoed by some of Burroughs' own gibes in his published works. In *The Man-Eater* (1915)[4], a rich and indolent young man muses on how to spend the day:

"Golf's an awful bore. Let's not play today."
Tiresome game, tennis."
"Ha! I have it! Great morning for a ride!"

Then there is also Carson Napier's unforgettable definition in *Lost on Venus* (1932), when Duare heard him mention *golf* and asked what it was. "Golf," he replied, "is a mental disorder."

Such heartfelt emotion in 1932 was probably to some extent also due to the fact that Burroughs had just recently acquired (by foreclosure) the ownership of a championship golf course adjacent to his own property. He had sold this land to the country club prior to the Depression, and now, fully developed, it was back on his hands again.

Moving from Chicago to Los Angeles at the end of the First World War, the Burroughs family had purchased the extensive San Fernando Valley property of General Harrison Gray Otis, publisher of the *Los Angeles Times* and who served as its editor until his death in 1917. Located in outlying Reseda, the estate was given the name "Tarzana Ranch" by its new owner. Within ten years, however, he had started selling off parts of it (at a profit) for the country club, and for new residential developments as Los Angeles continued its northwestward growth through the Valley. But the name had caught the public fancy, and in 1930 the expanding community was accorded the dignity of a separate post office of its own—*Tarzana, California*. The population of Tarzana is 16,000 today, but it was only 300 in 1930.[5] Its "chief industry" then, and still recognized as such by the local press in 1962, is the

---

4. Dates in parentheses are dates of *writing*.
5. According to the 2000 census, it is approximately 26,000.

small but prosperous firm of *Edgar Rice Burroughs, Inc.* at 18354 Ventura Boulevard.

Edgar Rice Burroughs, Upton Sinclair, and Mark Twain all sometime-Californians, seem to have been the major American novelists who published their own books. In Burroughs' case, this step did not materialize until 1931, twenty years after he started writing, and thus there are no "Burroughs" editions of the earlier Tarzan books. This is ironic in a way, for ERB's fame had speedily been established by the best-selling of all his books, *Tarzan of the Apes*, which first appeared between hard covers a half century ago in June 1914.

The last new Tarzan story, *Tarzan and the Madman*, was published fifty years later (almost to the day) in June, 1964, although this forgotten manuscript had been written by Burroughs back in 1940. It is of interest to note that both the first and the last of the Tarzan books have something in common with a very unlikely third party: *Portugal*.

Tarzan and the Madman, a story with a "lost city" background, features a decadent Portuguese fiefdom in the heart of Africa. *Tarzan of the Apes*, on the other hand, seems to have no Portuguese aspect at all—until one looks at a map. Exactly where, dear reader, was Tarzan born? While never mentioned by name, the location of the little cabin on the shore of the landlocked harbor on the west coast of Africa is given in Jane Porter's letter in chapter xviii of *Tarzan of the Apes* as "About 10 Degrees South Latitude." Now there is only one place in the Southern Hemisphere where the Tenth and adjacent parallels intersect the west coast of Africa. *Tarzan was born in Portuguese Angola.*

It is understandable that we always think of him as domiciled in British territory, but this was not the case at the very beginning when the elder Lord and Lady Greystoke were marooned at that isolated spot on the west coast. After he came into his title, wealth, and a family of his own, Tarzan built and settled down on a ranch across the continent somewhere in British *East Africa* (either Kenya or Uganda). This became his base of operations for almost all succeeding forays into the jungle, from *The Eternal Lover* (1913) onward.

It might be of interest to interject at this point a comment on Tarzan's British title. "John Clayton, Lord Greystoke" was not his real name. Many readers have overlooked the fact that on page 1 of the first Tarzan story, Burroughs wrote that "in the telling of it to you I have taken fictitious names for the principal characters." And on page 2 of the same book, *Tarzan of the Apes*, he introduces Tarzan's father as a "certain young English nobleman, *whom we shall call* John Clayton, Lord Greystoke . . ."

The author stated that his reason for using fictitious names in the story of Tarzan was to evidence "the sincerity of my own belief that it may be true." This statement at the start of the book was part of the literary framing device, certainly. But I had the pleasure of discovering amid ERB's papers in the office safe at Tarzana (and first reporting in an obscure footnote on page 191 of my *Golden Anniversary Bibliography of Edgar Rice Burroughs*), that before he settled on the fictitious title of "Lord Greystoke," Mr. Burroughs had originally outlined the first Tarzan story with its hero as heir to the title of . . . *Lord Bloomstoke*.

Burroughs' writing career spanned both the First and the Second World Wars. Indeed, Tarzan was a veteran of both conflicts, although he did not serve with the uniformed regulars. But ERB wrote him into entanglements with German troops in *Tarzan the Untamed* (1918), and with the Japanese in *Tarzan and "The Foreign Legion"* (1944). Needless to say, the foe did not fare too well under these arrangements.

The author's own semimilitary background—the Michigan academy days; trailing the Apache in the Southwest; in the home guard as an Illinois militia captain during World War I; a Pacific correspondent in World War II—gave his stories of fighting men, espionage, and the cavalry a certain degree of authenticity. And yet there are examples in his writings which can be quoted to prove that he was basically a man of peace.

One of the most stirring and impassioned pleas for human brotherhood that I have ever read came from the pen of Edgar Rice Burroughs. (It could also be thought of as evincing an anti-communist message, although the communist movement of today was hardly off the ground when this was written in 1911.) The passage occurs in chapter ten of *A Princess of Mars*, where John Carter hears for the first time the voice of his future wife. Dejah Thoris, as a solitary prisoner of the green men, bravely beseeches her captors in the audience chamber:

> "Why, oh why will you not learn to live in amity with your fellows? Must you ever go on down the ages to your final extinction but little above the plane of the dumb brutes that serve you? You are a people without written language, without art, without homes, without love; the victims of eons of the horrible community idea. Owning everything in common, even to your women and children, has resulted in your owning nothing in common. You hate each other as you hate all else except yourselves. Come back to the ways of our common

ancestors, come back to the light of kindliness and fellowship. The way is open to you; you will find the hands of the red men stretched out to aid you. Together we may do still more to regenerate our dying planet. The granddaughter of the greatest and mightiest of the red jeddaks has asked you. Will you come?"

Lorquas Ptomel and the warriors sat looking silently and intently at the young woman for several moments after she had ceased speaking. What was passing in their minds no man may know, but that they were moved I truly believe, and if one man high among them had been strong enough to rise above custom, that moment would have marked a new and mighty era for Mars.

Together with its old-fashioned eloquence, this passage from his very first story also serves to illustrate the very credible, if ponderous, eye-witness style in which Burroughs penned the earlier Martian tales, by couching them in the first person singular as the personal memoirs of John Carter.

In marked contrast to that "granddaughter" sequence written in 1911, and bridging all the Mars books in between, is the pleasantly flippant, easy-going style which Burroughs (and two worlds) had reached a generation or two later. Here are some lines written by ERB in 1940, with John Carter (again in the first person) telling of an unexpected meeting with *his* grand-daughter, in Book One of *Llana of Gathol*:

"Llana!" I cried; "what are you doing here?"

"I might ask you the same question, my revered progenitor," she shot back, with that lack of respect for my great age which has always characterized those closest to me in bonds of blood and affection.

Pan Dan Chee came forward rather open-mouthed and goggle-eyed. "Llana of Gathol!" he whispered as one might voice the name of a goddess. The roomful of anachronisms looked on more or less apathetically.

"Who is this person?" demanded Llana of Gathol.

"My friend, Pan Dan Chee of Horz," I explained.

Pan Dan Chee unbuckled his sword and laid it at her feet . . . .

"Well," interrupted Kam Han Tor, "this is all very interesting and touching; but can't we postpone it until we have gone to the quays?"

This great difference in style is very characteristic of Burroughs, who remained young in heart all his days. His work at any given period reflects the popular idiom of that period quite well. This is equally true whether it be his early writings prior to World War I, or in the 1920s when he turned out probably his greatest works, or his valued contributions to the entertainment of the Depression-minded thirties, or his war stories of the forties. It almost seems that the older he got, the more light-heartedly he wrote. Perhaps, after all, it was a conscious effort on his part to avoid being taken seriously.

Many of his later writings—in between jungle perils and scientific sword-play, that is—were cast in the unpretentious mold of good-natured philosophizing. There was something of Will Rogers in him, too. Consider the contribution he once submitted when asked to participate in a collection of "Famous Recipes by Famous People":

> My tastes are uninteresting. I like ham and eggs, corned beef hash, fried chicken, plain hamburger on white toast. How they are properly prepared is more or less of a mystery that I have no desire to solve. Culinarily speaking, I am a washout.
>   Edgar Rice Burroughs

One of the big "ifs" in reviewing ERB's career is the haunting question: would he have attained a more respectable niche in literary circles during the latter half of his long writing period, if he had not chosen to be his own publisher? Both through the advertising medium and through the providing of social contacts, an earnest publisher can often determine to a large extent any given author's "image" before the public. But by publishing his own books in California from 1931 onward, Burroughs (who was never one to blow his own horn too loudly) inevitably withdrew to a considerable degree from the rest of the literary world, which was centered more in the East.

He himself acknowledged something of this situation in a typical letter to Cyril Clemens in 1940:

> I am very sorry that I have no personal recollections of Zane Grey, inasmuch as I never met him.
>   Sorry I didn't get around more.
>   Yours, Burroughs.

For these and other reasons, Edgar Rice Burroughs is very little known to the general public even to this day, a decade and a half after his death. The first full-length, hardcover book exclusively about Burroughs did not appear until 1964, and that was merely a glorified bibliography of his works. The present extraordinary opus by Richard Lupoff marks the first serious

book ever published to examine *in depth* the literary contribution which
Edgar Rice Burroughs has made to the world. As pleased as I was to have
been responsible for the above-mentioned 1964 volume, I feel even more
gratified to have been invited to have a part in this one.

* * *

In the course of his excellent work in this book, Mr. Lupoff deals at
some length with the possible *sources* which may have inspired the creation
of the various Burroughs characters and situations. If I may be permitted
to do so, there is one other such possibility that I would venture to put
forward, although it bears on only one aspect of a single book: *Thuvia,
Maid of Mars*.

Thuvia was illustrated, as were so many other of the Burroughs first
editions, by J. Allen St. John. This eminent Chicago artist was himself the
author of one book published in 1905 (before ERB had ever started to write).
St. John's 156-page tour de force, entitled *The Face in the Pool, A Faerie Tale*,
consisted of theme and variations on the standard fairy-tale motif of the
bewitched princess in need of rescue.

When Burroughs wrote *Thuvia* in 1914, he created the phantom Bowmen of Lothar, those amazing illusions which could be materialized out of
thin air and withdrawn again the same way by mental concentration of the
Lotharians, and yet who (while visible) were great fighters who could inflict
actual injuries and death on real men. It is thus of more than passing interest
to note that J. Allen St. John wrote, in his "faerie tale" which was published
in 1905 in Burroughs' home town of Chicago, the following passage:

> The Prince, seeing himself likely to be overpowered by sheer force
> of numbers, seized the tiny bag the Wise Man had given him, and,
> tearing the red cord from it with his left hand and teeth, scattered
> the black peas broadcast; then, setting his lance in rest, he charged
> swift as an eagles swoop, shield and body lying low to saddle, and
> the mighty battle-axe of Kelmet swinging from its steel chain at his
> wrist.
>
>   . . . Yet even so, the issue hung in the balance, as instantly a foe
> went down before the fury of his arm, another sprang to fill the gap,
> while from the castle men completely armed, shouting hoarse battle
> cries, rushed to join the fray.
>
>   But the tide was turned suddenly in his favor by the blackpeas
> he had scattered from the small green sack. These had no sooner
> touched the ground than in their place appeared the twenty men in
> sable armor, mounted in their steeds. Uttering no sound, silently they

swung into the press, dealing such fearful blows with sword or mace and seconding Hardel so skillfully that in a little, the pass growing easier, the Prince, with a last charge and swing of his gleaming axe, beat down the few that still opposed, to thunder over the bridge and gain the forest road just beyond, followed by his twenty black-mailed henchmen. Nor did they draw rein till, the wood left far behind, they halted in a quiet valley some leagues away.

Hardel here turned, and facing them as they drew up in military order, each sitting motionless in his proper place, spoke words of praise and heartfelt thanks, to which they listened mutely. As he ceased speaking, one of the company drawing the little green bag from his gauntlet cast it before him on the turf, at which the knight at the extreme left rode up till he stood over the spot whereon it lay, and saluting the Prince with drawn sword, instantly vanished. The next in line did the like, and so on, till only the one who had thrown down the bag remained; then he, dismounting, picked it up, and handing it to Hardel, disappeared immediately it was in the Prince's grasp, leaving him amazed, to peer into the sack and find the twenty small black peas lying innocently in it, as before.

Although the foregoing is a mere variant in the dragon's teeth legend from Greek mythology, it has one significant difference. While the dragon's teeth sown by Cadmus produced hostile warriors who fell upon each other, the black peas in St. John's version produced friendly troops who fought on the Prince's side against his enemies, and whose services could evidently be utilized again and again in the same manner as often as desired.

This was exactly the way Burroughs depicted the phantom bowmen in *Thuvia, Maid of Mars*, the only major difference being the method of their materialization. J. Allen St. John stood very high in Burroughs' esteem as a man and as an illustrator. Was he also one of ERB's sources?

Before we leave the subject of illustrations, something should be said about the great advantage that Burroughs enjoyed in writing his particular type of story. There is nothing which can "date" a book so quickly, and remove it from popular interest, as illustrations or a dust jacket (particularly the latter) depicting out-moded fashions of dress. But the Burroughs jackets successfully, and probably unintentionally, skirted this pitfall. Inside the early Tarzan editions there were a few small St. John sketches showing long skirts and high collars, but even here these were far out-numbered by jungle scenes where relative freedom from clothing was the rule. There was no such problem at all in the Mars, Pellucidar and Venus books, which illustrated characters with different forms of dress entirely. Perhaps only in a single one of the Burroughs books was there a prominent picture which is "dated" in terms of American civilization: the frontispiece and jacket of *The Girl from Hollywood* (published in 1923); and even here the "Hollywood" aspect gives it some leeway. The more one thinks about this, the more concrete becomes the realization that a major factor in the continuing popularity of the Burroughs novels across decades of changing fashions was this matter of illustrations. There were plenty of them, but the unique "fashions" they depicted never went out of style.

ERB drew occasionally from real life, and in at least one instance he brought a contemporary world figure into the plot of a story. This was his use (presumably unauthorized) of one J. Stalin in the first chapter of *Tarzan Triumphant* (1931), in which Burroughs actually depicted him by name— "Stalin, the dictator of Red Russia"—in his Moscow office, and quoted him in the process of sending an OGPU emissary to Africa to *liquidate Tarzan*. What befell the OGPU man and his expedition constitutes one of the main plotlines of the book. The United States had not yet recognized the Soviet Union when this was written, but the Russian people had been reported in the mid-1920s as going mad over Tarzan, and it is rather strange to see Burroughs putting Stalin in the position of trying to kill him off. Did ERB intend this as a satire against Soviet copyright violators by implying that, in bilking him of his proper royalties, the Russians were killing the goose that laid the golden eggs? Or, in the light of Mr. Lupoff's perceptive comments in this volume, was the Stalin plot against Tarzan simply another manifestation of a thinly-veiled wish on the part of the tired author? At any rate, the title of the book tells the inevitable outcome.

On another occasion (1927), an entire Burroughs work was instigated by a development in his own family life. His daughter Joan (pronounced "Joanne") was thinking of a stage career at the time, and was acting with a stock company in small legitimate playhouses.

As a fatherly gesture, Edgar Rice Burroughs wrote a complete three-act play, *You Lucky Girl!* as a possible starring vehicle for her. Nothing came of it, however, and as the years passed even Joan herself forgot all about its existence; never published nor performed, the play exists today only in manuscript. [6] While its plot as a love story is a very ordinary one (two small-town girls facing the dilemma of stage aspirations versus family responsibilities), *You Lucky Girl!* does have two or three distinctions. It marks Burroughs'

---

6. It has now been performed and was published in 1999 by Donald Grant. See Chapter XXI, "Forty More Years of Adventure," for details.

only real venture into the field of drama; he made no record of it in his working notebook, but it is the only one of his unpublished works which he had *copyrighted* in manuscript form. While hardly of Broadway caliber, the play would lend itself readily enough either to stock company performance or to amateur theatricals in schools or churches. Unfortunately, one of its best lines occurs at a point which would never reach an audience seeing it performed. This consists of one of the *stage directions* in Burroughs' dry wit:

(Act I, page 13)

Anne:
> Good!
> (*Goes to door up R. and turns*).
> There are some magazines on the table
> and—the piano has just been tuned.
> (*Note: See that it has.*)

Farther on in the play the dialogue includes a tirade about the dangers of world over-population, which would probably have been played for laughs back in the 1920s, but ERB's message would be both timely and serious to an audience today.

* * * *

The later life of Edgar Rice Burroughs was not marked with the family contentment which had been such a happy feature of younger days.

After thirty-four years of marriage, he divorced his wife Emma in 1934. A later remarriage also ended in divorce. By this time ERB was in Hawaii, where on December 7, 1941, he witnessed the actual bombing of Pearl Harbor, and where he spent the war years as the oldest accredited United Press correspondent in the Pacific theater. By the end of the war in 1945 he was 70 years old, and had been invalided home to California with a heart condition.

Here a final irony awaited the creator of Tarzan: there was no place in Tarzana for him to live.

Not wanting to move in with any of his children, he proudly insisted upon having his own home. But the post-war housing shortage was already presenting difficulties. The old Tarzana Ranch had been completely sold off into residential developments, and they were all full. ERB's three children, while still very close to their father, had homes and families of their own in neighboring communities. Out of all the former Burroughs property in Tarzana, only the office in Ventura Boulevard remained.

Immediately adjacent to Tarzana, however, is the community of Encino, and here the old story-teller found a suitable house for sale. In fact it was situated in Zelzah Avenue, the last street in Encino, with its back yard bordering on the Tarzana line. In this tantalizing location Burroughs saw three more of his books published, and lived out his remaining years as a semi-invalid.

There in his Zelzah Avenue home, on March 19, 1950, he died. None of his family was with him at the time. He was reading the Sunday comics in bed, right after breakfast, when the end came suddenly.

* * * *

It was said of Abel in the Bible, "He being dead yet speaketh."

This had never been brought clearer to mind, as far as Edgar Rice Burroughs is concerned, than in the summer of 1964 as one final new Tarzan story was read with nostalgic gratitude by many of us who thought that we had already read the last. And perhaps, with all the respect to his agnostic views, we may take the closing line of this posthumous Tarzan tale as the author's own unintentional valedictory to a very meaningful life:

"Thank God for everything."

RICHARD A. LUPOFF

Introduction

For much of the past hundred years, one of the more popular American authors has been Edgar Rice Burroughs. From the appearance of Burroughs' first story in 1912 until just a couple of years before his death in 1950, hardly a year passed without the publication of some new Burroughs yarn, either in the lamented pulp magazines of that era, or in book form.

He was best known, of course, for his jungle adventure stories, most of them featuring the famous character Tarzan. There were two dozen Tarzan books, and then there were a few others featuring such Tarzan-like creations as Thandar, Bulan, and the revived prehistoric hunter Nu.

John Carter, an earthly adventurer on the red planet Mars, runs a close second to Tarzan in popularity among Burroughs fanciers; a good many, in fact, place Burroughs' science fiction above even his jungle stories in their personal favor. And it's a fact that Burroughs wrote plenty of science fiction—the John Carter stories, the Pellucidarian adventures of David Innes at the earth's core, Carson Napier's Venusian sojourn, the *Moon Maid* and *Land that Time Forgot* trilogies, and more.

And, almost as if in moments of whimsy, Burroughs poured out other kinds of stories, too—historicals, westerns, realistic novels, even a few detective stories. His words were marked with vivid characters, colorful backgrounds, breathtaking pace and suspense, and almost always a thinly submerged sense of humor and satire that provides a second level of appreciation of any Burroughs book for the reader whose taste calls for other than simple action-and-adventure stories.

Burroughs died peacefully in the spring of 1950, full of years, fame, and accomplishments. Let other authors make profound social statements in their works; *his* contribution had been the entertainment and stimulation of two generations of readers in his own lifetime, and many more to follow.

Almost immediately upon Burroughs' death a strange thing happened.

His books began disappearing. Burroughs' own publishing company had been producing all his new books for some years, the last only two years before in 1948; the company also maintained many older titles in reprint editions. The great paperback publishing boom had not yet reached major proportions, but a few Burroughs titles had been reprinted in that format.

Now the "Burroughs" Burroughs editions began disappearing from bookstores. Book dealers active in the field both then and now recount their experiences of being unable to obtain books ordered from Edgar Rice Burroughs, Inc. Reprint editors tell of comparable experiences. Donald A. Wollheim, soon to be with Ace Books but then with Avon, tells of attempting to secure paperback rights to Burroughs' works and receiving for reply only rebuffs—or total silence.

It seemed almost as if Edgar Rice Burroughs, Inc., was attempting to bury the writings of Burroughs, and attend to more lucrative matters such as the licensing of the Tarzan character for motion pictures, comic strips and magazines, and other commercial exploitations.

For 12 years this was the situation, while Burroughs, except for the Tarzan adaptations, became virtually a forgotten man. A coterie of loyal fans kept the lamp of memory flickering, and a semi-professional publisher would now and then risk lawsuit with an underground edition of a few hundred copies of some "lost" Burroughs work.

In 1962 everything changed. Jack Biblo and Jack Tannen, operators of a used book store in New York, learned through a copyright search that approximately half of the Burroughs canon was in the public domain. That is, the copyright had lapsed 27 hears after first publication, and had not been renewed as legally required. Anyone who wanted to reprint Burroughs could, permission or no, providing only that they stayed within the out-of-copyright list.

Biblo and Tannen set up a publishing house called Canaveral Press and announced an ambitious program of reprinting Burroughs in hard-bound, illustrated editions. In short order Wollheim of Ace Books announced a similar and even more ambitious program of paperback reprints. Ballantine Books produced a trump card with the claim that they *had* obtained Burroughs Inc.'s permission, and thus would reprint copyright as well as public domain material. Dover Books announced its own, somewhat smaller, Burroughs program.

For a time there was utter chaos. From a drought of Burroughs there was now, suddenly, a flood. Where a given title had been out-of-print for decades, there were now two, three, four competing editions on sale at once. Eventually, fortunately, a measure of order was restored when a new administration at Burroughs, Inc. negotiated settlements with the various publishers involved.

Canaveral obtained exclusive hardcover publishing rights for a time. They eventually produced two dozen Burroughs titles including several first editions. Dover limited its program to a few omnibus volumes of Burroughs, then retired from the field.

Ace and Ballantine split the paperback rights more or less down the middle—Ace got Pellucidar and Venus series, Ballantine got Tarzan and Mars. Other titles were parcelled out one by one. For hardcover first editions of remaining Burroughs manuscripts, Burroughs Inc. published a single title, and in recent years has allowed various small presses to produce others.

In his fashion, this immensely popular author came back into his own after a hiatus of 12 years. If Edgar Rice Burroughs sits in some writers' Olympus (not with Socrates and Shakespeare, but more likely with Doc Smith and Zane Grey and Frederick Faust), he must look down on this world and derive some satisfaction from being remembered and reprinted again, after all those years in limbo.

A word about *Master of Adventure: The Worlds of Edgar Rice Burroughs*, and my own involvement in the Burroughs revival. In 1962, when Canaveral Press had just begun its Burroughs reprinting program, I had the fortune of meeting Messrs. Biblo and Tannen, and of making a number of suggestions, some of them slightly pointed, about the books being issued. To my astonishment (and pleasure) I found myself invited to become editor of the Canaveral series.

I felt, at the time, that the hardcover editions of Burroughs being produced were a basically sound product, but needed dressing up in terms of "package" . . . and a great deal of better promotion and distribution. Unfortunately, Canaveral lacked the resources in terms of both manpower and budget to do this job with complete success, which is one of the reasons why Canaveral did not add further volumes to its existing Burroughs list.

Still, under the circumstances I found myself immersed in Burroughs, reading first those readily available titles of his which I had never before got around to, then tracking down the scarcer books, the magazine stories that had never appeared in book form, and finally the unpublished manuscripts. The more I got to know Burroughs, the more convinced I became that he was an author worthy of attention, who was simply not receiving it.

I began writing about him. First, copy for the dust-wrappers of Canaveral editions. Then introductions to newly-issuing books of Burroughs material. A number of magazine articles. But finally the realization dawned that only by writing at full book length would it be possible to say what needed to be said about Burroughs. I began such a book, received encouragement from Biblo and Tannen, and finally the book appeared under the Canaveral imprint of 1965.

That book was *Edgar Rice Burroughs: Master of Adventure*. For the latest edition, the book has been retitled and expanded.

The book received a rather favorable greeting at the time. Many newspapers ran reviews praising it and agreeing that it was an overdue treatment of an overlooked author. A number of feature articles were written, using the book as a focus and as a jumping-off point for comments on Burroughs himself. A few—*very* few—treated both *Edgar Rice Burroughs: Master of Adventure* and the entire Burroughs revival phenomenon as a species of camp. It is possible, of course, to read Burroughs in this context, but this is not the viewpoint from which I wrote, and I think it does injustice to the man to regard him in this light.

The major area of hostility to the book lay surprisingly within the Burroughs fan community itself! Here, the book was roundly criticized for presenting a balanced appraisal of Burroughs . . . instead of the unqualified adulation that was expected. Worse yet, considerable space was devoted to seeking out the precursors and sources of Burroughs' inspiration . . . why, the man must be treated as an original. To do other is no less than accusing him of theft! (Or so the argument ran.)

I can only say that the dedicated Burroughs idolator is in for some rude moments as he reads this book. So is the "judge" who seeks to condemn Burroughs' works without first reading them. The course followed traces a middle ground between uncritical admiration and unfair condemnation of Burroughs. I think it is a valid perspective on the man's works, and it is those works that this book is about.

CHAPTER I

Who Was Edgar Rice Burroughs

At some future date, perhaps twenty-five years hence, perhaps two or three times that, descendants of today's community of literary critics will evaluate the American authors of the first half of the twentieth century. The vast majority will be long forgotten by then, the remainder will be sorted out in the many-years-long process that determines who will survive, who will perish. From the vantage point of 1965 it seems certain that one twentieth-century American is assured of survival, for his historic impact on narrative technique if for no other reason: Ernest Hemingway.

Almost as secure seems William Faulkner, and not too far behind are Scott Fitzgerald and Sinclair Lewis. Beyond these, one can guess. John Steinbeck? Theodore Dreiser? Willa Cather? The list might go on, and there is certainly no way of being really sure of who will still be read in the next decade, no less the next century. Authors come and go, their admirers become more and then less numerous, eventually most authors fade from notice while only the few attain a lasting place in the world of books.

Will James Branch Cabell be read in the year 2000? Will James Gould Cozzens? Will Katherine Anne Porter's *Ship of Fools* be considered an enduring masterpiece or a flash in the pan?[1]

It may seem impudent to suggest the addition to this list of candidates for lasting literary life of an author whose self-appointed task was mere

---

1. A note from the twenty-first century: Despite the temptation to update this page and make myself look less foolish than I really am, I have decided to let the text stand. It seems to me that Hemingway is fading badly, Faulkner is holding his own, Fitzgerald and Lewis are seen increasingly as period pieces. Cabell is of interest only to cultists and antiquarians. Katherine Anne Porter, to borrow a sports metaphor, is "on the bubble." As the great W. Somerset Maugham said in *The Summing Up*, you can never tell who will be remembered and who will be forgotten. Nevertheless, almost a century after his writing career began and some fifty-five years after his death, Edgar Rice Burroughs is still being read and his works are still being adapted for the amusement of nonliterary fans. He has already outlasted ninety-nine percent of his contemporaries, and he's still in the game.

entertainment. But such a man seems these days to be running a strong chance of permanence: Edgar Rice Burroughs. Long popular with the non-classics reading public, Burroughs throughout his lifetime received little critical notice, and that almost unanimously unfavorable.

He was regarded as barely literate, pilloried by critics, banned by librarians, proscribed by teachers as totally without merit of any sort, literary, moral or social. Only in very recent years has a re-evaluation begun; it is far from complete and acceptance of Burroughs by any sort of Establishment is still far off, but the condemnation is no longer unanimous nor in many cases as nearly unconditional as it was for so long.

And of course there is that still enduring public popularity. This in itself, without its duration, would mean little. Back in the late 1940s and early 1950s the largest selling author in the world was Mickey Spillane. He caught a mood. He was a sensation. Today he is largely forgotten. His more recent books have found a still loyal but far more modest readership; his older ones, in spite of a paperback revival in the 1970s, are little remembered and little read. While still actively writing, he is a forgotten man as far as any real impact is concerned.

What authors *are* read for decades upon decades? One might make a very surprising list of those whose works strike past the trappings of temporary fashion. One might suggest L. Frank Baum, another condemned figure whose children's fantasies of Oz retain their appeal after a century. One might suggest John Dickson Carr, whose historically-oriented and fantastic tales as much as his conventional detective novels are as good fifty or more years after their first appearances as they were when new.

The praise of critics is sometimes misplaced, their condemnation as well. Styles come and go as well as individual works or authors, and Salinger the hero becomes Salinger the fool, yet Holden Caulfield does not change, nor the Glasses. Rather the critics assess, and reassess, and one is led to wonder if they will determine anything, or whether it is the reading public, the only slightly less grimy portion of the great unwashed, who will decide for themselves whom to keep and whom to take up and examine, and toy with and finally cast aside.

When an author survives for nearly a century, not only without the support of the critical or academic community but in the face of these communities' adamant condemnation, it is time to begin asking if a legitimate folk-author has not been here. It is time to start thinking of permanence. And surely it is time to attempt an evaluation of some length, and of some depth.

Also, if the figure involved is one concerning whose life and works is as little known as is the case with Burroughs, and in particular if as much false is "known" as is the case with Burroughs, a general guide to him, and to his literary output is appropriate.

To hundreds of millions around the world the name Tarzan is a household word. It represents manliness, strength, courage, and perhaps just a touch of bestiality, and perhaps more than just a touch of stupidity. It is the name of the lord of the jungle, John Clayton, Lord Greystoke, one of the most phenomenally successful fictional creations of all time.

What these hundreds of millions know about Tarzan, unfortunately, is largely a concoction of ignorance and error, based chiefly on a long and vastly successful series of inaccurate motion picture adaptations of the Tarzan stories, and to a lesser degree upon television, comic strip and other adaptations of the original works. Far fewer of the multitudes who "know" Tarzan know that Burroughs, in addition to writing *Tarzan of the Apes* in 1912, and some two dozen additional Tarzan books over the following thirty-five years, was one of the most popular, prolific, and influential science-fiction writers of all times, a figure to stand with Verne, Wells, and few others as an all-time master of scientific romance.

The first half of this book, dealing mainly with Burroughs' science fiction, is an attempt to list and describe, and to a degree to analyze and evaluate his works in this field. His output consists of more than thirty volumes comprising one series of eleven books, another of seven, another of four, plus a variety of non-series books. Burroughs' science fiction ranges from his earliest published work—antedating Tarzan in both authorship and initial publication—to the last work of Burroughs published in his lifetime, and beyond, to a number of stories found in manuscript and published as late as 2001, fifty-one years after Burroughs' death.

Interwoven with Burroughs' science fiction (and his Tarzan stories) were a third category, or better a "non-category," a miscellany of works ranging from historical romances to westerns, detective stories, realism and satire. Such works will be discussed "as they fall," eschewing only the Tarzan stories which will receive separate treatment in the latter half of this book. A few of the works discussed have not yet been published in any form. Discussion of these is based upon manuscript copies furnished by Mr. Hulbert Burroughs, the author's son. Between 1962 and 1965 Canaveral Press reissued many out-of-print Burroughs books, and beginning late in 1963 issued a number of posthumous first editions of Burroughs works. As editor for Canaveral I had the opportunity to examine many of the manuscripts left by the author, and it may be hoped that even more of the works discussed in the present volume as existing only in manuscript form will eventually see print.

Master of Adventure is not intended, primarily, as a critical work, although it does contain criticism. I have attempted to avoid the totally unquestioning acceptance of Burroughs' total output which marks the uncritical ideologue, and the reader will note that some of Burroughs' works are credited with only special-interest value while others are considered to be worthwhile only for the "completist" reader. At the same time, synopses of many of Burroughs' works are presented; again, this book is conceived with a higher ambition than a mere compendium of synopses.

Rather, *Master of Adventure* is intended as a comprehensive guide to the worlds created by Burroughs. For the librarian, for the teacher or student, for the general reader whose interest in Burroughs has been piqued by the remarkably durable popularity of his creations, this book should prove a single compact source of information on Burroughs' works. It includes, in addition to descriptions of Burroughs' books, discussions of the various characters, environments, and basic rationales he utilized. It delves into sources which Burroughs may have drawn upon, and traces to some degree the influence which he in turn exerted over later authors, and continues to exert to this day.

For the already dedicated Burroughs fan, *Master of Adventure* may contain a number of previously unknown bits of Burroughs lore and information. Certainly the sections on sources in particular will be of interest to the Burroughs enthusiast; tracing of sources other than those named in this book may be a sport to engage in for long times to come, and dispute as to whether a possible source was ever actually read by Burroughs, and whether any given earlier work was a meaningful influence upon him, must almost certainly remain a moot, albeit a fascinating, question for all time.

CHAPTER II

The Beginning of a Career

This book is not intended primarily as a biography of Edgar Ride Burroughs. For one thing, that matter was handled to an extent by Pastor Heins in his introduction; for another, three full-length biographies of Burroughs exist as well as his own unpublished autobiography (heavily referenced by his biographers), and to attempt a more detailed portrait of him than Heins provides would probably be superfluous in view of such extensive coverage.

Nonetheless, it is appropriate to present at least a lightning sketch of Burroughs' life in order to get a few dates and circumstances settled, and in order to obtain some perspective for later evaluation of Burroughs' works.

In brief, then, Edgar Rice Burroughs was born in Chicago on September 1, 1875. The son of a former Civil War major (Union) who after the war became a successful businessman, the young Burroughs received a fine education, attending first the Brown School, then due to a diphtheria epidemic, Miss Coolie's Maplehurst School for Girls (yes!), and in turn the Harvard School, Phillips Andover, and finally the Michigan Military Academy.

In his various schools Burroughs tended to be at best a mediocre scholar, caring little for studies, but at the military academy he found the vigorous life and the opportunity to ride frequently much to his liking—he had already put in a period as a real cowboy on a family ranch in Idaho—so that he not only lasted through graduation, but actually returned for a time as Assistant Commandant of Cadets.

At the same time he taught a course in geology—doing research for his classes that later served well in providing the background for a number of stories with "lost world" settings.

It must have been a combination of admiration for his father and enjoyment of his days at Michigan Military Academy that imbued Burroughs with a feeling for the "military virtues" of courage, honor, skill in combat both with and without arms, spartan endurance of imprisonment if captured by an enemy, and indomitable hope and confidence in the face of adversity. At the same time these same influences seemingly implanted a love of combat and an admiration of warlike attributes which persisted through most of Burroughs' writing career.

As a mere boy he had served briefly in the army, until it was discovered that he was under age, but he indicated in later writings that he saw little or no action during his enlistment, and it was not until World War II that he ever actually saw war with his own eyes.

This must have been a traumatic experience for the inveterate romancer that Burroughs was, but although nearing seventy at the time (he was the oldest accredited war correspondent in the Pacific theater) he nonetheless assimilated new and horrifying sights, apparently changing a basic attitude. Even earlier than the actual outbreak of the war, Burroughs' attitudes were apparently undergoing a change from the romantic to the more realistic, for his *Carson of Venus* written in 1937 reflects much of the European tyranny that preceded the war, and the two novelettes that make up *Beyond the Farthest Star*, both written in 1940, demonstrate a total rejection of the glamor theory of warfare.

But this is getting far ahead of the outline of Burroughs' life and work, some thirty years ahead in fact.

Between his early boyhood and the beginning of his writing career, Burroughs worked at the traditional variety of professions regarded as prerequisite to literary success. To speed over his pre-literary career, let me quote two paragraphs from a characteristically wry autobiographical note that appeared in *Amazing Stories* magazine for June, 1941:

> Somewhere along the line I went to Idaho and punched cows. I greatly enjoyed that experience, as there were no bathtubs in Idaho at that time. I recall having gone as long as three weeks when on a round-up without taking off my boots and Stetson. I wore Mexican spurs inlaid with silver: they had enormous rowels and were equipped with dumbbells. When I walked across a floor, rowels dragged behind and the dumbbells clattered: you could have heard me coming for a city block. Boy! was I proud!
>
> After leaving Orchard Lake (Michigan Military Academy), I enlisted in the 7th U.S. Calvary and was sent to Fort Grant, Arizona, where I chased Apaches, but never caught up with them. After that, some more cow punching; a storekeeper in Pocatello, Idaho; a policeman in Salt Lake City; gold mining in Idaho and Oregon; various

clerical jobs in Chicago; department manager for Sears, Roebuck & Co.; and, finally, *Tarzan of the Apes*.

In 1941, wealthy, famous, and elderly, Burroughs took a humorous view of his early days. But there is revealed nonetheless a young man who achieved little success and little happiness in the many occupations he tried. By 1911, in his mid-thirties, Burroughs might well be forgiven for indulging in the age-old pastime of the frustrated: daydreams.

The traditional story of the beginning of Burroughs' literary efforts, which exists in several slightly varied versions, is this. As part of his work, he was required to check advertising in the pages of the pulp magazines of the day. At the same time he habitually made up wildly implausible adventure stories for his entertainment.

Letting his eye stray, from time to time, away from the advertisement which he was checking and onto the columns of text adjoining them, Burroughs read enough pulp adventures to become convinced that he could write stories just as good, if not better. His first effort was, literally, a day-dream written down. So wild was this story, *Under the Moons of Mars*, that Burroughs feared to be known as its author—he was afraid that his very sanity would be doubted!

He therefore sent the story to the *Argosy* magazine, under the by-line *Normal Bean*, intending the pseudonym as a thinly disguised hint that the author was not after all a madman. The manuscript found its way to the *Argosy*'s sister magazine, the *All-Story*.

Another legend of Burroughsiana is that either the editor of *All-Story*, Thomas Newell Metcalf, or else an anonymous proofreader or typographer, took *Normal* for a typographical error and considerably changed the spelling to what it should logically have been, *Norman Bean*. Metcalf paid Burroughs $400 for magazine rights to the story, and ran it as a six-part serial from February through July, 1912.

By so doing, Metcalf gave first public exposure to a science fiction classic, a story that, despite the passage of nearly a century, is still read as vivid high adventure, not as an historical curiosity nor merely as a work profoundly influential on the development of a whole school of science fiction, although it is this, but purely on its own merits as an engrossing story.

The romance, better known under its book title *A Princess of Mars*, is a remarkably constructed fiction. It opens with a foreword signed by the author—that is, by *an* "Edgar Rice Burroughs." But not by the actual ERB, for in the foreword we read of "Burroughs'" first meeting with John Carter on the Virginia plantation of "Burroughs'" father. "Burroughs" writes that the time was "just prior to the opening of the civil war," and that he "was then a child of but five years."

But Burroughs was born in Chicago—in 1875!

Thus, from the very beginning of Burroughs' first work we see a blurring of reality and fantasy, of truth and dream. This odd characteristic, psychologically understandable in the light of Burroughs' known real-world frustration and his daydreaming, pervades much of his work. It may well be the key to the marvelous rapport which he achieved, through his stories, with his readers' imaginations.

Burroughs—or rather, "Burroughs"—tells of his admiration for John Carter, a Confederate cavalry captain who was to him "Uncle Jack," a "tall, dark, smooth-faced, athletic man" of about thirty. He tells of John Carter's reported death twenty-six years later, on March 4, 1886, and of taking charge of John Carter's estate, of his papers, and of his funeral arrangements.

The burial, in accord with John Carter's written instructions, is held in Virginia, where the unembalmed body is placed in an open coffin. "A strange feature about the tomb," we are told, "is that the marble door is equipped with a single, huge gold-plated spring lock which can be opened *only from the inside.*"

Among his papers, John Carter had also left a thick manuscript, which "Burroughs" " . . . was to retain sealed and unread, just as I found it, for eleven years; nor was I to divulge its contents until twenty-one years after his death." John Carter having died in 1886, the twenty-one years would run out in 1907, five years before Burroughs' (or was it *really* "Burroughs"?) story was published by Metcalf in *All-Story*. The web is woven more and more complex, truth and fancy become more and more intertwined. (And in a sequel to *Princess*, titled *The Gods of Mars*, it is implied that the manuscript in question was read immediately upon John Carter's death.)

The main narration of *A Princess of Mars* now commences, given by John Carter in the manuscript which he had left to his nephew. It begins with the narrator, mustered out of the defeated Confederate army, seeking wealth and adventure. "Masterless, penniless, and with my only means of livelihood, fighting, gone, I determined to work my way to the southwest and attempt to retrieve my fallen fortunes in search for gold."

Captain Carter and his partner, Captain James K. Powell, of Richmond, do quite well, late in the winter of 1865, discovering over a million dollars worth of ore. March 3, 1866, however, brings a sad reversal of their luck, as they are attacked and vastly outnumbered by a band of Apaches. Powell is killed outright but John Carter rescues his body to save it from mutilation at the hands of the Apaches, and makes his way to a cave. There in that Arizona setting, by morning it is necessary only for the Apaches to enter the cave and take John Carter, who has fallen victim of a mysterious paralysis. But something behind the former officer, which he, due to his mysterious debility, is unable to turn and see, so terrifies the advancing Indians that they leave him unmolested in the cave.

With a final, convulsive wrench, John Carter strives desperately to turn about, but instead records that "something gave, there was a momentary feeling of nausea, a sharp click as of the snapping of a steel wire . . ." and he stood, free, able to look down at his own body lying on the floor of the cave!

Before dawn on the morning of March 4, 1866, the disembodied soul of John Carter stepped from the mouth of that cave in Arizona, turned his face toward the heavens, and felt himself "drawn with the suddenness of thought through the trackless immensity of space." He tells of "an instant of extreme cold and utter darkness," and then, "I opened my eyes upon a strange and weird landscape."

John Carter was on Mars!

The gradual movement from the mundane to the outre, from the easily acceptable to the utterly fantastic, is performed by Burroughs in *A Princess of Mars* with consummate skill, with an insidious fraying of the bonds of reality so deft as to be virtually undetectable by the unwary reader. First we have the foreword, actually little more than a letter of transmittal of a manuscript, containing nothing more exceptional than a rather eccentric set of burial instructions.

The manuscript itself opens with a self-introduction by John Carter who cites a most curious fact about himself: that, while to all appearances, he is a man of about thirty, he has no recollection of ever having been younger. He *thinks*, therefore, that he must be very much older than he looks, but, he tells us, "I feel that I cannot go on living forever . . . some day I shall die the real death from which there is no resurrection. I do not know why I should fear death, I who have died twice and am still alive; but yet I have the same horror of it as you who have never died."

Strangeness piled upon strangeness, but the reader does not refuse the bit; this is, after all, but a manuscript found by "Burroughs," and John Carter *is* dead.

Then the fight in the Arizona hills, the cave, the strange disembodiment, and the mysterious flight to Mars. What John Carter found when he arrived on Mars is best summarized by David G. Van Arnam in his excellent study of the series, *The Reader's Guide to Barsoom and Amtor*. Van Arnam says:

Barsoom (Burroughs' Martian name for Mars) is a dying planet of vast dead sea bottoms covered with ochre moss, of dead cities visited only by savage hordes of green Martian barbarians, of constantly warring kingdoms, tiny city-states, and empires, where the remnants of a once-mighty race linger on, fighting desperately against the perils of a vanishing atmosphere, the terrible green men, and each other.

A million years ago the planet was rich and prosperous; the blond, white-skinned Orovars held sway over virtually the entire planet and ruled the five seas with mighty fleets. All was peaceful.

Then the seas began to recede; Horz, the capital of the most magnificent of the Orovar empires, built out towards the sea as Throxeus, mightiest of the five seas, gradually evaporated. The powerful civilization began to crumble under this inevitable threat and doom. The previously small and controllable groups of green men, great savage manlike tusked monsters that grew to a height of fifteen feet, began attacking their former masters, vengefully, terribly. The Orovars were almost entirely wiped out. Those that remained alive (apart from the Lotharians, who lost all their women in a desperate trek across half a world, and one group who successfully defended themselves in Horz to the present day) gradually merged with two of the minor races of that time, a reddish-yellow race and another, almost black, to finally become the dominant red race today.

In the process most of the Orovar civilization was lost, but, although the white race was virtually destroyed, the new race of red men survived hardily, recapturing many cities from the green men and slowly rebuilding the lost science.

At the time of *Princess*, the red men hold uneasy sway over most of the civilized portion of the planet, from such centers as Ptarth, Dusar, Amhor, Duhor, Toonol, Phundahl, and the great Empire of Helium. The green men are in control of much of the actual surface of the planet, but the red men have built a system of fertile and well-defended walled waterways, lacing the globe.

At the north pole survives a black-bearded yellow race, in the land of Okar. At the south pole live the Holy Therns (white-skinned offshoots of the Orovars) in the Mountains of Otz ringing the Valley Dor and the Lost Sea of Korus. Underneath is the domain of the Black Pirates, on the underground Sea of Omean which drains Korus.

In short, Burroughs had created a fully-visualized hero—thirty years in apparent age but actually ageless, a professional soldier, an adventurer—and had transported him to a fully visualized alien world, the planet Barsoom, which we call Mars. Barsoom was fully equipped, far beyond even Van Arnam's description, with geography, history, mythology, flora and fauna, human and inhuman inhabitants, science, politics, religion, architecture, law, and every other institution to be expected in a fully developed world.[1]

Once landed John Carter is captured by a band of the green nomads, but wins his freedom and rank among them by virtue of his fighting prowess (enhanced not trivially by his earthly muscles' greater effect in the lighter-gravitied environment of Mars).

The Barsoom upon which John Carter finds himself is a sorrowfully decadent world. The science is inherited from earlier days of Orovar rule; the pattern of survival of scientific devices is not a consistent one. Thus, while the modern Martians possess "fliers" operated by anti-gravitational and propulsive rays and capable of an airspeed of 200 miles per hour, they have no form of mechanized ground transportation, and must go either on foot or on *thoat*back, the thoat being an eight-limbed Martian beast roughly equivalent to the horse, but subject to control only by telepathic influence rather than by reins, bridle and bit.

There are, similarly, radium pistols, which fire explosive shells, but which are, to say the least, highly unreliable. Further, sunlight is required to activate the explosive, so that if the pistol is used at night, the shell will act virtually as an inert projectile, although it will explode the next morning if it lands in an exposed spot. As a result of the unreliability of the pistols, expediency, reinforced by a rigid Barsoomian code of honor, dictates that a variety of bladed weapons—lances, longswords, shortswords, daggers and dirks—are the primary means of combat. There is also some use of bows and arrows, but except among the nearly legendary Bowmen of Lothar, bow and arrow are not popular.

The human inhabitants of Mars (that is, those intelligent races other than the green men) resemble earthly humans in every detectable way with the exception of being oviparous, the incubation period for their eggs being several years and the maturation rate of the offspring very rapid. Martians live for a thousand years, retaining the appearance of youth and its full vigor until near the very end. The fact that those few who survive to this age show signs of deterioration would indicate that they would probably die soon of natural causes, but constant wars produce a high mortality rate, and a religious stricture causes those Martians who reach the age of one thousand

1. Dave Van Arnam passed away in 2002; at the time he was planning to revise his *Reader's Guide to Barsoom and Amtor*. Two other Martian studies exist: *A Guide to Barsoom* by John Flint Roy (1976) and my own *Barsoom: Edgar Rice Burroughs and the Martian Vision* (1976; reissue 2002).

John Carter battles green men of Barsoom

to make a final pilgrimage down the sacred River Iss . . . a pilgrimage from which none ever returns.

It is not necessary further to rehearse the plot of *A Princess of Mars* except to state that John Carter, through courage and skill, wins free of the green men, makes league with the red people of Helium, and near the end of the book is apparently going to live happily ever after as the husband of Dejah Thoris, princess of Helium. Unfortunately, through a complexity of circumstances, at this point the atmosphere plant, a sort of air factory that constantly replenishes Barsoom's attenuated oxygen blanket, ceases to function. John Carter, the only man alive who knows the secret telepathic combination of the impenetrable lock on the single entrance to the atmosphere plant, sets out to save the entire population of the planet from oxygen starvation.

John Carter succeeds in reaching the plant, delivers the "nine thought waves" that will open the seals, and expires as an oxygen-starved companion crawls forward to restart the vital machinery.

John Carter reawakens in his own body, back on earth. (What body he used on Mars is not clear; perhaps an astral one, but in the entire period of his experiences on Mars it seemed to be as solid as the original.) At this time, then, he obviously writes the manuscript which "Edgar Rice Burroughs" received upon Carter's death in 1886.

It is curious to note that while the introduction of all book editions of *Princess* is signed Edgar Rice Burroughs, the original magazine version bore the by-line Norman Bean. In the *All-Story* version the full introduction (it runs to six pages in standard book editions) does not appear, but is replaced by a brief editor's note signed, appropriately, Editor's Note.

In the manuscript the full introduction appears, signed only by "the author."

As a first work *A Princess of Mars* is an admirable creation. To the perceptive reader it is doubly rewarding, first as a story of considerable pure entertainment value, and secondly as a revelatory exhibit of a self-taught writer learning his craft. The portions of the "manuscript" following John Carter's advent on Barsoom tend to be distressingly stationary, as the author has John Carter walk about the camp of the green men, engaging one or another in conversation whereby the Barsoomian landscape is sketched in for the reader.

As the novel progresses—and obviously, as Burroughs developed his craft with remarkable speed—the narration begins to move in several senses of the word, and by the end of the book an obvious sense of pacing and a narrative drive are evident which contribute greatly to the appeal of many of Burroughs' better works, and which a number of his imitators worked hard, but without success, to duplicate.

In two sequels to *Princess*, *The Gods of Mars* and *The Warlord of Mars* (serialized in *All-Story* in 1913 and 1914 respectively) John Carter does return to Mars (ah, that curious tomb!) and undergoes various further adventures, rising ultimately to the position of Warlord of Barsoom, an unique position supreme to that of all the kings and emperors of the world. One might speculate on the purpose of such a post: if the Warlord stands above *all* nations, what war can there be, and without war, what use is a Warlord? Burroughs did not bring in the theme of interplanetary war until the proposed eleventh novel of the Martian series, introducing the idea in *Skeleton Men of Jupiter*, an introductory novelette. The rest of the novel was never written.

But even without an interplanetary menace, the Warlord has a job in subduing defiant monarchs, rebels and outlaws of all sorts, as well as uncivilized savages.

En route to the position of Warlord of Mars John Carter destroys the false religion of the Holy Therns and the goddess Issus. (That pilgrimage down the River Iss led to the temperate Valley Dor at the south pole of the planet. There, amidst sylvan beauty, a race of hideous semi-human creatures, not green men but a sort of anthropophagous plant-men, devoured the pilgrims promptly upon their arrival.)

The second book, *Gods*, ends with another cliffhanger, as Dejah Thoris is imprisoned in a strange cell beneath the south pole where, surrounded by mountains and ice fields there are an underground sea and an underground city, kept habitable by constantly pumping the water from the ever-fed sea back to the surface. A secondary hero of the book is Carthoris, son of John Carter, and Dejah Thoris. (In later books they also have a daughter, Tara, and ultimately a grandchild, Llana.)

In *Warlord*, the third book, Dejah Thoris is rescued, John Carter goes off adventuring again, and conquers virtually the entire planet, including the hermit empire of Okar at the north pole.

Thus ends the original trilogy of the Martian series, and it might be of interest to ask if the fascinating hero John Carter and the marvelously complete planet Barsoom were created out of the ether by Burroughs or if some source of inspiration, fictional or historical, might not have contributed to the characterization or the setting. If the latter should prove to be the case, it need not reflect discredit upon ERB, for the combining of known elements into new combinations and patterns is the whole basis of the creative act, from the most elementary tale-telling of the small child to the complex narration of the novelist.

CHAPTER III

A Phoenician on Mars

The literature of space flight has a long and honorable history, with stories of visits to the sun, the moon, and even other planets surprisingly antedating the existence of astronomical theory to support them. In the classical era and indeed for centuries after, scientific and religious thought were so intermixed that supernatural and what we would today consider superscientific elements appear in indiscriminate juxtaposition, so that the borderline between fantasy and science fiction becomes blurred. Yet this is true of many more recent works, including *A Princess of Mars* with John Carter's apparently astral voyage to Mars, his unexplained longevity and his apparent deaths and resurrections.

At least five historians of science fiction do agree that the oldest works that can reasonably be termed science fiction are those attributed to Lucian of Samosata, a Hellenized Syrian who flourished circa 200 A.D. In one tale Lucian portrays a flight to heaven by means of bird's wings, but more important from our viewpoint is his *True History* in which a ship is carried aloft by a waterspout and deposited on the moon. Subsequently the crew visit the planet Venus, colonization rights to which are the subject of warfare between the armies of the sun and the moon!

The historians who agree on Lucian as a sort of great-great-great grandfather of modern science fiction are J. C. Bailey in *Pilgrims through Space and Time* (1947), Marjory Hope Nicolson in *Voyages to the Moon* (1948), L. Sprague de Camp in *Science Fiction Handbook* (1953), Roger Lancelyn Green in *Into Other Worlds* (1958) and Peter Leighton in *Moon Travellers* (1960).

From Lucian's hands the theme of space flight passed through many others, but interplanetary stories seemed to give way once more to lunar and solar expeditions. Neither de Camp nor Green cites any title for over fifteen centuries, with the possible exceptions of "spiritual" journeys, fairly excludable from the ken of science fictionists. In 1880, however, Percy Greg published *Across the Zodiac*, a huge novel in which an anonymous narrator travels to Mars in his spaceship the *Astronaut*. The ship is a giant, its walls alone being of metal three feet thick, and the total dimensions of the *Astronaut* being one hundred feet length, fifty feet breadth, and twenty feet height.

Greg's hero finds a civilized race on Mars, and involves himself substantially in the affairs of the Martians, to the point that he eventually feels it politic to return home, which he does in his *Astronaut*. The ship was powered by a form of repulsive energy called apergy.

Other Martian voyagers followed Greg's anonymous hero, and while any direct influence on Burroughs is doubtful until a 1905 work, the general development of the theme is of interest. Further, influence of one pre-Burroughsian author upon another may be adduced, leading to an influence, albeit an indirect one, upon Burroughs.

In 1891 Robert Cromie, a friend and admirer of Jules Verne, produced *A Plunge into Space*. In it his heroes build a great globular craft in the Alaskan wilderness. The site is chosen for privacy, but results also in the prospective space travelers' having to fight off an Indian raid early in the book. The ship, christened the *Steel Globe*, is powered by " . . . the law of gravitation [which] may be diverted, directed, or destroyed."

With a fairly sizable complement on board, the *Steel Globe*, carrying a carefully measured supply of air, food and water, takes off for Mars. The trip is generally uneventful, and when the voyagers reach Mars they find the natives to be friendly, advanced beyond any society on earth in both science and organization, and living an idyllic life.

In fact, the Martian life is so perfect that, except for an apparently harmless dalliance between one of the earthly visitors and a pretty Martian maiden, an overwhelming boredom sets in. The visitors (who are by this time no less bored than the reader) again carefully provision their ship, climb aboard, and set out for home.

Part way back to earth they take a routine check of air consumption and discover that the supply is below its proper level, and go on a regime designed to cut consumption. Still, the level continues to run below normal, and the cold equations of the captain and engineer tell the story: unless the crew is reduced in size, *all* will suffocate before reaching Earth.

At this point the Martian sweetheart appears, revealing that she had stowed away in order to be with her lover. All anguish and heroics notwithstanding, there is no solution for the air shortage but for the ship's complement to be reduced, and it is, by the exit of the Martian maiden through the airlock. The *Steel Globe* then succeeds in returning to Earth.

Although generally a poor book, Cromie's *A Plunge into Space* is to my knowledge, the earliest story in which the coldly and ruthlessly scientific outlook is applied to questions of space flight. And, oddly, sixty-three years later, in the August, 1954 issue of *Astounding Science Fiction* magazine, there appeared a story by Tom Godwin titled *The Cold Equations*. It treated of precisely the same theme, coming to precisely the same bitter conclusion, and created a furor in the science fiction community for the powerfully developed sensation of inevitability in its outcome. *The Cold Equations* has since been anthologized innumerable times.

In 1894 John Jacob Astor published *A Journey in Other Worlds*, a sort of unauthorized sequel to Greg's *Across the Zodiac* in which an apergy-powered craft reaches Jupiter and Saturn. Astor's book is a remarkably advanced work for its time, delving into many changes on our own planet before taking up the theme of space travel. By the year 2000 disease is virtually unknown, thanks to the blessing of universal inoculation. Giant mechanical "water spiders" riding on air cushions have supplanted conventional ships for oceanic navigation. Apergy-powered ornithopters fill the air, and it is possible for the hero to drive his electric phaeton from his Manhattan home, up the "improved post road" and reach Vassar College "in the beautiful town of Poughkeepsie" in just two hours. His fiancée is a junior at Vassar.

The nations of the western hemisphere have one by one joined the United States, turning this nation into a sort of super Pan-American Union, while in Europe the mutual suspicions of Germany, France and Russia have led these countries into a perpetual cold war, permitting Britain to spread her influence throughout Africa and Asia, thereby far outweighing the loss of Canada.

The greatest project taking place on Earth is the venture of the Terrestrial Axis Straightening Company. By building great complexes of dams about the Arctic and Antarctic Oceans, and by shifting massive volumes of water between the poles, the Earth's tilt will be reduced from 23° to a mere 11°. This will eliminate the extremes of summer and winter in the temperate zones, and substitute a climate of perpetually alternating spring and autumn.

Aboard the *Callisto* Astor's space travelers debate the best method of interstellar flight, settling upon the idea of creating an artificial sun from two asteroids, giving their sunlet an apergetic push toward a distance star, and then orbiting themselves in either a large and comfortable spaceship or a hollowed-out asteroid, and traveling thus warmed and lighted to another solar system.

In *A Journey in Other Worlds*, however, the *Callisto* travels only as far as Jupiter and Saturn, landing on both. Jupiter is found to be an alien world in anticipation of the finest traditions, replete with weird landscape and strange beasts. Saturn, unfortunately, is found to be an abode of departed spirits, and much of the visit is given over to conversations with a former bishop.

In 1899 Ellsworth Douglass returned to Mars, this time with a gravitation-powered craft, no longer round like Cromie's *Steel Globe* or dome-shaped like Astor's *Callisto*, but cigar-shaped, as were the majority of fictional space craft for the next sixty years. (Only very recently, comparatively speaking, has the idea of assembling a spaceship in orbit become popular. This technique, avoiding a passage through a planetary atmosphere on takeoff, obviates the need for streamlining, and current thought on the topic, both in and out of fiction, is that spaceships need not be streamlined.)

Douglass' book, intriguingly titled *Pharaoh's Broker*, is a curious little gem. The travelers in it are Isidor Werner, a Jewish grain speculator from Chicago, and Dr. Hermann Anderwelt, his old physics professor. Werner finances Dr. Anderwelt's project to build a spaceship and fly to Mars, which the two of them do. Arriving there they find Martian civilization to resemble that of Biblical times, down to a "Hebrew" prime minister in "Egypt." He and Werner converse in Hebrew.

Werner learns that the Martian "Egypt" is in the midst of its seven fat years, and against the anticipated lean years, he corners the entire planet's wheat market. The coup backfires, however, when a revolution threatens. Werner decides to convert his holdings to cash, but Martian money is iron, and hence worthless on Earth, while the Martian gold supply is almost nil—mostly consisting of the small change that was in Werner's pockets when he arrived. It would be impossible to carry home his holdings in kind, and even if this were not the case, lacking the corner on Earth, Werner would hold relatively little value.

He instead gives away his possessions, and with Dr. Anderwelt returns to Earth where each writes a book, Dr. Anderwelt's a scientific treatise and Werner's the very tale we have just read. Dr. Anderwelt's treatise deals with "parallel planetary life," the theory that each planet experiences essentially similar historical development, beginning with those nearest the sun, and working outward in turn.

Thus, the trip to Mars had been tantamount to a trip into Earth's own past. A trip to Venus would give the traveler a picture of Earth's future. The two men prepare for a trip to Venus, Werner promising to write a similar report upon their return from the planet. Unfortunately, it seems that the sequel to *Pharaoh's Broker* was never written, or at least was never published.

Still, the existing book is remarkable for its witty style, and for at least one element of remarkable scientific prediction. During the trip to Mars, Douglass has Werner take daily exercise with equipment brought along for that purpose. Dr. Anderwelt confines himself to astronomical observations and intellectual exercises, and as a result nearly dies of atrophy and general deterioration of the system, brought about by the weightless conditions aboard ship, and called *Space Fever!*

H. G. Wells of course had his great *The War of the Worlds* a year before *Pharaoh's Broker*, but the travel was solely from Mars to Earth in this novel, and the action of the book takes place entirely on Earth, removing it generally from our sphere of interest.

In reading seriously in turn-of-the-century interplanetary tales, a great difficulty exists in locating copies of many books. *Pharaoh's Broker*, for instance, apparently had only one edition, and that in England, and the modern reader is unlikely to obtain a copy, or for that matter even to hear of the book. (A 1976 reissue should make the novel a bit less difficult to obtain.) None of the historians named a few pages ago seems to know of Douglass' book, nor is it mentioned in any other source I have read. My own discovery of it was by merest chance, and what other early works of serious influence or of passing interest were published and forgotten can only be speculated upon, and occasionally rediscovered by the diligent searcher or the fortunate stumbler.

Prior to 1964 one of the scarcest of all science fiction novels, and one of the least known (although Green describes it with full appreciation) was *Lieut. Gullivar Jones: His Vacation* by Edwin Lester Arnold. Edwin Lester Arnold was the son of a distinguished English diplomat, Sir Edwin Arnold. The senior Arnold served in Asia for some years, making a home in Tokyo, and produced a number of literary works influenced by Eastern life. These included *The Light of Asia*, *The Light of the World*, *The Song Celestial*, and *The Voyage of Ithobal*. The last is an epic poem of Egyptian theme, running to some 226 pages, and containing such execrable doggerel as the following:

For the name of that Lady was plain to view—
Nesta, the Priestess of Amen-ru—

And Gods and Kas had been set to guard her
Asleep, while the slow-footed years crept through.

When the younger Arnold set himself to literary work, he wisely avoided his father's footsteps and confined himself to prose. He produced only four books in a literary career that spanned the years 1890 through 1905; *Gullivar Jones* was his last published work.

The hero of the story, an American naval lieutenant on leave in New York, is wandering through a slum neighborhood when an old man apparently comes tumbling out of the sky, to land on his head practically at Jones' feet. Jones takes him to a hospital, but he is dead. A carpet found near the body somehow devolves into the officer's possession, and as Jones, despondent at an overdue promotion blurts out "I wish I were anywhere but here, anywhere out of this red-tape-ridden world of ours! *I wish I were in the planet Mars!*" the carpet flies into the air, wraps itself into an air-tight cocoon with Jones inside, zooms out the window and does not release the lieutenant until he *is* on (or "in") Mars.

As science fiction purists have tried, over the years, to rationalize John Carter's trip to Barsoom away from the mystical, astral explanation, so a similar attempt may be made concerning Gullivar Jone's carpet. Arnold's description of the carpet's behavior is hardly that associated with the customary magic carpet of Arabian nights fame. Instead of a sedate floating ride, Gullivar Jones tells us that:

> I gave a wild yell and made one frantic struggle, but it was too late. With the leathery strength of a giant and the swiftness of an accomplished cigar-roller covering a "core" with leaf, it swamped my efforts, straightened my limbs, rolled me over, lapped me in fold after fold till head and feet and everything were gone—crushed life and breath back into my innermost being, and then, with the last particle of consciousness, I felt myself lifted from the floor. . . .

Written today, such a tale would be easily rationalized. The carpet would be a telepathically-controlled device lost, strayed or planted by a superior alien culture for devious motives revealed later in the story. But in 1905 the impression given was that of a magic carpet, and such we must accept as Arnold's intent unless we wish to construct a modern fantasy with Edwin Lester Arnold as its central figure.

Dumped by the carpet on Mars, Gully makes the acquaintance of the local residents, a peaceful but strangely indolent race who quickly accept him into their society. Jones notices that everyone has the appearance of young adults, and asks why no children or old people are seen about. He is told that Martians mature very quickly, and retain their youthful appearance and vigor throughout their lives. Only at the time of death do they suddenly show the signs of age.

Dead Martians are dressed in the finest robes, seated on wooden thrones mounted in turn upon rafts, and floated down a sacred river on which no living Martian is permitted to sail, and from which, of course, no deceased Martian ever returns.

Roving bands of semi-human barbarians operate in the wastes between the cities of Arnold's Mars; little by little they are tearing apart the remnants of a once-great civilization, although at the time of Gullivar Jone's arrival a truce exists between the "Hither people" among whom he lands, and the barbaric "Thither people" whereby peace is bought at the price of an annual tribute. This tribute is the most beautiful maiden of the Hither people, selected each year and presented to the chief of the barbarians.

With this background filled in by his Martian friend An, and with the annual selection of the sacrifice approaching, Jones is alone in urging the Hither folk to stand up for their national pride, and break their shameful treaty. He is precipitated upon the face of the scared river, and in one of the most chilling yet eerily beautiful scenes in all fantasy, floats downstream in the company of the beautiful, pallid corpse of a Martian girl who had died in the first bloom of life.

After days of being swept along by the current, Jones reaches the ultimate destination of the river, a gigantic ice field, into which the corpses of hundreds of generations of Martians are frozen in ever-receding ranks.

Jones returns from his strange pilgrimage, only to find that the Princess Heru, his Martian sweetheart, has been taken as this year's tribute to the Thither folk. Unwilling to accept her loss with Martian detachment, Jones rescues the maiden from the clutches of the barbarians, returns with her to the city, and as a result of a desperately voiced "I wish I were in New York!" is whisked home again by the same carpet that had carried him to Mars.

In addition to his misadventures in Arnold's book, poor Gully Jones seems doomed to alternate forever between brief periods of discovery and long years of obscurity. When it was first published in 1905, in England, *Lieut. Gullivar Jones* was unsuccessful; it never had an American edition, and it was Arnold's second failure in a row. He was apparently so discouraged that he never wrote another word for publication, although he lived until 1935.

As far as I have been able to determine, the book went into obscurity almost immediately upon publication, and was not recalled for fifty-three years, until Green's *Into Other Worlds*. Green calls the novel "a gay, fey dream-story, with the least memorable of plots and the sketchiest of scientific backgrounds: but it is the most haunting and convincing picture of the immeasurably ancient world of Mars, before the discovery of [C. S. Lewis'] *Malacandra* . . . compellingly vivid and highly colored . . . delightful fantasy."

I had not yet read Green when I discovered *Lieut. Gullivar Jones* through the guidance of Stephen Takacs, one of the more knowledgeable science fantasy book collectors and dealers. Once I had read the book, and Green's as well, I agreed fully with Green, but added one more observation which he apparently failed to notice: there is an uncanny prediction, in the Mars of *Lieut. Gullivar Jones*, of the Barsoom of Edgar Rice Burroughs' great trilogy, *Princess, Gods, Warlord*.

In each case there is a formerly elevated civilization, the descendents of the great people now living in deteriorating splendor. In each case semi-human barbarian nomads control the countryside and bear implacable enmity toward the city-dwellers. In each case there are few or no children about, due to rapid maturation, nor aged to be seen, for age does not appear until near or at the end of life.

The element of the sacred river of death is nearly identical (although in Burroughs the pilgrimage is performed as the final act of life, while in Arnold it is a pilgrimage of the already-dead), and the destination of the river, an ice field in both cases, is all the more remarkable. And of course the crucial plot element of the "civilized" princess rescued by the earthly military man (Arnold's lieutenant, Burroughs' captain) from the barbaric nomads, while not in itself to be assigned too much weight, is nonetheless an additional point of similarity to be placed in the scales.

Greatly impressed with the Arnold book, both as a work in its own right and as a hardly disputable source of Burroughs, I brought it to the attention of my friend Donald A. Wollheim, himself one of the world's leading authorities on science fiction, possessor of an enviable collection of early publications in the field, and a great Burroughs enthusiast. Wollheim at the time was also editor of the paperback Ace Books.

Wollheim read my copy of the original edition of *Gullivar Jones* and promptly announced its first American edition under the title *Gulliver of Mars*. Invited to write an introduction for the paperback, I pointed out the likely relationship between Arnold's Mars and Barsoom, continued:

> As for publishing dates, *Gullivar Jones* appeared in 1905. Burroughs wrote *A Princess of Mars* in 1911, and it was first published the follow-

ing year in *All-Story* magazine. How a copy of *Gullivar Jones* found its way from England to America and Burroughs' possession will probably never be known. The book never had an American edition before now. Nor did ERB ever refer to it, as far as available records show . . .

Perhaps the only major flaw in the comparison of *Gullivar Jones* with Burroughs' Martian books, is the central character. John Carter, as we all know, is immortal, daring, the greatest swordsman of two worlds. Gully Jones is no John Carter.

The search for Carter would seem to be a hopeless task, for the heroes of adventure tales from mythical times onward might be investigated, turning up here an immortal hero (remember Carter's "having died twice, yet still living"), there a great swordsman, and yet never uncovering a single, specific source for John Carter. Of course there was the possibility that there was no single source, that John Carter was an original, a conglomerate of characteristics put together by Burroughs for the first time.

But the astonishing find of Barsoom in Arnold presented such an intriguing prospect of additional finds that I felt constrained to make an effort, at least a perfunctory one, and the first obvious place to look was the other works of Edwin Lester Arnold.

In 1901, four years before *Gullivar Jones*, Arnold had published *Lepidus the Centurion: A Roman of To-day*. The idea behind Lepidus is a promising one: Louis Allanby, a modern (i.e., Victorian) English squire, stumbles upon a Roman grave at his country estate. More than a simple grave, this is actually an underground mausoleum, and within it, apparently perfectly preserved, lies the body of a Roman officer.

Allanby peers closely into the Roman's face, and the Roman, Lepidus, somehow absorbs part of the Englishman's soul, is revived, and returns with Allanby to his home, where he is passed off as a visiting member of the Italian branch of the family. From this promising start, unfortunately, the story goes nowhere. Louis is a totally brainless, spineless mama's boy, interested in nothing more vigorous than an afternoon's tennis match. The book is filled with dull dinner parties with the local vicar, with dull picnics, dull hunting parties. Louis is a nobody and Lepidus is seen too little to serve as a prototype for anyone, although what is seen of him is promising.

Tracking back to 1895 we find *The Story of Ulla*, a collection of ten shorter works by Arnold from such sources as the *Graphic*, *Pall Mall*, *Idler*, *Lloyds*, and *Atalanta*. Most of the ten are rather slight romances. One story, *Rutherford the Twice-Born*, has a basis in reincarnation and/or heredity memory, with a family ghost as well; another, *The Vengeance of Dungarvan*, offers a marvelous villain, Black John Hackett, worthy of the later H. P. Lovecraft or Robert E. Howard.

But no John Carter.

A year earlier, in 1894, Arnold had seen published *The Constable of St. Nicholas*, a tale of crusaders on the island of Rhodes. The hero, Oswald de Montaigne, is a swordsman of some note, but only superficially similar to any Burroughs hero. Less a man of action than any Burroughs hero, tending to ponder overlong, to react rather than to initiate action, he cannot be considered a Burroughs source.

Back farther, back to 1890 for Arnold's first book and our last hope, *Phra the Phoenician*, or more fully *The Wonderful Adventures of Phra the Phoenician*.

Opening *Phra* one finds a prologue, in which the title figure asserts that "When I say that I have lived in this England more than one thousand years, and have seen her bud from callowest barbarity to the height of a prosperity and honour with which the world is full, I shall at once be branded as a liar. Let it pass! The accusation is familiar to my ears. I tired of resenting it before your fathers' fathers were born, and the scorn of your offended sense of veracity is less to me than the lisping of a child."

In the novel Phra tells us that "The first thirty years of my life, it will be guessed in extenuation, were full of the frailties and shortcomings of an ordinary mortal; while those years which followed have impressed them-selves indelibly upon my mind by right of being curious past experience and credibility.

"Looking back, then, into the very remote past is like looking upon a country which a low sun at once illuminates and blurs. I dimly perceive in the golden haze of the ancient time a fair city rising, tier upon tier, out of the blue waters of the midland sea."

Phra seems to be about thirty years of age. He loses his earliest youth in the shifting sands of ancient memory. In the course of the book we learn that he is an expert swordsman and soldier, that he lives and dies again and again, only to revive after the passage of years, and resume his life—always a soldier—always thirty.

The clincher: John Carter is convinced that "Someday I shall die the real death from which there is no resurrection," while Phra, after living life upon life, dies truly while laboring over his memoirs. "It is over," he writes, "and I in turn have time to laugh. I have come here, to my secret den in the thickness of these great walls, staggering slowly here by dim, steep stairs, and rare-trodden landings—here to die; and I have double-locked the oaken door, and shot the bolts and pitched the key out of my one narrow window-slit, and gently, rocking and swaying as the strong poison does its errand, I have thrown my belt and sword and opened my great volume once again."

So ends *Phra*. So ends Phra.

The book is far different in tone from *Gullivar Jones*; the earlier book is heavily sensual, pervaded by a dreamlike, almost narcotic atmosphere. It is, in its own, a masterpiece. And Phra the Phoenician is John Carter.

There is no evidence that Edgar Rice Burroughs did read and admire the works of Edwin Lester Arnold, but the dates of publication are right and the internal evidence is massive. There are those who deny the influence of Arnold. Hulbert Burroughs sat across a desk from me a year after the present work first appeared, with a copy of the paperback *Gulliver of Mars* in his hand, and said "You pulled this out of thin air."

A good many purchasers of *Gulliver of Mars* took the trouble to send me letters challenging the assertions made in my introduction. A typical correspondent is Miss Georgia Covington, whose comments I quote here:

> . . . the differences between the two putative civilizations of Mars are far greater and more numerous than the similarities. Mr. Arnold's "Hither people"—soft, decadent, inbred, overcivilized, languid, effeminate—are strikingly similar to H. G. Wells' study, in *The Time Machine*, of our putative descendents of about 1,000,000 A.D. So too the doom which finally overtakes them.
>
> The struggle for life of Mr. Burroughs' Martians, quite on the other hand, under the grimly inhospitable conditions offered by "their dying planet," has rendered them vigorous, virile and aggressive; dynamic, energetic, and inventive to a degree.
>
> The similarities between the two studies are no more than may safely be attributed to the workings of blind coincidence combined with the two authors' fanciful inferences from what had been observed, of the planet's surface, through the telescopes of the period in which the stories were written. Their differences are so enormous that to attempt to draw a parallel or comparison between them is absurdly far fetched.
>
> Again: Teleportation (the process by which John Carter purports to journey between planets) *may* be possible. One reads of instances in which it is speculated actually to have occurred. Although the existence of this power is a possibility extremely doubtful, on the potential capabilities of the human mind it is best to keep an open one. But magic carpets are *not* possible. They belong, together with magic itself and all things magical, in the realm of pure fantasy. . . .

Other correspondents than Miss Covington point out the similarity between Arnold's Hither and Thither people, and the Eloi and Morlocks of Wells' *The Time Machine*. The Wells book was published in bits and chunks in many periodicals before the appearance of *Gullivar Jones*. While I would not care, on my own initiative, to assert that Arnold was influenced by Wells, I can clearly see the similarities pointed out by these people, and would not deny their case.

I think there is no contradiction here. If Wells did influence Arnold, there is no reason why Arnold in turn might not have influenced Burroughs, and in fact I rather hope that Wells *did* bear upon Burroughs, for he is indeed a worthy literary ancestor for any science fiction author.

One other case which has been made: Fritz Leiber in the fan journal *Amra* has published an article amusingly titled *John Carter: Sword of Theosophy*. In this article Leiber makes a rather good case for Madame Helena P. Blavatsky as a source for Burroughs, starting with John Carter's "astral" trip to Mars (astral flight being a favored Theosophical theme) and continuing through various aspects of Barsoomian history and their resemblance to Theosophical teachings.

No occult scholar myself, I can still easily conceive of Burroughs stumbling across the weirdly mystical teachings of this cult, and grafting some of the enchanting (albeit absurd) ideas onto his own stories. Still, I will hold with Edwin Lester Arnold as the primary source for Burroughs' Martian trilogy (in later books of the series Burroughs went far beyond his original concepts). To any who disagree, I ask only that they first read five books: *Phra the Phoenician, Lieut. Gullivar Jones, A Princess of Mars, The Gods of Mars*, and *The Warlord of Mars*. Then, let's talk.

CHAPTER IV

To the Earth's Core—and Elsewhere

During the period in which he wrote the first Barsoomian books (*Princess* in 1911, *Gods* in 1912, and *Warlord* completed July 8, 1913) Burroughs was active with other fiction as well, a total, in fact, of six other novels.

The first of these, also written in 1911, was *The Outlaw of Torn*. An historical novel set in thirteenth century England, *Outlaw* is a generally routine novel of Saxons versus Normans, a kidnapped princeling, the raising of an outlaw army, bloody battles and tearful reconciliation. Such avatars as *Gullivar Jones* notwithstanding, *A Princess of Mars* had offered something new to the world of pulp fiction; with *Princess* Burroughs had a real impact on the magazine fiction field, establishing a solid place for the scientific romance which that type of story held well for decades, and which experienced a significant revival, along with Burroughs, during the paperback boom of the 1960s and 1970s.

Burroughs had no such revolutionary contribution to make to the historical novel, and had difficulty marketing *The Outlaw of Torn*. It was not published until 1914, by which time Burroughs was selling everything he could write and magazines were crying for more; it did not see book publication until 1927, the only historical novel published by Burroughs during his life.

The only other noteworthy element concerning *Outlaw* is the appearance, in a single scene, of Lord Greystoke. Not Tarzan, of course, but likely an ancestor of his, a fact seriously enough regarded by some Burroughs enthusiasts that they place *The Outlaw of Torn* in the Tarzan series. This early Lord Greystoke becomes involved in a minor controversy with the Outlaw of Torn, and is dispatched with a single stroke of the Outlaw's sword.

Burroughs' practice of including such connecting links between his various books provides material for a fascinating hobby (if one is a Burroughs fan) in attempting to see just how many of the works can be drawn into a

single gigantic fabric of counter references and character crossovers. Later
on he did provide links among all his major series, as well as tying in many
non-series stories.

The third work Burroughs produced was *Tarzan of the Apes*, commencing
work on December 1, 1911, and completing the story on May 14, 1912.
Burroughs alternated his successful series for a while. He wrote *The Gods
of Mars*, then *The Return of Tarzan*, but before going on to *The Warlord of
Mars* he produced three other stories, two of which were distinctly science
fiction, and the third marginally so.

The first of these, and by far the most important, was *At the Earth's Core*,
completed in February, 1913, and published in *All-Story* fourteen months
later. It is the first novel of seven in Burroughs' Pellucidar series, a group
of adventure stories laid inside the earth.

The idea of another world within (or beneath) the earth is of course
a very old one. Wherever caves are known, and they are known in most
parts of the world, superstition tends to grow up about dwellers in them,
and secret places to which caves lead. Other natural phenomena lead to
speculations as to what—or who—lies beneath the earth. Volcanoes and
earthquakes may give rise to one class of story and belief; springs, animal
burrows, even common growing things may lead to others.

Further, the common association of death with a return to the earth or
an under-earth through burial is widespread and not recent in origin.

In specific works of the developing science fiction genre the theme of
under-world adventure is not neglected. Nicholas Klimius (or Nils Klim)
experienced a wonderful *Journey to the World Under-Ground*. The earliest
appearance of this classic is difficult to ascertain, but an English language
edition is known as early as 1742. The original, in Danish by Ludvig Baron
von Holberg, is cited by de Camp as dating from 1741.

At any rate, Klimius falls through a hole in the Earth and finds it hollow,
and inside a central sun with a number of inhabited planets. The inner shell
of the Earth is also inhabited. Klimius has a number of adventures in "inner
space," upon the inner planets, and on the inner shell of the Earth. The
happenings are largely of a socially satirical nature, rather than what we
today consider entertainment fiction.

Perhaps the first English-language document dealing with a hollow
Earth (other than in translation) was an 1818 circular by Captain John
Cleves Symmes, as cited by Bailey, seriously advancing the hollow-earth
theory (and there are people to this day who believe in it, some of them
even maintaining that we live on the inside, according to Martin Gardner's
Fads and Fallacies in the Name of Science, 1957).

Captain Symmes published a non-fiction volume about his theory in 1826, but six years earlier there had appeared *Symzonia* by Captain Adam Seaborn, whom Bailey suggests to be Symmes himself. In this novel a ship enters the inner world through an opening at the south pole, and finds it inhabited and civilized, lighted by two suns and two moons—presumably our own sun and moon, reflected by the atmosphere through openings at both poles.

Poe make use of the Symmes theory in three different works. In *Hans Pfaal* (1835) he makes mention of a balloonist's noticing a great hollow at the pole. In *MS. Found in a Bottle* (1833) he describes a sort of zombie-ship manned by living dead, being sucked into a whirlpool near the south pole, presumably to emerge inside the Earth.

Finally, in the *Narrative of Arthur Gordon Pym* (1838), Poe again portrays a fantastic sea voyage, replete with wonders, terrors and disasters of various sorts, and generally hinting that a visit to the inner world through the southern polar opening is in store. However, Poe does not provide such an episode. A number of authorities (including Bailey) suggest that the *Narrative* was only the opening section of a planned longer work, and Jules Verne wrote a sequel, *The Ice Sphinx* (1897; sometimes rendered *The Sphinx of Ice*) which does not, however, include any inner-world element.

Verne's own *Journey to the Center of the Earth*, however, antedates *The Ice Sphinx* by over three decades, appearing first in 1864, and is perhaps the most famous of all inner-world stories. In it, entry to the inner world is achieved through an extinct volcano in Iceland, and the inner world consists of a series of caves, some so large that a sea is found, and clouds form under the roof of the cave. Light is provided largely by vulcanism, although there are also electrical discharges providing light. The inner world contains survivors of primitive forms of life, both animal and vegetable, and even giant primitive humans.

The introduction of prehistoric survivors is apparently Verne's and will be seen to be a major element in Burroughs.

Actually, "hollow Earth" or "inner world" stories were surprisingly common late in the nineteenth and early in the twentieth centuries. To cite just a few more: John Uri Lloyd used the inner-world format for his *Etidorhpa* (spell it backwards) in 1895. Lloyd's book is written as a journey, the narrator being guided through various allegorically significant settings beneath the Earth as a kind of penance and purgatory for having revealed Masonic secrets.

Willis George Emerson in *The Smoky God*, 1908, used the hollow Earth for a social allegory (Lloyd's lessons had been mystical in nature), but to little better effect. Emerson's inner world is populated by a race of civilized and tranquil giants who scorn the outer world's inhabitants as barbarous and unworthy of contact.

The main flaw in both the Lloyd and Emerson books is that they are, above all, dull. Not so the earlier volume by William R. Bradshaw, *The Goddess of Atvatabar* (1891). At least in its earlier portions, this novel of an inner world reached through a polar opening moves with a good pace and considerable humor. As usual, an inhabited inner world is found, and a fascinating picture is given of the people, their science (they ride to war on "magic" powered mechanical ostriches forty feet tall), and, intriguingly, a number of inhabitable inner moons suspended between the crust of the Earth and the inner sun. Unfortunately, *Atvatabar* also bogs down in turgid mysticism in its middle portions, but is an amusing curiosity to the antiquarian reader.

To my knowledge Charles Willing Beale, in *The Secret of the Earth* (1899), was the first author to take his adventurers through the polar opening by means of an aircraft.

In 1908 Howard Garis, writing under the house name of Roy Rockwood for the Edward Stratemeyer syndicate, published *Five Thousand Miles Underground or The Mystery of the Center of the Earth*, a rather outrageous copy of Verne's *Journey* and adding only one element of any particular significance, that being the vehicle used to enter the inner world (again, through a natural opening in the Earth).

Rockwood's voyagers consisted of Professor Amos Henderson, two youngsters, Mark Simpson and Jack Darrow, a hunter friend, and a Negro chef named Washington White.

Washington is included for comic relief, and perhaps we ought not to condemn Rockwood for practicing the literary conventions of his time, which ran to racial stereotypes of many sorts. Nonetheless there is still something remarkable about such lines as this one of Washington's:

> "Yas sir Professer, I'se goin' t' saggasiate my bodily presence in yo' contiguous proximity an' attend t' yo' immediate conglomerated prescriptions at th' predistined period. Yas, sir!"

The line is not lifted unfairly from context. It appears in fact, on the first page of the book, and is clearly intended to delineate character. Washington is cowardly, superstitious, simple, faithful, etc. The perfect comic darky.

Professor Henderson's craft, the *Flying Mermaid*, is a ship with a large rigid gas container mounted above the hull in place of sails. When on water it is driven by propellers; when the captain wishes to fly, an electric generator is used to fill the cylinder with a super-light gas. Rockwood's science was a bit backward, for he has the ship growing lighter as more and more gas is generated, with apparently no limit to the lifting power of the cylinder. Unless he had in mind a substance with negative weight (which is not indicated in the book), packing the cylinder with more and more gas would have reduced its lifting ability, not increased it.

At any rate, *Five Thousand Miles Underground* brings the inner-world theme into the twentieth century, and leads up to Edgar Rice Burroughs, with perhaps mention of only one more early adventure under the Earth, that of R. E. Raspe's *Baron Munchausen* (1786?). Munchausen's travels were so extensive, and their telling so fast paced, that Raspe gives no more space to a complete incident than many a novelist to the most petty moment. Nonetheless, the Baron jumps into Mount Etna, falls through its bottom, meets Vulcan and Venus, displeases Vulcan who throws him into a well, through which he passes, emerging in the South Seas, having passed entirely through the Earth. One of the quickest of all visits to the world underground!

But to return to 1913, and *At the Earth's Core*, Burroughs commences his narration with a framing sequence, a literary device little used nowadays, but quite popular in the past, and one which Burroughs used a number of times. *A Princess of Mars* was a manuscript read by a dutiful nephew; *Tarzan of the Apes*, to be discussed more fully later, was a tale begun in a saloon. *At the Earth's Core* is a second-hand tale recounted by an anonymous narrator (presumably Burroughs himself, or perhaps "Burroughs" the nephew of John Carter).

In a fashion reminiscent of Professor Challenger's young friend the reporter Edward Malone, in Arthur Conan Doyle's *The Lost World* (1912), the narrator has given his tale to "a Fellow of the Royal Geographical Society on the occasion of my last trip to London." But

"You would have thought that I had been detected in no less heinous a crime than the purloining of the Crown Jewels from the Tower, or putting poison in the coffee of His Majesty the King.

"This erudite gentleman in whom I confided congealed before I was half through—it is all that saved him from exploding—and my dreams of an Honorary Fellowship, gold medals, and a niche in the Hall of Fame faded into the thin, cold air of his arctic atmosphere.

"But I believe the story, and so would you, and so would the learned Fellow of the Royal Geographical Society, had you and he heard it from the lips of the man who told it to me. Had you seen, as I did,

the fire of truth in those gray eyes; had you felt the ring of sincerity
in that quiet voice; had you realized the pathos of it all—you, too,
would believe. You would not have needed the final ocular proof that
I had . . ."

Here is the introduction of what soon becomes a most unlikely story,
carefully arranged to nurture the suspension of disbelief. *All* fiction is, by
definition, untrue, or therefore not to be believed by readers, but realistic
recountings of ordinary events in fiction are, if not believed, at least easily
accepted by the reader. The more extravagant the narration, the more difficult this acceptance, and most of the stories of Edgar Rice Burroughs, if
they are nothing else, are at least extravagant.

To overcome this obstacle to acceptance, Burroughs has his anonymous
narrator tell the reader "In the first place please bear in mind that I do not
expect you to believe this story."

Seventeen centuries earlier Lucian opened his *True History* with "I write
of things which I have neither seen nor suffered nor learned from another,
things which are not and never could have been, and therefore my readers
should by no means believe them."

In both cases the reader, through a natural sort of contrariness native to
us all, is likely to reply: "Oh, I dunno, maybe I just *will* believe your story."
Which is, of course, exactly what the author wants, not in order to deceive
the reader, but in order to get him to accept, as he reads, the characters and
situations of the extravagant tale.

Burroughs' anonymous narrator quickly bows out of *At the Earth's Core*,
leaving the story to its protagonist, who opens with a quite mundane and
believable statement:

> I was born in Connecticut about thirty years ago. My name is David
> Innes. My father was a wealthy mine owner. When I was nineteen
> he died. All his property was to be mine when I had attained my
> majority—provided that I had devoted the two years intervening in
> close application to the great business I was to inherit.

The sentences are short, clear, solid. The delivery is calculatedly matter
of fact, almost dull. None of the convoluted prose for which Burroughs
is criticized, not a single comma appears, four of the five sentences in the
paragraph are less than ten words in length. After being warned of the
unbelievability of the story we are given an opening which seems unworthy,
not of belief, but of doubt.

Innes tells of being approached by Abner Perry, an amateur paleontologist, learned and devout, and an inventor who "had devoted the better part of a long life to the perfection of a mechanical subterranean prospector."

The subterranean prospector, or iron mole, is in reality a vehicle something like a tank, something like a drill, and perhaps just a tiny bit like a submarine or even a spaceship. The iron mole is housed in a silo-like structure, the drill point of the vehicle downward. With Perry and Innes inside it is to be used as a sort of "land submarine" boring here and there in the Earth's crust in search of mineral deposits worth commercial exploitation.

The story by now begins to sound just the least bit like a travelogue, with a heavy dose of scientific instruction thrown in for good measure. Not quite the experience in "mundania" that was first indicated, but still far from an extravagant romance.

The late Lin Carter, himself a science-fiction author and one of the most perceptive critics of imaginative literature, stated in his classic study of epic fantasy (*Notes on Tolkien*, *Xero* magazine, 1961, 1962): "One such traditional plot device is to open your tale in surroundings, or among characters, familiar to your audience, and by degrees (once the reader has 'identified' and become 'comfortable' with them) to carry him further and further into your make-believe world."[1]

Burroughs indeed opens *At the Earth's Core* "in surroundings, or among characters, familiar." Connecticut. A young man hoping to run an inherited business successfully. An absent-minded professor who has invented a somewhat radical machine, but one designed nonetheless to serve a perfectly mundane purpose. Undeniably, Burroughs' reader is by now "comfortable," and so the author sets out "to carry him further and further" into a land of extravagance and wonders.

David Innes and Abner Perry take the iron mole on a test run, boring straight down into the Earth. The machine seems a total success, far outstripping Perry's fondest hopes, until some distance below the surface, an attempt is made to turn from their straight descent, and explore for a while on the horizontal. A design flaw in the machine prevents its being steered, and it continues to plunge downward.

What to do? It is impossible to climb back to the surface from the depth already reached. To stand still in the mechanical prospector is merely to

---

1. Carter's series of Xero articles served as the basis for his book-length study *Tolkien: A Look behind the Lord of the Rings* (1969), which in turn led to his stint as Consulting Editor on the fondly remembered Ballantine Adult Fantasy series (1969–1973). Carter was a talented and perceptive literary man who devoted the majority of his energies to producing a barrage of pastiches of the Burroughs and Robert E. Howard variety (touched upon elsewhere in this book). He died in 1987, leaving his potential not merely unfulfilled but virtually untouched.

await death by suffocation or starvation. To turn back is impossible. And to continue ahead . . . what hope is there in that?

Little or none, it would seem, but David Innes, in common with Burroughs' other heroes, is an activist. Better to go out bravely struggling against fate in however hopeless a cause, than to surrender. Tarzan of the Apes meets every adversity with grim and silent determination to struggle on; John Carter of Mars, with a motto bearing far more import than its simple declarative "I still live!" fought free of every entrapment.

And David and Abner?

"If the crust is of sufficient thickness we shall come to a final stop between six and seven hundred miles beneath the Earth's surface; but during the last hundred and fifty miles of our journey we shall be corpses. Am I correct?" I asked.

"Quite correct, David. Are you frightened?"

"I do not know. It all has come so suddenly that I scarce believe that either of us realizes the real terrors of our position. I feel that I should be reduced to panic; but yet I am not. I imagine that the shock has been so great as to partially stun our sensibilities."

After traversing some 500 miles, however, including alternating bands of terrible cold and frightful heat, the mechanical prospector breaks surface. David breathes fresh air, realizes that he and Abner are safe, and faints.

When they recover, David and Abner attempt to discover just where they are. At first they think that their machine must have been deflected from its downward path by some subterranean obstacle, and returned to the surface on some unknown diagonal course, breaking free at an indeterminate point. However, they gradually realize that this is not the case, and by various evidences finally grasp the weird truth that they are in a totally unknown world inside the Earth.

Perhaps the greatest charm and appeal of Burroughs is the discovery of new worlds. This will probably emerge a minority opinion among his admirers, most of whom give their greatest enthusiasm to his characters, the heroic Tarzan, John Carter, and others, the beautiful Dejah Thoris, barbaric La of Opar (who seems to hold more popularity among Tarzan fans than the more conventional Jane). But in my own reading of Burroughs, I have been most impressed by his ability to create exotic worlds, complete with geography, ecology, and history.

Of Burroughs' many worlds, Barsoom is likely the most thoroughly realized, but Pellucidar is a close second, if indeed it is not a match for Barsoom. For its general geography, Burroughs provides major land and water masses the "mirror image" of those on the outer surface. Thus the greatest land mass of Pellucidar is the equivalent in position and area to the Pacific-Indian ocean complex, with other large land masses "under" the Atlantic Ocean, the major seas, and so on, while the great ocean of Pellucidar lies beneath the Asian-European-African continental land masses, with smaller oceans and seas equivalent to the American continents, Australia, Antarctica, and other smaller land masses of the outer world.

The element of a polar opening or openings as found in the Symmes theory occurs in the third book of the series, again in the fourth, and once again in the seventh and final book of the group.

As the outer surface of the Earth is covered predominantly with water, so the inner surface of the world, Pellucidar, is predominantly composed of land, making for a "larger" inner world within a "smaller" outer one, just one of the curiosities of this conception.

Pellucidar is lighted by a miniature sun which hangs suspended in the center of the hollow Earth. In the outer world the phenomenon of alternating day and night is of course caused by half the Earth's blocking the other half from the light of the sun at all times, the rotation of the planet bringing any given point into the lighted—day—or the shadowed—night—side once every twenty-four hours.

In a hollow sphere lighted from a central point, however, there is no shadowing effect, and no night, only a single eternal day. From this premise Burroughs theorizes that, without day and night to give him the idea, man would never have developed the concept of time. And since time exists only as a human concept, there is no time in Pellucidar.

This leads to endless oddities. Sequence still exists but duration is purely subjective. Even aging is capricious: one might go for a stroll while one's wife prepares lunch, only to come home and find her dead of old age, children grown and perhaps parents themselves . . . or one might go off on a complex adventure, experiencing innumerable dangers and performing endless deeds of heroism, and return home to find nothing changed, and the next meal not even cooking.

The closest a Pellucidarian can come to time is knowledge that a meal or a sleep, or a number of meals or sleeps have past. Other than that, it is always noon, everywhere in Pellucidar except one place, the Land of Awful Shadow. The inner sun of Pellucidar has a single satellite, the Pendent World, which revolves about the inner sun once every twenty-four hours, thus remaining stationary over a single point on the ground. The area thus shadowed exists in a state of perpetual eclipse, the only "night" in the entire world.

Because Pellucidar is the inside of a globe rather than the outside, its horizon rises rather than dropping off, and if it were not for the atmosphere inside the Earth, one could, theoretically, see all the way to the opposite side of the world, as nearly directly overhead as the sun permits looking. Actually, because of atmospheric haze, the rising land becomes gradually less distinct as one looks farther and farther away, until vision is lost in the mists of distance.

As in Verne, primitive plants and beasts survive in Pellucidar, but of greater interest, Burroughs populates his inner world with a number of creatures, including intelligent ones, that never existed on the outer surface at all, at least as far as is known.

These include the Mahars, a race of hideous artificially parthenogenetic female winged reptiles who live in ancient cities in Pellucidar, carrying out the hideous investigations of their cold-blooded science and the barbaric anthropophagous rites of their bloody religion.

The Mahars are served by Sagoths, a race of terrible apelike creatures with whom they communicate by a sort of fourth-dimensional thought transference which is specifically stated *not* to be telepathy.

The Sagoths in turn act as slave masters and drivers for the Mahars, capturing and ruling Pellucidarian humans who are used by the Mahars as forced laborers, gladiatorial sacrifices, and ritual as well as nutritional meals. The Mahars are unable to transfer their thoughts to humans, and thus consider them to be paradoxical beings. Their behavior at times seems obviously intelligent, and yet, lacking the power of thought-transference, they cannot be intelligent beings. Thus, a major problem for Mahar philosophers is to determine whether humans are truly intelligent, or merely clever beasts whose behavior bears an uncanny resemblance to that of intelligence.

Although the Mahars are of high order of intelligence themselves, and are of considerable scientific attainment, their cities occupy relatively little area, and beyond these enclaves Pellucidar is a primitive world, for the most part of only stone-age level. Burroughs carries David Innes and Abner Perry through many strange experiences in Pellucidar, including the usual enslavement and escapes, and larding an otherwise straight adventure story with a delightful dose of wryly satirical comments on the relative merits of the primitive Pellucidarian life as against the civilized existence of the outer world.

David falls in love with an excellently realized Pellucidarian maiden named Dian the Beautiful, wins her favor after much travail, and sets out with Dian disguised in a lion skin to return to the outer world in the iron mole. Here he plans to gather the books and implements of civilization,

David Innes, hyaenodons, and man-apes of Pellucidar

and then return to Pellucidar, rejoining Abner Perry who will stay behind, in an effort to civilize the savage inner world.

Unknown to David Innes, however, his rival for Dian's affection, a Pellucidarian named Hooja the Sly One, had abducted Dian and substituted for her a Mahar, in the co-pilot's seat of the iron mole. As David sets out for the surface with the quiet figure beside him, the reader may be tempted to moan rather loudly at the stupidity of Burroughs' heroes. One of the most perceptive commentators upon Burroughs, Harold V. Lynch, holds that Burroughs caused his heroes to perform their frequent boneheaded blunders not merely as a *deus ex machina* to make his plots work, but rather as a deliberate ploy designed to give his readers a moment of superiority over the hero, especially since most Burroughs heroes are so skillful, courageous, muscular, etc., as to threaten to destroy empathy.

If one's hero is a superman, there must be a similarly super villain to provide any challenge, and once this happens, there is a tendency to make the hero doubly super, and the villain triply so, and so on until the reader loses all sense of identity with the characters. One solution for this problem, in addition to a relentless pace and a dazzlement of novel ideas, is to provide one's heroes with faults as gigantic as their talents. Perhaps Burroughs' treatment of his own protagonists springs from just such a motive, whether fully conscious or not.

At any rate, by the time David discovers that a hideous Mahar is beside him in place of Dian the Beautiful, he finds himself once more helpless to alter the iron mole's course. The vehicle, bearing David and the Mahar, emerges in the Sahara, where the anonymous narrator had met David and received his strange story.

Stocking the mechanical prospector with the goods needed by himself and Abner in Pellucidar, David Innes once again turns the prow of the machine downward towards the center of the Earth, and sets out once more for Pellucidar. He leaves behind him, in the Sahara sands, a shallowly buried box containing a telegraph set. This is attached to a very long, thin cable which in turn is connected to a reel inside the iron mole.

With the wire playing out behind the machine, and David headed back to Abner, Dian and Hooja in Pellucidar, an obvious hook is left from which to hang the thread of a sequel to *At the Earth's Core*. The story is an intriguing one, original in some aspects despite the wealth of earlier inner world stories, and the sequel could well be anticipated by the readers of *At the Earth's Core* ninety years ago.

The same is true today.

Having to date started his three major series (Mars, Tarzan, Pellucidar) and written only one story, *The Outlaw of Torn*, which was not part of a series, Burroughs turned out a new serial for *All-Story*. Completed in March, 1913, *The Cave Girl* was published that summer; a sequel, predictably titled *The Cave Man*, was written a year later, but was not serialized (in *All-Story Weekly*) until the spring of 1917.

The book version combines the two stories under the title *The Cave Girl*; it was published in 1925. Even this relatively minor Burroughs work has appeared in approximately twenty editions in the United States and Great Britain.

The cave girl of the title is one Nadara, but she is not actually the focal point of the story. That character is Waldo Emerson Smith-Jones, a very un-Burroughsian hero indeed. Scion of a wealthy Back Bay family, trained by his domineering mother to eschew all physical exertion as crude, Waldo is on a Pacific cruise by order of his physician when a storm arises, sweeping Waldo overboard. He is washed ashore on a tropical isle, where:

> Now he slunk, shivering with fright, at the very edge of the beach, as far from the grim forest as he could get. Cold sweat broke from every pore of his long, lank, six-foot-two body. His skinny arms and legs trembled as with palsy. Occasionally he coughed—it had been the cough that had banished him upon the ill-starred sea voyage.
>
> As he crouched in the sand, staring with wide, horror-dilated eyes into the black night, great tears rolled down his thin, white cheeks.
>
> It was with difficulty that he restrained an overpowering desire to shriek. His mind was filled with forlorn regrets that he had not remained at home to meet the wasting death that the doctor had predicted—a peaceful death at least—not the brutal end which faced him now.

Faced with the challenge of surviving in a primitive environment, Waldo overcomes his weakness and timidity, and is gradually transformed into a powerful giant who lives in the island jungle, stalks game with craft and courage, and in general adapts himself totally to his new surroundings. In due course he meets a tribe of primitive humans, cut off from contact with the outer world for untold millennia, and rises to the state of being able to hold his own in mortal combat with the most powerful and bestial of the sub-men.

Among the primitives is a beautiful girl of distinctly non-primitive features, Nadara, whom Waldo finds highly attractive. Nadara renames Waldo, Thandar the Brave One, when, early in the tale, she observes Waldo's encounter with a panther. Waldo's shrieks of terror are so blood-curdling that they frighten the beast away, and are taken by Nadara for an unconventional war cry.

By the end of *The Cave Man* Waldo—or Thandar—and Nadara are mated, rescued and returned to Massachusetts. Nadara is revealed to be the daughter of the lost Count and Countess of Crecy. And " . . . they are living in Boston now in a wonderful home that you have seen if you ever have been to Boston and been driven about in one of those great sight-seeing motor busses. For the place is pointed out to all visitors because of the beauty of its architecture and the fame that attaches to the historic and aristocratic name of its owner, which, as it happens, is not Smith-Jones at all."

The Cave Girl and *The Cave Man*, beyond the change in Waldo's character as he is gradually transformed into Thandar, offer little different from *Tarzan of the Apes*. Perhaps this is why the reception of the stories was not too enthusiastic, and why, also, Burroughs never brought Thandar back in any further adventures. He wrote most of his tales in such a fashion that a sequel could be written, and when one was not, one can assume that it was omitted because there was little demand for one.

The later *Jungle Girl*, for instance, is full of loose ends, obviously planted by the author to provide material for a sequel, but one was never written. And in the case of *The Cave Girl*, once the two novelette-length serials were out of the way, there seemed little reason to go on. Thandar was nothing but another Tarzan, and Nadara's island offered none of the lost lands and hidden kingdoms later found in Tarzan's Africa.

But to return to 1913, the prolific Burroughs devoted only a little over a month—from March 31 to May 10—to writing a story that he called *Number Thirteen*. It was published complete in the November *All-Story* as *A Man Without a Soul*, and appeared in its first book edition in 1929 as *The Monster Men*. The last title has been retained in all succeeding editions.

The Monster Men is a curious tale, crudely told even for Burroughs whose style was more frequently admirable for its vigor than for its polish. A mad scientist with a deliciously wicked assistant and a very beautiful daughter are the major characters, along with one other. One is led to wonder if Burroughs was not satirizing certain science fictional clichés, but so early in his career—and so early in the development of modern science fiction—this seems unlikely.

Burroughs' mad scientist, Professor Maxon, is obsessed with the creation of artificial life, and he is not interested in synthesizing protozoons either. He is out to make a man. Perhaps because of these weird experiments Maxon, his assistant von Horn, beautiful young Virginia Maxon, and Sing the Chinese cook, set out to establish a base for combined rest and work in the Pamarung Islands, just north of the equator in the western Pacific.

Maxon creates a series of hideous experiments, each, however, approaching more closely to perfection (and all surviving), until he reaches Number Thirteen: an initially mindless but otherwise completely and perfectly formed artificial human. Number thirteen is trained, showing remarkable intelligence; he leads the other twelve experiments away from their inhuman treatment at the hands of von Horn. The twelve monsters try to get themselves adopted as brothers to the local jungle-dwelling baboons, but even these apes will not have them, and, one by one, the twelve perish in the jungle.

But Number Thirteen, by now dubbed Bulan (another Tarzan!), returns to human company, saving Virginia and Professor Maxon from von Horn's carefully nurtured treachery, and behaving with characteristic heroism in a series of bloody encounters with hostile natives.

In the end all is well, and the expected romance between Bulan and Virginia Maxon flowers . . . only to be given pause by Bulan's moral compunctions. Part of his education as Number Thirteen had been some religious training, and Bulan knows that only God can breathe an immortal soul into a living person. Bulan therefore doubts that he can share with Virginia the sacrament of marriage. This is a serious question, and receives serious treatment.

Regarding it, P. Schuyler Miller has written that while reading Burroughs modern readers can laugh at the naiveté of such questions as "Would a man created by science have a soul?" more sophisticated science fiction writers today ask much more meaningful questions, such as "Are androids people?"

Touché!

And Burroughs' solution to the problem is so ingenious that the reader is inclined to shout "Foul!" If such is your reaction, I refer you to a bit of seemingly minor byplay in a railroad station way back on page 4 of the Canaveral Press edition of *The Monster Men*.

After *Number Thirteen / A Man without a Soul / The Monster Men* Burroughs wrote *The Prince of Helium*, which was published as the third Barsoomian novel, *The Warlord of Mars*. He then produced one of the most remarkable stories ever written by *any* author, a story which combined so disparate a variety of themes and locales as very nearly to defy belief. It is also one of the finest books of Burroughs' long and varied career.

The Mucker was written in the late summer of 1913, and was serialized in *All-Story Cavalier Weekly* a year later. In 1916 Burroughs wrote a sequel, *The Return of the Mucker*, which appeared in *All-Story Weekly*.

[The many references to such titles as *All-Story, Argosy All-Story, All-Story Cavalier*, etc., arise from a single family of pulp magazines originally published by the Frank A. Munsey company. As periodicals were added, combined, or dropped, schedules changed, etc., a bewildering aspect is presented. All of these magazines were more or less interchangeable. In their heyday they published much of the adventure fiction of the times, featuring the works of many writers whose works deserved a more permanent form than that provided by ephemeral periodicals printed on fast-disintegrating paper. From the pulp era a few publishers survive, but not as purveyors of popular fiction. Of the Munsey group, *Argosy* magazine was revived in 1997 by film director Francis Ford Coppola as *Zoetrope Argosy* to serve as a showcase for new short fiction. In recent years many small-press magazine and book publishers have exhumed an astonishing amount of old pulp fiction. Much is also posted on the Internet, although often in violation of copyright laws.]

The mucker of Burroughs' story (the word is seldom encountered now; the dictionary entry defining it as an epithet for "a coarse, vulgar person" may soon carry the obsolete tag) is Billy Byrne, a Chicago punk, purse-snatcher, second-story man, part-time sparring partner and drunkard. Billy has to leave Chicago to avoid a murder rap (although he is innocent of his crime), and makes his way to San Francisco where an attempt at drunk-rolling backfires and Billy awakens from a mickey finn to find himself shang-haied.

A wild and fast-moving adventure follows, involving a fire at sea, piracy, kidnapping, a typhoon and Billy's being cast away with the beautiful and refined Barbara Harding of New York . . . on a Pacific island inhabited by a lost race of Japanese Samurai who have kept much of their language, armor, and famed swordsmanship over the isolated generations, but who have forgotten much of the outside world, and have largely reverted to savagery and cannibalism.

Through a pure and idyllic life in the wilds with Barbara, Billy undergoes a moral and physical regeneration, until succeeding in holding at bay both the Samurai and a band of cut-throat sailors with whom he and the kidnapped Barbara were shipwrecked. The two are rescued by the timely arrival of the United States Navy, steaming majestically into the harbor.

Billy and Barbara return to the United States but Billy (reminiscently of Bulan in *The Monster Men*) renounces any romantic entanglement with Barbara because he regards himself as socially unworthy of her. A curious social commentary, in that it is the reformed hooligan who rejects the society girl because of their differing backgrounds, rather than the other way around.

Billy returns to the prize ring, no longer as a sparring partner but as a serious professional, and works his way up to a championship fight, but decides to return to Chicago and clear his name against the old murder charges before taking on the champion.

That is the end of the first story of Billy Byrne. In *The Return of the Mucker* Billy does stand trial, is found guilty, escapes from a speeding train *en route* to prison, makes his way to Mexico, joins a revolutionary army, quits to take a job on a Yanqui-owned *rancho* . . . and is ready to die defending the owner of the ranch from an attacking party of blood-and-lust crazed bandits when they are saved by a fortuitous across-the-border raid by the United States Army (this last inspired perhaps by Black Jack Pershing's expeditions in search of Pancho Villa . . . or perhaps by Burroughs' own brief border service years earlier).

The owner of the *rancho*, rescued along with Billy, is none other than Barbara Harding! At last Billy and she are married and presumably live happily ever after. At least one assumes so, as no further sequel appeared. As a small bonus Billy's murder conviction is also wiped out by an off-stage deathbed confession by the *real* killer.

Now I have devoted this much space to one of Burroughs' lesser-known stories, and frankly one of his less influential ones, because I regard it as a most remarkable technical achievement on the author's part as well as being an entertaining adventure yarn. The disparate elements in the book are none of them particularly original. Gangster stories, piracy, south sea adventure, lost races, prize-ring stories, court-room drama, hobo life, ranch romance . . . are plentifully available in pulp literature and in more respected media as well.

But why any author would essay the use of *all* these elements in one book is a puzzle to wonder at. Harold Lynch has speculated that Burroughs set himself as a task, to take as many of the classic themes of adventure writing as he could, and mold them all into a grand heroic cycle for a single protagonist to survive. One would fear that such a work would inevitably reduce itself to a group of unrelated incidents, dragged together into a hodgepodge book.

Instead, the well handled development of Billy from a petty hoodlum into a strong and decent human being, and the parallel development of his relationship with Barbara Harding give the book a focus and continuity which it would otherwise lack. The flow of incidents, further, is handled with a degree, at least, of logical consistency, resulting in a work which holds together far better than it seemingly ought to.

Following *The Mucker* Burroughs turned his hand to royal romance in a mythical European kingdom with *The Mad King*. Following closely in the tradition of Anthony Hope's *Prisoner of Zenda* and *Rupert of Hentzau*, Burroughs' *The Mad King* is pleasantly readable, but added little to the earlier works of Hope, and is therefore of no particular note for us. If it was Burroughs' intention to prove that he could write a Graustarkian romance, he succeeded, but he is of interest to us for the fields in which he excelled, rather than those such as this, where he merely followed the lead of others, and produced imitation products, however competently.

However, Burroughs certainly derived more from *Zenda* than the basis of a single mediocre novel. Much of the verve and style of the Hope book is detectable in Burroughs' better adventure tales, and the swordsmanship of Rudolf Rassendyll is sometimes seen aiding the exploits of John Carter and other Burroughsian swordsmen, including Barney Custer in *The Mad King*.

If *The Mad King* was unremarkable, Burroughs' next story, *Nu of the Neocene* was the very opposite. *Nu* appeared in *All-Story Weekly* complete in the issue of March 7, 1914 (it was written in just twenty days, from November 27 through December 17, 1913). A sequel, published under the title *Sweetheart Primeval*, is included in the book version, which has carried both the titles *The Eternal Lover* and *The Eternal Savage*.

Whatever name one applies to the story (and admittedly, neither *The Eternal Lover* nor *Sweetheart Primeval* is a very effective title; *The Eternal Savage* is a bit better, but it was applied by a paperback publisher many years after Burroughs' death), it is a remarkable one for a number of reasons. For one thing, Tarzan appears in the book as a minor character, as do his wife Jane Porter Clayton and their son, Korak the Killer, although in *The Eternal Lover* Korak is a tiny babe in arms. Even Jane's Baltimore nursemaid Esmeralda is present, caring for the new baby.

Also present are two characters who had first appeared in *The Mad King*, Barney Custer of Beatrice, Nebraska, and Lieutenant Butzow of the Luthan army. The story is told by an anonymous narrator, very likely our old friend "Edgar Rice Burroughs."

The narrator, together with a Mr. William Curtiss, Butzow, Barney Custer, and Barney's sister Victoria, is visiting at the African estate of Lord Greystoke, Tarzan.

Victoria Custer is subject to strange dreams in which she lives a primitive but contented life in the company of a cave man. She is obsessed with a fear of earthquakes, and in particular experiences a curious reaction to certain places near Tarzan's home. She becomes terrified, or strangely depressed, at evidences of past geological changes. Nonetheless, in describing one such moment to her brother Barney, Victoria states that "Through all my inexplicable sorrow there shone a ray of brilliant hope as remarkable and unfathomable as the deeper and depressing emotion which still stirred me."

Victoria's strange feelings are explained—if explained is the right word— by the occurrence of a minor earthquake in the vicinity. An ancient cave, apparently sealed by a similar temblor in the long-ago Neocene Era is opened by the new quake. In the cave, preserved over the millennia by a gas which seeped into the cave, is Nu, the son of Nu, a young cave man who had been out hunting and wandered into the cave, apparently, just before the ancient upheaval.

Nu can speak the language of the animals, as can Tarzan—the ancient language was shared by men and beasts; today the languages of men have evolved, but Nu can speak with the modern apes and monkeys. He and Victoria are soul-mates. Whether she is a reincarnation of Nat-ul his Neocene love, or whether some other explanation is to be sought, is subject to individual judgment.

There is a strange romance, with the primitive Nu competing against the suave but somewhat underhanded Curtiss for Victoria's favor. Burroughs includes his accustomed conflict and adventure—Nu is hardly ready to join even the limited "civilization" of the Clayton estate, while Barney Custer is not exactly ecstatic at the prospect of his sister's marrying a cave man.

After some vacillation Victoria decides to abandon her inhibitions; Nu is her fated lover and she will live with him regardless of convention. Seeking to run away with Nu, Victoria realizes that Barney and the others will search for them.

And it was instinct that drove Victoria Custer deeper into the jungle with her savage lover as she sensed the nearer approach of her brother—one of the two master instincts that have dominated and preserved life upon the face of the Earth. Yet it was not without a struggle. She hesitated, half turning backward. Nu cast a questioning look upon her.

"They are coming, Nat-ul," he said. "Nu cannot fight these strange men who hurl lead with the thunders they have stolen from the skies. Come! We must hurry back to the cave of Oo, and on the morrow we shall go forth and search for the tribe of Nu, my father, that dwells beyond the Barren Cliffs beside the Restless Sea. There, in our own world, we shall be happy."

And yet the girl held back, afraid. Then the man gathered her in his mighty arms and ran on in the direction of the cave of Oo, the sabre-toothed tiger.

A recurrence of the ancient earthquake renders Nu and Victoria/Nat-ul unconscious, and they recover in Nu's time. Now, in the second part of the book (or in terms of original publication, the sequel) there is further adventure, including a conflict between migrating tribes rather anticipatory of William Golding's *The Inheritors* (1955) and the recent wave of "anthro-pological fantasies" sparked by Jean Auel's *Clan of the Cave Bear* (1980).

Throughout, the narrative theme of Nu's obsessive hunt of Oo, the sabre-tooth, continues. A veritable Ahab, he refuses to take Nat-ul for his mate until he has laid the head of Oo before her father's cave in evidence of his worthiness as a mighty hunter. At the end of the book Victoria returns to modern times, with the implication that her entire stone-age experience was merely a dream . . . until Barney and the others find the cave of Oo, and in it the severed skull of a sabre-tooth . . . and the skeleton of a Neocene hunter.

One of Burroughs' very few tragic stories, *The Eternal Lover* is also one of his finest works. A minor curiosum is the use of *Back to the Stone Age* as a chapter title. Twenty-two years later Burroughs wrote a novel with the same title in his Pellucidar series.

Following *The Eternal Lover* Burroughs wrote another Tarzan novel and then *The Lad and the Lion*. Despite its title, this latter is not intended as a juvenile; it is a rather Tarzan-like adventure of a youngster who grows up with a lion as his companion. It is not very good.

Next came *The Girl from Farris'*, a novelette of contemporary (1913–14) realism. Not very good as a work of fiction, *The Girl from Farris'* does include some revealing pictures of the Chicago business world as ERB saw it in those days of struggle, as well as a partially autobiographic description of a broken businessman leaving Chicago for an Idaho ranch where he tries gold-mining. (Burroughs had previously left Chicago to work on his older brothers' ranch in Idaho, and had tried gold-mining as well.)

One other oddity of *The Girl from Farris'* is the appearance, a very brief one, of a Chicago police lieutenant named Barnut (shades of Normal Bean!). The story existed only in its original (1916) magazine version, and a news-paper serialization of 1920, until the issuance of a tiny pamphlet edition in 1959. In this edition, photo-reproduced from typewritten copy, Barnut is erroneously rendered "Darnut," leading some Burroughs students (myself included) to wonder if ERB intended a subtle tie-in between "Darnut" and Tarzan's friend Paul D'Arnot, a French naval lieutenant. The correct spelling of Barnut of course rules this out.

The 1959 edition, by the way, is so crudely produced and so small (both in dimension and circulation) that argument is possible as to whether it is the first edition of the story, or a mere pamphlet, the first edition being a far more elaborate large-size paperback published in 1965.

After *The Girl from Farris'* Burroughs returned to his first successful series with a fourth Martian novel.

CHAPTER V

Barsoom Resumed

One might reasonably conclude that the first three books of the Barsoomian series were intended to represent a single, complete saga. The first two tales, *A Princess of Mars* and *The Gods of Mars*, had both ended with classic cliffhangers, the former with John Carter's loss of consciousness at the Atmosphere Plant and the latter with the imprisonment and possible death by stabbing of Dejah Thoris at the Martian south pole.

A single hero and heroine were featured in the three books, while about them Burroughs built his marvelously complete picture of Barsoom, its monstrous fifteen-foot tall green barbarians, its various civilized races of dominant red men, admirable though isolated yellow and black men, and nearly extinct whites, its ancient culture and the limited survival of that culture into later times.

With the romance of John Carter and Dejah Thoris as a continuing theme pervading the adventures of the Earth man, the main focus of the three books is upon the latter's fantastic rise in the society of Mars: from a literally naked and weaponless newcomer, unable even to speak the language of the planet, rising to the Warlordship of all Mars. The question then arises, What do you do for an encore?

If Burroughs had dropped his Martian series with the completion of the trilogy, I suspect that those books would hold an even higher place in the general field of science fiction than they do (as might the earliest Tarzan books if there were not the numerous later pot-boilers of that series to dim their lustre). A similar case was that of Burroughs' contemporary pulp writer, George Allan England.

[A discovery of Munsey publications editor Robert H. Davis, England broke into the Munsey *Cavalier* magazine in 1912 with *The Vacant World*, a novel of the future in which a natural disaster destroyed civilization and very nearly annihilated mankind. Two survivors, an engineer and his secretary, awaken after a sleep of centuries and struggle to survive in the hostile and primitive world in which they find themselves.

[England produced two sequels to *The Vacant World*. They were *Beyond the Great Oblivion* and *The Afterglow*, issued in 1914 as an omnibus volume as *Darkness and Dawn*. The *Darkness and Dawn* trilogy has been regarded ever since as a science fiction landmark; the three stories were reprinted in latter-day successors to the old Munsey magazines in the 1940s; the most recent complete book edition was in 1974.

[The great length of the trilogy was required to give full scope and power to England's concept of universal desolation and the indomitable spirit of his protagonists in their struggle to survive and rebuild the destroyed civilization of former times, but if the author had gone on with sequel after sequel it is more than likely that the effect of the three books would have been diluted and their appeal reduced for later readers. He did not continue the series.]

Edgar Rice Burroughs saw fit to continue his Martian stories beyond the original trilogy. And if his doing so robbed the initial epic of its unique and concentrated appeal, the appearances of further adventures on Barsoom were met with delight on the part of readers who had enjoyed *Princess*, *Warlord* and *Gods*.

The new Martian novel was conceived with a working title of *Carthoris* (the son of John Carter and Dejah Thoris), and was written in April, May and June of 1914. It did not appear in print, however, until April, 1916, when it was serialized in *All-Story Weekly* as *Thuvia, Maid of Mars*, the title which has been retained on all published editions of the novel. In setting out to produce this "encore" to the previous trilogy, Burroughs faced a serious problem in deciding what he could do in the Barsoomian context that would not be merely redundant.

He had faced essentially the same puzzle in producing sequels to *Tarzan of the Apes*, and in continuing to produce them, as he did, for thirty-five years. The solution Burroughs adopted for Tarzan was to plunge the ape man into a series of adventures in new and wildly exotic settings. A separate study of the Tarzan books and Tarzan's Africa would show that continent dotted with lost cities and civilizations, from Opar the orphaned colony of lost Atlantis (introduced early in the series and revisited several times) to Alemtejo the forgotten stronghold of descendants of the Portuguese da Gamas (introduced in the sole completed Tarzan manuscript found among Burroughs' posthumous effects, *Tarzan and the Madman*).

Indeed, Burroughs even took Tarzan to Indonesia (*Tarzan and "The Foreign Legion"*) and to a lost Mayan outpost of Uxmal in the Pacific (*Tarzan and the Castaways)*, as well as to England, France, America, and (*Tarzan at the Earth's Core*) Pellucidar.

With the Martian series, Burroughs went off on a different tack, one which I regard as more daring than that which he used for Tarzan, and one which was, in my pleased opinion, completely successful. Within the framework of the already-published works, and using many of the characters introduced in the earlier books, Burroughs created a number of wholly new characters and built up other, formerly minor, figures into the heroes and heroines of succeeding books.

Similarly, within the established geography, culture, science, etc., he carried his new characters to previously unexplored sections of the Barsoomian landscape, introducing fresh and intriguing elements into the successive tales. Thus, while John Carter and Dejah Thoris appear in *Thuvia*, they are not central figures, and the book rings clearly with an excitement and freshness that the later Tarzan novels lack despite the author's vigorous and ingenious story-telling.

The title-character and heroine Thuvia had been introduced in *The Gods of Mars* as a pathetic plaything of the Holy Therns, a thoroughly corrupt cult-priesthood. Rescued by John Carter, Thuvia was later imprisoned with Dejah Thoris and the beautiful but wicked Phaidor at the end of the book, their common cell a compartment in a giant horizontally-revolving wheel.

As John Carter lost sight of the three, Phaidor lunged at Dejah Thoris, plunging a dagger murderously toward her breast. Thuvia threw herself between Dejah Thoris and Phaidor, seeking to accept the blade herself rather than permit the Princess' death. In *The Warlord of Mars* Burroughs revealed that both Dejah Thoris and Thuvia escaped, and by the fourth book in the series Thuvia was sufficiently rehabilitated from her former unhappy existence among the Holy Therns to become a lead heroine, conveniently "a princess in her own right."

The hero of *Thuvia, Maid of Mars* is Carthoris, whose name had been Burroughs' working title for the book. With an earthly father and a Barsoomian mother, Carthoris (who was hatched, as are all Barsoomians) has a skin of moderately ruddy hue, less red than his mother's, less white than his father's. His muscles, too, partake of half-earthly heredity, so that Carthoris is stronger than an ordinary Martian, able to leap distances nearly incredible to an ordinary Martian . . . but less endowed in these characteristics than is his purely earthly (or Jasoomian, to use the Barsoomian word) father.

The story opens in the beautiful court gardens of Thuvan Dihn, Jeddak (emperor) of Ptarth, a Martian city-state. Thuvia, previously discovered to be the daughter of Thuvan Dihn and hence a Martian princess herself, is being paid unwelcome court by the wily Astok, Prince of Dusar. Thuvia will have none of Astok; she is already promised to Kulan Tith, Jeddak of Kaol, whom she admires but does not love.

Carthoris is also in the picture, being greatly attracted to the lovely Thuvia. But Carthoris knows and obeys the Barsoomian honor code, and he will not interfere between Thuvia and Kulan Tith. Astok presses his suit so insistently that Thuvia calls out for assistance, Carthoris turns up, humiliates Astok, and of course makes the latter his moral enemy.

Astok arranges the abduction of Thuvia and simultaneously plants evidence to frame Carthoris for the crime. Carthoris must thus first escape from Ptarth, where he is a hunted criminal, then find and rescue Thuvia from Astok and return her to Ptarth . . . where she will be married to Kulan Tith! A pretty grim prospect, and it is made the more so by Astok's sabotage of Carthoris' proud invention, a sort of autopilot for the Martian flier. The sabotage is undiscovered until Carthoris, having gotten away from Ptarth in his flier, becomes hopelessly lost in unknown regions of Barsoom.

The plot builds with considerable complexity, and the outpouring of imaginative devices on Burroughs' part does not falter. Perhaps the finest concept in the book is that of the Bowmen of Lothar. Lothar is an ancient city-state far to the west of Helium, west and south of Ptarth. Its inhabitants are an ancient race, few in number and slowly approaching extinction in their isolated city. All of their women are dead; the few men who survive exist in a slow-paced, almost dreamlike world awaiting the inevitable—but distant—end.

The Lotharians' traditional enemies are the Torquasians, a tribe of green barbarians normally inhabiting the region of the now dry Gulf of Torquas to the east of Lothar. When the Torquasians conduct one of their periodic sieges of Lothar they are met by the Bowmen, a fantastic army of mentally projected phantoms created by the sheer will power of the few living Lotharians. So realistic is the phantom army of Bowmen that a vast number of casualties are inflicted upon the Torquasians in each battle, and the green men are repeatedly driven off.

Burroughs' description of a battle between the Bowmen of Lothar and the marauding Torquasians is one of the finest sequences of the Martian series, and one of Burroughs' more ingenious characters emerges from the battle. He is Kar Komak, a Bowman whose pseudo-existence was so powerfully supported that he took on a real life, participated in the remainder of the book, and came to stand as a memorable and intriguing character.

Carthoris invades the city of Lothar, rescues Thuvia from the Lotharian

Jeddak, Tario, and his jealous heir-apparent, Jav, only to be astounded to behold Thuvia disappear as they set out for Ptarth. Again Carthoris enters Lothar and rescues Thuvia all over again, an exercise in repetition which Burroughs manages to make great fun rather than the boresome task one might anticipate.

Carthoris returns Thuvia to her home, Kulan Tith recognizes the true love between Thuvia and Carthoris and renounces his claim upon the princess of Ptarth:

"Take back your liberty, Thuvia of Ptarth," he cried, "and bestow it where your heart already lies enchained, and when the golden collars are clasped about your necks you will see that Kulan Tith's is the first sword to be raised in declaration of eternal friendship for the new princess of Helium and her royal mate!"

Thuvia, Maid of Mars lacked the creative power of *Princess*, *Gods* and *Warlord*; Burroughs was no longer driven to write by the day-dreams and the underlying frustrations that had led to the creation of Barsoom. But *Thuvia* showed an increased skill in both plotting and expression, and made a most enjoyable novel, as well as attaining considerable commercial success (some thirty editions have appeared to date in the United States and England, although with the advent of print on demand public-domain editions this number—as with all Burroughs titles—seems ever-changing).

CHAPTER VI

The Return to Pellucidar

The success of *Thuvia* gave evidence that the Mars stories could be spun out beyond the scope of the original trilogy, and in fact Edgar Rice Burroughs continued the series throughout his entire career. Although there were many more Tarzan books than Martian volumes, the first of the latter (*A Princess of Mars*) was the first Burroughs work ever published when it appeared in *All-Story*, while the last of Burroughs' books to appear in the author's lifetime was the tenth of the Mars series, *Llana of Gathol*. An eleventh Barsoomian volume, *John Carter of Mars*, appeared in 1964, although one of the two novelettes it contains is of dubious authenticity. (The book is discussed more fully in a later chapter.)

Even before *Thuvia* was published, however, Burroughs was back at his desk, his production quite prolific. Three projects attended to over the summer and early autumn of 1914 were sequels to *The Cave Girl*, *The Eternal Lover*, and *The Mad King*. The sequels were titled, respectively, *The Cave Man*, *Sweetheart Primeval* and *Barney Custer of Beatrice*. Because the two stories of each pair have appeared in combined editions ever since their first publication, they are generally regarded as complete novels rather than novelette pairs, and indeed the assignment of chapters and the general treatment of each book has been such as promote its being regarded as single novel.

The Cave Man has already been discussed along with *The Cave Girl*. The other stories involved present a curiously tangled sequence of fictional happenings as well as a remarkable interplay of characters. The actual sequence of writing—and of the events described in the stories—is (1) *The Mad King*, (2) *The Eternal Lover*, (3) *Sweetheart Primeval*, (4) *Barney Custer of Beatrice*. In other words, the two tales of Nu and Victoria take place *between* the two Luthan adventures; a number of the characters from the first half of *The Mad King* (as it appears in book versions) turn up in *The Eternal Lover*, meet the Clayton family, participate to varying degrees in the African adventure, and then return to Lutha for *Barney Custer*—the second half of *The Mad King*.

Read in this sequence—the first twelve chapters of *The Mad King*, then *The Eternal Lover* complete, and finally the remainder of *The Mad King*—the stories make a reasonably coherent whole, despite the disparity of locale and theme. The unwary reader who reads the books unaware of this sequence is likely to emerge more than mildly bemused.

From November 23, 1914, through January 11, 1915, Burroughs worked on a sequel to *At the Earth's Core*. The sequel was titled simply *Pellucidar*. The elapsed time for writing *Pellucidar*, some forty-nine days, was typical for Burroughs, who usually spent anywhere from a month to three months on a book. His speed record for a full novel was set on *Carson of Venus*, produced in twenty-six days in July and August of 1937. Burroughs turned out *The Outlaw of Torn* even more rapidly, in seventeen days in November, 1911, but the story was rewritten the following year; Burroughs does not record the additional time spent on it, so we do not know how much total time was involved.

Other quick writing jobs were *The Deputy Sheriff of Comanche County*, a poor western turned out in twenty-eight days in 1930, and the excellent *The Warlord of Mars*, written in thirty-one days in 1913. The longest period ever devoted to one book by Burroughs was over ten months in 1921 when Burroughs wrote *The Chessmen of Mars*.

Of course "elapsed time" may be deceptive; we do not know how many actual work days and off days Burroughs allotted himself during the periods covered, nor how many hours constituted a work day at a given stage of his writing career. Burroughs did maintain a notebook for most of his life, recording the dates of beginning and completing each story, but the other details which would be so interesting to learn are not available.

In these early days Burroughs wrote his stories out in longhand, often on the reverse sides of unused letterheads from defunct businesses of his own. The original handwritten manuscripts of *A Princess of Mars* and *Tarzan of the Apes*, among others, are preserved by the Burroughs family in Tarzana, California. The cliché story of the hit tune written on the back of an old envelope finds a remarkable parallel in Burroughs' case!

Later on Burroughs switched to a typewriter, and at various times exper-imented with "writing" by dictating stories to a secretary or into an office dictating machine. (There is a classic publicity photo of Burroughs, by this time world-famous, "talking a story" into a Dictaphone. He generally preferred to type his own material.)

Burroughs did not outline extensively, nor did he place very much emphasis on redrafting and polishing his stories. The results of this rather
casual attitude towards his craft are somewhat mixed, as are the opinions of
ERB's admirers (and his critics). There are those who lament these habits,
maintaining that if only Burroughs had worked harder on his stories they
would have been even better than they are, that the occasional slip of style,
the over-reliance on coincidence as a crutch in plotting and the repetitious
use of such devices as the lost cities endlessly stumbled upon by Tarzan
and the innumerable mad kings of the Martian stories, might have been
eliminated, or at least reduced.

A counter argument is made that the very casualness of Burroughs' work,
the loose ends, the melodramatic twists, are an important part of his appeal.
Extensive polishing and revision might have "slickened" Burroughs' books
but might also have destroyed the spontaneous vigor and the naive appeal
of the natural storyteller.

Both sides can make a case of some strength, and examples from among
the author's best works can be cited by both. My personal opinion, somewhat
tentatively held, is that Burroughs would have done better to work harder
and longer on his stories, and might even have done better to attempt
a smaller output than was the case, devoting the effort expended on his
numerous works to producing fewer but better books.

Still, this attitude is one of a reader seeking the best possible product
of a great natural gift. Burroughs' own attitude was a combination of pure
economic motivation and, especially in his earlier years, the outpouring of
the daydreams of an unhappy man. Indeed, in his several published articles
and interviews in which he discusses his own literary philosophy Burroughs
displays a strongly "un-literary" outlook, indicating that his only motivation
in writing was to earn a living and the only objective of his stories was to
entertain readers.

Yet I would gladly trade *Synthetic Men of Mars*, *Back to the Stone Age*, *Land
of Terror*, the whole Venus Series, *The Deputy Sheriff of Comanche County*, *The
Bandit of Hell's Bend*, and easily a dozen of Burrough's latter-day formula-
ridden Tarzan novels for another single volume of the best Martian, Tarzan,
or Inner World quality, or one matching the best of ERB's non-series work.

But to return to 1915 and *Pellucidar*, the latter was Burroughs' seventeenth
book produced since 1911. Discounting the two novels finished in 1911,
he was averaging five complete novels annually. In 1913, his peak year, he
turned out some 413,000 words of fiction (as stated in an article, *How I Wrote
the Tarzan Books*, in 1929). He did not maintain this early pace for many

years, but in the first creative outburst of Burroughs' career the result was
the production of a large number of books in a remarkably short period
of time, their quality ranging from pleasant light entertainment to truly
memorable and enduring fiction.

Whether Burroughs thought the Inner World stories of Pellucidar less
believable and hence more in need of buttressing, or merely wished to
continue the practice of *At the Earth's Core*, the author furnished *Pellucidar*
with an elaborate and complex frame, one of the finest he ever created for
any story. He calls once more upon his anonymous narrator, revealing him
to be the author of the previous book of the series. As in the case of *A
Princess of Mars*, the doorway is opened to endless puzzling over identities.

Specifically, *Pellucidar* opens with the narrator (*is* he "Burroughs" or *Burroughs?*) preparing to leave his home (location not specified) for a hunting
trip abroad:

> And then came a letter that started me for Africa twelve days ahead
> of my schedule.
>
> Often I am in receipt of letters from strangers who have found
> something in a story of mine to commend or condemn. My interest
> in this department of my correspondence is ever fresh. I opened this
> particular letter with all the zest of pleasurable anticipation with which
> I had opened so many others. The post-mark (Algiers) had aroused
> my interest and curiosity, especially at this time, since it was Algiers
> that was presently to witness the termination of my coming sea voyage
> in search of sport and adventure.

The letter itself is presented in full in the framing sequence, as it was
received by "Burroughs." The writer introduces himself, then offers his
impression of the first Inner World novel:

> I became interested in your story, *At the Earth's Core*, not so much
> because of the probability of the tale as of a great and abiding wonder
> that people should be paid real money for writing such impossible
> trash. You will pardon my candor, but it is necessary that you under-
> stand my mental attitude toward this particular story—that you may
> credit that which follows.

The writer of the letter, Cogdon Nestor, then proceeds to report that
on a Saharan expedition of his own he had come across a mysterious box,
shallowly covered by the drifting sands of the desert. Opening it, he finds
within a perfectly ordinary telegraph set, the receiving key clicking cease-
lessly. Having forgotten whatever little Morse Code he ever knew, Nestor

is unable to understand the message, but the patterned clicking is clearly an attempt at communication, so Nestor clicks the sending key a few times to let whoever is on the other end know that contact has been established.

Nestor recalls the closing incidents of *At the Earth's Core*, in which David Innes, accompanied by the Mahar, had returned to the Inner World in the mechanical prospector, leaving behind a telegraph set in the Sahara, its wire playing out behind the prospector as the machine bored its way down to Earth. Half-convinced against his will that the events described in *At the Earth's Core* were not merely "impossible trash" but actual occurrences, Nestor returns to Algiers. There he sends his letter, concluding:

> I arrived here today. In writing you this letter I feel that I am making a fool of myself.
>
> There is no David Innes.
>
> There is no Dian the Beautiful.
>
> There is no world within a world.
>
> Pellucidar is but a realm of your imagination—nothing more.
>
> But—
>
> The incident of the finding of that buried telegraph instrument upon the lonely Sahara is little short of uncanny, in view of your story of the adventures of David Innes . . .
>
> . . . It is maddening!
>
> It is your fault—I want you to release me from it.
>
> Cable me at once, at my expense, that there was no basis of fact for your story, *At the Earth's Core*.

And "Burroughs' " response? "Ten minutes after reading this letter I had cabled Mr. Nestor as follows: '*Story true. Await me Algiers.*' "

Up to this point, the reader is likely to identify, in viewpoint, with Cogdon Nestor. Having read *At the Earth's Core* one is, of course, fully aware that it is merely an extravagant romance (if not "impossible trash") without a grain of truth and without value except as popular entertainment. To the reader who accepts Cogdon Nestor's outlook, "Burroughs' " two words, *story true*, are nearly as stunning as they must have been to Nestor himself.

Burroughs seldom mixed the real world into his romance, and when he did, as in a few of the Tarzan novels and in *The Girl from Hollywood*, the result tended to range from somewhat less than fully successful to wholly disastrous. But he often attempted the opposite feat of mixing his fiction into the real world, and with great success. He had a knack for reaching his reader's credulity, for making the most obvious fantasy seem as if it might, just *might*, be true.

He had done this in *The Cave Girl* not with a frame, but with his closing paragraph, his reference to "the historic and aristocratic name . . . which, as it happens, is not Smith-Jones at all."

For *At the Earth's Core* he accomplished the same effect even more powerfully, with just two words, *story true*, words that appeared in another book altogether! Obviously an author does not achieve verisimilitude by simply passing off fiction as truth. The attempt is often made, as it occurs (or has occurred) regularly in the "true" adventure story magazines of the "man's sweat" variety. No one is fooled.

Nor was it Burroughs' serious intention to make his readers believe that his novels were other than entertainment fiction. But part of the effectiveness of fiction lies in its believability, which becomes increasingly strained as the fiction becomes more and more extravagant—as Burroughs' surely is. The various devices employed by Burroughs, the frames, the story-within-a-story, the sealed manuscript, all were designed to support the believability of his highly extravagant stories, and to a good degree, they worked.

Such devices are currently out of style in fiction, and perhaps in an age when much of past years' science fiction is not only true but outpaced by truth, they are no longer needed. A century ago extravagant romance needed more support, and in the devices of Burroughs this support was provided.

In the prologue to *Pellucidar* "Burroughs" meets Cogdon Nestor in Algiers, they hire a telegrapher to serve as decoder for David Innes' message and as an operator to send their own reply, and the three proceed back to the telegraph set Innes had left in the Sahara desert.

The entire prologue fills only seven pages (perhaps one or two more or less depending upon the typography in various editions of the book), the main text of *Pellucidar* being the report sent by David Innes to "Burroughs" and Cogdon Nestor in the Sahara.

David and the Mahar had made the return trip to the Inner World in safety. David had been uncertain about transporting the intelligent reptile back to Pellucidar: "It has been, of course, impossible for me to communicate with her since she had no auditory organs and I no knowledge of her fourth-dimension, sixth-sense method of communication.

"Naturally I am kind-hearted, and so I found it beyond me to leave even this hateful and repulsive thing alone in a strange and hostile world. The result was that when I entered the iron mole I took her with me."

The trip itself is relatively uneventful, but when the machine breaks surface in Pellucidar David realizes that they are nowhere near Sari, the land where Abner, Dian, and Hooja the Sly One are presumably still resident. The reason for this distressing displacement is that the mechanical prospector, when it plunged downward did not travel *straight* down but, deflected from time to time by various strata of rock, might emerge in the other world at a point far away from that directly opposite that from which it had started, and in an entirely unpredictable direction. Just this had happened.

David's problem, then, is to find Sari in a huge world whose maps are few and unreliable, where compasses are useless, and where every human native is endowed with a "homing sense" but with no particular talent for finding any place other than his own home. David, being a native outer-worlder, has no homing sense at all.

The basic structure of the book is thus set in a pattern that might be classed as the *Odyssean*. Basically, as in Homer, the hero is set at Point A, motivated to reach a distant Point B, and turned loose. The author can run him through as many strange adventures and encounters with weird beasts and peoples in weird lands as he wishes. As many and as varied incidents can be inserted as the author sees fit, and when the author considers that enough has been written, he brings his adventurer to the elusive Point B, generally engages him in climactic battle, and the story is complete.

The *Odyssey* provides a model for this primitive travel story, and as a framework for fiction it has never lost its popularity. Burroughs used the Odyssean pattern in many of his books, especially the science fiction volumes, and to this day the pattern is favored by leading science-fiction authors. [Two of the most successful applications are Jack Vance's fascinating *Big Planet* and Philip José Farmer's humorous *The Green Odyssey* (both 1957, although the Vance had had magazine publication in 1952).

[Vance's Big Planet is just that, a gigantic low-density world divided among innumerable tiny principalities set up by non-conforming Earth colonists. Vance's hero Claude Glystra, a commissioner sent from Earth to investigate conditions on Big Planet, is involved in a spaceship-wreck and has to make his way across the surface of Big Planet to the Earth headquarters, thus setting up a classic Odyssey.

[Farmer's hero Alan Green (hence *The Green Odyssey*) is also a shipwrecked spaceman; John Carter-fashion he works himself up to a fairly comfortable position among the inhabitants of his adopted planet, but unlike John Carter he does wish to return to Earth. Green sets out across the planet in hopes of finding another crashed spaceship and possible survivors of its landing, and takes passage on the *Bird of Fortune*, a "windroller" or landship, in hopes of making the trip. The *Bird of Fortune* bears an uncanny resemblance to the *Fortuna*, a windroller used to explore the interior of South America in Lloyd Osbourne's 1907 novel *The Adventurer*, and Burroughs can hardly be credited with inspiring the story (although Farmer is an admirer of Burroughs) but the travel-tale persists in science fiction as one of the most popular structures.]

In Burroughs' *Pellucidar* the Odyssean structure worked with grand success. Perhaps the most fascinating land visited is the Land of Awful Shadow.

Pellucidarians, because of the location of their miniature sun, inside a hollow sphere on the inner shell of which they make their homes, know no such phenomenon as night. To them, the closest approximation of night would be to crawl to the back of a deep cave where sunlight could not penetrate.

However, there hangs in the sky of Pellucidar a tiny globe, an "inner moon" or miniature planet which orbits the inner sun *à la* Ludvig Holberg's *Nils Klim* or Bradshaw's *Atvatabar*. David Innes is able to perceive plant life and water on the Pendent World as he dubs it, and surmises that there may also be animals or human inhabitants.

The period of revolution of the Pendent World about the inner sun is such that it remains eternally over a single area of Pellucidar. From the viewpoint of the outer world, it might thus be said that the "year" of the Pendent World is twenty-four hours, but of course in Pellucidar there is no time, so such a statement would be meaningless. At any rate, the area beneath the Pendent World is bathed in perpetual shadow just as the rest of Pellucidar is bathed in perpetual light. The shadow is not full darkness; it is in fact the eerie half-light of an endless eclipse, and the country thus darkened is known throughout the countries near enough to know of it as the Land of Awful Shadow.

As for the Pendent World itself, one could only hope that some day Burroughs would carry David Innes or some other character to its surface. Would it be a miniature, inhabited globe? David's observation would indicate as much. Would it be hollow, with yet another Inner World, another inner sun, another Pendent World, leading down into the infinitesimal?

We do not know.

Six novels of Pellucidar were published in Edgar Rice Burroughs' lifetime, plus three interconnected novelettes which appeared only in magazine form during the author's life. A fourth novelette of the group appeared posthumously, and the stories were collected to make a seventh Pellucidar volume (*Savage Pellucidar*, 1963), but in none of them does the obvious trip take place.

Rumors circulated among science fiction aficionados in general and Burroughs enthusiasts in particular, of yet another Inner World tale, *Emperor of*

Pellucidar, but no such manuscript is known, nor is there any mention of the title in Burroughs' working notebook. In all likelihood, *Emperor of Pellucidar* is merely a likely title, one which might have been applied to an existing Inner World story, but which was not used. Otherwise, we will probably have to consign *Emperor of Pellucidar* to the Great Library of Pseudobiblia at Oz.

By the end of the second Inner World novel, *Pellucidar*, David and Dian are finally united, and an "Empire of Pellucidar" has been established, a loose confederation of primitive states with David as "Emperor." Abner Perry is merrily seeking to bring all of the benefits of civilization to the entire Inner World.

Except for the obvious sequel-hook of the Pendent World, which Burroughs never did utilize, the ending of *Pellucidar* seemed a fine and final solution to the Inner World saga. And so it was for a period of thirteen years, until 1928, before Burroughs ventured once more to resume the series, with *Tanar of Pellucidar*. During those thirteen years Burroughs wrote two dozen books.

The first of these was *The Son of Tarzan*, which is discussed in later chapters along with the other books of that series. The next was *The Man-Eater*, a very Tarzan-like story set partially in the African jungle and partly in Virginia. There exists even the possibility of tying *The Man-Eater* into the Tarzan series, for there is a cryptic reference to a "Mrs. Clayton and her daughter," grist for the mill of the exegesis.

Perhaps the most interesting aspect of *The Man-Eater* is the story of its loss and recovery to the Burroughs canon.

The story—it is of novelette length—was written in May and June of 1915 as *Ben, King of Beasts*, but appeared as *The Man-Eater* as a daily serial in the New York *Evening World* from November 15 to 20, 1915. There was, apparently, no magazine publication, nor any reprint of any sort of the story. The working title *Ben* was its listing in the author's notebook, and with the passage of years even he, apparently, forgot all about an *Evening World* serial called *The Man-Eater*.

In 1955 two paperbound pamphlets were published anonymously in strictly limited editions of 300 copies each. One contained the text of *The Man-Eater* and the other, another Burroughs story, *Beyond Thirty*. The "print" was nothing but duplicated typewriter output and the general production quality, while adequate for reading purposes, was strictly spartan.

The reason for the underground nature of the project was fear of prosecution for copyright infringement, although later developments proved that this fear was unwarranted—both stories had lapsed into the public domain. Some years later, in researching Burroughs bibliography, Heins learned that the anonymous publisher was Lloyd Arthur Eshbach, a some-time science-fiction author, editor and publisher whose lamented Fantasy Press was one of the leading specialty houses that sprang up (and, almost without exception, quickly wilted) in the late 1940s and 1950s.

Two years later a hardbound book edition containing both stories appeared, this time from Science Fiction & Fantasy Publications, a tiny house that had previously specialized in issuing bibliographic compilations by its owner, Bradford M. Day. Again the question of copyright infringement arose, but Day had done the homework which Eshbach had apparently failed to do, and, after totally unsuccessful attempts even to open negotiations with ERB Inc., openly produced an edition of 3000 copies.

It seems astonishing that the appearance of the Eshbach and Day volumes did not immediately precipitate the flood of public domain Burroughs publishing that led, ultimately, to the renewed authorized publishing of Burroughs, and, even more important, the release of many previously unpublished Burroughs manuscripts, which took place in the early 1960s. It seems astonishing, but nothing of the sort happened in 1957, or for several years more, at which time the revival took place without apparent regard for either the Eshbach or the Day publications.

The companion pamphlet to Eshbach's *Man-Eater*, and co-feature of Day's omnibus volume, was *Beyond Thirty*, a science-fiction yarn written in July and August, 1915, and published complete in *All Around* magazine for February, 1916.

The story takes place in the year 2137; hero and narrator, Jefferson Turck, fills in the 222 years of elapsed time, and through Turck, Burroughs presents a startling prediction of world developments which may yet prove more accurate than those of many more serious self-proclaimed prognosticators.

Looking forward from the early days of the First World War, Burroughs could see only violence and turmoil in Europe and the entire Old World, with a hemispheric policy of isolation adopted by the powerful Pan-American Federation as the inevitable American response. At the same time a new force entered upon the world picture: "the military power which rose so suddenly in China after the fall of the republic, and which wrested Manchuria and Korea from Russia and Japan, and also absorbed the Philippines . . ."

By 1971 affairs have reached such a condition that a treaty, or actually more of a unilateral proclamation, is issued by the Pan-American Federation to the rest of the world, the latter represented by China. Under its terms the Federation claims absolute control over the portion of the world from 30° east longitude to 175° west longitude. Within these boundaries, which encompass all of North and South America plus generous chunks of ocean for buffers, the Federation rules absolutely; beyond them, the Federation seeks no authority or influence, nor is any shipping, immigration, or other contact permitted to enter the territory claimed by the Federation.

No travel is permitted across the lines from within the Federation either, under severe penalty. Even radio contact is cut off, references to the Old World are dropped from Federation schoolbooks, and the entire continents of Europe, Africa, Asia and Australia are virtually forgotten in the West.

At the time of the story Turck is commander of the Federation aero-sub *Coldwater* on the Atlantic anti-commerce patrol, when a terrible storm wrecks the craft and Turck and his crew are blown "across 30." They make land in the British Isles, the first men in a century and a half to make the crossing.

Here they find that endless combat has led inevitably back to virtual barbarism. The ancient British monarchy is little better than a savage tribal domain currently held by Queen Victory (Victoria?), the daughter of King Wettin who was murdered by the wicked Buckingham, who now has designs upon the crown itself.

Burroughs paints a fascinating picture of the degenerated land of Gra-britin (several spellings are given, to correspond with local pronunciations), and after some involvement in the royal intrigues Jefferson Turck makes his way across the Channel. On the continent he is made captive by the forces of Menelek XIV, Emperor of Abyssinia. (Menelek II, a real emperor of Abyssinia, had died in 1913).

Menelek's empire has expanded to cover all of Africa, continental Europe, eastern Russia, Turkey and Arabia. His rule is represented as preferable to the outright barbarism of the British Isles, but the Abyssinian Empire is threatened by the growing power of the Chinese Empire which presses ever westward.

Although enslaved by the Abyssinian, Turck is highly regarded by his captors because of his obvious military skills, and the American secures an interview with Menelek himself. The Emperor reveals that his domain is a bulwark of Christianity standing between the malign forces of Caucasian barbarism and Asian materialism!

Turck, however, sees in the expanding Chinese Empire a more scientifi-cally-oriented and flexible attitude than that of the Abyssinian Empire, and making his cause with the Chinese against his captors, Turck is instrumental in bringing about a major victory of the Chinese over the Abyssinians.

Turck then appoints himself *de facto* ambassador plenipotentiary of the Pan-American Federation to the triumphant Chinese Empire, and negotiates a treaty reopening contacts between the hemispheres.

He returns to the Federation, word of conditions in the Old World having preceded him with members of the *Coldwater* crew who made their way back during Turck's captivity. His treaty with the Chinese is fully accepted in the Federation, and a new era of world-wide cooperation and enlightenment dawns. (Turck also brings home Queen Victory of Grabritin as his bride.)

The remarkable anticipation of Orwell's *1984* in Burroughs' idea of wiping entire portions of history from schoolbooks was noted by Paul Mandel in his excellent article for *Life* magazine on Burroughs, published in November, 1963. The equally remarkable anticipation of the growth of Chinese power "after the fall of the republic," the new Chinese Empire turning first to Manchuria, Korea, and the Philippines, and then westward to Europe, is positively chilling in its accuracy. And the prediction of an African Empire challenging China for supremacy is a matter which may be presaged today in the fledgling Organization of African Unity—with its headquarters in Addis Ababa, the ancient seat of the Meneleks!

If Burroughs has a claim to more value than that of "mere" entertainment, *Beyond Thirty* (also published as *The Lost Continent*) stands as a work of prediction in the front rank of speculative literature.[1]

1. In recent decades China has made great strides as an economic power, and the pro-democracy riots of 1989 indicted a desire, as yet unfulfilled, to move away from that nation's automatic form of government. The African continent is also a mixed story, with some bright spots of progress overshadowed by tragic instances of corruption, genocide, famine and plague. Burroughs' predictions for the future of both China and Africa must remain in the category of the indeterminate.

CHAPTER VII

Wieroos and Kalkars

In the years following *Beyond Thirty* Burroughs continued to turn out a steady stream of widely differing works. These were the years of his great success; the first Tarzan motion picture was made in 1917, and opened in January, 1918. With Elmo Lincoln as the original screen Ape Man and Enid Markey as the first Jane the picture initiated a successful series which continues to this day as a standard Hollywood product.

From poverty and obscurity to wealth and fame, and from his home in Chicago to permanent residence in California, these were eventful years for Burroughs but the production of stories never let up. Burroughs' notebook shows that he kept works in progress almost continuously, sometimes overlapping projects, and generally beginning new stories almost immediately upon the conclusion of earlier ones.

Seven Tarzan books were produced between 1915 and 1925; in the same decade Burroughs wrote two more Martian novels (*The Chessmen of Mars* and *The Master Mind of Mars*) and a number of miscellaneous works of little lasting importance in relation to his overall output, but perhaps worth at least a passing note for each.

H.R.H. The Rider was written late in 1915 and serialized in *All-Story Weekly* three years later. It is a pleasant but extremely lightweight—even by ERB's standards—romance in the derivative tradition of *The Mad King*. Again a mythical European kingdom is the setting, and the themes are those hallowed in the genre: the bored princeling exchanging personalities with the dashing bandit, the Unwanted Princess, the American millionairess in search of a European title, and a marvelously heroic character: Prince Boris of Karlova!

Although *H.R.H. The Rider* contains neither supernatural nor superscientific elements, its reading today presents far more feeling of fantasy than do the most extravagant of Burroughs' tales. The kind of world-view that made possible a story like *H.R.H. The Rider* is extinct.

The Oakdale Affair was not written until early in 1917, but it was actually published before *H.R.H. The Rider*, appearing complete in *The Blue Book* for March, 1918. The hero of this tale is Bridge, the enigmatic friend of Billy Byrne in *The Mucker*. Aside from Bridge's reappearance (and precious little is revealed about him) there is almost nothing to recommend this story of a banker's daughter disguised as a boy and her exploits among hoboes and criminals.

These two works were issued in a combined volume, *The Oakdale Affair and The Rider*, in 1937.

The Efficiency Expert (written late in 1919, published in *Argosy All-Story Weekly* for October 8 through 29, 1921) is another attempt, like *The Girl From Farris'*, to depict realistically the world of big business. The hero this time is Jimmy Torrance, Jr., a young athlete. Again, the remaining interest of the book must be for the specialist only; the story itself, not very good in its time, has become dated as well. (Again, the tie-in: Jimmy's home town is the same as Barney and Victoria Custer's: Beatrice, Nebraska.)

The Efficiency Expert and *The Girl from Farris'* were announced several years ago for publication in an omnibus volume, for sale on a limited basis to members of the Burroughs Bibliophiles only. The volume was repeatedly delayed and postponed, but finally appeared in 1965 as two separate volumes, eliciting a sigh of relief from Burroughs completists but little interest from anyone else.

The Girl from Hollywood was written in November and December, 1921, and January, 1922; it was published as a six-part serial in *Munsey's Magazine* beginning with the June, 1922 issue, and the first book edition appeared the following year.

The story is another attempt at realism, its setting patterned on the Tarzana Ranch near Los Angeles, which Burroughs had bought from General Harrison Gray Otis. The incidents involved the motion picture industry, with a heavy infusion of dope addiction, rum runnings, illicit sex and violent death. As a work of fiction the main value of *The Girl from Hollywood* is its clear illustration of a Burroughs trade mark: when dealing with farfetched occurrences in distant and exotic settings, Burroughs was a masterful spinner of yarns; when dealing with less unlikely events in realistic settings, he was unable to bring his gifts to bear at all effectively.

Although *The Girl from Hollywood* was unsuccessful as fiction, it is of interest for its autobiographical aspect. The central character of the book,

Colonel Custer Pennington, is a sort of dream-Burroughs, perhaps with a touch of General Otis added to his nature.

A wounded veteran, Colonel Pennington is sent home to Virginia to die. Instead he migrates to California where he buys a battered ranch near Los Angeles and makes a full recovery through the beneficent influence of a clean and vigorous outdoor life. Pennington's wife and children, their characteristics and ambitions, their acquaintances with film people, are all more or less traceable to reality.

The Colonel is obviously Edgar Rice Burroughs, but not as he actually was. The native Chicagoan whose ambition to military glory had been sublimated into a highly lucrative career writing romances about sanguinary adventures metamorphosed into the retired hero who "might have been" but never really was.

We can sympathize with Burroughs' disappointed military ambitions, yet such regrets are really minimal. After all, there have been innumerable Colonel Penningtons . . . and only one Edgar Rice Burroughs.

Beware! a murder mystery novelette written in 1922 failed to find a market. It deserved to fail. It was a routine locked-room mystery in essence, with the intrigue of a European revolution added for extra interest. Sixteen years later a pulp editor for Ziff-Davis publications, Raymond A. Palmer, was looking for a big name in the science fiction field to perk up a new magazine, *Fantastic Adventures*.

Palmer remained a lifelong Burroughs fan (he passed away in 1977), and *Amazing Stories*, a Ziff-Davis magazine edited by Palmer, had featured Burroughs' science fiction over a decade earlier, while under a different editor and publisher. (*Amazing* had reprinted *The Land that Time Forgot* and the *Amazing Stories Annual* had featured an original Burroughs story, both in 1927.)

Burroughs had no science-fiction stories available to meet Palmer's request, but Palmer was willing to take *Beware!* even though it had no relevance to the field. Palmer then made a number of superficial changes in the story, altering the names of several characters, changing the time setting from 1921 to the year 2190, and renaming the result *The Scientists Revolt*. The revised story appeared in the second issue of *Fantastic Adventures*, July, 1939. The magazine has become extremely difficult to obtain and does not repay the effort required to do so.

The Bandit of Hell's Bend was another venture, like the second tale of Billy Byrne, into the West. Written in 1923 it was serialized in *Argosy All-Story Weekly* the following autumn, and published in its first book edition in 1925. The western setting has been praised for its authenticity, based as it was on Burroughs' own experience as a cowboy on his older brothers' Idaho ranch.

As a western novel *The Bandit* is routine fare: two cowboys vie for the favor of the pretty daughter of their employer, mysterious cattle rustling activity and an enigmatic masked bandit, etc. This book is definitely worthwhile for the Burroughs enthusiast, as a sample of the author's versatility, but as one more entry in the giant catalog of western novels, it is unexceptional.

Burroughs' longest single story is 125,000 words in length, double the size of a typical novel. Titled *Marcia of the Doorstep*, this is the story of a stagestruck girl, her struggles and problems. Written in 1924, it never found a publisher in his lifetime, not even Edgar Rice Burroughs Inc. in the years when Burroughs was publishing his own stories.

During this same period, 1915–1925, Burroughs wrote the two science-fiction novels which are generally regarded as his greatest contributions to this field, books which, paradoxically, might have won him an even higher standing among science-fiction enthusiasts if he had not written any others to dilute their impact on decades of readers. Each was actually a trilogy of interconnected short novels or long novelettes.

The first was *The Land that Time Forgot*, consisting of the title portion, written in 1917, its sequel *The People that Time Forgot* (1917–18), and *Out of Time's Abyss* (1918). All three were published originally in *The Blue Book Magazine* in 1918, reprinted in Hugo Gernsback's *Amazing Stories* in 1927; the first book edition appeared in 1924 and the book has been in and out of print ever since, several new editions appearing almost simultaneously between October, 1962, and September, 1963, when it was discovered that the book was in public domain.

Of all Burroughs' science fiction up to its time, *The Land that Time Forgot* is by far the most concerned with scientific speculation; specifically it is devoted largely to weird conjecture about evolution.

The novel opens, in indirect fashion, as a very well turned out war adventure story involving the capture of a surfaced German submarine, the *U-33*, by an English *tugboat*. The sub's crew are captured along with their craft, and pressed to serve until port can be made safely.

Burroughs offers a series of hair-raising nautical adventures, mutinies and counter-mutinies, sabotage to navigational equipment, until finally, completely lost, the *U-33* approaches an uncharted, mountainous body of land. The island is heavily laden with magnetic materials; so strongly is its influence felt that not only is the *U-3*'s compass rendered useless but the entire ship is drawn irresistibly toward the mountainous coastline.

Addressing the English mate of the prize submarine, the American narrator Bowen Tyler, Jr., asks:

> "What do you make of it?"
>
> "Did you ever hear of Caproni?" he asked.
>
> "An early Italian navigator?" I returned.
>
> "Yes; he followed Cook about 1721. He is scarcely mentioned even by contemporaneous historians—probably because he got into political difficulties on his return to Italy. It was the fashion to scoff at his claims, but I recall one of his works—his only one, I believe—in which he described a new continent in the south seas, a continent made up of 'some strange metal' which attracted the compass; a rockbound inhospitable coast, without beach or harbor, which extended for hundreds of miles. He could make no landing, nor in the several days he cruised about it did he see sign of life. He called it Caprona and sailed away. I believe, sir, that we are looking upon the coast of Caprona, uncharted and forgotten for two hundred years."

Unlike the Italian Caproni, Tyler and the *U-33* do find a way to make port in Caprona, or Caspak as its inhabitants call it, by cruising beneath the cliffs, up a tortuous channel entered through a subterranean opening. They emerge safely in Caspak only to face terrifying attack by huge, vicious monsters, mostly reptiles long since extinct in the rest of the world.

To this point *The Land that Time Forgot* seems like nothing more than a new version of Sir Arthur Conan Doyle's Amazonian *Lost World*, Verne's *Mysterious Island,* or for that matter Burroughs' own Pellucidar. Indeed, one is led to wonder if Burroughs intended an eventual tie-in of Caspak and Pellucidar, but such was apparently not the case. At least, no tieing-in story ever appeared.

Having entered Caspak at its southern extremity the *U-33* crew move northward from their newly established base, Fort Dinosaur. (And I must say that the ludicrous name, Fort Dinosaur, never fails to nettle when I delve into *The Land that Time Forgot*). The visitors encounter a tribe of man-like apes which they later learn to call in the Caspakian language, Ho-lu. Continuing northward they come upon primitive humans, or Alus. (The irregular and inconsistent use of hyphens and formation of plurals in the language of Caspak is as given in the book.)

The Alus have no speech, no weapons or other implements, and are obviously in the most primitive stage of development.

At the same time that Bowen Tyler and his sweetheart the actress Lys La Rue (who entered the story by being rescued from a ship torpedoed by the *U-33* before its capture) continue northward along with the English and German crews, they of course experience such dangers and adventures as are to be expected of Burroughs. But the chief value and interest of the book is the continuing mystery of the progressively more advanced peoples discovered in the course of the northerly trek.

In turn Burroughs introduces the Bo-lu, who are capable of elementary speech, and have armed themselves with clubs. Next come the Sto-lu whose speech, although in the same language as that of the Bo-lu, is more complex and sophisticated, and whose implements include a stone hatchet.

Then come the Band-lu, who have the spear; and the Kro-lu, who have the bow and arrow; and finally the Galus, men fully the equals of those in the outer world, armed with ropes as well as other weapons, speaking the most advanced form of the Caspakian language.

Throughout the book there is repeated mention of the females of Caspak bathing for long periods in sacred waters, of individuals being "cos-ata-lu" (literally, *not-egg-man*) or "cor-sva-jo" (*up-from-the-beginning*), and of being "batu," or finished, but all of these terms used in a sense which the narrator fails to comprehend.

Whatever the meaning of the mysteries of Caspak, the plot continues with a switch in viewpoint for the second novelette, *The People that Time Forgot*, to Thomas Billings, secretary to Bowen Tyler, Sr., who sets out to search for the younger Tyler, who is his close friend as well as his employer's son.

Billings' plane is downed over Caspak by the attack of a pterodactyl of huge size, which mistakes the aircraft for a rival aerial reptile.

The concluding story of the trilogy, *Out of Time's Abyss*, is narrated by Bradley, one of the original English crew, and is the eeriest of the three. It tells of the *U-33* party's encounter with the Wieroos, a race inhabiting a large island in the Inland Sea of Caspak. Terrible, winged, man-like creatures who delight in working unspeakable atrocities on the humans they kidnap to their island stronghold, the Weiroos are described as a blighted offshoot of human evolution, but the reader is left with the distinct impression that these cruel and loathsome folk are intended by Burroughs to represent not an offshoot of humanity but its successor. Consider the Wieroo:

> The creature stood about the height of an average man but appeared
> much taller from the fact that the joints of his long wings rose fully

a foot above his hairless head. The bare arms were long and sinewy, ending in strong, bony hands with claw-like fingers—almost talon-like in their suggestiveness. The white robe was separated in front, revealing skinny legs and the further fact that the thing wore but the single garment, which was of fine, woven cloth. From crown to sole the portions of the body exposed were entirely hairless, and as he noted this, Bradley also noted for the first time the cause of much of the seeming expressionlessness of the creature's countenance—it had neither eyebrows nor lashes. The ears were small and rested flat against the skull, which was noticeably round, though the face was quite flat.

Needless to say, by the end of the third segment the various interpersonal conflicts of the lost party are resolved in various ways, Bowen Tyler and Lys La Rue are permanently matched, as are Thomas Billings with Ajor, a Galu woman, and Bradley with Co-Tan, another Galu woman. All members of the party return to the outer world by means of a second rescue expedition, this one sent by sea.

The mysteries of "cor-sva-jo," "cos-ata-lu," and "batu," of the subdivisions of Caspakian humanity and the strange survivals of primitive species are explained in suitably audacious manner. In Caspak evolution is not a titanic, eons-long process in which each individual member of each species plays but a tiny role.

Rather, each individual undergoes the full development of his species in a sort of raw proof of the principle that ontogeny recapitulates phylogeny. The mysterious bathing of Caspakian females is actually egg-laying; the eggs are swept downstream to the southern end of the continent where they grow into primitive life forms. As each Caspakian creature proves its right to survival by the very fact of survival it fights its way northward, periodically undergoing a metamorphosis into a more advanced life-form. After moving upward through various reptilian and mammalian forms the individual reaches the state of Ho-lu, then Alu, Bo-lu and so on.

A Caspakian who has undergone the complete process is indeed "cor-sva-jo," come up from the beginning.

A Caspakian of any stage of development who has reached the maximum development of which he is individually capable is "batu"—finished. He will remain, for the rest of his life, in the state of Band-lu, Sto-lu, or whatever level was last attained before becoming *batu*.

Only those Caspakians who have reached the final state of development, that of *Galu*, are capable of bearing live children instead of laying eggs

The Land that Time Forgot

which must begin the cycle anew. Thus a Caspakian *Galu*, a fully developed human, may have attained that state by evolving "cor-sva-jo," from the beginning, *or* by being "cos-ata-lu," *not-egg-man*: born alive.

If *The Land that Time Forgot* had been published as a treatise in imaginary biology it might have been regarded as a piece of fascinating fantasy. As the science-fiction novel that it is, it is no less a fascinating fantasy while also being a thrilling adventure story of the finest sort produced by its author.

Burroughs' second great science fiction trilogy novel is in my personal estimation his finest effort in this field, and one of the best of all his books. The three component tales had a curious history. The first of them was written in 1919, apparently intended to stand alone as a political satire of the then-recent communist revolution in Russia. The story, *Under the Red Flag*, pleased no editor, for it never appeared under its original title or in its original form.

In 1922 Burroughs wrote *The Moon Maid*, which did find a home in *Argosy All-Story Weekly* where it was serialized in the issues of May 5 through June 2, 1923. In February and March, 1925, the same magazine carried Burroughs' sequel to *The Moon Maid*, *The Moon Men*—which was actually a reworking of the six-year-old unsuccessful *Under the Red Flag*. The same year, in September, *The Red Hawk*, the concluding novelette of the group, was serialized in the same magazine.

The first book edition appeared in 1926, titled *The Moon Maid* but including all three stories.

In introducing *The Moon Maid* Burroughs again uses his anonymous narrator, a passenger on the great Chicago-Paris overnight flier *Harding* on Mars Day, June 10, 1967. The world holiday has been proclaimed in celebration of the first complete exchange of messages between Earth and Mars via radio transmission, the Martian message of greeting being date-lined Helium, Barsoom.

The complete and successful communication between the planets is the product of over twenty years of refinement of a superior directional radio receiver and transmitter on Earth. Contact is made with John Carter of Mars, concerning whom another traveler remarks to the narrator, "That we were able to communicate intelligibly with [the Martians] is due to the presence upon Mars of that deathless Virginian, John Carter, whose miraculous transportation to Mars occurred March 4, 1866, as every school child of the twenty-first century knows."

Of all the passengers aboard the *Harding* the lone melancholy soul is Air Admiral Julian, who explains his unusual sadness to the narrator, prefacing the explanation with an exposition of his unconventional beliefs concerning reincarnation, ancestral memory, and what might be termed transtemporal telepathy:

> My theory of the matter is that I differ only from my fellows in that I can recall the events of many incarnations, while they can recall none of theirs other than a few important episodes of that particular one they are experiencing; but perhaps I am wrong. It is of no importance.

I will tell you the story of Julian 5th who was born in the year 2000, and then, if we have time and you are still interested, I will tell you of the torments during the harrowing days of the twenty-second century, following the birth of Julian 9th in 2100.

The anonymous narrator—in this case really an anonymous auditor sitting in for the reader—agrees, whereupon Admiral Julian's descendant tells his story through his ancestor.

"My name is Julian. I am called Julian 5th. I come of an illustrious family—my great-great grandfather, Julian 1st, a major at twenty-two, was killed in France early in The Great War. My great-grandfather, Julian 2nd, was killed in battle in Turkey in 1938. My grandfather, Julian 3rd, fought continuously from his sixteenth year until peace was declared in his thirtieth year. He died in 1992 and during the last twenty-five years of his life was an Admiral of the Air, being transferred at the close of the war to command of the International Peace Fleet, which patrolled and policed the world. He also was killed in line of duty, as was my father who succeeded him in the service.

"At sixteen I graduated from the Air School and was detailed to the International Peace Fleet, being the fifth generation of my line to wear the uniform of my country. That was in 2016, and I recall that it was a matter of pride to me that it rounded out the full century since Julian 1st graduated from West Point, and that during that one hundred years no adult male of my line had ever owned or worn civilian clothes.

"Of course there were no more wars, but there still was fighting. We had the pirates of the air to contend with and occasionally some of the uncivilized tribes of Russia, Africa and central Asia required the attention of a punitive expedition. However, life seemed tame and monotonous to us when we read of the heroic deeds of our ancestors from 1914 to 1967, yet none of us wanted war."

In this fashion the narration continues, drawing a "future history" of generations-long endurance, created decades before similar projects were undertaken by such science-fiction authors as Isaac Asimov and Robert A. Heinlein.

In 2015, after forty-eight years of radio communication, the Martians launch a ray-propelled ship toward the Earth. Designed to attain a maximum speed of 1000 miles per hour, the ship should take five years to reach its goal, and is provisioned appropriately. Unfortunately the ship goes astray, but with air recycling machinery and other equipment, may sustain life indefinitely. [Again, a remarkable anticipation of the "generations ship" so brilliantly portrayed by Heinlein in *Universe* (1941) and Harry Martinson in *Aniara* (1956).]

On Christmas Day, 2025, an Earth ship, *The Barsoom*, sets out for Mars. Its commander is the young Julian 5th. His first officer, Lieutenant Commander Orthis, is a brilliant but unstable engineer whose scientific genius was responsible for the construction of *The Barsoom*.

Nearly insane with resentment and jealousy at his appointment as first officer rather than captain of *The Barsoom*, Orthis sabotages the craft, and only a combination of good fortune and brilliant piloting permit Julian to bring the craft safely to an emergency landing on the moon. Desperately seeking a safe landing place, Julian makes the astonishing discovery that many of the moon's craters are not mere pockmarks on the face of a solid sphere. Rather they are shafts leading to a hollow and inhabited world within the moon, conceptually similar to the earthly Pellucidar.

There are two major differences between the Inner Worlds of Earth and Luna. First, there is no inner sun within the moon, warmth and light being provided by an all-pervasive, harmlessly radioactive atmosphere. Second, the inhabitants of the moon are not simple primitives as are the denizens of Pellucidar, but instead have a fairly advanced civilization.

Again, as in his earlier novels of Mars and Pellucidar, Burroughs was operating in a time-honored tradition in providing an inhabited moon; perhaps the most relevant earlier work was H. G. Wells' classic *The First Men in the Moon* (1901). Wells' earthly visitors Cavor and Bedford were indeed the first men *in* the moon for the civilization of the insect-like Selenites existed mainly in a honeycomb of caverns leading from the surface of the moon all the way down to a postulated central sea. (The sea is not visited in Wells' book. Nor, for that matter, is the moon visited at all by Bedford's girl friend, an otherwise generally faithful 1964 motion picture adaptation notwithstanding.)

Burroughs' moon is shared by three intelligent races of varying levels of civilization. The Va-gas, a race of vicious centaurs, are relatively barbaric. The Kalkars, a human-like race, are only slightly more advanced than the Va-gas. The U-gas, true humans, have attained a relatively advanced level of development.

Julian and the outwardly penitent Orthis are captured by the Va-gas. While they are held the centaurs take another captive, a beautiful girl who, flying over with artificial wings, falls into the clutches of the Va-Gas.

The girl is Nah-ee-lah, the daughter of Sagroth, Jamadar (king) of the city-state of Laythe. She and Julian become acquainted and their conversations provide Burroughs with an excellent opportunity to present the cosmogony of the inhabitants of the moon, or Va-nah. The Lunarians believe that the universe is a gigantic rock extending to the end of creation; their world is an inhabited hole in its center.

When Julian insists that he is a visitor to Va-nah, the girl admits the possibility of there being other worlds within the all-encompassing rock, with communication possible between them by means of the *Hoos*, or craters. Julian explains that worlds are not holes in any universal rock, but globes in space; he goes so far as "to explain the whole thing to her, commencing with the nebular hypothesis, and winding up with the relations that exist between the moon and the Earth." But all to no avail:

> "Suppose," she said, "that I should take a handful of gravel and throw it up in the air. According to your theory the smaller would all commence to revolve about the larger and they would go flying thus wildly around in the air forever, but that is not what would happen. If I threw a handful of gravel into the air it would fall immediately to the ground again, and if the worlds you tell me of were cast thus into the air, they too would fall, just as the gravel falls."

Such astronomical or metaphysical discussions aside, Julian and Nah-ee-lah are in dire peril, for the Va-gas relish no food better than fresh tender girl, nor, apparently, would they turn up their noses at juicy leg of Earthman in a pinch. Julian and Nah-ee-lah manage to escape in a terrible storm which strikes the Va-gas encampment, and after experiencing a series of frightening adventures make their way through an army of besieging Kalkars and enter the city of Laythe.

Here we learn of lunar-wide revolution; Kalkars everywhere have risen and overcome the governing U-gas, establishing a communistic system in the place of the U-gas' feudal-paternalistic regime. Laythe alone has held out, but is besieged and faced with the choice of surrender or slow death. The plight of the Laytheans is worsened by internal revolt, and the city falls; the U-gas are destroyed.

Julian, however, escapes to *The Barsoom*, taking Nah-ee-lah with him, and the couple returns safely to Earth.

At this point in the narration Air Admiral Julian interrupts his own story to note that the *Harding* has reached its destination, Paris. He and the narrator-auditor of the book leave the ship, Julian promising that, should they ever meet again, he will give the tale of a later descendant, Julian 9th.

Two years pass before the two men meet again. When they do Admiral

Julian proves true to his word, but prefaces the story of Julian 9th with the final chapters of that pertaining to Julian 5th. He tells of the years following Julian 5th's return to Earth with Nah-ee-lah, of the arrest of all scientific progress by pressure brought by an anti-science cult.

And then, in 2050—disaster!

A huge fleet of spaceships descends upon the Earth. Orthis, having remained on the moon when *The Barsoom* returned to Earth, had not been lost as believed by Julian. Instead, Orthis had made league with the Kalkar horde, had directed them in the construction of space craft and, now twenty-five years after leaving the Earth as first officer of *The Barsoom*, Orthis returns as the commander of a conquering space fleet.

The planet is virtually disarmed, there having been no war since 1967, eighty-three years earlier. The International Peace Fleet, under command of the aging Julian 5th, makes a gallant and sanguinary defense, but their case is hopeless. Both Julian and Orthis are killed in a final, climactic battle, and Orthis' now leaderless Kalkars settle their barbaric, exploitative rule upon the conquered planet, disguising beneath the trappings of a collectivist "brotherhood" a vicious feudalism.

Four generations pass, and Julian 9th, descended from Julian 5th and Nah-ee-lah the Moon Maid, tells his story through Air Admiral Julian. This story, with its portrayal of an agrarian, collectivized, alien-ruled America, the original *Under the Red Flag*, is the best of the three in the book, although all three are excellent. Burroughs' obvious deep feeling about communism, his revulsion at its tyranny and terror in the names of justice and brotherhood, is a powerful force in making *The Moon Men* an outstanding example of that form of imaginative literature dubbed "social science fiction" by Asimov.

Through the eyes of Julian 9th we see a fully developed picture of life beneath the Kalkar heel. The "Americans" as the Earth people are called, are forced to bow to any whim of their Kalkar masters. The form of address required in speaking to Kalkars is "brother," Burroughs' bitter commentary upon the communist "comrade." Earthly collaborators receive preferential treatment from the conquerors and authority over their fellow humans, but are held in contempt by Kalkar and "American" alike.

Loyalty to any former earthly authority or tradition is forbidden, and the result is the growth of a clandestine religion in which "Americans" worship a secretly preserved American flag and sing the proscribed "Onward Christian Soldiers" in forbidden religious services conducted by Orrin Colby, a blacksmith. Their prayer:

A scene from *The Moon Men*

God of our fathers, through generations of persecution and cruelty
in a world of hate that has turned against You we stand at Your right
hand, loyal to You and to our Flag. To us Your name stands for justice,
humanity, love, happiness and right and The Flag is Your emblem.
Once each month we risk our lives that Your name may not perish
from the Earth. Amen.

Although not himself religious, and although many of his books are
dotted with wry comments and slams against sham and exploitation in the
name of religion, Burroughs shows a very different attitude in *The Moon
Men*, when he deals with spontaneous religious feeling, distinct from insti-
tutionalized, and corrupted (in his opinion) practice.

In another area Burroughs uses *The Moon Men* as an outlet for social
comment, this area being that of anti-semitism. Burroughs has been criticized, especially for the anti-semitic caricature Adolph Bluber in *Tarzan and*

the Golden Lion. But in *The Moon Men* he offers Moses Samuels, a tragic, heroic figure, one of the most believable of all his characters.

Samuels is a tanner who buys hides from Julian and others and sells them to the Kalkars; such commerce is not regarded as collaboration as the Kalkar influence is so pervasive as to be unavoidable. Further, the Kalkars only cheat and exploit those "Americans" from whom they buy. A new Kalkar commander has just arrived, and Moses Samuels is speculating to Julian, about what sort of ruler he will be: "Sometimes they are liberal—as they can afford to be with the property of others; but if he is a half-breed [half Kalkar and half human], as I hear he is, he will hate a Jew, and I shall get nothing. However, if he is pure Kalkar it may be different—the pure Kalkars do not hate a Jew more than they hate other Earthmen, though there is one Jew who hates a Kalkar."

Samuels' martyrdom at the hands of the Kalkars is a scene of great power, and his role in *The Moon Men* might well raise Burroughs to a higher regard among critics who judge fiction by social as well as literary standards, were it better known. [At this point, in order to avoid confusion, I should mention that Moses Samuels' role in *The Moon Men* is not the same in all editions. The original magazine versions of the three stories tended to be some-what more episodic than the combined book version. In the smoothing and polishing process that created the book version, Samuels' part is unfortu-nately diminished, even though the general quality of the text is somewhat improved. A 1962 paperback edition contains the magazine version rather than the standard book version. While the book is generally recommended as better reading, anyone with a special interest in the social content of the original stories would do well to check the magazine text as well. Details are given at the end of this chapter.]

At the end of *The Moon Men* the "Americans" revolt against the Kalkar rule. The rebellion is crushed by overwhelming Kalkar power and Julian, a leader of the rebels, is beheaded, partly as a result of the treachery of another villainous Orthis, now Brother General Or-tis.

By the time of Julian 20th, the central figure of the concluding portion of the trilogy, *The Red Hawk*, civilization has deteriorated further. When the original Lieutenant Commander Orthis had led the Kalkars in building their triumphant war fleet in the moon, he had effectively presented them with a complex technology which they had neither the industrial base nor the education to sustain. Following the death of Orthis in his final battle with Julian 5th the Kalkars were unable to build additional ships, and could repair those already in service only by cannibalizing other ships.

Over the years some of the craft on the Earth-moon run were lost or

A scene from *The Red Hawk*

crashed, each such loss reducing the Kalkar fleet by one irreplaceable unit. Fewer and fewer ships remained, finally none at all. Contact between Earth and moon ceased; conditions on the moon remained unknown, while upon the Earth the organization of the Kalkars degenerated and repeated revolutions by Earthmen succeeded where their first had failed.

In the time of Julian 20th we learn that the Kalkars have been reduced to control only of small enclaves on the east and west coasts of North America. The feudal agrarian culture of earlier years has slipped back even farther into a nomadic tribalism closely resembling that of the ancient Amerinds while the *original* American Indian survives also, serving the "Americans," waiting for them, too, to pass from the scene, so that the red man might finally regain the continent.

The plains life, its description based upon Burroughs' experiences as a cowboy and a soldier, is wholly convincing and wholly fascinating. The final push against the Kalkars and their last stand in a ruined California city are equally effective, bringing *The Moon Maid* to a completely satisfying close.

The Moon Maid trilogy is, in my opinion, Burroughs' masterpiece of science fiction and a too-often overlooked pioneer work of the modern school of social extrapolation in science fiction.

[A few words concerning bibliography. Both *The Land that Time Forgot* and *The Moon Maid* appeared originally as three separate stories.

[*The Land that Time Forgot, The People that Time Forgot,* and *Out of Time's Abyss* appeared in a combined edition under the first title in 1924; in 1962 a Canaveral Press edition was issued under the same name. The following year *three* paperbacks appeared under the Ace Books impress, containing the three original stories split apart once again, and restoring the original titles to the separate slim volumes.

[*The Moon Maid, The Moon Men,* and *The Red Hawk* appeared in a combined edition under the first title in 1926. The first of the three magazine stories was also reprinted in a magazine in 1928 as *Conquest of the Moon.*

[All book editions used the title *The Moon Maid* until 1962, when the Canaveral edition appeared titled *The Moon Men,* but still containing all three stories. In the same year Ace Books produced two paperbacks, *The Moon Maid* and *The Moon Men,* the former containing the original (magazine) version of that story only, the latter containing the magazine versions of its title story and *The Red Hawk.*

[In 1963 Dover Publications issued a sort of superomnibus, *The Land that Time Forgot and The Moon Maid,* containing the book versions of both trilogies. This volume was available in both paperback and clothbound editions.

[Finally, the University of Nebraska Press issued a "complete and restored" *Moon Maid* in 2002, reinstating all passages excised from both the magazine and book versions.

[Thus the material in question is available in anywhere from one to six volumes, paperbound and clothbound, magazine versions and book versions, or a combination thereof.]

CHAPTER VIII

The Good Pot-Boilers

In *The Reader's Encyclopedia* William Rose Benet defines a pot-boiler as "A literary or critical term meaning an inferior piece of work . . . done merely for the sake of money: in other words, to keep the pot boiling, that is, to eat." By this standard most of the literary output of most of the authors of the past several centuries must be regarded as pot-boilers.

The word inferior in Benet's definition is purely relative in its meaning, if any one work of a given man is regarded as his best, then all else he ever created is inferior to that one, or if Benet's intent is to mean below average, then exactly one half of any author's output is, by definition, inferior. As for writing for the sake of money, certainly every professional author writes for the sake of money, "that is, to eat," and this is certainly not a sign of wickedness.

With the possible exception, then, of the one word *merely*, the greatest number of Edgar Rice Burroughs' works were pot-boilers. Of necessity they were inferior to his very best works, and there is no denying that they were written for money. Burroughs was a fairly prolific author. His lifetime output of approximately seventy books (*approximately* only because of bibliographic quibbles, such as whether unpublished works count, and whether connected stories published at various times in both separate and combined editions should count as single or multiple works), although by no means a record or anything like one, is a considerable amount of prose.

It is to be expected, then, that the majority of Burroughs' works do not contain the creative values of the few best. Especially in view of his penchant for series stories, most of Burroughs' books are set in already established fantasy-worlds—Barsoom, Pellucidar, Tarzan's Africa—and feature already established characters, or new characters not really too different from those already familiar to the reader.

The later books of Burroughs' various series then lack somewhat in the fascination of meeting new folks and exploring new worlds, as Burroughs' characters, settings, and largely stereotyped plotting patterns become increasingly familiar to the reader.

This is hardly to say, however, that the later stories of all Burroughs' series are devoid of merit. At best, a good many of them do contain considerable imaginative content, and certainly plenty of color and action. For those who enjoyed the earlier books of a series, often the later ones can provide the pleasure of meeting again the old friends, and of visiting once more the lands of enjoyment first encountered in the earlier books.

In the period 1915–1925 that we have been considering, Burroughs continued his Martian series with two more novels, *The Chessmen of Mars* and *The Master Mind of Mars*.

Chessmen was written in 1921 and published in both magazine serial form and a book edition the following year. It is told by John Carter to Burroughs when Captain Carter returns to Earth for a visit, via teleportation. The hero of the tale is Gahan, Jed of the city-state of Gathol. The heroine is Tara of Helium, younger sister of Carthoris and daughter to John Carter and Dejah Thoris.

No major change in the overall picture of Barsoom comes about in *Chessmen*, except perhaps for carrying on the John Carter family tree through the romance of Tara and Gahan, but the book offers a fast-paced and imaginative adventure story with several exotic settings, a good amount of swordplay, and periodic bursts of humor.

The rather odd title of the book comes from the Martian city of Manator, where much of the action occurs. The inhabitants of Manator are obsessed with the game of *Jetan*, a Barsoomian chess. Burroughs worked out the pieces and moves of Jetan in considerable detail, and in addition to the description of the game woven into the story he provided an appendix to the book detailing Jetan at some length.

The pieces which he describes, are the Warrior, Padwar, Dwar, Flier, Chief, Princess, Thoat, and Panthan. All are references to military or royal grades in Martian society except for the Flier, which is based upon the Martian aircraft, and the Thoat, based upon the Martian beast of that name.

The game is played with twenty black pieces by one player and twenty orange by his opponent, and is presumed to have originally represented a battle between the Black race of the south and the Yellow race of the north. On Mars the board is usually arranged so that the Black pieces are played from the south and the Orange from the north.

A companion of Tara and Gahan for much of their peripatetic adventuring is Ghek the Kaldane, a hideous creature for whom the reader's initial revulsion is turned gradually to admiration and liking by his conduct.

In a Martian area known as Bantoom, Burroughs places two races living in weird symbiosis; these are the *rykors* and the *kaldanes*. A rykor is, to all appearances, a normally—indeed, an exceptionally—formed human, male or female; handsome, muscular—and headless! A kaldane, by contrast, would appear to be a bodiless human head, equipped with a pair of crab-like chelae and six short, spider-like legs on which to crawl about.

These two hideous life-forms coexist by the mind-wrenching device of the kaldane seating itself upon the neck of the rykor, its chelae entering the rykor's spinal column through the top of the neck. The head and the body thus work together, the kaldane providing sight, intellect, and direction while the rykor provides locomotion, manipulation, and whatever brute force might be needed.

A stock of rykors are kept by their master, the kaldanes, in pens when not in use. A rykor, totally mindless and without purpose or personality except as lent by a kaldane, receives no more consideration or care than any piece of machinery. A given kaldane might use any rykor that he cared, male or female, moving to another at will.

These two repulsive forms of life would seem to be as unpleasant and unsympathetic a pair of creatures as imaginary evolution has ever developed, but in *The Chessmen of Mars* Burroughs causes Tara and Gahan to join forces with Ghek, a kaldane who has grown tired of the life in Bantoom and decided to join the humans in their travels.

In Manator the three adventurers become involved in the great tournament, for the Manatorians are so fond of Jetan that they have built their entire society upon its principles. Periodically great games are held in which live chessmen and women play upon a giant board of Jetan in the stadium, the battle of the game being performed, often to the death, by the "pieces."

Is *The Chessmen of Mars* a pot-boiler? Probably it must be rated as such; by no means does it compare with so fine a work as, for example, *The Moon Maid*. But it is a most commendable adventure story, its imaginative touches well mixed with its direct action sequences. In this case, pot-boiler is hardly a term of disparagement.

The sixth Barsoomian novel, *The Master Mind of Mars*, was written in 1925, and first appeared in the 1927 (and only) edition of Hugo Gernsback's *Amazing Stories Annual*. Burroughs' Caspak trilogy had been reprinted in the *Amazing Stories* monthly earlier in 1927, but when the annual appeared in July of that year it marked Burroughs' first appearance with new material in any specialized pulp magazine.

All of the Munsey magazines were general-interest pulps, where science fiction appeared side-by-side with western stories, jungle adventures, sea adventures, detective tales, and stories of endless variation in theme and setting. The other publications to which Burroughs strayed from Munsey—Street and Smith's *New Story*, MacCall Corporation's *Red Book*, *Blue Book* under several publishers, etc.—were similarly varied in content.

To lure Burroughs into the specialty market Gernsback not only offered the top rates that his publication could afford, but gave Burroughs a terrific play in the magazine itself. The *Amazing Stories Annual* may well have been the greatest science fiction bargain of all time; it certainly contained one of the top lineups of authors ever to appear in a magazine of its type, some of the authors featured having since slipped into obscurity but others still in print and high in favor with connoisseurs of the field.

(In addition to the Burroughs novel the annual contained two stories, *The Face in the Abyss* and *The People of the Pit*, by the master fantacist Abraham Merritt. Austin Hall contributed *The Man Who Saved the Earth*. The explorer and anthropologist A. Hyatt Verrill was represented by *The Man Who Could Vanish*, Jacque Morgan offered a scientific farce, *The Feline Light and Power Company is Organized*, and H. G. Wells himself had a short story in the issue, *Under the Knife*.)

But the Burroughs tale received the full play of the issue. The cover illustration, a beautifully lurid painting by Frank R. Paul, showed a weird laboratory scene. In the foreground a beautiful red girl, minimally draped in a wispy material, lies unconscious. Bending over her, manipulating a strange apparatus that includes a tank of fresh blood, is a wizened red man of Mars, assisted in his mysterious work by an Earthman. In the background an ancient red Martian woman lies on a similar table, while what appear to be row upon row of Martian bodies stretch behind them, into the distance.

Blazoned across the top of the cover in huge yellow letters are the words EDGAR RICE BURROUGHS, and in red lettering not much smaller, *Master Mind of Mars*. The story received first position in the magazine, and was illustrated with six full-page drawings by Paul, plus a number of smaller sketches.

The story itself is prefaced by a letter to Burroughs, dated Helium, (Barsoom), June 8, 1926. The correspondent is Ulysses Paxton, a former captain of infantry. In the letter, which is transmitted from Paxton to Burroughs "with the aid of one greater than either of us," Paxton reveals that he is himself a fan of Burroughs' stories. His favorite story is *A Princess of Mars*, and he has always harbored a hope and half a belief that there might be some grain of truth in the saga of John Carter.

In the trenches of France during the Great War, Paxton had been mortally wounded; lying waiting for death, he had experienced a largely delirious daydream, had yearned inexpressibly for Barsoom, and had miraculously found himself whole and naked upon that planet, just as had John Carter half a century before him.

On Barsoom Paxton is taken on as a laboratory assistant to Ras Thavas the most brilliant scientific wizard of the red planet, the Master Mind of Mars.

Quite aside from his intellectual attainments, Ras Thavas is an unusual character even for a Barsoomian. A curious and crotchety old man nearing his life's limit of 1000 years, Ras Thavas is intent upon achieving a perfect technique for transferring a brain from one body to another, thus indefinitely prolonging human life. Brain transfer as a science-fictional theme was of course not new in 1927; it can be traced at least to its use in *Frankenstein* in 1818, but in 1927 it was still not the tired device that myriad low-budget horror films have since made it.

The plot deals, rather predictably, with Ras Thavas transplanting the brain of the powerful Xaxa, hideous Jeddara (queen) of Phundahl, into the beautiful body of the innocent Valla Dia, leaving the latter the withered husk of Xaxa's body in exchange. Ulysses Paxton, renamed Vad Varo by Ras Thavas because his earthly name is "meaningless and impractical," shares Valla Dia's excitement and travail as she eventually regains possession of her rightful body.

In the process Vad Varo destroys the corrupt Cult of Tur, paralleling John Carter's overthrow of the Cult of Issus in *The Gods of Mars*. And of course by the end of the tale Vad Varo is the husband of Valla Dia, who happens by happy happenstance to be a princess.

The first book edition of *The Master Mind of Mars* appeared in 1928. In it the date of Ulysses Paxton's letter to Burroughs is given as June 8, 1925 (rather than 1926, as in the magazine version); and since the earlier date is the one given in Burroughs' notebook as the day he started writing *Master Mind*, it can be kept as one example of Burroughs' custom of mixing real elements into his fictional worlds.

The story itself, although a bit silly in its bare-bones description, is once more a colorful and action-filled romp, certainly enjoyable if not particularly significant.

Rude bows and arrows, stone-shod spears, gaudy feathers, the waving tails of animals accentuated the barbaric atmosphere that was as yet uncontaminated by the fetid breath of civilization—pardon me!—that was as yet ignorant of the refining influences of imperial conquest, trained mercenaries and abhorrent disease.

Skipping forward rapidly to the nineteenth century, Burroughs picks up Jerry MacDuff a descendant of the ancient Caledonians, pushing westward from his parents' home in Georgia. Jerry marries Annie Foley who is one-quarter Cherokee; they have a son Andy, born in Missouri in 1863 while his parents are en route to California, but the trip is never completed. Apaches ambush the wagon and massacre its inhabitants except for the infant, who is adopted by the Apache Go-yat-thlay and his youngest squaw, Sons-ee-ah-ray.

The boy is raised as an Apache. His name is Shoz-Dijiji, and he grows to be a great warrior. The growth and young manhood of Shoz-Dijiji are chronicled in two books, *The War Chief* and *Apache Devil*, both of which are of excellent quality. For once Burroughs drew upon his real-life experiences for background information with great success and conviction.

He mixed in a number of real persons, particularly such Apaches as Cochise, Mangas Colorado, and Geronimo, giving a picture of the hopeless struggle of the proud Apaches against the overwhelming power of the advancing white men. Shoz-Dijiji's two romances are handled better than most of Burroughs' rather stilted love interests. The little Indian girl with whom Shoz-Dijiji grows up is effectively portrayed and the tragic end of her love for Shoz-Dijiji is genuinely touching.

The final defeat of the Apaches is depicted with an effective portrayal of the hopelessness of their situation, and the final decision of Shoz-Dijiji to renounce the reservation life to which the Apaches are doomed, and join the white man's world by marrying the white girl Wichita Billings, carries convincing tragic overtones despite its apparent happy resolution of his problems.

The War Chief was written in 1926, was serialized in *Argosy All-Story Weekly* in 1927, and appeared in book form in 1928. The sequel, *Apache Devil*, was written in 1927, serialized in the same magazine in 1928, but book publication was delayed until 1933.

Although far out of the mainstream of Burroughs' works, these two Apache novels show him at or very near the top of his form; they are far superior to his few conventional westerns, and stand in the top rank of all his books.

Also in 1928 Burroughs revived his Inner World series with *Tanar of Pellucidar*, the first story in this series since 1915. *Tanar* was serialized in *Blue Book* in 1929, and was published in book form the following year.

Adopting the policy he had used in the Martian series, of moving the original hero to a subordinate role and setting up new featured characters, Burroughs billed Tanar, a native of Pellucidar, in the book's title, and gave him major attention in the story, although David Innes does appear in the book.

This third Inner World novel is of particular interest for it is in this volume that Burroughs introduces his young inventor friend Jason Gridley, whose experiments with advanced radio design offer the frame for the book. Gridley picks up strange and inexplicable transmissions of several sorts, unearthly languages and weird music, that are *never* explained and that might well provide a springboard for imagining whole shelves of books that Burroughs might have written, but never got around to.

Jason Gridley also picks up a transmission from David Innes' mentor Abner Perry at "the Imperial Observatory at Greenwich, Pellucidar." This transmission of course provides the body of the novel, another excellent Inner World tale, its believability enhanced by the lengthy and ingenious introduction.

An opening between Pellucidar and the outer world at the North Pole is introduced in this story. Through it at some uncertain time in the seventeenth or eighteenth century a pirate fleet was swept. The descendants of the crews, their hereditary title gradually corrupted from Corsairs to Korsars, still practice piracy on the high seas of Pellucidar, led by The Cid and by Bohar the Bloody, whom Tanar the Fleet One must face if he is to win the lovely Stellara for his mate.

By the end of the story all is well for Tanar and Stellara, but poor David Innes, who had gone to Tanar's aid and himself fallen prisoner to the Korsars, is now rotting in a snake-infested dungeon in a stronghold of the pirates.

"Think of it," cries Jason Gridley back in the sunny comfort of Tarzana, California. "Think of that poor devil buried there in utter darkness, silence, solitude—and with those snakes! God!" he shuddered. "Snakes crawling all over him, winding about his arms and nothing else to break the monotony— no human voice, the song of no bird, no ray of sunlight. Something must be done. He must be saved."

"But who is going to do it?" asked Burroughs.

"I am!" replied Jason Gridley.

And there, in a brief passage, Burroughs provided the lead-in for the

next book in the Pellucidar series, one of the most remarkable entanglings
of the threads of his gigantic web of stories, *Tarzan at the Earth's Core.*

Written directly after *Tanar* (Burroughs' notebook shows *Tanar* completed
on November 21, 1928, and *Tarzan at the Earth's Core* begun December 6)
this latter book takes up in plot directly where *Tanar* left off. Indeed, these
two books plus the next two in the series, *Back to the Stone Age* and *Land of
Terror*, are all cut from the same cloth.

Tarzan at the Earth's Core opens in the Ape Man's African domain with
Tarzan sniffing the breeze, seeking to identify an odor which no ordinary
man could even detect. He meets a safari headed by Jason Gridley who,
true to his word to Burroughs at the end of *Tanar*, has set out to rescue the
prisoner of the Korsars, David Innes. (Heins has commented that the length
of time, or what passes for time in eternal Pellucidar, that David spent with
the snakes before being rescued must certainly mark the greatest epic of
man's endurance in all of Burroughs' writings.)

Jason Gridley and Tarzan hold a lengthy discussion of the possibility of
there really being an Inner World beneath their feet, and of the possibility
of there being polar openings to any such Inner World. Gridley gets his
case across, citing references as old as 1830, and reading to Tarzan portions
of the manuscript of *Tanar of Pellucidar* in order to convince the Ape Man of
the desperate plight of David Innes, and of the need for action to rescue him.

Tarzan finally agrees to make the try, and joins Jason in planning the
vehicle in which they will undertake the long journey. Rather than attempt
to duplicate Abner Perry's iron mole and bore through the equatorial crust,
Tarzan and Jason Gridley feel that they would have a better chance to
enter Pellucidar at the northerly land of the Korsars. In order to do so
they determine upon an aircraft which will carry them through the polar
opening.

The result is a great dirigible, the *0–220* named thus in honor of Edgar
Rice Burroughs' real-life telephone number. The airship is built of Harbenite, an ultra-light, ultra-strong metal discovered in Africa by the son
of a missionary friend of Tarzan's. The metal is strong enough to hold the
ultimate lifting "substance"—a total vacuum. There is no need to worry
about replenishing supplies of hydrogen or helium: all that is needed is
a set of valves to admit air into the vacuum tanks when the *0–220* is to
descend, and a set of pumps to expel the air and restore the vacuum when
the ship is to rise again.

The *0–220* carries an airplane for short-range scouting in Pellucidar.
The ship is crewed by German officers and men, perhaps as an attempt by

Burroughs to counter the anti-German elements of several earlier books. These were the years of the Weimar Republic and hopes existed that a peaceful and stable Germany would emerge.

In addition to the flying crew, the *0–220* carries Chief Muviro and nine of his Waziri warriors, Jason Gridley and Tarzan, engineers, cabin boys and a chef, Robert Jones, an American Negro who remained in Germany after the Great War. Robert Jones is a sort of later-day avatar of the comic Negroes who appeared in *The Man-Eater* and several early Tarzan novels; he is contrasted with the courageous and dignified Waziri.

Flying from a base in Friedrichshafen the *0–220* proceeds due north. The ship follows the curvature of the Earth, and in a scene slightly reminiscent of the climax of Poe's *Narrative of Arthur Gordon Pym*, and rivalling the earlier work in its almost hypnotic power, the *0–220* is swept over the brink of the polar opening, the miniature sun of Pellucidar becoming visible just as Sol drops below the southern horizon of the outer world. To the hardened science fiction fan, mourning for his lost sense of wonder, that splendid and frightening moment when, amidst the bitter whiteness of the arctic, the *0–220* noses over and emerges in the Inner World is a fleeting instant of heart-filling marvel, a moment in which the science adventure novel reaches its full dimensions as a wonder tale!

Once in Pellucidar the party began to unload the *0–220* and to prepare their airplane for reconnaissance missions. Tarzan, happily freed of the fetters of airshipboard life, takes off through the undergrowth of Pellucidar, only to find that his African-bred sense of direction is useless in this new land. Further, with no moon, no stars, with the sun eternally at high noon, with no compass and no magnetic pole to give it meaning if he had one, Tarzan is completely lost!

To the reader accustomed to the Ape Man's virtual infallibility in the jungle, this is a jolt of considerable proportion. To Tarzan it is the same. Similarly, the rest of the *0–220* party undergo unexpected difficulties, losing another of their number, Lieutenant Wilhelm Von Horst, in a great stampede of hunting tigers seeking to bring down a gigantic woolly mammoth.

The various members of the expedition undergo their respective adventures and hardships, the most effective sequence being a chilling encounter with the Horibs, an intelligent race of terrifying anthropophagous lizards who customarily fatten their prospective dinners in underwater caverns where trapped air bubbles keep them alive until the Horibs see fit to slaughter them.

Ultimately Tarzan does succeed in rescuing David Innes from the Korsars, the *0–220* expedition is reunited, and all are ready to leave for the outer world once more when it is realized that Lieutenant Von Horst is still unaccounted for! Jason Gridley, whose charitable concern for David Innes brought about the *0–220* expedition, now announces that he is going to stay in Pellucidar and find Von Horst, and apparently is setting out in this new quest as the volume ends.

In *Back to the Stone Age* (written 1935, *Argosy* serialization and first book edition in 1937) the scene flashes back to the moment of the tiger-mammoth fight in *Tarzan at the Earth's Core*. This time the focus is on Von Horst, and the reader is carried through his exploits up to and including the time of his discovery in the distant land of Lo-har by David Innes. By this time Von Horst has passed through a series of hair-raising perils raised by strange beasts and stranger men, has won the love of the beautiful La-ja of Lohar, and has attained the chieftanship of La-ja's tribe.

David calmly explains to Van Horst that Jason Gridley changed his mind at the last minute, and returned to the outer world with the *0–220*. This is the only such outright "cheat" I have come across in Burroughs' works, although there are a number of slips and inconsistencies elsewhere in them.

Von Horst is invited to return with David to Sari, there to await a possible second *0–220* expedition. Von Horst replies that he is perfectly content to remain in Lo-har with La-ja, and he is presumably there to this day.

Between October, 1938, and April, 1939, Burroughs wrote the sixth Pellucidar novel, *Land of Terror* (no magazine publication, first book edition in 1944). In it, Burroughs continued to mine the *0–220* theme, this time recounting the experiences of David Innes on his trip from Lo-har back to Sari. *Land of Terror* is a typical Inner World adventure, spiced by the attempts of various Pellucidarian maidens to win David's affections, and his continual refusal to be untrue to Dian the Beautiful.

In quality, the Pellucidar series had started extremely well, but unlike Burroughs' novels of Barsoom the Inner World stories did not keep up in quality as they continued to appear. The first Inner World novel, *At the Earth's Core*, is a thrilling adventure tale, packed with astonishing imaginative concepts as well as with humor, satirical asides, and excellent characterizations.

The second book of the series, *Pellucidar*, closely rivals the first in all aspects, perhaps the novelty of its predecessor alone rendering it the superior of the two. The third book, *Tanar*, does not present quite the imaginative stimulation of the earlier volumes, but is nonetheless quite readable.

With *Tarzan at the Earth's Core*, despite a number of high points, the imaginative fabric of the earlier volumes starts to break down. Pellucidar, unfortunately, loses much of its feeling of being a cohesive world with institutions of its own. Instead, the impression is given of a dangerous primitive land, divided into enclaves of various sorts, with little of the cohesion and interest of the first three volumes.

Back to the Stone Age continues this trend, and *Land of Terror* brings the series to a nadir. Plotting is perfunctory, pace is poor, and whatever reader involvement survived the poor performance of *Back to the Stone Age* is totally annihilated in the debacle of *Land of Terror*. It is certainly Burroughs at his worst.

There is a seventh Pellucidar volume, and happily to report, it shows considerable improvement over the fifth and sixth. *Savage Pellucidar* is actually a group of four inter-connected novelettes.

Three of them were published in *Amazing Stories* in 1942. Editor Ray Palmer felt at that time that serials were lacking in reader appeal, and he convinced Burroughs to write a number of novelette-length stories in all of his science fiction series. Each was published in *Amazing* or its companion pulp *Fantastic Adventures* as a "complete novel," later grouped for book publication, four novelettes to the volume. The stories thus collected make up the final Pellucidar and Venus books, and the tenth Barsoomian volume.[1]

In the case of the Inner World stories, after the appearance in 1942 of the novelettes *The Return to Pellucidar*, *Men of the Bronze Age*, and *Tiger Girl*, no book edition was forthcoming for over twenty years, and during those years the three stories ranked among the most difficult of all Burroughs' works to obtain. In 1963, with the retirement of Cyril Rothmund as general manager of Edgar Rice Burroughs, Inc., a routine office inventory produced the astounding discovery of over a quarter million words in unpublished manuscripts.

Among these was *Savage Pellucidar*, a fourth novelette in the 1942 *Amazing* series. Even a dedication, *To my first grandson, James Michael Pierce*, was found. The novelette was published in the fall of 1963, appropriately in *Amazing Stories*, although Palmer had long since departed as editor and Cele Goldsmith was now at the helm. Shortly thereafter the first book edition appeared, the first of the Canaveral Press first editions.

1. The attribution of this change from serialized novels to linked novelettes is credited by most pulp scholars to Palmer's influence. Irwin Porges, however, suggests Cyril Ralph Rothmund influenced Burroughs to make the change.

Too late for use with the book, a jacket blurb by Burroughs himself was discovered. He had intended to call the book *Girl of Pellucidar*, and his intended blurb follows:

> While this could scarcely be called 'A collection of flowers of literature,' it might still be called a sort of anthology—an anthology of adventure. It is a tale not alone of the adventures of the girl, O-aa; but of those which befell Hodon the Fleet One and Dian the Beautiful and Abner Perry and David Innes and the little old man from Cape Cod, whose name was not Dolly Dorcas, and many others.
>
> It will take you to strange lands across the nameless strait in the Stone Age world at the Earth's core, and to adventures upon the terrible seas of Pellucidar. It will take you from the terrors with which you have been for years accustomed—the terrors of a world gone mad with hate—to the cleaner, finer terrors of prehistoric hunting beasts and savage, primeval men.
>
> The primary cause of many of the adventures which befell the nice and un-nice characters whose stories unfolded between these covers was Abner Perry's insatiable urge to invent. Had he not invented a balloon, very little of all this you are about to read would have happened.
>
> On the other hand, the ships he built, the cannon and muskets and gunpowder he produced made it possible for many of these characters to live to tell of their adventures.
>
> But maybe you do not like adventure? Then do not read this story. For it is replete with adventure and mystery and despair and courage and loyalty and—love.
>
> We think you will love little O-aa and her astounding mendacity. Perhaps you will be shocked by the little old man whose name was not Dolly Dorcas and who had an inordinate appetite for human flesh, especially Swedes, a lovely old gentleman from Cape Cod where the cranberries come from.

Savage Pellucidar is necessarily episodic, but its quality is considerable. Several of Burroughs' better characters appear in it. The girl O-aa is an incredible liar, delighting in spinning tall tales regarding the number and ferocity of the male members of her family. She is also an incessant chatterer.

Ah-gilak, the old man whose name was not Dolly Dorcas, is another traveler from the outer world, a nineteenth century sailor whose ship was swept through the polar opening, and whose survival is credited to the fact that Pellucidar is timeless.

Savage Pellucidar opens with Abner Perry's attempt to build a Pellucidar-ian airplane and continues with a disastrous flight in a natural gas balloon made of saurian peritonea. It ends, after much flashing back and forth between various scenes and sequences, with the focus back on the inventor who had, indeed, been responsible for the entire Inner World adventure with his invention so long before of the iron mole.

> Abner Perry was so happy that he cried, for those whom he had thought his carelessness had condemned to death were safe and at home again. Already, mentally, he was inventing a submarine.

Some note is also due to a borderline science fiction novel that Burroughs wrote in 1929, published as *The Land of Hidden Men* in *Blue Book* in 1931. The book edition, published 1932, was called *Jungle Girl*. This is the story of Gordon King, an American physician who becomes lost in the jungle of Cambodia and discovers a lost race dwelling there.

The plot hinges upon King's knowledge of jungle medicine and nutrition, for the monarch of the lost people suffers from a nutritional ailment brought on by his living entirely on mushrooms. The symptoms of his nutritional ailment are outwardly indistinguishable from those of leprosy, and the American secures royal favor by "curing" the Cambodian's "leprosy" by convincing him to vary his diet.

Jungle Girl is an enjoyable bit of fluff, with good color and not entirely lacking in suspense. There are a number of loose ends in the book, calling for a sequel, but *Jungle Girl* obviously created no wild clamor among concerned editors, readers, or publishers, and the commercially-minded Burroughs left the sequel unwritten.

It is difficult to take *Jungle Girl* seriously, but then Burroughs himself advised his readers repeatedly not to take any of his works seriously, so it is not going against the author's wishes to have a good laugh at *Jungle Girl* and romp through its pages for fun.

Still I suspect that I would hold the book in higher regard if I were not myself inordinately fond of mushrooms.

CHAPTER IX

Barsoom Concluded

After the enjoyable *Master Mind* and its initial appearance in 1927, there remained five volumes in the Martian series, three real novels, one "novel" composed of four interconnected shorter tales from *Amazing*, and a final, posthumous volume containing two additional novelettes.

The first of these remaining books was *A Fighting Man of Mars*, written in 1929, serialized in *Blue Book* the next year, and published in book form the year following. In introducing this tale Burroughs doubled and redoubled the complexities of his interlocking series by explaining that when Jason Gridley left Tarzana, California, for Africa, in order to convince Tarzan to accompany him to Pellucidar, he had left an automatic transmitter and receiver turned on in his Tarzana laboratory.

The set endlessly broadcasted Gridley's initials. The receiver was set to pick up whatever reply Gridley might receive—previously it had been Abner Perry's distress call from Pellucidar, this time it might be a message from Barsoom.

During Gridley's absences from Tarzana, Burroughs dropped in occasionally to see that all was well in the lab, and on one such visit found the receiver operating at full speed, bringing in a Morse-coded message. Over a decade earlier Burroughs and Cogdon Nestor had needed a telegrapher to translate David Innes' message to them in the Sahara, as recorded in *Pellucidar*. Apparently Burroughs had taken a lesson from that experience, and studied Morse in the intervening time, for he was able to transcribe the Gridley Wave message as it came in.

The transmission itself was made by Ulysses Paxton/Vad Varo, but the story was that of Tan Hadron of Hastor, the Martian fighting man of the book's title. Basically *A Fighting Man of Mars* falls into the same category as *Thuvia*, *Chessmen*, and *Master Mind*. None of these four middle novels of the series are vital to the Martian mythos set up by Burroughs in his original trilogy, but all are entertaining and imaginative works.

Fighting Man offers a number of excellent action scenes, two marvelous lost cities on Mars not described in earlier works, an excellent suspense device in which Tan Hadron and a friend Nur An are condemned to The Death, a mysterious and horrible form of execution. The companions fight monsters, encounter a race of giant spiders, spend some time with a de-lightfully sadistic mad monarch, and of course win through at the end.

To cap his triumph, Tan Hadron wins the love of Tavia, a slave girl, and Tavia then turns out to be a long-lost princess. In short, *A Fighting Man of Mars*, is another Barsoomian pot-boiler, and a fine one.

The eighth Barsoomian book, *Swords of Mars*, is a different story altogether. Written in 1933, serialized in *Blue Book* in 1934–35, first published in book form in 1936, *Swords* is a very remarkable book, near the top of the Martian series in imaginative content and a good story as well.

Beginning with an Arizona camping trip by Burroughs, the book de-scribes yet another visit to Earth by John Carter. In the story which Captain Carter narrates he is himself the lead actor for the first time since *Warlord*.

The novel deals, for once, with the problems which John Carter en-counters in his capacity as a responsible civic official, specifically with the situation in Zodanga. This city had been razed once by the Warlord, but in the rebuilt metropolis John Carter saw evidence that the Guild of Assassins was completely out of hand, and set out to break up the Guild.

Always an exponent of direct action, John Carter proceeds to Zodanga disguised with body makeup as a native red Martian. He infiltrates the Guild of Assassins under the alias of Vandor, a *panthan* or freelance fighting man, and through the Guild becomes involved with Fal Sivas, a Zodangan scientist who is building a spaceship in which he hopes to embark upon a campaign of interplanetary conquest.

Through the eyes of John Carter the reader sees Fal Sivas' spaceship and hears the inventor explain the guidance device of the craft, an artificial brain which, described by Burroughs in 1933, has almost the precise size, function, and even programming characteristics of the electronic computers used to guide today's spacecraft!

Perhaps the only major difference between Fal Sivas' guidance com-puter and today's equivalent is that Fal Sivas' research techniques involved removing the tops of the heads of beautiful Martian girls and studying the convolutions of their living brains, hardly accepted methodology in modern labs. Still, consider Fal Sivas' description of his device, as reported by "Vandor."

"I have given that seemingly insensate mechanism a brain with which to think. I have perfected my mechanical brain, Vandor, and with just a little more time, just a few refinements, I can send this ship out alone; and it will go where I wish it to go and come back again.

"Doubtless you think that impossible. You think Fal Sivas is mad; but look! watch closely."

He centered his gaze upon the nose of the strange-looking craft, and presently I saw it rise slowly from its scaffolding for about ten feet and hang there poised in midair. Then it elevated its nose a few feet, and then its tail, and finally it settled again and rested evenly upon its scaffolding.

I was certainly astonished. Never in all my life had I seen anything so marvelous, nor did I seek to hide my admiration from Fal Sivas.

"You see," he said, "I did not even have to speak to it. The mechanical mind that I have installed in the ship responds to thought waves. I merely have to impart to it the impulse of the thought that I wish it to act upon. The mechanical brain then functions precisely as my brain would, and directs the mechanism that operates the craft precisely as the brain of the pilot would direct his hands to move levers, press buttons, open or close throttles."

. . . The interior of the control room, which occupied the entire nose of the ship, was a mass of intricate mechanical and electrical devices.

On either side of the nose were two large, round ports in which were securely set thick slabs of crystals.

From the exterior of the ship these two ports appeared like the huge eyes of some gigantic monster; and in truth, this was the purpose they served.

Fal Sivas called my attention to a small, round metal object about the size of a large grapefruit that was fastened securely just above and between the two eyes. From it ran a large cable composed of a vast number of very small insulated wires. I could see that some of these wires connected with many devices in the control room, and that others were carried through conduits to the after part of the craft.

Fal Sivas reached up and laid a hand almost affectionately upon the spherical object to which he had called my attention. "This," he said, "is the brain."

" . . . In one respect, however, the brain lacks human power. It cannot originate thoughts. Perhaps that is just as well, for could it, I might have loosed upon myself and Barsoom an insensate monster that could wreak incalculable havoc before it could be destroyed, for this ship is equipped with high-power radium rifles which the brain has the power to discharge with far more deadly accuracy than may be achieved by man."

"I saw no rifles," I said.

"No," he replied. "They are encased in the bulkheads, and nothing of them is visible except small round holes in the hull of the ship. But, as I was saying, the one weakness of the mechanical brain is the very thing that makes it so effective for the use of man. Before it can function, it must be charged by human thought-waves. In other words, I must project into the mechanism the originating thoughts that are the food for its functioning.

"For example, I could charge it with the thought that it is to rise straight up ten feet, pause there for a couple of seconds, and then come to rest again up its scaffolding."

"To carry the idea into a more complex domain, I might impart to it the actuating thought that it is to travel to Thuria, seek a suitable landing place, and come to the ground. I could carry this idea even further, warning it that if it were attacked it should repel its enemies with rifle power and maneuver so as to avoid disaster, returning immediately to Barsoom, rather than suffer destruction.

"It is also equipped with cameras, with which I could instruct it to take pictures while it was on the surface of Thuria."

In the light of progress since 1933, Burroughs' description of a spacecraft designed for remote exploration is astonishingly accurate. What Fal Sivas calls a mechanical brain we would call a computer, but the equivalence is obvious. The telepathic input which Fal Sivas uses has not been developed successfully as yet, but work has been done in attempting to decode, with computers, encephalographs. Telepathic input is not entirely beyond the pale.

As for the "eyes" of Fal Sivas' ship, such sensory devised are carried by space craft, as of course are cameras such as those described.

Weapons on spaceships? We hope not, but computer-directed naval gunnery is commonplace, while research into space-based weapon systems is an ongoing facet of modern military planning. And the "brain" itself, "about the size of a large grapefruit," is quite the size of the guidance computers in actual use right now. The instructions which Fal Sivas discusses, involving complex sequences of "if this occurs, then do that," are perfect prototype computer programs.

Burroughs seldom attempted any "heavy science" type science fiction, but on this occasion when he did attempt it, the result was a bull's eye of accurate prediction. As for the story: Fal Sivas, Vandor, and several others do travel successfully to Thuria, the nearer moon of Barsoom (called Phobos by astronomers on Earth). Here, by a fantastic bit of pseudoscientific mumbo-jumbo they shrink to a size proportionate to their normal sizes as the satellite is proportionate to Barsoom itself.

They run through a fairly routine (for Burroughs) series of battles, captures, and escapes, encounter a nation of invisible people, meet new monsters unlike those found on Barsoom, and finally get home where John Carter's forces triumph over the malevolent Guild of Assassins. This time, however, story value is secondary. In *Swords of Mars*, the imaginative content is the main appeal.

Synthetic Men of Mars is the last full-fledged novel of the series. Written in 1938, it was serialized in *Argosy* in 1939 and appeared in book form in 1940. It involves a new attempt by Ras Thavas, the Master Mind, to work mischief in his laboratory by growing synthetic men in vats of chemicals, harking all the way back to Professor Maxon of *The Monster Men*. Unfortunately these *hormads* do not come out any better than had Maxon's monsters and Ras Thavas produces all manner of horrors, the worst of which is a great creeping mass of protoplasm that threatens to grow until it overcomes the entire planet.

The hero of the book, Vor Daj, has his brain transferred into the body of a *hormad* by means of Ras Thavas' surgical talent, and Vor Daj then works to thwart a plot by the rebellious monsters to take over Barsoom. He destroys the growing blob, and finally secures his own body in order to marry the beautiful maiden Janai.

Synthetic Men of Mars has little to recommend it.

The tenth Martian "novel" is actually a compendium of four *Amazing Stories* novelettes written in 1940 and published in 1941. The book version, *Llana of Gathol*, was published in 1948, the last of Burroughs' books to appear in his lifetime. The book version has a new, and touching, introduction, in which John Carter visits Burroughs for the last time. Burroughs, old and ill, realizes that John Carter, his favorite Uncle Jack of so many years before, is still a young and vigorous man, while Burroughs himself has not long to live.

John Carter recounts the adventures of his granddaughter Llana, the daughter of Tara of Helium and Gahan of Gathol whom he had met in *Chessmen*.

Again an episodic book as it must be, *Llana of Gathol* still makes enjoyable reading, certainly far better than *Synthetic Men*.

The finest sequence of the book is an eerie incident in which the Orovars (white Martians) of ancient Horz, preserved in the millennia-long hypnosis *à la* Poe's M. Valdemar, awaken to discover their world lost, the great seas receded, their ships long forgotten along with the extinct oceans of Mars.

Two more Barsoomian novelettes remain to be accounted for.

Skeleton Men of Jupiter appeared in *Amazing Stories* for February, 1943. In it John Carter and Dejah Thoris travel to Jupiter. Here Burroughs introduces a new interplanetary theme to the canon, new races, new geography, new life forms. The "feel" is distinctly good, and the story, while not particularly rich in new devices, is satisfactory.

It was Burroughs' very obvious intent to develop the theme of John Carter's Jovian experiences into a book-length adventure through a series of novelettes which would then be published as an eleventh Martian "novel," *Llana*-fashion. But the succeeding novelettes were never written, and *Skeleton Men of Jupiter* remains, a highly readable start but no more.

The only other story in the Barsoomian sequence is *John Carter and the Giant of Mars*, a novelette of highly dubious authenticity from the day of its appearance in the January, 1941, *Amazing*. The geography of Barsoom, the sound of the descriptions and the dialog, the general pacing and flow of the story, the plotting devices used . . . all have a distinctly unBarsoomian feel to them.

Repeatedly the reader finds himself thinking "Burroughs would not have described that incident that way," or "John Carter would never say that."

In 1941 readers wrote to *Amazing* challenging the authenticity of the story, but Palmer replied that the manuscript had been published exactly as received from Edgar Rice Burroughs, Inc. And over twenty years later I had a letter from Palmer still insisting that *Giant of Mars* was wholly authentic, at least inasfar as any tampering by Palmer was concerned.

Only in 1964 was the final clarification of the matter offered by Hulbert Burroughs:

> Although twenty-four years have passed and memories are dim, my brother (John Coleman Burroughs) recalls that at his Dad's suggestion, he and ERB collaborated on a *John Carter of Mars* story for

Whitman Publishing Company. This story appeared under the title *John Carter of Mars* in Whitman's Better Little Book No. 1402. Whitman had a very set formula for this—exactly 15,000 words—with text so arranged that the drawings on the opposite page depicted what was being told in the text. My Dad was never happy to write to such a strict formula. Apparently, therefore, he worked with my brother on it. John also did all the illustrations for the book.

Later, *Amazing Stories* was clamoring for a new Martian story from ERB; so he and JCB worked out a new ending to the Whitman story by adding 5,000 or 6,000 additional words to bring it up to a length of 20,000 required by *Amazing*.

The explanation provided after so many years explained the incongruities of *John Carter and the Giant of Mars*. The main credit for its authorship belongs to John Coleman Burroughs, but the story cannot be wholly discounted, as Edgar Rice Burroughs did have a hand in it.

The two stray novelettes *Skeleton Men of Jupiter* and *John Carter and the Giant of Mars* were finally issued in book form in 1964, under the title *John Carter of Mars*. By a production error the first 1500 copies of the first edition were stamped *John Carter and the Giant of Mars*. The title appears correctly on later copies and on a paperback edition, leaving those 1500 copies a final curiosity of the Martian series.

It is worth noting that unlike the Inner World series, Burroughs' Martian stories did not deteriorate as he went along. With the two exceptions of *Synthetic Men* and the mainly spurious *Giant of Mars*, every tale in the series, from *Princess* written in 1911 right on to *Skeleton Men* written in 1941, shows a continuing vigor and inventiveness. Of his four major series of books, Burroughs maintained a higher overall quality in the Martian tales than in any other.

CHAPTER X

Wrong-Way Carson

There is a third science-fiction series by Edgar Rice Burroughs, which I have not discussed to this point because the stories were written relatively late in Burroughs' career. This third series, concerning the deeds of Carson Napier on the planet Venus, date from the early 1930s, constituting four books plus an additional novelette which appeared in the posthumous collection *Tales of Three Planets*.

According to Sam Moskowitz's *Explorers of the Infinite*, Burroughs' Venusian stories were written as the result of a squabble between Burroughs and one of his imitators. Certainly the breadth and success of Burroughs' prolific writing gained for him the admiration and the emulation of many writers, and to this day the influence of his many adventure tales is visible in new works appearing in the fields of scientific romance and jungle adventure.

During his own lifetime Edgar Rice Burroughs held an equivocal opinion of such sincere praise as imitation proverbially constitutes. He was a personal friend, for instance, of the late Ralph Milne Farley, whose stories of Myles Cabot the "radio man" show a strong Burroughsian influence. But one such imitator whose efforts were not appreciated was the late Otis Adelbert Kline whose novel *The Planet of Peril*, very much in the Barsoomian tradition although laid on Venus, appeared in *Argosy* in 1929. The following year a sequel, *The Prince of Peril*, ran in *Argosy*.

And in 1931 Kline produced not one but two pseudo-Tarzans, *Tam, Son of the Tiger*, which was published in *Weird Tales* magazine, and *Jan of the Jungle*, which ran in *Argosy*.

Now Burroughs wrote a Venus novel himself, completing it in November, 1931, and sent it off to *Argosy*. The story, *The Pirates of Venus*, pre-empted the pages "reserved" for Kline's third Venus novel, *Buccaneers of Venus*. The Kline work appeared instead in the lesser-paying *Weird Tales*.

Stung now, Kline retaliated for Burroughs' invasion of his Venusian domain by moving in on Burroughs' original science-fiction locale with *The Swordsman of Mars*, a carbon-copy of Barsoomian derring-do which was taken by *Argosy* for publication in 1933.

Thus went the feud, probably to the benefit of both writers and unquestionably to the delight of their readers, as Kline and Burroughs blasted back and forth at each other with hundreds of thousands of words of enthralling prose.

All of this is according to Moskowitz. We shall return to the "feud" shortly.

But of immediate concern is the legacy of three novels and five novelettes which might otherwise never have been written, chronicling the curious adventures of Carson Napier on the planet Venus.

The opening volume of the series, *Pirates of Venus* (the *The* was dropped from the book version), includes a "frame" of considerable complexity, involving Burroughs, Jason Gridley, and Burroughs' real-life friend and associate Cyril Ralph Rothmund.

Carson Napier is an attractive young man of twenty-five to thirty, blond, intelligent, and friendly. He is the son of a British army officer and an American girl from Virginia. Carson was born in India while his father was stationed there, and raised by a Hindu mystic, Chand Kabi, who taught him the art of mentally projecting human images.

Carson explains that he is building a giant rocket ship on Guadalupe Island off the coast of Baja California with the aid of the Mexican government. The ship is just about ready to go, and Carson has contacted Burroughs in order to arrange with him for the reporting of Carson's progress through space by telepathic contact. Carson's goal: Mars!

This completes the framing sequence and the main story begins.

The description of Carson Napier's final preparations for his flight, the countdown, blastoff, and first hours in space are told in solidly realistic fashion quite different from Burroughs' usual romantic approach. Shortly after beginning his journey, however, Carson realizes that he is not following his predetermined course.

He cannot imagine what is wrong, for his plans were calculated, checked and rechecked in conclave of the greatest scientific brains of the world. And then the light dawns: "With all our careful calculation, with all our checking and rechecking, we had overlooked the obvious; we had not taken the moon into consideration at all.

"Explain it if you can; I cannot. It was just one of those things, as people say when a good team loses to a poor one; it was a *break* and a bad one."

At least Carson is not given to dramatic overstatement.

The voyage continues. Carson narrowly escapes crash-landing on the moon (and one wonders if he would have found Va-ga hordes in the lunar depths if he had crashed). He passes by the moon and resigns himself to incineration in the sun, but instead achieves a landing on Venus, the orbit of which is intersected by Carson's trajectory at the convenient moment of the planet's presence at just the right point. A *good* break, that.

Carson parachutes from his craft as it plunges through Venus' atmosphere, and Carson lands safely in a tree so gigantic that it alone houses the major part of an entire city: Kooaad, principal municipality of the kingdom of Vepaja. Mintep is *jong* (king) of Kooaad and Vepaja. His beautiful daughter the *janjong* Duare, is sacred by the laws of her country.

The Venusians are given very nearly as complete a culture by Burroughs as were the Martians. Their name for their own world is Amtor; they have writing and maps, but the maps are based on the Amtorian notion that their world is in the shape of a bowl with a terrible burning center and an icy rim.

This is nothing more than an inverted conception of half the planet, with the torrid equatorial belt reduced to a point and the icy pole stretched out to surround the hemisphere. Thus the maps of Amtor portray only half the planet's surface, one entire hemisphere left a great *terra incognita*, while the territory included is depicted in highly unreliable fashion.

Amtor is surrounded by a great double envelope of cloud. Rarely does the sun break through the outer covering, and almost never through both. When it does, terrible storms occur beneath the double opening, caused by a focusing effect similar to that of a pinhole camera. Because of their permanent cloud cover the Amtorians have no astronomy nor concept of any world beyond their own or any universe beyond the terrible burning occasionally glimpsed through the double cloud openings.

Not all Amtorian science is as backward as geography or astronomy, however. They have an immortality serum, for instance, periodic injections of which can prolong life indefinitely. Carson Napier receives a dose shortly after landing.

John Carter, you will remember, is apparently immortal as a result of unknown events in some ancient time. Tarzan is doubly protected against aging and death. In one of his adventures he captures an immortality potion from a lost tribe and in another deathlessness is bestowed upon the Ape Man by a dying (!) witch doctor.

Again, in Pellucidar the phenomenon of timelessness obviates aging although there is plentiful death by violence. And in *The Moon Maid* the theme of reincarnation, an alternate sort of quasi-immortality, is advanced by Admiral Julian. *The Eternal Lover* strongly hints at reincarnation although the treatment is not definitive. And the story *The Resurrection of Jimber-Jaw* deals with the indefinite prolongation of human life by a combination of refrigeration and drugs.

At any rate Carson, having adapted to the life of Kooaad, seeks to earn his place in the city's life and is assigned to gather *tarel*, the useful webbing material spun by the *targo*, a giant Amtorian spider. Carson and a companion, Kamlot, encounter a *targo* and in the ensuing battle the monster is killed. Kamlot too, is killed, to all appearances, and left for dead.

Carson makes his escape but before he can reach Kooaad again he becomes involved with a group of Thorists, Amtorian communists, aboard a pirate ship. The Thorists have already captured Duare, and Carson enters a conspiracy to overthrow the Thorists. The revolt succeeds, at least to the extent that Carson and Duare escape from the Thorists with the assistance of a group of *klangan*, manlike flying creatures somewhat resembling the Wieroos of Caspak.

At the end of *Pirates of Venus* Duare is apparently saved, but Carson is carried off to captivity in the country of Noobol, once more a prisoner of the Thorists.

The Pirates of Venus was serialized in *Argosy* in 1932; a sequel, *Lost on Venus*, the following year. *Pirates* first appeared in book form in 1934 and *Lost* in 1935.

In plot, *Lost on Venus* is a direct continuation of *Pirates*, carrying Carson and Duare through further adventures. The basic structure, if the term is even applicable, is extremely simple. Carson and Duare wander about the largely unknown lands and seas of Amtor, visiting various strange city-states. Most of the time they are either in hiding or in flight.

Two Amtorian city-states of particular interest are described in *Lost on Venus*, Havatoo and Kormor.

Havatoo is Burroughs' satire on the perfect, planned society. The society of Havatoo is run along lines of scientific objectivity by a well-intentioned but literal-minded and rather inflexible government. The rulers are a council which examines each citizen for socially desirable characteristics, and assigns to each a station appropriate to his personality, physique, skills, etc. The social utility of each life determines its length through the administration or withholding of the immortality serum each time a new dose is due.

Carson's stay in Havatoo is rather pleasant, and the picture of the planned society is surprisingly favorable, coming from a man of Burroughs' rather primitive Republican sentiments. But when Duare is sentenced to death by the ruling council she and Carson flee Havatoo.

Across the river from Havatoo is the terrible city of Kormor, ruled by the mad jong Skor. Kormor is populated almost entirely by zombies, created by Skor in order to have more docile subjects. Duare and Carson find refuge among the few surviving normal humans in Kormor, but are discovered by Skor and forced to flee back to Havatoo, from which city they finally escape in an *anotar*, and atomic-powered airplane of Carson's design.

Carson of Venus, the third and final novel in Carson's saga, was serialized in *Argosy* in 1938 and published in book form in 1939. Hitler was threatening all Europe by the time this novel was ready (it was written in the summer of 1937) and Burroughs satirized the Nazi movement in this novel. The Venusian equivalents of the Nazis were the Zanis; the equivalence went as far as an unusual salute and a special greeting, "Maltu Mephis" instead of "Heil Hitler."

Although Burroughs used the framework of his Venus series, the setting of Amtor and the characters Carson and Duare, the book is really a war novel with little or no science fictional content. The kingdom of Korva has managed to preserve its independence from Mephis and his Zanis but is in grave peril. Carson takes a hand in the conflict, serving as a spy as well as a military leader and in the end the Korvans defeat the Zanis and preserve their freedom.

In gratitude for Carson's service to the cause of Korva, he is appointed *tanjong*, crown prince. Actually, the royal situation in Korva is rather muddled. Earlier the jong Kord was captured by Mephis; Kord's nephew Muso succeeded temporarily to the throne but was overthrown upon news of Kord's death. Mephis himself is poisoned and the post of jong develops upon Kord's son-in-law Taman.

Alert readers of the time presumably did not fail to identify Mephis (Mesphistopholes) as Hitler and Muso, obviously, as Benito Mussolini.

At the end of the novel Carson and Duare determine to adopt Korva as their permanent home, abandoning Vepaja.

This seeming end of the series paralleled other Burroughs series which were resumed after apparent completion, and in 1941–42 *Fantastic Adventures* magazine ran a series of Carson of Venus novelettes, four in number, which were issued in book form as *Escape on Venus* in 1946.

The pattern of these stories resembles *Lost on Venus* somewhat, in that Carson and Duare visit a series of bizarre societies, face peril and captivity, eventually make good their escape, and then go on to new, if similar, ad-

Carson Napier and the klangan of Amtor

ventures. The four novelettes in the group feature a variety of monstrous races: fish men, plant men, amoeba men . . . and by the end of the volume, Carson and Duare, their Amtorian friends Ero Shan and Nalte, are united, all is well, and the series seemed once more to be completed.

However, Burroughs had started another cycle of Carson novelettes, completing one and barely beginning a second when the United States entered World War II. He put the stories aside and never returned to them, and the new novelette, *The Wizard of Venus*, lay forgotten for twenty years.

It was discovered in the same cache that produced *Savage Pellucidar*, and published in 1964 in *Tales of Three Planets*.

The wizard of the title is Morgas, a feudal ruler whose sinister influence is spread by hypnotic means. Carson Napier and Ero Shan become involved with him when an experimental *anotar* they are testing is blown off course and lands in the country of Donuk, "at least ten thousand miles from Sanara and almost due west of Anlap." Seeking to rescue the lovely Vanaja from Morgas, Carson and Ero Shan fall prisoner to the wizard.

The key to their escape, and cause of the ultimate downfall of Morgas, is Carson's occult talent, first demonstrated in the frame of *Pirates* and used ever since to transmit his memoirs to Tarzana, but never previously utilized in the stories themselves. In *The Wizard of Venus* Burroughs was beginning to break new ground in a series previously rather dull; it is a pity that he did not go on to develop the Amtorian sequence with newer and more imaginative ideas than those in the earlier books.

A bit more information is in order concerning the Burroughs-Kline "feud." In preparing the current book I attempted to check out the report of it which appeared in *Explorers of the Infinite*; unfortunately neither of the principals in the alleged feud is alive, but in each case a member of the author's immediate family took an interest in the matter, and offered an opinion based upon personal recollection of the principal at the time of the alleged feud.

Edgar Rice Burroughs' son Hulbert Burroughs had this to say:

> You have dealt to some extent with Sam Moskowitz's account of a supposed literary feud between Edgar Rice Burroughs and Otis Adelbert Kline. When I first read Moskowitz's account of this in his excellent book, *Explorers of the Infinite*, I was very much surprised because I had never known of such a "feud." I have no recollection of my Dad ever having mentioned anything about it. I am not inferring that you should delete this item. I am merely intrigued and curious to research the matter in ERB's correspondence of that era to determine if he make any reference to it.
>
> I could be wrong, but I personally think this may have been a mythical feud created by a very enterprising magazine editor to build up interest, magazine sales—and Otis Adelbert Kline!

In a later letter from Hulbert Burroughs:

> I have just finished reviewing the *Argosy* file [of ERB's correspondence]

from the years 1931 through 1935, and find no mention whatever of Otis Adelbert Kline and the great feud.

In Kline's case I was able to make inquiry of E. Hoffman Price, a longtime close friend and frequent collaborator of Kline's. Price had no recollection of Kline's ever mentioning any feud with Burroughs, but referred me to Kline's daughter, Mrs. Ora Rossini. Mrs. Rossini, when I wrote and asked her if she could shed any light on the matter, sent quite a lengthy and detailed reply, the gist of which is contained in these paragraphs:

> I have also seen reviews of my father's stories being compared to Burroughs' material, but always inferring that he was an imitator of ERB. Perhaps it was so, in a way, on the Tarzan character, but as far as I know, it was not meant to be that way. In any event, there never was a feud that I heard of. The two were contemporary writers and therefore, competitors in a sense . . .
>
> In any event, the only thing I can recall was that OAK was working on a story and before it was completed, he was very surprised that ERB had one published first with the same location. If ERB was first with the Mars background, then this must have been the story. As far as I know the two had never met nor had any contact with each other and I don't think they had any mutual acquaintances. Certainly, they had no friends in common. I do remember OAK's comment on the coincidence of ERB coming out with the same locale . . . Since apparently OAK took longer to bring out a story working part time it is possible that the ideas occurred about the same time with each of the writers, but ERB got into print first.

In a note to Moskowitz I passed on the general negative views of both authors' families to the feud theory, and asked if he could document the feud story in any way. (*Explorers of the Infinite*, perhaps because it covers so much ground is riddled with unsubstantiated assertions which the reader is left to accept or reject solely on the author's word. This of course does not make the statements *false* but it leaves them open to serious doubts, especially in such cases as the present one, where persons closely involved challenge the unsupported statements.)

Moskowitz replied with a letter offering no fewer than ten points in substantiation of the story of the feud. Unfortunately, this "evidence" is far more impressive in its massiveness than in its conclusiveness.

The first four items grouped by Moskowitz under the headings of "Original" sources consist of the enumeration of four persons active in the science-fiction field or related areas at the time of the alleged feud. These are Kline himself, Farnsworth Wright (editor at the time of *Weird Tales*), Albert J. Gibney (associate publisher of the Munsey magazines, including *Argosy*), and Mort Weisinger, long-time science fiction fan and editor.

Unfortunately although the *names* are impressive no document or quotation is present and the list of names alone constitutes no evidence at all.

The next category, "Secondary" sources, consists of a list of four fan-press items published between 1936 and 1952. The oldest article of the four is the "master source" of the group. The science fiction fan press, like more seriously regarded scholarly institutions, is notoriously inclined to pass-along scholarship rather than more difficult research. At any rate the article in question is *The Kline-Burroughs War* by Donald A. Wollheim, which appeared in *Science Fiction News* for November, 1936. Moskowitz asserts that "there were references . . . before this but this was the first substantial treatment of the subject."

At any rate, I asked Wollheim what *his* source was, and he replied simply "I made it up!"

Asked if he did not regard this as somewhat irresponsible journalism, he explained that by "made it up" he did not mean out of whole cloth, but rather that he had viewed the circumstantial evidence and concluded that there was indeed a feud, or "war," between the two authors.

This, it would seem, throws the "Secondary" evidence into Moskowitz's third class, "Circumstantial." His points here are that (a) Burroughs never wrote a Venus story until *immediately* after the appearance of *Jan of the Jungle*, a blatant imitation of Tarzan in *Argosy* and *Tam, Son of Tiger*, a similar copy of Tarzan in *Weird Tales*." (b) "Kline had never written a Mars story until *immediately* after the *Pirates of Venus*."

When Sam Moskowitz first sent me his letter with the ten points, I was frankly overwhelmed by the volume of his evidence. I sent him a letter saying that, as far as I was concerned, he had proved his case. But as time passed and I studied the Moskowitz document, I found myself becoming more and more skeptical about the case he had made—as the preceding paragraphs indicate.

What I should have done at the time was send Moskowitz another letter informing him that I had reconsidered my position and intended to express a more negative opinion, but by now my book was in production and I thought it would be a bad idea to stir up more controversy. I was absolutely wrong. The result was a new "feud over the feud," which went on for three decades. In the end, I recognized my discourtesy and apologized to Sam Moskowitz, who most graciously accepted my apology. We wound up seated side-by-side at a Burroughs conference at the University of Louisville in 1994, and discovered that once the ill-will of the prior incident was cleared away, we could become fast friends.

Not very long after that, Moskowitz died. I will be endlessly grateful that we parted, that last time, as friends not enemies.

To return to the original dispute, however, I must maintain that of all the "evidence" presented it seems that this circumstantial argument, not really direct "evidence" at all, is actually the strongest and most convincing in the dispute. The nature of the stories, the time and place of their publication, all point to a relationship beyond that of mere coincidence.

Nonetheless, I think that the case is far from proved.

CHAPTER XI

The Last Hero

In November, 1940, Burroughs began writing a fourth series of scientific romances which might ultimately have stood beside his Barsoomian, Amtorian, and Pellucidarian tales in interest and in extent, had the author not become a war correspondent after witnessing the bombing of Pearl Harbor. Late in 1940 Burroughs completed two novelettes in his new series.

He then put them aside, and once war broke out, although he did not completely abandon fiction writing (in fact he wrote a complete Tarzan novel in 1944 and several shorter items during the war) he never returned to this new series, and all that exist are two novelettes. The first, *Beyond the Farthest Star*, appeared in *Blue Book* for January, 1942. The second, *Tangor Returns*, remained unpublished until the first book edition in 1964 of *Tales of Three Planets*, which included both these novelettes.

The hero of the new series was to be an earthman whose true name, at least in the existing material, was never revealed. On the planet Poloda where the stories take place, he is known as Tangor, a local neologism coined to serve as his name, and meaning "from nowhere."

Nowhere is the place of Tangor's origin, as far as the Polodans are concerned. He appeared, naked, on the surface of their planet, quite suddenly, and without mechanical assistance of any sort. The reader learns that this man was a World War II fighter pilot "fatally" wounded in a dog-fight with a group of *Luftwaffe* Messerschmitts. A bullet through his heart, his plane about to crash, the earthman estimated his remaining life span at fifteen seconds. Instead—Poloda.

The parallel to both John Carter and Ulysses Paxton, particularly the latter, is obvious.

On Poloda Tangor finds a modern industrialized civilization equal in technology to contemporary Earth. This was a departure for Burroughs, in that all the new worlds discovered in his previous stories were either primitive in most regards (Pellucidar, Caspak, Va-nah in *The Moon Maid*, Amtor, the lost Cambodian domain of *Jungle Girl* and most of the many lost civilizations discovered by Tarzan) or, having formerly operated at an advanced level, were now decadent (Barsoom, Opar).

Poloda is suffering a hundred-year war when Tangor arrives. On one side the leading power is Unis, with whom Tangor makes cause. The Unisans are obviously the allied powers, and particularly the United States, in a patterning of the Polodan situation to that of Earth as it would be after the United States entered World War II, a development which Burroughs obviously expected by November, 1940, when he wrote the first Tangor story.

The Axis powers are represented in opposition, Nazi Germany in particular being represented by the brutal, totalitarian state of Kapara.

Instead of painting war as a glorious exercise in heroic adventure, as he had in many of his earlier interplanetary tales, Burroughs pictures the Polodan hundred-year war as a bitterly cruel, murderous process, not only destructive of life and property but utterly sapping the spirit of the living.

So eager to have done with warfare on any terms but abject surrender are the Unisans that they plan a mass migration to another planet of their sun Omos. In preparing to write the Tangor stories Burroughs had made very extensive notes on the imaginary astronomy of the Omos system. The peculiar characteristic of the planets circling Omos lie in the arrangement of their orbit.

Rather than circling their primary in concentric orbits, as the planets of our own system circle Sol, the planets of Omos share their orbit between those of Mars and Jupiter. The eleven planets of Omos—Poloda, Antos, Rovos, Vanada, Sanada, Uvala, Zandar, Wunos, Banos, Yonda, and Tonos—are only about a million miles from their sun, which is, of course, comparatively tiny as measured against ours.

Because the planets, with almost identical diameters of 7200 miles, share an orbit with a radius of only one million miles they are relatively close together, and share a common doughnut-shaped belt of atmosphere.

Burroughs devised a Unisan alphabet, complete government structure, dress, wildlife, and general cultural information, and had mapped the planet Poloda as well as charting the Omosian system. In working out the astronomical aspects of the planets he corresponded with Professor J. S. Donaghho, an astronomer. They thrashed out a problem involving disastrous tides on the planets of Omos, by having the pull of adjacent planets offset the tidal effects of their proximity, but Donaghho informed Burroughs that his doughnut-shaped atmosphere simply would not work. Each planet of Omos would capture all the atmosphere it could hold, and the rest would dissipate.

Burroughs was undaunted. He replied, "In the little matter of the atmosphere belt, there are two schools of thought on Poloda: One adheres to the Donaghhoan theory, while the other, hopefully anticipating inter-planetary navigation, clings stubbornly to the Burroughsian theory.

"I am glad that you found fun in answering my queries. I find fun in the imaginings which prompt them; and I can appreciate, in a small way, the swell time God had in creating the universe."

At the end of the second novelette in the series, Tangor is preparing to take off on an experimental interplanetary flight. By devising the doughnut-shaped atmosphere belt for the planets of Omos, Burroughs permitted interplanetary flights by conventional aircraft, providing only that sufficient fuel and provisions were carried on board; Tangor's flight was to have been by propeller-driven airplane. With eleven planets to populate with at least as many different races and cultures, Burroughs had given himself room for virtually unlimited variety in imaginings.

It seems likely that, if Burroughs had continued the Poloda series it would have stood with the best of his other interplanetary and Inner World stories. As it is, the two novelettes offer good reading, although an obviously unsatisfying ending, and a promise of more to come which will not be fulfilled.

One other curiosity concerning the Tangor stories is the method in which the manuscripts were produced. Once more, although by 1940 the technique was not only out-of-vogue but virtually antique, Burroughs used his old framing idea. This time the framing sequence dealt with his own attendance at a dinner party at Diamond Head.

Returning home, he finds himself unable to sleep, and goes to the typewriter instead to do a little work. Before he can begin to type, however:

> My hands were clasped over that portion of my anatomy where I once had a waistline; they were several inches from the keyboard when the thing happened—the keys commenced to depress themselves with bewildering rapidity, and one neat line after another appeared upon that virgin paper, still undefiled by the hand of man; but who was defiling it? Or What?
>
> I blinked my eyes and shook my head, convinced that I had fallen asleep at the typewriter, but I hadn't—somebody, or something, was

typing a message there, and typing it faster than any human hands ever typed.

The phantom typist is Tangor himself, although he never materializes in any way other than by operating the machine. Now the idea of spirit writing, or automatic writing, is quite an old theme, and seriously regarded in occult circles. The theory is that a denizen of the spirit world possesses a living medium, and through the medium writes messages to living persons, or even writes novels.

But the idea of a spirit working the keys of a typewriter is quite an offbeat variation of automatic writing. Yet Burroughs was not the first to use it. In fact in 1899 Harper and Brothers published *The Enchanted Typewriter* by the popular Victorian humorist John Kendrick Bangs. Bangs was a fairly prolific author who enjoyed considerable popularity for a time, but is now almost entirely forgotten, his most popular work today being *A Houseboat on the Styx*, a comic fantasy the theme of which is indicated by its title.

Many of his other books also contain fantasy elements, including several appearances of the ghost of Sherlock Holmes. In his short story "A Glance Ahead (being a Christmas tale of A.D. 3568)," first published before the turn of the century and included in Bangs' collection *Over the Plum Pudding* in 1901, he conceives a system of personality transference between multiple android bodies anticipatory of Burroughs' *kaldanes* and *rykors*.

And in *The Enchanted Typewriter* appears this scene:

> A type-writing machine of ancient make, its letters clear, but out of accord with the keys, confronted by an empty chair, three hours after midnight, rattling off page after page of something which might or might not be readable, I could not at the moment determine.

The typewriter of Bangs' hero is not operated by any interplanetary adventurer, but by the shade of none other than "Jim—Jim Boswell," temporarily returned from Hades. Later in the book, which bears no resemblance whatever to *any* Burroughs work except in these framing sequences, the typewriter is operated by Xantippe, or, as she prefers to be called, "Mrs. Socrates."

Unfortunately almost no information is available regarding just what Burroughs did or did not read before he began writing, and unlike the case of Barsoom and the works of Edwin Lester Arnold where internal evidence seems all but overwhelming, this one similarity between *Beyond the Farthest Star* and *The Enchanted Typewriter* may very well be merest coincidence. We do have the word of Hulbert Burroughs that his father was "an omnivorous reader," and again the date of publication of the Bangs book is right for Burroughs to have come across it. An idea might have been implanted that was given back forty years later.

In all likelihood this is mere coincidence, nothing more. But it is a remarkable coincidence that the idea of a spirit-operated typewriter should occur to these two authors. (Actually, Burroughs' first use of this general theme was in 1920, when he began a story titled *The Ghostly Script*. Nothing much ever became of this story, except that its general idea was worked into the framing sequence of *Beyond the Farthest Star* two decades later.)

One other oddity concerning John Kendrick Bangs. In 1901 he offered *Mr. Munchausen, An Account of Some of His Recent Adventures*. This collection of related tall tales includes *The Poetic June-Bug*, which contains this intriguing paragraph:

> The next morning, however, on opening the machine [a typewriter] I found that the June-bug had not only not been shaken out of the window, but had actually spent the night inside of the cover, butting his head against the keys, having no wall to butt with it, and most singular of all was the fact that, consciously or unconsciously, the insect had butted out a verse which read:
> "I'm glad I haven't any brains,
> For there can be no doubt
> I'd have to give up butting
> If I had, or butt them out."

Don Marquis' archy of *archy and mehitabel* started jumping on his boss' typewriter keys in 1916. Is this another source in Bangs, as suggested several years ago by its "rediscoverer," Mr. William Blackbeard of San Francisco, or merely another coincidence? We will probably never know.

In Burroughs' *Tales of Three Planets* the three worlds of the title are Poloda where the Tangor stories take place, Venus or Amtor where the *The Wizard of Venus* has its setting, and Earth itself. The story which takes place on Earth is *The Resurrection of Jimber-Jaw*, a short work first published in *Argosy Weekly* in 1937.

It is concerned with the disgruntled inventor of an experimental aircraft engine. Unable to secure backing in the United States, the inventor flies a plane powered by his advanced engine to Siberia, where he and his flying companion are forced down by carburetor trouble. They find a cave man frozen in the Arctic ice, and the scientist Stade revives him.

The two aviators return with "Jim" the cave man to the United States, and here Burroughs takes good advantage of the satirical opportunities inherent in the classic situation of the alien viewpoint of modern society. The story is distinctly offbeat Burroughs, but nonetheless highly enjoyable, written with so light a style that it seems almost a shaggy dog story.

It is a delight.

Tangor, if the Poloda series had reached substantial length, would likely have provided an insight into the later concept which Burroughs held of what a hero is like. In the two novelettes in which Tangor appears we do have a view of a man discouraged and disillusioned with the glories of war, and increasingly aware of its horrors. This was largely a departure from earlier Burroughs heroes, although Carson Napier was a long stride away from the protagonists of Burroughs' earliest stories. This is not surprising, as Carson was a product of the 1930s, when Burroughs was a successful author and quite a man of the world, while John Carter, David Innes, and Tarzan were all products of the era before the first world war.

John Carter is immensely capable, superhumanly strong and agile by Martian standards, the finest swordsman of two worlds by his own repeated admission, and a man of initiative and authority at all times.

The remarkable similarity between the early career of John Carter among the Barsoomian Tharks and that of T. E. Lawrence among the Arabs serves only to point up further Burroughs' romantic concepts of the nomadic life. Whereas Lawrence, at least to one theory, was actually sublimating homosexual tendencies in his rise to leadership of an essentially all-male society in the desert, John Carter acted from motives of purest heroism. He never had a "sick" day in any of his multiple lives. (Life, by the way, here imitated art. John Carter's exploits were published before Lawrence's were performed. Further speculation at this point, along obvious lines, might be fascinating but unfortunately is hardly subject to verification.)

In his Inner World experiences David Innes is not quite as capable nor as forceful a personality as is John Carter, yet as a modern man in a primitive world he possesses a far more sophisticated outlook than do the Pellucidarians. Further, with his friend Abner Perry, and with relatively advanced tools and weapons at his disposal, David does early in the series establish a sort of personal and organizational "power base" in Sari, and has generally a sufficient number of competent friends and allies to act with some strength in any situation.

Even Burroughs' one-shot heroes—Bulan of *The Monster Men*, Thandar of *The Cave Girl*, Nu of *The Eternal Lover*, Dr. King of *Jungle Girl*, Jefferson

Turck of *Beyond Thirty*, the three Julians of *The Moon Maid*, Tyler, Billings and Bradley of *The Land that Time Forgot*, the Apache warrior Shoz-Dijiji— are truly heroic. Burroughs' most famous creation, Tarzan, is virtually a symbol for courage and strength.

It is a symptom of Burroughs' deep romanticism, acting despite any bitterness caused by his early failures or any cynicism developed along with his later successes, that his heroes are *not* sublimating emotional distur- bances nor acting out psychological compulsions, but are *really* noble, *really* courageous . . . really *heroic!*

Similarly, the heroines, most particularly the handsome and regal women of Barsoom, but also such others as Barbara Harding whose influence is so strong over Billy Byrne, are comparable figures. They do not guard their virtue because they suffer from puritanical inhibitions, but because they are ideals, Victorian ideals perhaps, but inhabitants nonetheless of a finer, nobler, braver universe than the real world of *The Girl from Farris'* or *The Girl from Hollywood*.

Even Victoria Custer, who wears her very name as her label, runs off with Nu as his eternal soul-mate. All of Burroughs' "good" women are faithfully monandrous regardless of the question of clerical officiation at any mating ceremony. [The famous Downey case of the early 1960s, in which Tarzan books were temporarily banned from a public library because Tarzan and Jane were never officially married was one of the most absurd censorship cases of recent years. Among other factors, Tarzan and Jane *were* married by an ordained minister—no less than Jane's father—but quite aside from this, the general attitude in Burroughs' works, regarding sex, love and marriage, is positively Victorian.]

By the time of the Venus series, however, Burroughs had clearly come under the influence of modern realism, for Duare *does* exhibit considerable ambivalence in trying to reconcile her royal obligation as janjong of Vepaja with her attraction to Carson Napier, a problem transcending mere for- mality. And her solution of the problem is, to say the least, a compromise between love and duty.

Carson Napier himself is more of a Gullivar Jones than a John Carter. He is continually buffeted by forces totally beyond his ability to cope with; his solution to almost any problem is flight, not conquest.

This characteristic is exhibited in all four books, even though the volumes themselves are remarkably different from one another in overall structure. *Pirates of Venus* is a fairly conventional interplanetary adventure chronicling Carson's Guadalupe Project, his actual space flight, his landing on Amtor by a combination of incredible ineptitude and similarly incredible good luck, his introduction to the kingdom of Vepaja and his first encounter with the Thorists.

Lost on Venus is quite different, more of a social satire than a typical interplanetary adventure tale, and, with its utopia and anti-utopia of Havatoo and Kormor, probably the best book of the four. *Carson of Venus* is quite *un*fantastic, with its wartime realism (lacking the glamour of Barsoomian war although not quite as grim and bloody as Polodan), its bombings, spies, traitors, and interrogations. It could very easily have been transferred to Earth and published as a realistic novel. And *Escape on Venus*, with its episodic structure and return of the Odyssean mode, is a parade of wonders and menaces during most of which Carson and Duare are busy trying to get away.

For most of the series Carson is little better than a fugitive. He cannot return to Kooaad on pain of death, he is listed as an enemy by Thorists and Zanis alike, he will be killed if he returns to Havatoo, he will be made into a zombie if he re-enters Kormor, and he will be executed or at best re-enslaved if he is caught again by the fishlike Myposans of *Escape*.

Only in the posthumous *Wizard of Venus* does Carson show much spunk or much ability to handle himself in a tight situation. Maybe the boy was growing up at last.

To attempt a final evaluation of the massive science-fiction output of Edgar Rice Burroughs is not an easy task, but it can be a rewarding one. The pleasure of reading the thirty-odd books involved is considerable; there are several gems, many competent pot-boilers, and a mere handful, relatively speaking, of outright failures in the lot. In most of Burroughs' science fiction and borderline works there is a vigor in the narration and a convincingly unworldly atmosphere that make for simple pleasure reading of a high order.

But going beyond entertainment values alone, there is still ample to be found in these books. The character development in *The Mucker*, if not terribly subtle, is still evidence that Burroughs was aware of such matters, and utilized them in his works not entirely without skill. The stimulating pseudo-science of *The Land that Time Forgot*, the astonishing social and political extrapolation of *Beyond Thirty*, the scope and world-view of *The Moon Maid*, the bitter renunciation of the "glamour theory" of warfare in *Beyond the Farthest Star*, all warrant consideration in areas of science fictional endeavor far transcending "mere" entertainment.

Burroughs' influence on the development of science fiction has been an odd one. For some years, particularly in the 1920s and 30s, there was a great deal of Burroughs-type material produced, but as the years passed and science fiction "matured," the adventuresome themes of scientific romance, the wonder tales, gave way largely to introspective, social-satire material. It seemed that Burroughs was totally outdated.

Especially in view of almost all his science fiction's being out of print, and most of his other material as well, by the mid-1950s Burroughs seemed totally passé.

The outburst of public domain publishing in the early 1960s brought about a huge revival in Burroughs material, further stimulated by the granting of publication rights to copyrighted material, and especially formerly unpublished manuscripts. At the same time the pendulum in the general science fiction field had swung away from the material most popular in the 50s. A movement back to greater entertainment values in science fiction and associated fantasy publishing, generally called "sword and sorcery" (a term devised by a leading fan, George Scithers) became dominant, and in the sword and sorcery area the works of Burroughs were most influential.

Both within the science fiction field and in the entire publishing industry the Burroughs revival has been one of the most unusual phenomena ever recorded. Of course the high pitch of activity that characterized the revival at its peak could hardly be sustained and by the end of the decade had begun to slack off somewhat. Nonetheless, it seems unlikely that Burroughs will soon go out of print again.

For science fiction readers—and others—over the coming years, Burroughs' place seems assured as one of the few writers whose works will be perpetuated, not as creaking antiques, but as timelessly valid tales of great entertainment value and some value beyond that.

CHAPTER XII

The Backs of Old Letterheads

To this point I have minimized discussion of Edgar Rice Burroughs' most famous and successful creation, Tarzan. I have mentioned a few occasions of his writing Tarzan stories between other works in order to establish continuity, and substantial space was devoted to *Tarzan at the Earth's Core* because of that book's being part of the Pellucidar series.

However, Tarzan certainly deserves extensive consideration, and the next several chapters will be devoted to the Tarzan books.

First of all, it may be well to dispel a few false impressions. In 1917 the first Tarzan motion picture was produced, and from its release the following January an unending stream of Tarzan features in various adapted media have "educated" hundreds of millions of children and adults the world around to certain "facts" regarding the Ape Man, many of which are simply not in keeping with the character as created by Burroughs.

A few examples:

Tarzan is an American who lives in a crude tree-house in an African jungle. His jungle-law mate, Jane Parker, is the daughter of an English trader. Their adoptive son Boy was so named in preference to Tarzan's suggestion of Elephant. Boy was found by Tarzan and Jane in the wreckage of an airplane.

Conversation in the Tarzan ménage is severely limited by the Ape Man's miniscule vocabulary and proportionately small intellect.

. . . and so on, and on, and on. But a reading of even the first few of the many Tarzan novels offers this information regarding the matters discussed above:

Tarzan is an Englishman, one of the wealthier members of the House of Lords. His African home is a large and prosperous plantation.

Tarzan's wife, the former Jane Porter—not Parker—is American, from
Baltimore. She and Tarzan were duly married by Jane's father, Professor Archimedes Q. Porter, "who in his younger days had been ordained a minister." The couple's son Jack was conceived and brought
forth in perfectly conventional fashion (albeit discreetly offstage).

Conversation in the Tarzan family is on an elevated level, stimulated by Tarzan's fluency in French, Swahili, German, "animal language," and impeccable English, among other languages.

Rather than go on listing and correcting misconceptions in this piece-
meal fashion, let us undertake a moderately comprehensive survey of the
Tarzan books, similar to the preceding examination of Burroughs' science
fiction and miscellaneous works, considering in detail the original story
of the Ape Man, and devoting greater or lesser amounts of attention to
succeeding stories in the series as their contents warrant.

Before Burroughs created Tarzan he had written and sold *A Princess of Mars*,
and had written but not yet sold *The Outlaw of Torn*. The brief and fatal
appearance in this latter book of a Lord Greystoke has led a few Burroughs
enthusiasts to regard it, rather than *Tarzan of the Apes*, as the first volume of
the lengthy Tarzan saga. While this position can be justified by considerable
point-stretching and hair-splitting, it is obviously a scholarly game and
nothing more.

In a brief autobiographical article published many years later (*Open Road*
magazine, September, 1949) Burroughs told why he worked at producing
fiction, giving his readers a rather clear insight into his attitude toward
money and its absence. *Tarzan of the Apes*, was written between December
1, 1911, and May 14, 1912, while Burroughs was working as a department
manager for a business publication in Chicago. A few selections from that
autobiographical article:

> I was not writing because of any urge to write nor for any particular
> love of writing. I was writing because I had a wife and two babies . . .
> I loathed poverty and I would have liked to put my hands on the party
> who said that poverty is an honorable estate. It is an indication of
> inefficiency and nothing more. There is nothing honorable or fine
> about it . . .
>
> While I was working there, I wrote *Tarzan of the Apes* evenings
> and holidays. I wrote it in longhand on the backs of old letterheads
> and odd pieces of paper. I did not think it was a very good story
> and I doubted if it would sell. But Bob Davis saw its possibilities for

magazine publication and I got a check; this time, I think, for $700. [Burroughs had received $400 for magazine rights to *A Princess of Mars*.]

Tarzan of the Apes was Burroughs' second story to be published, appearing complete in the October, 1912, issue of *All-Story*, winning the cover-spot with an illustration by Clinton Pettee. Burroughs found soon that he could sell all the fiction he could write (although not always on the first attempt— a good many of his stories drew one or more rejections before finding a receptive editor) and soon left his job to write full time.

Selling stories to magazines provided a fair income for Burroughs and his family; in February, 1913, a third child and second son, John Coleman Burroughs, was born. After *Tarzan of the Apes* Munsey took *The Gods of Mars* for *All-Story*; *The Return of Tarzan* was rejected by the Munsey chain but taken by Street & Smith for their competing *New Story*. But a magazine sale is a one-shop proposition, and Burroughs hoped to get his stories into book form, where there was a prospect of long-term royalties. Still in his 1949 *Open Road* piece, he stated that:

> I met with no encouragement. Every well-known publisher in the United States turned down *Tarzan of the Apes*, including A. C. Mc-Clurg and Company, who finally issued it, my first story in book form.
>
> Its popularity and its final appearance as a book were due to the vision of J. H. Tennant, managing editor of the *New York Evening World*. He saw its possibilities as a newspaper serial and ran it in the *Evening World*, with the result that other papers followed suit. This made the story widely known and resulted in a demand from readers for the story in book form, which was so insistent that A. C. McClurg and Company finally came to me after they rejected it and asked to be allowed to publish it.

The first McClurg edition of *Tarzan of the Apes* was published on June 17, 1914; magazine sales were flowing along just as fast as Burroughs could write, and with the newspaper serialization just a small foretaste of the flood of subsidiary income to grow in the years that followed, Edgar Rice Burroughs was established at last.

As for those "old letterheads and odd pieces of paper" upon which *Tarzan of the Apes* was written in longhand, the manuscript remains in the possession of the Burroughs family in Tarzana, California. Its value in 1965 was estimated at amounts ranging anywhere from $15,000 to $50,000, prices many dealers today seek when offering a first edition of *Tarzan of the Apes*!

The surviving members of the Burroughs family continue to collect and preserve the wealth of Burroughsiana which constantly appears, with an eye to the possible establishment of a museum, in Tarzana, of the artifacts and curiosa of Edgar Rice Burroughs.

As for the actual text of *Tarzan of the Apes*, numerous versions and editions have appeared over the years, as the story has come into the hands of editors and adapters. Two versions are authentic, the original *All-Story* magazine version, and the standard book edition which was somewhat revised by Burroughs himself.

Some of the changes are of a purely literary nature, as Burroughs tried, I think rather successfully, to improve his style and his story-telling technique without substantially altering the story itself. An example, based upon the careful comparison and annotation by Henry Hardy Heins, occurs in the second chapter, where the *All-Story* version reads "As he turned to descend the ladder he was surprised to see his wife standing at his elbow," and the book version ends the same sentence with " . . . standing on the steps almost at his side."

The effect of the change, trivial though it may seem, is to give a greater concreteness to the situation, to add a corroborative and visual detail (the steps) to the scene. It may well be true, as so often stated, that Burroughs was no stylist, whatever merits he may have as a story-teller, yet such changes as this one indicate that he *was* aware of technical matters, and did attend to them.

The second category of changes in *Tarzan of the Apes* is the correction of certain errors in the African background. Burroughs had populated Tarzan's Africa with both tigers and lions, only to be told after the appearance of the magazine version of the story that there are no tigers in Africa. The result was the substitution in the book version of a lioness, panther, or leopard each time a tiger was mentioned in the magazine.

Again, Burroughs has been criticized for the inaccurate science in his science fiction stories and for the implausible jungle in his jungle tales. In fact, both hold up better under careful examination than they do under the rather cursory glance which they sometimes receive, but there is no denying that Burroughs was less than a stickler for total accuracy, as evidenced by his attitude in setting up the doughnut-shaped atmosphere of the Omosian planets in *Beyond the Farthest Star*; he was, first and last, a tale-spinner.

But to get to the contents of *Tarzan of the Apes*, putting aside all adaptations and second-hand opinions, and returning to the author's text, we find no simple tale of primeval adventure, but a surprisingly complex novel with a fairly large cast of characters and a locale ranging over three continents, and a sequence of events stretching over many years.

The story is opened, as are so many of Burroughs', with a framing sequence and, again as in many others of Burroughs' works, an anonymous narrator. The introductory pages of *Tarzan of the Apes* show a greater awareness of the tricks of the pulp trade than do those of *A Princess of Mars*. Whereas the Barsoomian novel began with a prosaic line, the first Tarzan story opens with an effective narrative hook. Consider the opening of *Princess*: "In submitting Captain Carter's manuscript to you in book form, I believe that a few words relative to this remarkable personality will be of interest."

By contrast, the opening words of *Tarzan*: "I had this story from one who had no business to tell it to me, or to any other." Beautiful! As the opening sentence of the book captures the reader's interest by appealing to his curiosity, Burroughs quickly substitutes a driving pace and a remarkable element of suspense which never releases the reader until the story is finished. The setting in which the narrator "had this story" is left somewhat indefinite, but reference is made to "the yellow, mildewed pages of the diary of a man long dead," "the records of the Colonial Office," and "written evidence in the form of a musty manuscript."

Aided by "the seductive influence of an old vintage," the anonymous narrator presents a story "painstakingly pieced . . . out from these several various agencies." The story of "a certain young Englishman, whom we shall call John Clayton, Lord Greystoke." This Clayton is the father of John Clayton, Lord Greystoke, Tarzan of the Apes, but Burroughs' curious wording, "whom we shall call John Clayton," leaves open the real identity of the jungle lord. Through two dozen books Tarzan is John Clayton, Lord Greystoke, with never another reference to a different "real" name. (Heins reports having read a paper in Burroughs' hand indicating that he originally contemplated the name "Lord Bloomstoke" before choosing Greystoke. Doubtless a good decision.)

One recalls another John Clayton, a very minor character in Conan Doyle's *The Hound of the Baskervilles* (1902). A number of admirers of "the greatest detective who ever lived" (the present author included) have attempted, in the delightful game of Holmesian scholarship, to establish, through *The Hound* and other stories, a link between the two so-different canons. But again, in seriousness, one can only shrug at the similarity, and guess that it is *probably* mere coincidence.

At any rate, Clayton and his bride, the former Alice Rutherford, set out from England aboard an unnamed steamer one "bright May morning in 1888." Clayton, recently having transferred from the Army to the Colonial Office in hopes of furthering his political ambitions, has been sent to investigate reports of slave trading by an unidentified foreign power (Belgium?) including the luring of young natives from a certain British West African colony (Nigeria?).

At Freetown the Claytons transfer to a chartered barkentine, the *Fuwalda*, "and here John, Lord Greystoke, and Lady Alice, his wife, vanished from the eyes and from the knowledge of men."

Two months later the wreckage of the *Fuwalda* is found upon the shores of St. Helena, and all hope for survivors is abandoned.

What had actually happened was a story of shipboard cruelty, a brutal captain and a rebellious crew, and a series of nearly mutinous incidents in which Clayton was forced to intervene to prevent murder—on either side. Finally driven beyond endurance the crew had mutinied, massacred their officers ("An axe in the hands of a burly Negro cleft the captain from forehead to chin") but spared the Greystokes in gratitude for former kindnesses.

Unsure of his own control over his men, the chief mutineer Black Michael had landed the Greystokes on "a beautiful wooded shore opposite the mouth of what appeared to be a land-locked harbor." Promising to spread word, after a discreet delay, of the whereabouts of Lord and Lady Greystoke, Michael assured them of an eventual rescue expedition, but the wreck of the *Fuwalda* prevented his keeping his word, if indeed he ever intended to keep it.

Left to their own devices, but with their possessions mercifully landed with them and with fresh water nearby, the Claytons proceed to make a home for themselves. John builds a strong cabin and furniture, and endeavors to supply food for himself and Alice. Their life is not too unpleasant a one after all as, Crusoe-like, they learn to live in their new surroundings. Eventually Alice is with child, and she and John prepare for the birth, carefully sorting the primers and picture books they had packed in their original luggage, just in case their colonial sojourn should prove a lengthy one.

As the child's birth drew near, Alice one day accompanied her husband on an expedition to fell a particularly choice tree needed for an addition to their cabin. They were attacked by a huge ape, and although they escaped, the shock of the experience was such that Alice never fully recovered. She survived for a year, giving birth to a son, nursing him, but Alice's mind was never again normal, her physical health was precarious, and finally she died.

To this point the story is not altogether implausible, although it is exotic and melodramatic. Now, however, Burroughs turns to a series of far-fetched coincidences that severely mar the story at the same time that they set up the circumstances needed for the development of the Tarzan character.

Upon the death of Alice Clayton her husband lies slumped over his diary, the usually bolted door of the cabin left unlatched. Without warning a huge and vicious anthropoid ape enters the cabin. It is Kerchak, king of a tribe of *mangani*, great apes. Although these apes are but loosely organized, they are of some intelligence and are capable of the speech which *all* animals understand, the size of their vocabulary varying with their respective species. The monkeys and apes, being the most advanced products of evolution next to man, have a fairly extensive vocabulary; lesser beasts have smaller vocabularies.

(Again, Burroughs' extravagant imaginings were not as silly as some critics allege. Repeated studies have shown that many species, not only apes and monkeys but dolphins, birds and even insects *do* communicate with one another, although not in a language common to different species.)

With the ape Kerchak is a female, Kala. Kala has but recently lost the tiny *bu-balu* (boy baby) which she bore her mate Tublat; in fact she still carries the tiny corpse in her arms. As Kerchak rushes Clayton, the Englishman springs for a gun, but the ape is too fast and kills him on the spot. To return to Burroughs' own words:

> When the king ape released the limp form which had been John Clayton, Lord Greystoke, he turned his attention toward the little cradle; but Kala was there before him, and when he would have grasped the child she snatched it herself, and before he could intercept her she had bolted through the door and taken refuge in a high tree.
>
> As she took up the little live baby of Alice Clayton she dropped the dead body of her own into the empty cradle; for the wail of the living had answered the call of universal motherhood within her wild breast which the dead could not still.
>
> High among the branches of a mighty tree she hugged the shrieking infant to her bosom, and soon the instinct that was as dominant in this fierce female as it had been in the breast of his tender and beautiful mother—the instinct of mother love—reached out to the tiny man-child's half-formed understanding, and he became quiet.
>
> Then hunger closed the gap between them, and the son of an English lord and an English lady nursed at the breast of Kala, the great ape.

Is the scene touching? Grotesque? Intolerably far-fetched? Sickeningly sentimental? I think that depends upon the reader's own ability and willingness to accept and empathize with the undeniably grotesque characters and situation. The suspension of disbelief required would seem to be an enormous one, and yet many cases of animal adoption across species are recorded, and cases of feralism—human children raised by animals—are very common in legend if not in fact.

Further, Burroughs' description of the instincts operating, particularly "the call of universal motherhood within [Kala's] wild breast," strike me as quite acceptable, however saccharine they may appear by today's anti-sentimental standards. When he wrote *Tarzan of the Apes* Burroughs was the father of two small children, with a third due. The struggles of the Claytons against their wild environment well paralleled those of the impecunious Burroughs family against the economic reverses that threatened to engulf them, and that led even to the real-life enactment of that cherished soap-opera scene, the pawning of Mrs. Burroughs' jewelry.

The love which Burroughs felt for his family, the sense of futility and frustration which repeated business failure had brought him, are transmuted into the sufferings of the Clayton family. The guignolesque fate of the infant John Clayton might well correspond, in a strange fashion, to the future which Burroughs fearfully contemplated for his own children.

Ensuing chapters of the book carry young Clayton, named Tar-zan (white skin) by the dark and hairy apes, through a long and danger-fraught childhood, for his growth is far slower and his strength less than that of the normal ape his age. Only the fierce defense given by Kala prevents Tarzan's death upon many occasions. Especially the jealous and brutal Tublat seeks to destroy his own foster-son.

But Tarzan survives, and, finding his way back periodically to the cabin in which he was born, acquaints himself with the relics of his infancy, and with his parents' books.

Here is one point upon which critics and educators focus a valid objection to *Tarzan of the Apes*. But it is a point of poignancy, amusement and perhaps, allegorically, of significance in indicating Burroughs' boundless faith in the ability of man to live up to a heritage, to rise above environment and improve himself so as to achieve the great destiny of humanity rather than the miserable fate of his surroundings.

For in the cabin the boy Tarzan finds his parents' books, including "a primer, some child's readers, numerous picture books, and a great dictionary. All of these he examined, but the pictures caught his fancy most, though the strange little bugs which covered the pages where there were no pictures excited his wonder and deepest thought."

Over a series of visits to the cabin he tries to puzzle out the mystery of the little bugs, until one day he makes the connection. He gazed at "a picture of a little ape similar to himself, but covered, except for hands and face, with strange, colored fur, for such he thought the jacket and trousers to be. Beneath the picture were three little bugs—
'BOY.' "

And eventually, although "he did not accomplish it in a day, or in a week, or in a month, or in a year; but slowly, very slowly, he learned, after he had grasped the possibilities which lay in those little bugs, so that by the time he was fifteen he knew the various combinations of letters which stood for every pictured figure in the little primer and in one or two of the picture books.

"Of the meaning and use of the articles and conjunctions, verbs and adverbs and pronouns he had but the faintest and haziest conception."

But eventually the boy Tarzan learns how to read and write English quite well, although he has no concept of the sounds of the language. Tarzan also finds his father's knife, and learns to use it as a weapon in compensation for the smallness of his teeth compared to the fighting fangs of the other apes, and learns to use agility and speed, and to spin strong ropes of grass for use in the hunt and fight.

In the course of growing up Tarzan engages in many fights, with other apes as well as with lower jungle animals. In one combat an ape rips loose a huge piece of Tarzan's forehead and scalp, so that even after the wound heals, it glows a bloody scarlet whenever the Ape Man is enraged. Eventually he fights and kills Kerchak, becoming king of the apes. Only the death of Kala, felled by a black African hunter, mars Tarzan's happy life as an ape. It also serves as his introduction to humanity, with a great preference in Tarzan's estimation for the beasts.

Tarzan embarks upon a campaign of revenge for Kala's death, first as-sassinating Kala's killer, then going on to "black-baiting." This latter is a continuing policy of torment and murder directed against the black Africans which would raise violent protest if it appeared today in a new work. And even in a book nearly a century old it is unquestionably in condemnable taste.

The question of racism in Burroughs is one which has been raised repeat-edly, and substantial evidence can be produced either to damn Burroughs or to save him. It must be realized that at the start of his career the stigmati-zation of racial and religious and even of national stereotypes was standard practice in popular literature, both in the pulp magazines for which Burroughs initially wrote and in the book field which he later attained. As a beginner, especially a beginner out to make a living rather than express any particular creative urge, Burroughs would naturally (whether consciously or not) follow the leading writers of the day.

And in the leading works of that day, "natives" of virtually any sort were treated as stupid but sly, superstitious, filthy, lustful, greedy, and so on for a long list of pejoratives. Similarly Jews were cheap, greedy, sly, treacherous; Irish were ruddy, jolly, stupid perhaps but good-natured and willing; English were noble, courageous, intelligent, in short paragons of virtue . . . unless they were of a certain element of the upper crust (not the true-blue Claytons, though) who were foppish, sissified, timid; and so on.

Certainly Burroughs used stereotyped characterizations. In *Tarzan of the Apes* and several other Tarzan books he portrayed Africans according to the accepted stereotype. He also portrayed American Negroes in the unfortunate "comic darky" vein in *Tarzan of the Apes* and several other novels including *The Eternal Lover* (the nursemaid Esmeralda), *Tarzan at the Earth's Core* (the chef of the *o–220*, Robert Jones), and *The Man-Eater* (Sophronia, Washington Scott).

But Burroughs also portrayed Negroes as heroic figures in many of the Tarzan novels, notably those featuring the Waziri, with whom Tarzan lived at one time as an adopted brother and even chieftain. There was also the Ethiopian empire of *Beyond Thirty*, portrayed with considerable respect and even a degree of admiration, even though Jefferson Turck sides against this empire, preferring the rationalistic philosophy of the competing Chinese empire to the Christian outlook of the Ethiopians.

Adolph Bluber in *Tarzan and the Golden Lion* is a classic anti-Semitic stereotype, but he is more than offset by the towering figure of Moses Samuels in *The Moon Maid*. Pat Morgan in *The Resurrection of Jimber-Jaw* is a "good" Irishman, contrasting with the low-life Kelley of *The Man-Eater*.

Arabs come in for rough treatment in a number of Tarzan novels, but are depicted with some sympathy in *The Return of Tarzan*. And in *The Lad and the Lion* the lost Prince Michael (the lad of the title) renounces a European throne to live as an Arab.

In *Tarzan the Untamed* and *Tarzan the Terrible*, Germans come in for some terrible licks, as they do also in *The Land that Time Forgot*. But these three novels were written during or shortly after the First World War, and wartime nationalistic sentiments ran high. In *Tarzan and the Lost Empire*, *Tarzan at the Earth's Core*, and *Back to the Stone Age*, Germans are portrayed heroically.

In later years the pendulum swung once again, so that both Germans and

Italians receive most unsympathetic handling in *I Am a Barbarian*, but again, World War II had started when the book was written, and although the United States was not yet a participant the nation's sympathies were obvious. And the United States *was* at war and Burroughs was a war correspondent in the Pacific when he wrote *Tarzan and "The Foreign Legion."* In this book Japanese are portrayed as sub-human "monkey-men," a popular stereotype of war propaganda. (Presumably ape-men are of a far higher order.)

Finally, Mexicans are ill-treated in *The Mucker*, referred to as "greasers" and generally given the treacherous native portrayal. But Indians, particularly Apaches, are treated with the greatest sympathy in *The War Chief* and *Apache Devil*; their historically confirmed atrocities against white settlers are largely justified as the reaction against the treachery and aggression of the whites.

What, then, may one conclude, regarding Burroughs as a racist? I think the late Dr. Thomas S. Gardner summarized Burroughs' racial attitudes in a statement offered at the annual meeting of the New York Science Fiction Association in 1963. Dr. Gardner was a member of a panel discussing Burroughs, and considerable had been said concerning racism in the Burroughs works. Gardner asserted that "Burroughs had good Negroes and bad Negroes, good Jews and bad Jews, good Germans and bad Germans. He had good people and bad people of every kind in his books, because there *are* good and bad people of every kind."

Dr. Gardner's statement may suffer a bit from cliché, but it is nonetheless valid, and I could not agree with it more with regard to the works of Edgar Rice Burroughs.

Still, the question arises: Should modern editors and publishers alter Burroughs' texts in preparing new editions of his works, in order to remove objectionable references? The 1963–1964 paperback Tarzan reprints published by Ballantine Books are expurgated of racial slurs; in fact the editing goes to lengths to remove racial references other than slurs. Consider this innocuous statement from the original text, most recently in 1962 Canaveral Press edition:

> As the three men seated themselves, Robert Jones entered from the galley, his black face wreathed in smiles.

In the Ballantine paperback edition of the following year, Robert Jones' face is described as *shining* rather than *black*. Yet Jones' outrageous dialect speech is retained!

I will myself take the credit or the blame for excising several vicious anti-Negro slurs from the 1963 Canaveral edition of *Tarzan and the Tarzan Twins*, with the permission and approval of ERB Inc. The book is specifically intended for children's reading, the theoretical justification for censorship being, in this case, that the critical faculties of children are not sufficiently developed to reject such prejudicial material.

Still, the act was performed with a second and, in truth, a third thought. And to this day I am not totally convinced that I did the right thing. It is one thing to ask a contemporary author to alter an unpublished work still in manuscript, or a published one for a new edition. It is another matter altogether to alter the works of a deceased author.

More importantly, if one once admits the *principle* of censorship there is little-telling where the censorship will stop. If one removes the anti-Negro comments from Burroughs' works, ought one not also to remove all the other slurs, those against Jews, Germans, Mexicans, Arabs, Japanese. . . . In *Tarzan and "The Foreign Legion"* Burroughs asserts that Indonesia, should she ever attain independence, will slip back into barbarism and savagery. One might or might not wish to remove this sentiment depending upon the momentary condition of the rather delicate relationship between Indonesia and the United States.

I have had a friendly disagreement with Pastor Heins over Burroughs' attitude toward religion. To my assertion that Burroughs was rather consistently anti-religious, Heins' reply is that "Burroughs hated . . . sham and hypocrisy, and these are pitfalls which all church people must guard against." In any case, considerable protest might be made against some of Burroughs' statements concerning the clergy, be they Martian, African, or Christian.

And nudism abounds in Burroughs. Will "decency" forces seek to clothe the naked Barsoomians, or the naked boy Tarzan?

What about the anti-communistic content of *The Moon Maid*, *Pirates of Venus*, *Lost on Venus*, *Tarzan the Invincible*? Or the anti-Nazi satire of *Carson of Venus* and *Beyond the Farthest Star*? Neither communism nor Nazism is particularly popular in this country, but both have had their periods of popularity, the Bunds of the 30s, the alliance of the 40s. As world conditions continue to change, who knows whether either movement may not attain momentum again?[1]

---

1. Communism as a world-spanning movement and threat to democracy seems positively quaint in the twenty-first century. By contrast, Nazism, with its absolutist and authoritarian doctrines, its use of brutal terror and violence against all resistance, its threat to all perceived rivals and its monstrously racist and anti-Semitic attitudes, seems to have been subsumed into the international network of Islamic extremism.

Finally, there is the unquestioned sanguinary tone of the great bulk of
Burroughs' tales. Whether it is Tarzan tearing out the throat of a jungle
adversary, John Carter or Carson Napier slashing his way across an alien
world, or some other Burroughs hero slaughtering foemen by the score,
there is hardly a Burroughs book without a liberal drenching, somewhere
in its pages, in freshly spilled blood.

The same charge was made against the earlier great writer of African
adventure, H. Rider Haggard, that his books were too gory. His reply was
that primitive life was indeed full of violence and sudden death, and that
his books mirrored this truth.

And if little blood is actually spilled in a typical realistic novel, or in real
life in a modern, civilized country, certainly the maimings of psyches and
souls portrayed in a realistic novel are hardly cleaner or pleasanter than the
honest combat of man against man, or man against beast, in a romance of
the Burroughs (or Haggard) type.

Burroughs wrote of primitive heroes facing a mortal challenge. They
meet it nobly, and survive. The survival of the young Tarzan was assured by
his killing his foster-father Tublat, with the knife of his blood-father John
Clayton. And the plot of *Tarzan of the Apes* is given another nudge forward
with the arrival of a ship at last, the *Arrow*. Once more there has been a
mutiny, and once more passengers are put ashore, this time, five.

They include a pair of absent-minded professors, Archimedes Q. Porter
and his secretary Samuel T. Philander; Professor Porter's beautiful nineteen
year old daughter Jane, the faithful but superstitious Negro Esmeralda, and
a young man in white ducks, William Cecil Clayton. Clayton happens to be
the current Lord Greystoke, his uncle John Clayton having disappeared at
sea in 1888 and the title thus having passed to William's side of the family.
Ah, coincidence!

By this time Tarzan is quite a practiced reader and writer, and, peeved
with the newcomers for having invaded his territory, the Ape Man posts a
no-trespassing sign on the cabin of his father:

THIS IS THE HOUSE
OF TARZAN, THE KILLER OF
BEASTS AND MANY BLACK
MEN. DO NOT HARM THE
THINGS WHICH ARE TARZAN'S.
TARZAN WATCHES.
TARZAN OF THE APES

Here is the one flaw in Burroughs' construction of the book which cannot be justified by any willing acceptance on the part of the reader. Tarzan is, at the time of the landing of the Porter party, possessed of two languages. He can read and write English, and he can speak and understand speech in "apish." The written English and the spoken apish, however, are totally unrelated to each other; Tarzan's comprehension of the written language is based upon direct association of "bugs" and meanings, initially pictures. There is no phonetic equivalence of "bugs" and spoken words, in Tarzan's mind. In fact Burroughs gives no indication of Tarzan's having any concept of a relationship between written and spoken language.

How, then, is he able to write *his own name*, which he knows only as a sound, having never seen it in print, and when he has no concept of any connection between sounds and "bugs?"

But I quibble. The readers of 1912 and 1914 seem to have made no protest against the technical error (although succeeding issues of *All-Story* rang with readers' praise of Burroughs). And generations of readers since have continued to overlook such quibbles in the name of literary license if they have noticed them at all.

The note from Tarzan is of course highly puzzling to the newcomers, but there is no halt in the action while they wonder about it. The sailors who landed the Porter party abandon them *post haste* when Tarzan puts an arrow through one who is about to murder William Clayton. They land again, bury a treasure (!), set out once more to sea, encounter a French naval craft and are captured.

Lieutenant Paul D'Arnot of the French navy lands with a party seeking to rescue the stranded passengers from the *Arrow*, but D'Arnot is captured by cannibals. Tarzan rescues the Frenchman, and while he nurses him back to health after D'Arnot's ordeal in captivity, the lieutenant teaches Tarzan to speak. He teaches him French, of course.

We now have Tarzan literate but for all practical purposes deaf and dumb in English, and articulate but illiterate in apish and French! All the while, Tarzan has been keeping watch over the little group from the *Arrow*, recognizing a kinship with them greater than that created by all his environmental conditioning as an ape. He rescues the two scholars who have wandered into the jungle and lost themselves, he protects Jane Porter and Esmeralda from marauding beasts, and carries Jane into the jungle for their classic inarticulate (but chaste) romance.

But when Tarzan is absent for several weeks caring for D'Arnot, the rest of the French party and all the Americans return to the rescue craft, and the *Arrow* passengers proceed back to the United States with William Cecil Clayton in steady pursuit of Miss Porter's hand.

Still in the jungle, their departure delayed by a by-play in which D'Arnot accidentally shoots Tarzan and nurses *him* back to health, the lieutenant trains Tarzan to act as a proper French gentleman. Together, D'Arnot and Tarzan find Father Constantine, a missionary priest, and after a week of his hospitality the two make their way back to France.

In Paris D'Arnot introduces "Monsieur Tarzan" to a police official who takes his fingerprints, provides a brief lecture on the new science of fingerprinting, and promises to analyze Tarzan's prints and compare them with "five tiny smudges" recorded by the deceased Clayton senior twenty years before, during the infancy of his son. (The infant fingerprints are in Clayton's diary, rescued by D'Arnot from the African cabin.)

Back in Baltimore an odd romantic contest is in progress. William Cecil Clayton, Lord Greystoke, has returned to America with the Porters and Esmeralda, and is pressing his suit with Jane Porter, who "respects but do(es) not love" him. Meanwhile a wicked old lecher named Canler (he is in his forties!), a creditor of the girl's father Archimedes Q. Porter, is making life miserable for the poor old professor. In finest melodramatic tradition, Canler offers to cancel the professor's debt in return for Jane in marriage.

Jane agrees to marry Canler for her father's sake, but several of the key characters are separated and menaced by a Wisconsin forest fire (the Porters having moved in the interim). Suddenly a mighty figure swoops from a branch and carries Jane from the hungry flames, through the treetops to safety. It is Tarzan, who has followed his true love to America.

Tarzan pays off Canler with money derived from the buried treasure of the *Arrow* (surely the reader remembers that buried treasure), but does not press Jane to marry him because he has no social standing to offer her. (Remember Billy Byrne, the mucker?)

William Cecil Clayton now proposes once more, and is accepted, when Tarzan receives "a message . . . forwarded from Baltimore; it is a cablegram from Paris." The message reads:

> *Finger prints prove you Greystoke. Congratulations.*
> *D'Arnot.*

As Tarzan finished reading Clayton entered and came toward him with extended hand [to thank him for past favors].

Here was the man who had Tarzan's title, and Tarzan's estates, and was going to marry the woman whom Tarzan loved—the woman who loved Tarzan. A single word from Tarzan would make a great difference in this man's life.

David Innes, Jubal the Ugly One, Dian the Beautiful

A brief conversation between the two men ensues, and at its conclusion William Cecil Clayton asks the man who he does not realize is his own cousin:

"If it's any of my business, how the devil did you ever get into that bally jungle?"

"I was born there," said Tarzan, quietly. "My mother was an Ape, and of course she couldn't tell me much about it. I never knew who my father was."

With these words, the novel ends. Whether Burroughs had originally planned to follow it with sequels is not known, but by the time of the first book edition in 1914 sequels were definitely slated, for the following publisher's announcement is appended to the last page of the story:

> The further adventures of Tarzan, and what came of his noble act of self-renunciation, will be told in the next book of Tarzan.

Certainly *Tarzan of the Apes* ends with no cliff-hanger such as that in *A Princess of Mars*; Clayton would marry Jane Porter and Tarzan, having tacitly abandoned his claim to the Greystoke title would return to oblivion in the African jungle. Perhaps, though, the fact that the wedding was left for "afterwards" is indication that Burroughs was deliberately leaving himself a sequel hook, should he ever wish to revive Tarzan. He left such hooks in many of his books, sometimes picking up the tale many years later, as in the Inner World series with its thirteen-year hiatus, between *Pellucidar* and *Tanar*. Sometimes, as with *Jungle Girl*, he never returned at all.

Taken alone, *Tarzan of the Apes* is a remarkable achievement. For all Burroughs' unconscionable reliance on coincidence, the reader who is willing to "roll with the punches" finds *Tarzan of the Apes* acceptable fantasy. For all the gross sentimentality of the book, its emotional content can be deeply touching for the reader able to accept the spirit of the Victorian romance.

For all the implausibility of the plot, the rapid pace of narration and the frequent scenes of conflict hold the reader from one incident to the next.

The characterization of Tarzan himself is a fascinating work; no simple primitive here, but a complex figure of introspective nature, a man whose development—in contact with the jungle, then with the artifacts of civilization, and finally with the representatives of humanity—is painstakingly detailed. *Tarzan of the Apes*, for all its fame as an adventure story, is at heart a novel of character!

CHAPTER XIII

Tarzan Returns

Burroughs may or may not have intended *Tarzan of the Apes* to have a sequel, but once the story appeared and reader reaction was heard there was no question but that there would be another Tarzan story. Burroughs had returned to his Barsoomian setting for *The Gods of Mars*, the second book of the trilogy, after writing *Tarzan of the Apes*. Once the second Martian book was out of the way he set to work on a new Tarzan story in December, 1912.

The story was completed the following month, and in view of the success of its predecessor the rejection of the sequel by *All-Story* is all the more startling. (In 1939 Alva Johnston reported that it was rejected by an anonymous subeditor at Munsey without ever being seen by Metcalf or Davis. Much more about Alva Johnston in a later chapter.)

At any rate the sequel (its working titles had been *The Ape-Man* and *Monsieur Tarzan*) ran serially in Street & Smith's *New Story Magazine* from June through December, 1913. Its title, as published, had evolved into the prosaic *The Return of Tarzan*.

While certainly not as significant as the first Tarzan novel—what sequel ever is?—*The Return of Tarzan* is of considerable interest. *Tarzan of the Apes*, for all its action, is essentially a novel of character, developing character of the boy Tarzan, human by heredity, and animal by companionship and surroundings. The heart of the book is Tarzan's development, first in his jungle foster-home among beasts and in periods of solitude, then in the companionship of his human discoveries, initially in Africa, then in France and finally in the United States.

Burroughs' belief was that heredity would overcome environment, that the generation of culture bred into young John Clayton would not yield to the accident of orphanhood. Modern anthropology and educational beliefs disagree with Burroughs' ideas of 1911, but he had his beliefs and he made an eloquent case for them.

The opening chapters of the first Tarzan novel meet Lin Carter's rules for epic fantasy precisely: the familiar surroundings of a convivial chat in which the anonymous narrator first receives the story of Tarzan, then the steamer from Dover, the *Fuwalda*, the solitary African home of the marooned Claytons, and finally the wholly exotic jungle life of Tarzan.

The latter portions of the book follow Carter's rules in reverse: from life with the beasts Tarzan turns to human companionship, first in the wild, then in Father Constantine's little mission, briefly in a coastal town, then back to Paris and finally Wisconsin. Even the language of Tarzan progresses from the exotic to the commonplace, from apish to French and finally to English.

We can wonder whether Burroughs was conscious of the familiar-to-exotic principle; unfortunately we do not know whether he was or not. From his own writings about his background and methods it seems that he had little or no *theoretical* knowledge of such techniques, but he did make reference to some earlier works, and his family testify that he was an omnivorous reader, so that it seems likely that Burroughs was familiar with the standard fictional techniques by example if not by precept.

In *The Return of Tarzan* Burroughs shows the now outwardly civilized Ape Man's attempts to make a full adjustment to human society. During the latter days of the first book, particularly in Wisconsin, Tarzan had learned to speak English. The second novel opens with Tarzan once more aboard an ocean liner, this time *en route* from New York to Le Havre.

On board are the wealthy Raoul, Comte de Coude, 40; his wife the Russian-born Countess Olga, 20, bored, loyal to her husband but not in love with him; Nikolas Rokoff and Alexis Paulvitch, the latter but recently deported from a German prison, the two Russians possessed of mysterious but undeniably evil intentions regarding the Countess Olga; and "M. Jean C. Tarzan."

The opening chapters of the book offer familiar shipboard adventure, with fascinating revelatory scenes in which the French-influenced M. Tarzan ruminates upon the characteristics he has observed in these strange creatures, men and women:

> *"Mon Dieu!"* he soliloquized, "but they are all alike. Cheating, murdering, lying, fighting, and all for things that the beasts of the jungle would not deign to possess—money to purchase the effeminate pleasures of weaklings. And yet withal bound by silly customs that make

them slaves to their unhappy lot while firm in the belief that they be the lords of creation enjoying the only real pleasure in existence. In the jungle one would scarcely stand supinely aside while another took his mate. It is a silly world, an idiotic world, and Tarzan of the Apes was a fool to renounce the freedom and the happiness of his jungle to come into it."

Aside from "stand supinely," a rather eloquent expression for a man only recently removed from the jungle! In Paris at last, Tarzan visits his friend D'Arnot, who, despite berating Tarzan for having given up his title, fortune, and love, takes him in charge and shows him the high (or low) life of pre-World War Paris.

Tarzan devotes alternate nights to frequenting the Paris music hall, cigar in mouth and absinthe in hand, and paying courteous but hardly proper court to Olga, Countess de Coude! Attacked one night by a gang of rowdies, Tarzan demolishes them in a burst of his former jungle savagery. It takes the full influence of D'Arnot with the prefect of police to keep Tarzan out of the pokey.

But the wages of Tarzan's public debauchery, the shocking contravention of his accustomed image, begin to cast a shadow when the villainous Rokoff and Paulvitch turn up again. Some carrying of tales, some misinterpretation of appearances, and Lieutenant D'Arnot receives a visit from the most courteous and proper M. Flaubert. Flaubert's purpose: to deliver the challenge of M. Le Comte, to M. Tarzan!

The duel is arranged, pistols at dawn. The duelists arrive with their seconds, Flaubert for de Coude, D'Arnot for Tarzan. The Ape Man and the Count take their positions, the signal is given, and the Count raises his weapon, aims carefully, and fires, again and again, until his pistol is empty. Now Tarzan, who has not fired once, offers to turn over his own firearm so that the Count may continue.

There is a rapid conversation at the end of which Tarzan produces a note in Rokoff's hand, proving that the entire matter was a wicked Russian plot. Tarzan was willing to offer the Count satisfaction anyway, realizing that even his innocent attentions to the Countess had compromised that nobleman's good name.

De Coude was a Frenchman. Frenchmen are impulsive. He threw his arms about Tarzan and embraced him. Monsieur Flaubert embraced D'Arnot. There was no one to embrace the doctor. So possibly it was pique which prompted him to interfere, and demand that he be permitted to dress Tarzan's wounds.

"This gentleman was hit once at least," he said. "Possibly thrice."

"Twice," said Tarzan. "Once in the left shoulder, and again in the left side—both flesh wounds, I think."

Well. All is now repaired between the Ape Man and the count, but it is clear that metropolitan France is no place for Tarzan, and D'Arnot arranges an appointment for Tarzan in French North Africa. The Ape Man proceeds to Oran, thence to Sidi-bel-Abbes, then Bouira, Sidi Aissa, Bou Saada, and Algiers. Rokoff and Paulvitch appear again, there is skull-duggery of various sorts, suspicion of treason in the French army, a romance between Tarzan and an Arab maiden, and finally Tarzan's departure for Cape Town under the assumed name of John Caldwell. On this trip he meets Miss Hazel Strong, Jane Porter's best friend.

We now flash back to the Wisconsin woods and the closing scene of *Tarzan of the Apes*. It is the moment between Tarzan's renunciation of Jane and his departure by motor car for New York and the ship which would carry him back to France.

William Cecil Clayton, Lord Greystoke, steps into the ante-room for a moment to fetch his coat, and his eye falls upon that fatal telegram of D'Arnot's, the one addressed to Tarzan: *Finger prints prove you Greystoke. Congratulations. D'Arnot.*

Stunned, fearing the loss of title, estate, riches, but most of all, of Jane, Clayton returns to the girl, eager to arrange an early marriage. But Jane puts him off repeatedly; finally Clayton returns to London where Jane follows, accompanied by Professor Porter. A friend, Lord Tennington, suggests a year-long cruise around the continent of Africa, aboard his ocean-going yacht the *Lady Alice*. Jane accepts enthusiastically, by adding only the condition that she will not marry Clayton until the cruise ends in London at the end of the year.

Clayton, who had had more the idea of a honeymoon cruise, is furious, but finally agrees to go along. And so the *Lady Alice* sails and, inevitably, is wrecked, and the survivors make their way in lifeboats to the African shore, where they prepare to take up a primitive existence pending rescue. For Clayton, Jane, and Professor Porter, this is becoming almost commonplace. For Tennington it is a new experience.

At the same time that the *Lady Alice* suffers disaster, Tarzan is aboard an ocean liner headed for Cape Town. His traveling companion (in a separate stateroom, of course) is Hazel Strong. And also on board are those two bad kopeks, Rokoff and Paulvitch. One night Tarzan is leaning against the rail, in solitude pondering the rolling sea. The wicked Russians sneak up behind their old nemesis, a quick rush, and *splash!*, Tarzan is in the drink swimming for the African coast himself.

He makes it, and swears off civilization. Well he might!

Tarzan wanders around the jungle for a while, simply reveling in the return to the primeval, and eventually joins forces with a tribe of fine natives, the Waziri. Tarzan helps them fight off a band of marauding Arab slavers, and is taken by the Waziri to their secret treasure-trove, the lost city of Opar.

In these sequences Burroughs introduced two themes which recur over and over in the ensuing Tarzan books. First are the Waziri, whose chief also bears the name Waziri. Upon the death of the old chief Tarzan becomes leader of the tribe, racial considerations quite aside, and hence accedes also to the name of Waziri, adding this new name to his already imposing list: John Clayton, Lord Greystoke, Tarzan of the Apes, M. Jean C. Tarzan, and John Caldwell.

Later Tarzan relinquishes direct command of the Waziri to a magnificent warrior named Muviro, but Muviro never takes the name Waziri, implying that Tarzan is still in truth Waziri, chief of the Waziri. And, indeed, these warriors play their role in many of the Ape Man's adventures, a squad commanded personally by Muviro accompanying Tarzan on the *0–220* expedition to Pellucidar.

The second element, and even more fascinating than the white Englishman's chieftainship of a black African tribe, is the city of Opar itself. Opar is a treasure city, a gold-mining colony of the continent of Atlantis. When Atlantis sank the colonists of Opar were stranded amidst their useless wealth. Isolated ever since, they have lived on, ruled by a priestess-queen in a sun-worshipping theocratic state. The women of Opar are beautiful creatures, perfect replicas of their Atlantean ancestors.

The men of Opar are monstrous. Increasingly base and lustful, the male Oparians have mated even with female apes to produce a race of semi-animal brutes. Their language is a mixture of the high speech of Atlantis and the apish. When children are born in Opar the male infants are selected for their brutishness, the females for the purity of their human features. Those who do not qualify are destroyed.

Tarzan's early adventure in Opar involves the beautiful priestess-queen La, whose force of bestial priests capture the Ape Man. La is to sacrifice Tarzan, but instead falls in love with him. He escapes, at length, and he and his Waziri carry off a vast treasure in Oparian gold.

There is much marching and counter-marching in the jungle as the focus shifts from Tarzan and the Waziri to Jane Porter and the other *Lady Alice* survivors, and back, in a fashion which became a trade-mark of the Tarzan books. Eventually, however, William Clayton conveniently dies, D'Arnot turns up with another French rescue party, and in a double wedding ceremony officiated over by Professor Porter (who is a clergyman as well as a scholar), Tarzan marries Jane and Lord Tennington marries Jane's best friend Hazel.

All board a French cruiser commanded by the same Captain Dufranne who commanded the rescue ship of the previous book, and they leave Africa with a vast golden treasure while the Waziri wave their spears in farewell to their chief Waziri, no longer Tarzan of the Apes but now John Clayton, Lord Greystoke.

There is even less apparent reason for a sequel this time than there was at the end of *Tarzan of the Apes*. Burroughs seemed to have had enough of Tarzan, and one may wonder what the world's response to the Ape Man would have been if he had no more adventures. As in the case of the initial Barsoomian trilogy, the first two books of Tarzan seem a logical unit, beyond which further extension of the series is risky business.

And Burroughs did turn away from Tarzan, turning his hand in January, 1913, to *At the Earth's Core*, the first Pellucidar novel, which he followed with five more books before Tarzan was seen again. Even then it was in a minor role in *The Eternal Lover*, written in 1913, and not completed until December 27 of that year.

But Tarzan was too strong a character to remain in retirement. The popularity of the Ape Man was such that Burroughs was all but forced to call him back, just as Conan Doyle was forced to continue his Sherlock Holmes stories long after he wanted to quit, and even to revive the great sleuth after Doyle had, in desperation, killed him off.

CHAPTER XIV

And Returns and Returns

In the first two Tarzan books Burroughs had presumably accomplished all he had set out to do. Above all he had created a magnificent fictional personality. Despite the gross over-simplifications of later adaptations—the Weissmuller-era motion pictures in particular rise again and again, but other motion pictures and other adapted versions share the blame—Tarzan is a very complex character.

He was of the finest tradition of English aristocracy by his heredity and heritage, and Burroughs' strong belief in the effects of innate quality is apparent in all his works. By virtue of Tarzan's natural intelligence he could never feel fully comfortable living the primitive bestial existence of his boyhood and youth. And yet those jungle years, for all their ferocity, had taught the Ape Man a different code, a more honest and simpler code than that of man. A code and an outlook that would prevent him from fully acclimating himself to human society.

Thus we see the mature man-beast, at once John Clayton, Lord Greystoke, yet, despite the implication at the close of *The Return of Tarzan*, still Tarzan of the Apes, mighty hunter, mighty killer. Partaking of two worlds, never fully at home in either, the melancholy figure of Tarzan stands far above the simple jungle adventurer of screen and cartoon page.

Further, in terms of his own development as a writer, Burroughs had largely perfected a narrative structure new for him, although very old in the development of the novel. For the Tarzan tales Burroughs used a technique of introducing several sets of characters—Tarzan alone, the Porter party elsewhere, D'Arnot in the clutches of cannibals—starting each upon a separate course of action and then "cutting" from sequence to sequence in a style very like that used in motion pictures. Gradually drawing his characters together, Burroughs would finally reveal the grand pattern in which each element played its part, however humble or exalted that might be.

Readers of the Tarzan series who have wondered at the mysterious appearance of the boy Jack Clayton in *The Beasts of Tarzan* need to go afield to *The Eternal Lover* for his first appearance, as a tiny babe hovered over by the faithful Esmeralda as Lord and Lady Greystoke retire to the role of gracious hosts on their African estate. The Greystokes play no major role in *The Eternal Lover*, and the story contains a curious lapse in logical continuity as Burroughs portrays the primitive Nu, apparently time-traveled from the neocene to modern times and able to speak with animals, yet unable to converse with Tarzan.

Perhaps they needed a good hairy translator.

In the brief return of Tarzan in *The Eternal Lover* Burroughs likely intended to show the Ape Man in comfortable obscurity, where he would remain for all time, but instead the opposite effect was achieved. Tarzan came back for a thorough workout in *The Beasts of Tarzan*, written in just over a month in January and February, 1914. The story appeared in *All-Story Cavalier Weekly* in May and June, the final installment appearing just a few days before the publication of the first book edition of *Tarzan of the Apes*.

The story, unfortunately, shows signs that the series was beginning to run downhill, as Burroughs, seemingly at a loss for new imaginative devices, merely reshuffled familiar characters in familiar patterns, producing little of particular note. D'Arnot is back again and it is in his company that Tarzan receives a frantic telegram from Jane:

> *Jack stolen from garden through complicity of new servant. Come at once.*
> *Jane.*

At the news of the disastrous occurrence in London, Tarzan bids a quick good-bye to Paris where he has been visiting D'Arnot and returns to his English home. He and Jane attempt to unravel the mystery of their infant's kidnapping, only to have a second abduction perpetrated: that of Jane herself!

The mystery is unveiled when the identity of the criminals is revealed: it is Nikolas Rokoff and Alexis Paulvitch at work again, this time seeking revenge for former defeats at the hands of the Ape Man by stealing the two things he holds dearest in the world, his wife Jane and their son Jack.

The trail leads inevitably to the African jungle, where Tarzan enlists the aid of a number of ferocious animals (the *Beasts* of the title) in tracking down Rokoff and Paulvitch and rescuing their two victims. Perhaps the most noteworthy innovation of the book is the ape Akut, whose intelligence and fidelity mark him as an anthropoid far above the average of his fellows.

The Beasts of Tarzan is an adequate jungle adventure story, but of no particular significance in the development of the character of Tarzan or the total trend of the series. Burroughs must have recognized the downward trend of the Tarzan lineage, for after *Beasts* he once more dropped the Ape Man, devoting the remainder of 1914 to a wide variety of other writings: *The Lad and the Lion*, *The Girl from Farris'*, and new volumes in the Martian and Pellucidar series. He also turned out a group of sequel novelettes, "second halves" for *The Cave Girl*, *The Eternal Lover*, and *The Mad King*.

When Burroughs felt ready to return to the Tarzan series early in 1915 he attempted the Barsoomian technique of switching focus to a new hero. As he had turned in *Thuvia* from John Carter and Dejah Thoris to their son Carthoris, so he moved now from Tarzan and Jane to their son Jack. *The Son of Tarzan* opens with the rescue of an aged and broken Paulvitch from a miserable existence in the African jungle.

Paulvitch is taken aboard the *Marjorie W*. He gives the name Michael Sobrov, and insists on taking with him an intelligent ape who has been hanging around him in the jungle. Arriving in London, Paulvitch sufficiently rehabilitates himself to make a living touring music halls exhibiting a trained ape, Ajax. Ajax, who of course is really our old friend Akut from *Beasts* (unknown to Paulvitch), habitually studies the faces of his music-hall audiences. In truth, he had clung to Paulvitch only because the Russian represented Akut's sole link to the beloved Tarzan.

One night the young Jack Clayton, now a splendid boy although of a somewhat rebellious nature, defies his parents in order to attend a music-hall performance, and he and "Ajax" experience an electrifying experience that can only be described as love at first sight.

Skipping over a few details, we shortly find the boy and the ape back in Africa, where Burroughs follows Jack Clayton through the years of development in which he earns a sobriquet far superior to that of his father. Where the elder Clayton was dubbed Tar-zan, "whiteskin," young Jack is known to the beasts as Korak, "the killer!"

Let me digress now for a little while to compare the son of Tarzan as created by Burroughs with his screen and comic book counterpart. Korak, Jack Clayton, is a normal boy. His parents seem to have a Lysenkoesque fear that he may have inherited some of his father's bestial experiences and resultant feral tendencies. This fear is well founded, it turns out, and fortunately so, for with Akut's assistance the boy makes a thorough adjustment to jungle life and shows signs of becoming another Tarzan.

He ages normally (although there is a rather distorted time sense in the Tarzan stories when one attempts to match the chronology against real-world dates and occurrences mentioned in the books), reaching manhood before his adventure ends. He even marries at the end of the novel, taking as a bride a seeming Arab maiden named Meriem, who turns out to be the long-lost daughter of a French general.

And although he loses top billing after this one starring role, Korak is seen again rather prominently in *Tarzan the Terrible* and in the later *Tarzan and the Ant Men* (written in 1923) with Meriem and *their* little son Jackie.

A fifteen-chapter motion picture serial *The Son of Tarzan* was released in 1920, starring P. Dempsey Tabler as Tarzan and Gordon Griffith as the young Jack. Oddly, Griffith had played Tarzan as a boy in the first Tarzan picture, and Elmo Lincoln played the adult Ape Man.

The most famous screen son of Tarzan was Johnny Sheffield, introduced in the film *Tarzan Finds a Son* (1939). And Tarzan does find him, literally, in the wreckage of a crashed airplane. When Jane (Maureen O'Sullivan) hints to Tarzan (Johnny Weissmuller) that the boy should have a name, and Tarzan asks how a name is chosen, Jane tells him that a name should be suggestive of those noble characteristics which the parent hopes to see in the child. Tarzan suggests, with considerable astuteness, Elephant.

But with the rejection of such a fine name as Elephant, Tarzan and Jane settle on Boy, and Boy it was through picture after picture, with Sheffield growing taller and more absurd in his role, and Weissmuller growing fatter and more absurd in his, with each passing production. Finally Sheffield went on to play Bomba the Jungle Boy, a sort of junior-grade Tarzan, in a series of films of his own, and Weissmuller became Jungle Jim, a characterization which permitted him to keep his shirt on in his jungle peregrinations.

More recent Tarzan films have dropped both Jane and Boy altogether, making Tarzan a sort of world-traveling freelance professional do-gooder. By 1966 and the inception of the hour-long weekly Tarzan television series, further transformations had taken place. Jane remained lost; the Korak/Boy figure had undergone still another metamorphosis into one Jai, a kind of boy-companion for the Ape Man, but without a clearly specified relationship.

The source of *this* boy is one that requires some tracing. In a Tarzan film released shortly before the television series made its debut, the Ape Man (played by Mike Henry) encountered Ramel, a Latin American youth played by Manuel Padilla, Jr. The film was *Tarzan and the Valley of Gold*, with a script by Clair Huffaker. A novelization of the film, by Fritz Leiber, retained the character of Ramel.

When the television series was constructed, Ron Ely replaced Henry as Tarzan. The *character* of Ramel was dropped, but the actor, young Padilla, was retained, the new character of Jai being created to keep him in the series. The reason for this might take considerable discussion; suffice to say that the boy companion of the adult hero is a long established device for securing audience identification on the part of youngsters.

For a number of years the newspaper comic strip Tarzan drawn by Hal Foster followed the Burroughs books fairly closely, but in later years both the strip and the separate comic magazine Tarzan were written and drawn independently of the Burroughs texts, taking their inspiration largely from the motion pictures. Thus they were adaptations of adaptations, and any resemblance to the original was proverbially coincidental. Also, the art and the writing have been very bad much of the time.

Only since the early 1960s has the comic magazine Boy grown up sufficiently to demand that he be called by his "right" name, and a series paralleling the Tarzan comic began in 1964, titled *Korak Son of Tarzan*.

In 1965 with the accession of Russ Manning as artist and writer of both the comic strip and magazine versions, the Tarzan feature regained much of its quality, and fidelity to the Burroughs creation.

The present book is concerned with the works of Burroughs in their authentic form rather than their adaptations, however interesting the latter may be. However, in the case of *The Son of Tarzan* the popular impression has been so sadly distorted by adapted versions that this discussion seems appropriate.

At any rate, after *The Son of Tarzan* came *The Man-Eater* with its cryptic references to Mrs. Clayton and Charlotte. If Charlotte was intended to be the daughter of Tarzan, she never turned up again, while Korak appeared in at least five books, *The Eternal Lover* (as an infant), *The Beasts of Tarzan* (still a tiny child), *The Son of Tarzan* (as a growing boy and then as a young man), *Tarzan the Terrible* (full grown), and *Tarzan and the Ant Men* (now a father himself).

In September and October, 1915, Burroughs wrote *Tarzan and the Jewels of Opar*, which may be considered the last novel in the original Tarzan chronology. The quality is not very great, the plot is still a continuation of the original elements introduced in earlier books. There is a new villain, Albert Werper, a disgraced former lieutenant in the Belgian army in Africa.

Werper poses as a Frenchman and gains the hospitality of the Clayton plantation. Tarzan moons around distracted by financial reverses which have all but wiped out the fortune founded upon the gold looted from Opar in

The Return of Tarzan (which in turn had gone to replace the depleted fortune of the treasure buried by the *Arrow* mutineers in *Tarzan of the Apes*). Setting out with Werper in tow, Tarzan determines to revisit Opar and renew his gold supply, but gets a crack on the head and spends most of the novel wandering around the jungle as an amnesiac simpleton.

La of Opar, half crazed with love for Tarzan, sets fifty of her bestial priests after the amnesic Ape Man, a group of villainous Arabs make the scene unpleasant for Jane, and there is vast confusion until Tarzan regains his memory and saves the day.

On Saint Patrick's Day, 1916, Burroughs started work on his first short story, which concerned an incident in Tarzan's boyhood.[1] A year and a day later, March 18, 1917, he completed the twelfth short story in the series, all of which appeared in *Blue Book* magazine, one in each monthly issue, starting in September, 1916. The stories were illustrated by Herbert Morton Stoops, and in 1919 were collected and published by McClurg as *Jungle Tales of Tarzan*.

The *Jungle Tales* are a charming group of vignettes, more than coincidentally reminiscent of the Mowgli stories in Kipling's *The Jungle Book* a quarter century before. Each *Tale* reveals some trait in the development of the youthful Tarzan. The titles are indicative of the themes of the stories, and if any prove more mystifying than enlightening, I can heartily endorse a reading of the stories themselves. They are:

Tarzan's First Love
The Capture of Tarzan
The Fight for the Balu
The God of Tarzan
Tarzan and the Black Boy
The Witch-Doctor Seeks Vengeance
The End of Bukawai
The Lion
The Nightmare
The Battle for Teeka
A Jungle Joke
Tarzan Rescues the Moon

1. Since the first publication of this book, more information has surfaced on Burroughs' early attempts at short story writing. Both "The Avenger" and "For the Fool's Mother" were written in 1912, the former composed during the writing of *Tarzan of the Apes* and the latter during the composition of *The Gods of Mars*. Neither sold at the time; completists can find them in *Forgotten Tales of Love and Murder* (2001).

So durable have these little stories proved that one of them, *The Battle for Teeka*, was reprinted in the May, 1964 *Ellery Queen's Mystery Magazine* under the title *Tarzan, Jungle Detective*.

With the *Jungle Tales* Burroughs seemed to have completed a phase in the Tarzan series. The first logical grouping of books closes with this return to the beginnings of Tarzan. With the next book in the series, *Tarzan the Untamed*, the adventures of the Ape Man entered an entirely new phase, with new settings, new themes, and a substantially different tone.

It therefore seems appropriate to pause in the examination of the Tarzan stories, and inquire into the literary antecedents of this immensely popular character. Just as Burroughs' science-fiction novels are seen to occupy a place in the continuing development of that *genre*, so also his tales of jungle adventure form part of a literary tradition stretching back many years.

A few of Edgar Rice Burroughs' more fanatical admirers have been known to fly into raging denunciation of any attempt to place Burroughs in *any* literary tradition, maintaining (at least implicitly) that he performed his acts of creation in a total intellectual vacuum. Such fanaticism flies in the face not only of all logic and precedent, but also all evidence. In the case of the science fiction, internal evidence in Burroughs' works and those of earlier authors is clearly indicative of sources, however much we might debate the importance of given sources (e.g., Arnold *vs.* Wells *vs.* Blavatsky).

In the case of Tarzan's lineage, there is direct written evidence signed by Edgar Rice Burroughs himself.

CHAPTER XV

Ancestors of Tarzan

In 1963 when I was working on the early chapters of this book I happened to mention to Mr. Camille Cazedessus, a leading Burroughs devotee, the presence of two likely sources for Burroughs' Martian series in the works of Edwin Lester Arnold. Cazedessus was highly interested in the find, and asked if I was aware that a similar source for Tarzan was known. I was not aware of such a source, and requested details.

Cazedessus referred me to our mutual friend Pastor Heins, but Heins denied knowing of such a source. Was he certain? Quite certain . . . but oh, Cazedessus must be referring to Altrocchi: not a source of Tarzan, but a work dealing with possible sources of Tarzan, brought to Heins' attention by yet another Burroughs fan, Richard Wald.

Altrocchi, Heins explained, was Rudolph Altrocchi, a professor of Italian at the University of California. In 1944 Harvard University Press had issued Professor Altrocchi's book *Sleuthing in the Stacks*, "Strange information unearthed by a scholar turned sleuth." *Sleuthing*, although hardly a very old book, happens to be a very scarce one, and apparently seldom read by Burroughs enthusiasts or science fiction people. Prior to writing the present work, I had never before seen reference to it in either field, having at that time read in the science fiction field for over twenty years and in the Burroughs field for a shorter period.

Fortunately I was able to borrow a copy from the personal collection of my friend and sometime employer Jack Tannen; in fact the copy is autographed. *To my good friend Achmed Abdullah, in unfair exchange for his . . . * Nine Lives, *from Rudolph Altrocchi, Harbert, Mich. Aug. 26, 1944.* (Abdullah was a popular pulp writer of the 1920s and 30s, specializing in oriental themes such as *Mysteries of Asia, Steel and Jade, The Thief of Bagdad*).

Sleuthing in the Stacks is a collection of seven essays or academic papers by Altrocchi. The first, and typical, essay deals with a sixteenth century Italian book, heavily annotated by a hand which either did or did not belong to the late-renaissance poet Torquato Tasso. Altrocchi had bought the book in Rome, in 1930, the sale being conditional upon the authentication of the holographs.

Professor Altrocchi devotes some twenty pages to recounting his efforts and discoveries over a period of years in determining whether the writing is or is not truly Tasso's. He uses every conceivable test from comparisons of literary style and handwriting characteristics to dating references to known and datable literary works to chemical analysis of ink samples. (The ultimate finding is that the writing is a mere hundred-year-old forgery by Mariano Alberti, Count, Captain of the Papal Guard, and apparently quite a *cause celebre* in Italy in the 1840s.)

Other chapters in the book deal with the works of authors who interested Altrocchi, with the development of a painting in the north aisle of the Cathedral of Florence over a period of centuries, and with the correspondence between the Italian novelist Antonio Foganzaro and the American scientist Joseph Le Conte.

In short, *Sleuthing in the Stacks* is a potpourri of Professor Altrocchi's excursions into the arts, particularly into the historical background of certain literary themes. One theme so treated is that of feralism, or what Altrocchi calls "Aryan exposure." The wild man tradition in literature and legend.

The essay on this topic is fifty-three pages long, and Professor Altrocchi calls it *Ancestors of Tarzan*, which title I borrow for the present chapter.

Altrocchi is a very thoroughgoing scholar, and in his fifty-three pages (plus forty-eight referenced notes) he gives a history of feralism in fiction and reality which I can only hope to hint at here. He cites feralism in Shakespeare's *The Winter's Tale*. He refers to a treatise on the topic as early as 1603. He traces Romulus and Remus to a Greek story of Pelius and Nelius, whose mother was the nymph Tyro and father the God Neptune. (I might suggest that Poseidon might have been a more appropriate appellation than Neptune in the Greek context, but I assume Professor Altrocchi had a reason for using the Roman name, although the reason is not given).

He cites real, or at least allegedly real, cases of feralism and traces themes of feralism to Persian, Indian, and other literature, apparently finding an ultimate source in the folklore of Ceylon.

Unfortunately, Professor Altrocchi devotes most of his effort to searching for at best questionably related antiquities, and very little to any directly attributable sources for the Tarzan novels, most of which he admits he had never even read (!).

Altrocchi does, however, make two points of relevance to Burroughs. For one, he mentions Tarzan's remarkable feats of self-teaching, especially in the area of reading and writing, and traces this particular theme to a twelfth-century Arabic work *Hayy ibn Yaqzan*, by Abu Bakr Mohammed ben Abd-El-Melik ibn Thofail al-Guisi, or Tufail for short. The title character, a feral boy raised by a doe, dissects his foster-mother upon her death and makes various discoveries about internal anatomy by so doing.

Hayy ibn Yaqzan is traced in turn to *Salaman and Absal* by the earlier Ibn-Sina (Avicenna). In typical fashion Altrocchi also traces Hayy *forward*, through renaissance Italian literature and ultimately to *Tarzan of the Apes*, although the professor remarks that "similarity does not necessarily imply derivation." Considering his repeatedly expressed low opinion of Burroughs' works, Altrocchi may intend this remark to be other than entirely charitable.

Altrocchi's other point, a highly significant one, comes when he finally does come to grips with the question of Tarzan's very own ancestors. Altrocchi asks:

> What, then, were the sources of Mr. Burroughs? For his story did not spring full-grown from his imagination, no matter how fertile this may be. Indeed he frankly admitted his sources in two letters to me.
>
> First of all, as he says, he was always interested in mythology . . . Secondly he admits having been influenced by Kipling who, in his two *Jungle Books* (1894–95), developed most entertainingly the life of a boy, Mowgli, lost in the jungle, who fantastically hobnobbed with wild animals . . .
>
> There was another source for Tarzan. Somewhere perhaps in some magazine and certainly before 1912, Mr. Burroughs read a story about a sailor who, as the only survivor of a shipwreck, landed on the coast of Africa. There he tried to make the best of a difficult situation, *à la* Robinson Crusoe. During this forced sojourn in the jungle, a she-ape, which he had tamed, became so enamoured of him that when he was finally rescued, she followed him into the surf and hurled her baby after him. This modern story I have been unable to find.

Altrocchi then goes on to trace the shipwrecked-sailor-she-ape story, turning up versions involving a lady and a he-ape in the Canadian woods (!), an exiled Portuguese woman stranded by pirates, and so on for many

A Mahar casts her sinister spell

different versions of the basic story, occurring in many languages and locales.

Now I found Professor Altrocchi's citation of two letters and three sources particularly interesting, as might well be imagined. The references to mythological sources and to the shipwrecked sailor seemed perfectly acceptable, but Kipling . . . Kipling . . .

Why, it is practically an article of the Burroughsian faith, something that "everybody knows" that Burroughs did *not* have Kipling as a source. The first appearance of the statement that Burroughs had not read Kipling before creating Tarzan to my knowledge, was in *How to Become a Great Writer*, an article about Burroughs in *The Saturday Evening Post* for July 29, 1939. The author was Alva Johnston, who wrote that:

Burroughs was told that Kipling liked Tarzan and supposed that Tarzan was patterned after Mowgli of The Jungle Book. According to Burroughs, Tarzan is a literary descendent, not of Mowgli but of Romulus and Remus, who got such a raising from a she-wolf that they founded Rome.

Unfortunately, Johnston's "according to Burroughs," while it implies attribution to ERB, is not a direct quotation, nor does Johnston document his claim anywhere in the article. In fact, the article contains one long series of unsubstantiated assertions on Johnston's part, with nary a quotation nor a document to back him up. Still, the article has attained stature among persons interested in Burroughs, and its contents have been passed along as gospel in a number of respectable professional publications and in innumerable fan writings.

Even the erudite L. Sprague de Camp states in his *Science Fiction Handbook* (1953) that "The yarn [*Tarzan of the Apes*] deals with an English boy brought up by a race of African apes unknown to science. Kipling read and liked the yarn, supposing that Burroughs had paid him the compliment of imitation. Burroughs, however, swore that when he wrote *Tarzan* he had never heard of the *Jungle Books*, crediting his inspiration instead to the Roman legend of Romulus and Remus."

Asked some years later what *his* source had been, de Camp could not recall with certainty, but allowed that the Johnston piece "sounded right."

Roger Lancelyn Green, in *Into Other Worlds* (1958), reports that "*Tarzan of the Apes* is said to have been written as a joke, to see how far the assumptions made by Kipling in *The Jungle Books* could be driven without exceeding the bounds of popular acceptance."

This, of course, is diametrically opposed to the Johnston thesis, and when asked for substantiation Green refers to Kipling's autobiography *Something of Myself* (1937), which contains this passage:

> . . . if it be in your power, bear serenely with imitators. My *Jungle Books* begat Zoos of them. But the genius of all the genii was one who wrote a series called *Tarzan of the Apes*. I read it, but regret I never saw it on the films, where it rages most successfully. He had 'jazzed' the motif of the *Jungle Books* and, I imagine, had thoroughly enjoyed himself. He was reported to have said that he wanted to find out how bad a book he could write and 'get away with,' which is a legitimate ambition.

"He was reported to have said . . ." Kipling, then, was doing the same thing that Alva Johnston's readers did: pass on reports. But no source is given, and again, the trail dead-ends.

Sam Moskowitz, in *Explorers of the Infinite* (1963) does credit his source when he says:

> According to Alva Johnston, in his article *Tarzan, or How to Become a Great Writer* [sic], published in the July 29, 1939 issue of *The Saturday Evening Post*, Rudyard Kipling was a great fan of the Tarzan stories, believing that they were inspired by his own *Jungle Tales*. [Presumably Moskowitz has here confused Burroughs' *Jungle Tales of Tarzan* with Kipling's *Jungle Books*.]
>
> If the influence of any writer can be strongly discerned in the theme and style of *Tarzan of the Apes*, it would seem to be that of Kipling. But Burroughs stoutly and vigorously denied this. He has been quoted as saying: "I started my thoughts on the legend of Romulus and Remus who had been suckled by a wolf and founded Rome, but in the jungle I had my little Lord Greystoke suckled by an ape."

With four standard authorities in such violent disagreement, Altrocchi and Green citing Kipling and de Camp and Moskowitz denying him, the settlement of the dispute seems a worthy project. Three of the four lead to dead ends: de Camp and Moskowitz lead back to Alva Johnston, whose article is not documented, and who is unfortunately no longer alive to provide any testimony.

Green refers to Kipling himself, but Kipling seems to rely entirely on extremely loose inference and on hearsay.

But if Altrocchi could be located, and could provide copies of those "two letters" in which Burroughs "frankly admitted his sources," the mystery would be cleared up by the personal testimony of Edgar Rice Burroughs himself. My first effort to try and locate Professor Altrocchi was to send simultaneous letters of inquiry to Harvard University Press and to the dean of faculties of the University of California. Replies were quickly received from both institutions, but the news was bad. Professor Altrocchi had been dead for over a decade.

I next wrote to Hulbert Burroughs, and asked if he would check his father's files, to see if copies of the alleged letters existed there. He replied that fan letters were filed geographically, and apparently Burroughs regarded Altrocchi as a fan. Could I supply the professor's likely address as of the time of the correspondence?

I wrote back that the best bet would seem to be California, by virtue of Altrocchi's professorship at Berkeley, with Massachusetts running second on the possibility that he used his publisher's address as a mail drop. If both these failed perhaps the Harbert, Michigan notation in the inscription to Achmed Abdullah would offer another lead.

Happily the correspondence turned up on the first try. And in fact there were not just the two letters mentioned in *Sleuthing in the Stacks* but twelve letters, six from Altrocchi to Burroughs and a reply to each.

The first letter, from Altrocchi to Burroughs, was sent from the professor's office in Berkeley on March 29, 1937. Its style, a blend of scholarly deference and rambling conversation, resembles that of Altrocchi's book:

Please forgive this professor if he takes the liberty of writing to you.

To introduce myself let me say at once that I am *not at all* a fan-writer, but a student of literature, especially Italian literature. In the course of my studies, which have taken me into all sorts of corners of folkloristic and narrative motifs, I am now beginning to reflect on your extremely successful Tarzan books, and the question that presents itself to my mind is this: I wonder just whence you first got the idea of creating your Tarzan. On the one hand, the answer is obvious: from your imagination. But in the mysterious process of literary creation, which I love to delve into, the initial idea for even the most original of artistic creations may at times have come to the artists from the outside, from life or from literature. I hope you will not think it at all indiscreet of me, therefore, if I frankly dare to ask you whether you can tell me how the Tarzan type of story first revealed itself to your creative imagination.

I feel somewhat hesitant about making such an enquiry, but I do believe that often direct enquiry is the most honest and proper form of procedure. For similar reasons I have been in touch with Mary Roberts Rinehart, whom I have not the pleasure of knowing, personally, as well as my friends George Santayana, Richard Le Gallienne, and Edgar Lee Masters.

I do hope you will be so kind as to reply to this my letter; I thank you most eagerly in advance.

Let me take this opportunity to congratulating you on your success and of sending you my respectful wishes.

Burroughs' reply must have been written almost immediately upon receipt of Altrocchi's letter, for the date it bears is March 31, 1937. In clear

and unequivocal fashion, Burroughs answers Atrocchi's question regarding
sources, and it may be hoped that the publication here of the document
may settle forever the confusion and errors stirred up by Alva Johnston two
years later. Burroughs wrote:

> You need not have apologized for asking how I got the idea for Tarzan.
> I imagine that in the past twenty years several thousand people have
> asked me the same question which I wish I could answer definitely.
>
> I have tried to search my memory for some clue to the suggestions
> that gave me the idea, and as close as I can come to it I believe that
> it may have originated in my interest in Mythology and the story of
> Romulus and Remus. I also recall having read many years ago the
> story of a sailor who was shipwrecked on the Coast of Africa and who
> was adopted by and consorted with great apes to such an extent that
> when he was rescued a she-ape followed him into the surf and threw
> a baby after him.
>
> Then, of course, I read Kipling; so that it probably was a combina-
> tion of all these that suggested the Tarzan idea to me. The fundamental
> idea is, of course, much older then Mowgli, or the story of the sailor;
> and probably antedates even Romulus and Remus; so that after all
> there is nothing new or remarkable about it.
>
> I am sorry that I cannot tell a more interesting story concerning
> the origin of Tarzan.

The remainder of the correspondence between the men, carried on spo-
radically for over two years, dealt almost entirely with the story of the
shipwrecked sailor. Altrocchi traced the story to two possible sources:

> One is Guazzo's *Compendium Malefacarum*, written in Latin in the
> Early XVIIth Century and only recently translated; the other is an
> obscure French novel of adventure published in 1635, which I do not
> expect to find in this country.

Altrocchi doubted that Burroughs would have read either of these versions of the story, nor is Burroughs able to provide any better source, except
that "I may have found it in some book in the Chicago Public Library at the
time I was searching for material for a Tarzan book." Altrocchi's last letter to
Burroughs, dated November 13, 1939, was an invitation to a meeting of the
Philological Association of the Pacific Coast, in Los Angeles on November
24 of that year. Altrocchi was scheduled to read a paper titled *Ancestors
of Tarzan*. Burroughs wrote back thanking Altrocchi for the invitation but
stated that he was leaving town on the 21st.

Now of the three sources given for Tarzan, these being Romulus and Remus, Kipling, and the shipwrecked sailor, I think the first can be accepted at face value and passed by. And Professor Altrocchi beat that poor stranded swabby to death without finding the version that Burroughs read, and I shall have nothing to say about him with a single exception, to be mentioned in due time.

But if Burroughs obtained his Tarzan, at least partially, from Kipling's Mowgli, where did Kipling get Mowgli? On this point Altrocchi is just as silent as he is vociferous on the antecedents of Romulus and Remus and the shipwrecked sailor. But turning once again to Kipling's *Something of Myself* we find this statement:

> . . . somehow or other [when a small child] I came across a tale about a lion-hunter in South Africa who fell among lions who were all Freemasons, and with them entered into a confederacy against some wicked baboons. I think that, too, lay dormant until the *Jungle Books* began to be born.

And, much farther on in *Something of Myself*:

> It chanced that I had written a tale about Indian Forestry work which included a boy who had been brought up by wolves. In the stillness, and suspense, of the winter of '92 some memory of the Masonic Lions of my childhood's magazine, and a phrase in Haggard's *Nada the Lily*, combined with the echo of this tale. After blocking out the main idea in my head, the pen took charge, and I watched it begin to write stories about Mowgli and animals, which later grew into the *Jungle Books*.

The story of the Masonic Lions was uncovered, as far as I know, by Roger Lancelyn Green. It is reported in his 1965 volume *Kipling and the Children*. It was *King Lion*, a lengthy serial by James Greenwood running in Beeton's *Boy's Own Magazine* throughout 1864—the year before Kipling was born! Fortunately for the later conception of Mowgli, and indirectly of Tarzan, many magazines of that period issued bound volumes from time to time, and the complete *King Lion* could be found in the Midsummer and Christmas, 1864, volumes of the magazine. The hunter's name, by the way, was Linton Maberly.

One can well imagine the child Kipling, perhaps during his early years in British India, cutting his eye teeth on old *Boy's Own* volumes, even copies carefully preserved from past years, and marveling at the Greenwood serial.

Nada the Lily (1892) by H. Rider Haggard is readily obtainable. Like many of Haggard's African novels, *Nada* is a blend of fact and fancy, the factual content in this case extending beyond the verisimilitude of setting made possible by Haggard's years in Africa. In *Nada* Haggard actually depicts a number of historic personages and events, most important being the Zulu King Chaka (the "black Alexander") and a number of incidents of the Zulu wars of the late nineteenth century.

Leavening the book's authentic historical contents is a romance, based on African legend, of Galazi the wolf man. As a youth Galazi slays the leader or "king" of a very large wolf pack. Removing the hide and casting it over his own shoulders, wearing the wolf's head over his own, Galazi finds that he can command the wolves as if he were their king. Galazi's friend Umslopogaas similarly slays the "queen" of the wolves and wears her pelt and head.

In forays led jointly by Galazi and Umslopogaas, the "brothers of the wolf," Galazi leads and commands the dogs and Umslopogaas the bitches of the pack. (Galazi, it might be noted in passing, appears only in *Nada the Lily*, but Umslopogaas is a continuing figure in several of Haggard's romances. According to Morton N. Cohen in his excellent biography *Rider Haggard* (1960) Umslopogaas was based upon a real African friend of Haggard's early years as a colonist.)

The control and communication which Galazi and Umslopogaas achieve is not fantastic; in fact, it is little greater than that maintained by a trainer over a normally intelligent dog. The tale of *Nada* is narrated by Zweete the witchdoctor, an identity assumed in his old age by Mopo son of Makedama, Umslopogaas' uncle and foster-father. Zweete believes in ghosts and magic, and insists that the wolves of Galazi are the spirits of departed warriors, and that they have human intelligence.

The reader, however, is led by Haggard to take a skeptical view of this assertion. [In other books Haggard delved deeply into mystical and supernatural themes, most prominently so in his classic *She*, concerning which more will be said. However, *Nada* is subject to non-supernatural interpretation.]

At any rate, Kipling *did* read *Nada the Lily*, and was influenced by the book in creating Mowgli, as indicated by Kipling's own autobiography as well as a letter to the same effect which he wrote to Haggard, and which Cohen quotes in his book. Whether Haggard ever had a *direct* influence on Burroughs is subject to conjecture, but even without this I think we can trace a fairly authoritative "family tree" for Tarzan, as follows:

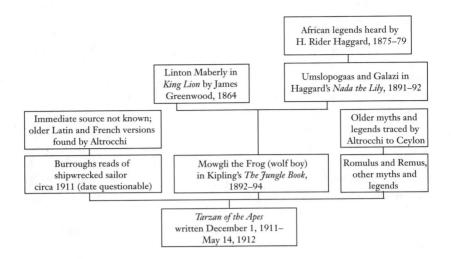

There is one major reason for suspecting a direct link from Haggard to Burroughs, and this centers on Haggard's novel *She* and upon Burroughs' several Tarzan novels involving the lost city of Opar. Opar is most prominently featured in *The Return of Tarzan* and *Tarzan and the Jewels of Opar*.

In *She* (1886) Haggard creates an immortal white goddess-queen in the lost African treasure-city of Kor. This goddess-queen is She-who-must-be-obeyed. A white explorer, Leo Vincey, makes his way to Kor, and She falls in love with him. The story comes to a tragic conclusion when She bathes a second time in the Flame of Immortality, and is destroyed by it; Vincey and a companion return to England.

Now Cohen reports that Kor has been identified by many scholars with the actual abandoned city of Zimbabwe, and that Zimbabwe is in turn identified by some with Ophir, the fabled treasure-city of King Solomon. (A theme of course dealt with by Haggard in *King Solomon's Mines* in 1885).

To explain the immortal white goddess-queen Cohen cites an African tribe, the Lovedu, which for many years was ruled by an "immortal" white queen, Mujaji. Cohen asserts that "there seems to be a reasonable explanation for both her colour and her immortality. All white visitors were, by royal decree, ushered into the Queen's dwelling. White male offspring were killed at birth and female offspring were retained to serve the Queen. One of the Queen's entourage secretly replaced her when she died."

In *The Return of Tarzan* and later books Burroughs created a white priestess-queen of the lost African treasure-city Opar. A white adventurer, Tarzan, makes his way to Opar, and its priestess-queen La falls in love with him. Although the story does not contain the death of La (in fact she recurs in later Tarzan novels) its ending is tragic from her own viewpoint in that her love is rejected by Tarzan.

The whiteness of La and the bestiality of the men of Opar are explained by selective preservation of children—girls for the purity of the white Atlantean strain, boys for the brutality of the crossed ape strain.

That the similarity here is more than coincidental seems obvious. But we cannot *know* that Burroughs borrowed Opar from Haggard. He might have got it directly from Ophir. And as for the white queen, while Cohen suggests Haggard's having had personal contact with the Lovedu prior to 1880, Burroughs might have come across a description of the tribe while doing his research for the Tarzan books in the Chicago Public Library!

There is a peg from which we may hang a final, albeit tentative, identification of the hereditary priestess-queen of Opar with the immortal goddess-queen of Kor. In Haggard's novel, the true name of the goddess-queen is Ayesha, but its pronunciation is taboo and the ruler is known as She-who-must-be-obeyed, or more succinctly, She.

Without the complication of the taboo or secret name, Burroughs calls his priestess-queen La. The word *la* is the feminine article in several romance languages including Spanish, French, and Italian. As a well-traveled and well-educated youth, Burroughs was exposed to languages; in his brief tour of military service along the Mexican border he picked up an elementary Spanish vocabulary. "About enough to curse," according to Hulbert Burroughs.

He was undoubtedly familiar with the word *la*, and although the article is normally translated *the*, a very rough equivalent, deliberately selected to indicate gender, a function which the English articles do not perform, would be . . . *she!*

She the white goddess-queen of Ophir.

La the white priestess-queen of Opar.

I would not suggest for a minute that Tarzan is Leo Vincey, but there is more than a coincidental touch of Kor in Opar, and of She in La.

Now to demolish Lupoff's Theory . . . or maybe just to add a previously unsuspected link to the chain, comes Mr. Samuel A. Peeples, another Burroughs devotee. Peeples cites *At the Queen's Mercy*, published in 1897. This novel by Mabel Fuller Blodgett concerns a lost civilization ruled by Lah, a high priestess-queen. Is Mrs. Blodgett's Lah a missing link between She and La of Opar? Or did Mrs. Blodgett and Burroughs both, coincidentally, have Haggard as a source? Or is the whole thing a case of multiple coincidence? Each reader must decide for himself.

I said some pages ago that I was going to resurrect Professor Altrocchi's poor old shipwrecked sailor just one more time. Now.

In 1888 an author long since forgotten, Harry Prentice, produced a book called *Captured by Apes; or, How Philip Garland Became King of Apeland*. In it, Philip Garland is shipwrecked on "the southernmost island of the Toukang-Basi group" in the Pacific. He discovers that the island is inhabited exclusively by a vast number and wide variety of simians. Prentice was apparently quite unaware of any distinction between monkeys and apes, and uses the terms indiscriminately.

Garland several times comes near to being killed as a result of the murderous antics of the beasts. He saves his skin by donning that of the deceased king of the apes, following which all the beasts obey him, Philip Garland, as if he were their king. When he is finally rescued there is a pitched battle between would-be colonists using modern implements of war and thousands upon thousands of apes hurling sticks and stones. Despite severe casualties, the apes completely overwhelm the humans, who flee the island and give it up to ape domination rather than face complete massacre.

This *very* curious blending of the shipwrecked sailor motif with the animal-skin ruler appeared four years before *Nada the Lily*, so Philip Garland could hardly be traced to Galazi the wolf man. Yet Harry Prentice had a very active interest in Africa. In 1890 he produced *Captured by Zulus*, a novel in which two white boys, Dick and Bob, share a harrowing experience with two African youths, Mapeetu and Kalida, before being rescued and returning to America. The similarity between *Captured by Zulus* and Edgar Rice Burroughs' *The Tarzan Twins*, 1927, is marked.

There is room here for endless conjecture, especially when one considers that Burroughs, born in 1875, would have been just the right age for reading Harry Prentice's boys books when they were published. But for all that such conjecture may be highly diverting for any documented ancestors of Tarzan, we shall have to settle, along with Professor Altrocchi, for Kipling, and Romulus and Remus, and that enigmatic, maddening shipwrecked sailor.

CHAPTER XVI

Tarzan's Greatest Adventures

By 1917 Tarzan was a huge success in magazine, newspaper, and book versions, and was well on his way to celluloid immortality, the first Tarzan film being released the following January. Burroughs was now doing extremely well as a writer, selling virtually every word he produced, whether jungle tale, interplanetary or inner-world science fiction, or one of his occasional attempts at other forms of fiction.

When the *Jungle Tales* were completed he turned away from writing about Tarzan for a time, and after producing two minor works (*The Oakdale Affair* and one of his rare unsold shorter works, *The Little Door*) he devoted seven months to the three segments of *The Land that Time Forgot*. Perhaps it was the success of the film *Tarzan of the Apes* with Gordon Griffith as the boy Tarzan, Elmo Lincoln as the grown Tarzan, and Enid Markey as Jane Porter, that rekindled Burroughs' interest in the Ape Man. Or perhaps it was the incessant demands of Burroughs' publishers—and his readers—for more Tarzan adventures.

But in August, 1918, Burroughs started a renewed series of Tarzan stories which attained heights of adventure, realism of motivation and atmosphere, and fantastic bounds of the creative imagination not seen in the earlier books of the series (nor, sad to say, in the later ones).

The first of these adventures was not completed until December, 1920, a total elapsed time of over twenty-eight months from its inception. It is published as two books, *Tarzan the Untamed* and *Tarzan the Terrible*, but its original appearance was somewhat protracted and more than a little complicated.

Nor did Burroughs work on this adventure continuously from August, 1918, to December, 1920. Between what eventually became the two volumes there was a period of eleven months during which Burroughs wrote *The Efficiency Expert* and worked on a fragment called *The Ghostly Script*, that eventually metamorphosed into *Beyond the Farthest Star*. In fact, he took time out between the next-to-last and last segments of *Tarzan the Untamed* to write *Under the Red Flag*, the original version of *The Moon Men*.

The first portion of the new Tarzan story appeared in *Red Book*, March through August, 1919, as *Tarzan the Untamed*. The second, under the title *Tarzan and the Valley of Luna*, was serialized in *All-Story Weekly* early in 1920.

When Burroughs began the epic in 1918 the First World War was still raging in a number of theatres, and ERB took for his background the East African campaign of British and German armies. The East African campaign was a real and bloody aspect of the war which was overshadowed by the European fighting, but deadly and dirty in its own right. In *On to Kilimanjaro* (1963), a survey of the campaign based on official records, Brian Gardner describes the fantastic difficulties of supply, communication, and training under which the campaign was fought.

The British poured in troops from all parts of the Empire, but a series of incredibly inept commanders combined with a terrific disease rate to render their forces impotent. The British suffered some 62,000 troops dead, over 48,000 of them due to disease. The only figure on the Allied side who emerges at all as a competent operator was a brilliant and daring Captain Meinertzhagen of the British intelligence branch.

The German force consisted of only 3,000 men, commanded by the brilliant Colonel Paul von Lettow-Vorbeck. Overwhelmingly outnumbered, von Lettow-Vorbeck used his troops as cadre for forces of native *askaris*, fought a guerrilla war that cost the Allies dearly in troops and equipment, and by the end of the war was in better condition than his enemy.

In the East African campaign cannibals were a menace to both sides, as were man-eating lions, and hippopotami that menaced river navigation. One major engagement was terminated when swarms of infuriated bees drove off both battling forces. A real incident in the campaign provided the basis for C. S. Forester's *The African Queen*, and the German guerrilla tactics provided the springboard for *Tarzan the Untamed*.

At the opening of the tale Tarzan is returning from Nairobi to his plantation. In Nairobi he had learned of the outbreak of war and, fearing German attack, was on his way home to pack Jane off to safer surroundings. He arrives home too late. German troops had arrived, been received with hospitality, and then turned on their hostess. They slaughtered the servants and burned the plantation. Lying within the wreckage of the bungalow Tarzan finds a corpse burned beyond recognition, but identifiable by Jane's wedding ring.

Tarzan tenderly buries the remains in Jane's rose garden and, swearing vengeance, sets out to aid the British in East Africa against their foe. He ravages behind the German lines, stealing silently past sentries, literally feeding Germans to the lions. There is a sub-plot involving a double agent known to the Germans as Bertha Kircher and to the British as Patricia Canby, a suggestion of romantic developments between the beautiful spy and the bereaved Ape Man, and a later developing romance between the girl and Lieutenant Harold Percy Smith-Oldwick, an English aviator who exhibits a marked resemblance to Waldo Emerson Smith-Jones of *The Cave Girl*.

But complications aside, the main feature of the first half of the book is simple bloody combat, inspired by wartime fervor, combat of man against man, and of man against beast as well. In what may be the most effective single scene in any of his works, Burroughs describes the fight between Tarzan of the Apes and Ska the vulture. Tarzan has been trekking across desert for days. For once he has underestimated the requirements of a trip. There has been no vegetation, no game, no water.

Above Tarzan in the merciless sky circles Ska, awaiting only the imminent demise of his prey. At times Tarzan falls and does not move. Ska circles lower and lower. When Tarzan moves again, Ska takes wing, but stays close above the Ape Man. Finally Tarzan falls once more. Minutes pass without motion except for the vulture's slow wheeling. Then:

> Ska, filled with suspicions, circled warily. Twice he almost alighted upon the great, naked breast only to wheel suddenly away; but the third time his talons touched the brown skin. It was as though the contact closed an electric circuit that instantaneously vitalized the quiet clod that had lain motionless so long. A brown hand swept downward from the brown forehead, and before Ska could raise a wing in flight he was in the clutches of his intended victim.
>
> Ska fought, but he was no match for even a dying Tarzan, and a moment later the ape-man's teeth closed upon the carrion-eater. The flesh was coarse and tough and gave off an unpleasant odor and a worse taste; but it was food and the blood was drink and Tarzan was only an ape at heart, and a dying ape into the bargain—dying of starvation and thirst.

Sustained by the vile blood and flesh of the vulture, Tarzan survives his trek, and after sanguinary adventures moves into a new exploit altogether, his visit to the lost city of Xuja. Xuja was not quite a replay of Opar, but the basic idea is essentially the same. A lost city in the wilds of Africa could provide a bizarre and exotic setting, permitting Burroughs to get away from the wild-man and wild-life theme developed in the original Tarzan story. Again, as Burroughs acknowledged the influence of Kipling's Mowgli upon Tarzan, so it is relevant to note that in the Mowgli stories Kipling too had included a lost city, the Cold Lairs.

But Kipling's lost city in India was ruined and long deserted except for animals, while Burroughs' (and Haggard's) lost cities in Africa were populated with exotic and eccentric races.

Xuja was located by means of a map found on the remains of an ancient Spaniard who had attempted to cross the desert to and from the lost city. He had visited Xuja and made good his departure, but had failed to survive the attempted return to the outer world, and lay now nothing but an armor-clad skeleton. Xuja is a remnant of an otherwise defunct and forgotten civilization where isolation and in-breeding have led to an endemic madness that centers upon the royal house itself. The Xujans practice a lion cult, with a lioness often serving as queen of the city, sharing the throne room with the human king. Mad Xujan monarchs have on occasion carried their totem to the point of mating with lionesses.

To complicate matters, Lieutenant Smith-Oldwick and Bertha Kircher turn up in Xuja, where Bertha makes the acquaintance of a crone who explains in English that she has been in Xuja for sixty years, and that during that time persons had occasionally made their way from the outer world to Xuja, but that none ever returned from Xuja to the world beyond.

Tarzan does eventually make his way out, and he brings Smith-Oldwick and Bertha/Patricia with him. At the end of the story the true identity of the girl is revealed, and she and the young English officer are suitably paired. At the same time a German document is discovered which contains the information that Jane is alive. The corpse which Tarzan found and buried was that of a murdered servant, left as a cruel joke while Jane was carried off by the German raiders.

Tarzan the Untamed ends at this point, but obviously it is an incomplete narration. Jane is still missing, the only clue to her whereabouts a document, now rather old, stating that she had been abducted by the German marauders. Rather than ending with the indication that a complete tale had been told, as had earlier novels in the series, *Tarzan the Untamed* ends with the Ape Man just setting out to find and rescue Jane.

The sequel volume, *Tarzan the Terrible*, opens after two months have passed. In this time Tarzan had traced Jane to a village in the Congo Free State, where she had been held by a German garrison. But she had escaped, the little garrison with its single officer had set out in a body to pursue her, and neither Jane nor the members of the German force had returned.

Only conflicting rumors hinted at the direction in which the fleeing girl and her pursuers had been headed.

Setting out nonetheless to attempt Jane's rescue, Tarzan finds his way into Pal-ul-don, the strangest of all the lands of the Africa which Burroughs described. Pal-ul-don is inhabited by the Waz-don, a race of tailed humans, completely covered with beautiful black fur, and by the Ho-don, similar white men with tails. In order to explain his own lack of a tail, Tarzan claims to be the son of their god, and because of his awesome feats of strength is given the name, in the language of Pal-ul-don, of Tarzan-jad-guru, *Tarzan-the-Terrible* (hence the title of the book).

The Ho-don princess is named O-lo-a (*like-star-light*), and the combination of syllables must have pleased Burroughs, for in the much later *Savage Pellucidar* his pair of inner-world lovers were named Hodon and O-aa.

Like Mars, the moon, Caspak and Pellucidar, Pal-ul-don comes fully equipped. Burroughs provided fauna (domesticated *Gryfs*—triceratops), language (a glossary of almost 150 terms is appended to the book), religion (mass human sacrifice, proscribed by Tarzan in his role of son-of-god), and excellent characters. Possibly the best is Pan-at-lee, a beautiful Waz-don maiden in whose romantic difficulties Tarzan takes a benevolent hand.

While Tarzan adventures among the peoples of Pal-ul-don, Jane has assumed a role of jungle hermit not unlike that acted by Tarzan himself in his earlier days. Surviving by her wits and her skill in bringing down jungle game, she even slays a lion. Aside from the perils of the wild, Jane is further menaced by the half-crazed German Lieutenant Erich Obergatz, who has fallen completely in love with his former prisoner. But the German is totally lacking in jungle lore, and his helplessness makes him a creature of mixed pity and revulsion for the capable Jane Clayton.

Through peril after cliff-hanging peril the Ape Man and his mate struggle to survive.

At one point, when death seems unavoidable for the now reunited couple, Jane asks Tarzan if he holds any further hope. His reply: "I am still alive." How like John Carter's motto, "I still live," and yet Tarzan is not just "John Carter on Earth." (Roger Lancelyn Green calls John Carter "merely Tarzan without the apes," but on his count he is uncharacteristically mistaken. Where John Carter is the simple fighting man, caring little even for his own immortality and accepting his miraculous transportation to Mars with little comment, Tarzan is always the strange one, often the loner, introspective and subject to irrational moods.)

Eventually Tarzan and Jane win free, aided by the timely arrival of their son Jack (Korak), home from the battle of the Argonne. Faced with the choice of returning to London and the civilized life, or of remaining in Africa to attempt, with the aid of the loyal Waziri, the reconstruction of their former plantation, Tarzan and Jane chose the latter, evidencing the finality of their commitment to Africa.

After *Tarzan the Terrible* Burroughs turned out *The Chessmen of Mars* and *The Girl from Hollywood*. Then, early in 1922, *Tarzan and the Golden Lion*. Another direct sequel, this opens with Tarzan, Jane, and Korak on their way home from Pal-ul-don. They find and adopt an orphaned lion cub, naming him Jad-bal-ja (*the-golden-lion* in the language of Pal-ul-don) and raise him in marvelous obedience.

The plot of the book hinges upon an attempt by a crew of shady characters to steal the treasure of Opar. It must be realized that the treasure of Opar is *immense*; after the fall of Atlantis the colonists had continued to accumulate riches for centuries, perhaps millennia, before they ceased to store up gold and jewels for the finally-forgotten mother nation. Tarzan's and the Waziri's repeated raids on the treasure vaults hardly scratched the surface of the hoard of Opar.

The criminal gang is made up of a collection of stereotypes and caricatures. There are Flora Hawkes, the beautiful but depraved schemer; Esteban Miranda, a hot-blooded Spanish actor; Dick Throck and John Peebles, former pugilists; Carl Kraski, another foul Russian cast in the mold of Rokoff and Paulvitch; and Adolph Bluber, a German Jew, the financier of the expedition.

The general level of the characterization is indicated by Bluber's dialog, a sample of which follows:

> Oh, vait, vait, Miss Flora. Don't be ogcited. But can't you see vere ve are? Two t'ousand pounds is a lot of money, and ve are good business men. Ve shouldn't be spending it vit'out getting not'inks for it.

Bluber is the perfect stereotyped Jew. He is short and fat, talks with an outrageous accent, is totally obsessed with money, cowardly, cheap, greedy . . . If anything can be said in extenuation of Burroughs' characterization, it is that Bluber is portrayed more as an object of scorn than of hatred. This provides small comfort.

The nature of the plot against Tarzan involves Miranda's impersonating the Ape Man, and in this role to secure the assistance of the Waziri in reaching Opar and removing and carrying away a fortune. Miranda is a physical match for his part, but the impersonation fails when it becomes evident that he lacks control of the animals that Tarzan commands, and that he is a coward. Before the Waziri realize that Miranda is an impostor Tarzan's reputation is severely damaged, but in the end Tarzan redeems his good name and the various villains are consigned to suitable fates. Miranda winds up a slave to an African tribe.

Tarzan and the Golden Lion was a step down in quality from *Tarzan the Untamed* and *Tarzan the Terrible*, but with the next book in the series, *Tarzan and the Ant Men*, Burroughs brought the series to its peak of invention. Written in the latter half of 1923, *Tarzan and the Ant Men* appeared, as was usual, in the Munsey *Argosy All-Story*. Both the magazine serialization and the first book edition of the tale appeared in 1924.

Tarzan and the Ant Men opens with a scene of Miranda's unhappy life in slavery, then switches to a homelike setting on the veranda of the Clayton bungalow. Tarzan, Korak, and Meriem are surveying the beauty of the restored Clayton establishment. Jane is in London but the younger Claytons and their young son Jackie are visiting Tarzan, now a graying grandfather.

Jack Clayton has brought his family in a private airplane, and Tarzan insists upon attempting to fly it, solo. He passes over an impenetrable thorn *boma* which has held a portion of the jungle in complete isolation for uncounted years. Then the plane crashes. Tarzan reverts from the modern aviator to the primitive man of the wild, and discovers the Alali, a tribe of primitive people living under a matriarchal system in which the feminized males are little above slaves to the domineering women.

Perhaps it was Burroughs' fear of and annoyance with feminine dominance that caused him to use this theme repeatedly, or perhaps it was his discovery, as he researched his stories, that such a reversal of the accustomed roles of the sexes actually exists in some primitive societies. But Burroughs portrayed similar matriarchal tribes in his Venus and Pellucidar series as well as in *Tarzan and the Ant Men,* and in each case the appropriate Burroughs hero set out to alter the society so as to establish masculine domination.

In the land of the Alali, Tarzan trains a young boy to assert normal male prerogatives, then goes off seeking new adventure. He finds it in the land of Minuni, the inhabitants of which are a human race eighteen inches high, who make war mounted on the backs of tiny antelope. Tarzan's sojourn among the Minunians is used to show their society, the entire adventure smacking of *Gulliver's Travels*. Perhaps because of the influence of Swift the book is wryly satirical. It also contains some remarkable pro-war propaganda, apparently not intended to be taken as satire, as Tarzan, in the land of the Minunians, learns that only by frequent war can a nation be kept strong, alert, and aggressive.

Tarzan and the Ant Men contains much of Burroughs' finest pseudo-scientific speculation. For instance, one nation of the Minunians dwell in gigantic beehive-shaped structures housing hundreds of thousands of individuals to each building. The problems of light and ventilation in the inner chambers of these buildings are both met by the use of unique Minunian candles, which burn atmospheric carbon dioxide and give off pure oxygen as a waste product!

These smallest Burroughs' characters also have the longest names: Komodoflorensal, Zoanthrohago, Elkomoelhago. Their warring nations are Veltopismakus and Trohanadalmakus.

Tarzan goes to war on the side of the Trohanadalmakusians but is brought down by vast numbers of Veltopismakusians and reduced by a Veltopismakusian scientist to the size of the tiny people. The treatment, which is a by-product of experiments directed to the enlargement of Minunians, is known to be of temporary duration, but just how long it will last is unknown.

In his Minunian size Tarzan rescues the beautiful slave girl Talaskar from the unwanted attentions of a jailer, in general has a grand swashbuckling adventure with the little people, and finally escapes from Minuni, being able to wriggle through the "impassable" thorn *boma* by virtue of his reduced size. Outside the *boma* Tarzan regains his normal size as the Veltopismakusian treatment wears off. He is captured by natives and has a little fillip of an extra adventure before making his way home to Jane, Jack, Meriem and little Jackie.

Even Esteban Miranda and Flora Hawkes turn up again; Flora has become Jane's maid!

If anything keeps *Tarzan and the Ant Men* from being the perfect Tarzan novel, it is perhaps the embarrassment of riches of the book that makes it just a bit too much to take. The opening sequences up to and including the plane crash, and the later adventure in the land of Minuni, are Burroughs at the top of his form, colorful, wry, action filled, imaginative, unbelievably believable. One runs out of adjectives. But perhaps the dual encounters with the Alali, before and after Tarzan's stay in Minuni, are too much for this book. And surely the post-climactic incidents with the superstitious natives and the reintroduction of Flora and Esteban from *Tarzan and the Golden Lion* makes the mixture too rich. The American book version was considerably rewritten and expanded from the magazine version (which text, oddly, is used unmodified as the British book version) but in the process of rewriting Burroughs only enriched the book even more.

EDGAR RICE BURROUGHS

PELLUCIDAR

Jacket design for a proposed edition of *Pellucidar*

Still, the virtues of *Tarzan and the Ant Men* so outshine its deficiencies that it must be regarded as a high point in the Tarzan series and for that matter in Burroughs' entire career. Again. for the reader who has been led to regard the Tarzan stories as mere recitations of primitive struggle, *Tarzan and the Ant Men* is a pleasant surprise.

Burroughs' next effort was *The Tarzan Twins*, a slim volume of greater curiosity value than literary. It should have been obvious long before now that Edgar Rice Burroughs did not usually write for children. His works have always been popular with younger readers, but they were originally

intended for adult consumption, published in magazines circulated mainly
to adult readers, issued and advertised in book publishers' regular (not juvenile) trade lists, and reviewed, when they were reviewed, as adult books,
not juveniles. In an editorial in 1924 the New York *Times* remarked that
Burroughs was read by the "tired businessman" audience.

A contemporary equivalent might be Ian Fleming or John D. Mac-
Donald, works not heavy in intellectual content or philosophical significance, but grand fun for a few hours reading on a commuter train, or on a
television-less evening at home.[1]

Once more the identification of Burroughs as an author of juvenile literature can be laid on the doorstep of the adapters. With motion pictures
pitched at the Saturday matinee level, comic magazine and newspaper strip
adaptations appearing regularly, and with innumerable "Big Little Books"
and other children's editions by the dozen, the entire Burroughs canon has
become identified as fit only for children to read. So far from accurate is
this impression that a case *might* be made for the very opposite contention,
that at least some of the gore-splattered pages of Burroughs are not fit for
children to read.

After *Tarzan and the Ant Men* Burroughs did not produce another Tarzan
story until 1927, and for once it was written expressly for juvenile readers.
The book was *The Tarzan Twins*, published by the P. F. Volland Company,
the volume being part of Volland's "Golden Youth Series." The publisher
stated that:

> These books conform to the Volland Ideal: while entertaining the
> reader with incidents of breathless interest, they inspire physical
> courage and spiritual bravery. They are full of thrilling action and
> color, but are never gruesome.

The Volland edition was extremely plush, printed on very high quality
coated paper, lavishly illustrated with color plates and line drawings by
Douglas Grant. (An English edition, published by Collins, was much less
elaborate, with a different set of inferior illustrations and no color.)

The "twins" themselves are not twins at all, but cousins whose *mothers*
are twins, one married to an American, the other to an Englishman who is a
distant relative of Lord Greystoke. The youngsters, Doc and Dick, attend
school together in England, and when vacation time nears the boys are
invited to visit Dick's distant kin Tarzan on the latter's African estate.

1. To these best-selling authors of the 1960s, one could add such contemporary favorites as Clive Cussler, Stephen King, Mary Higgins Clark or Dean Koontz. This list bears revision every few years.

When the train carrying Dick and Doc makes a brief unscheduled stop in the jungle the two boys wander off and become lost, are captured by cannibals, make good their escape in the company of Bulala and Ukundo, and are finally found in the jungle by Tarzan and a band of Waziri warriors. The similarity of the experience of Dick and Doc, Bulala and Ukundo, to that of Harry Prentice's Dick and Bob, Mapeetu and Kalida, is little short of uncanny.

Paradoxically, *The Tarzan Twins* was a financial failure despite running through several editions for Volland. It became a highly sought-after collector's item after it went out of print.

In July, 1927, Burroughs completed a manuscript he called *Tarzan the Invincible*, which appeared serially in *Blue Book* as *Tarzan, Lord of the Jungle*. The latter title has been retained in all book editions. (Burroughs later wrote a second novel called *Tarzan the Invincible*; to avoid confusion I will refer to the 1927 work as *Tarzan, Lord of the Jungle*, and reserve the *Invincible* title for the story written in 1930, which to muddle matters further, had *three* different titles.)

Tarzan, Lord of the Jungle, carries the Ape Man into the lost Valley of the Sepulcher, an isolated African land in which a band of shipwrecked English crusaders have lived since the days of Richard the Lion Heart. Tarzan attempts to rescue a lost American, James Hunter Blake, who has been taken prisoner and is living in the Valley. But Blake has made a happy adjustment to medieval life, establishing himself as being of noble lineage. ("My father is a thirty-second degree Mason and a Knight Templar," says Blake to substantiate his claim to nobility.) Before very long he is contesting for the hand of the Princess Guinalda herself.

The Valley of the Sepulcher contains two cities, the City of the Sepulcher at one end and the City of Nimmr at the other, and they are at more-or-less perpetual war, much as the Veltopismakusians and the Trohanadalmakusians of Minuni. The original English enclave in the Valley of the Sepulcher has kept up its population thanks to the happy fact that numerous wenches had been stowed away in their ships by the holy pilgrims. Their permanent stay in Africa is due to a stalemate over whether they had completed their duty as crusaders and should return to England, or whether they are still technically *en route* to the Holy Land.

As Richard Montmorency explains to Blake:

Godbred insisted that this was not the Valley of the Holy Sepulcher and that the crusade was not accomplished. He, therefore, and all his followers, retained their crosses upon their breasts and built a city and a strong castle to defend the entrance to the valley that Bohun and his followers might be prevented from returning to England until they had completed their mission.

Bohun crossed the valley and built a city and a castle to prevent Godbred from pushing on in the direction in which the latter knew that the true Sepulcher lay, and for nearly seven and a half centuries the descendants of Bohun have prevented the descendants of Godbred from pushing on and rescuing the Holy Land from the Saracen, while the descendants of Godbred have prevented the descendants of Bohun from returning to England, to the dishonor of knighthood.

Tarzan, Lord of the Jungle contains splendid color and action. Its atmosphere is a curiously disjointed one of mixed knighthood-in-flower, swashbuckling and typical African adventure in the accustomed mode of the Tarzan stories. The mixture is successful, and the book is most enjoyable and imaginative.

Burroughs followed it with a sequel to *The Tarzan Twins*, the sequel eventually appearing as a Big Big Book (just like the Big Little Books only Bigger) under the unlikely title of *Tarzan and the Tarzan Twins with Jad-bal-ja the Golden Lion*. It was not published until 1936, however, far out of sequence as far as writing is concerned, and long after the Volland Golden Youth Series had been buried by the depression.

Again, except as a bibliographic curiosity, the book is not of great interest. It does introduce "Kla," a sort of junior La of Opar. "Kla" is the kidnapped daughter of a missionary. Gretchen von Harben (the girl's real name) is rescued by Doc and Dick and returned happily to her father, while a band of Oparian separatists who had abducted her to be their unwilling priestess-queen are packed off to Opar in disgrace.

This second "Tarzan twins" story, when it went out of print, became an even scarcer item than the original twins book. In 1963 a combined edition of the two stories was issued by Canaveral Press, featuring superb illustrations by the award-winning Roy G. Krenkel. Again a new title was put on the combined edition to differentiate it from the 1927 and 1936 books combined in it. The 1963 volume is called *Tarzan and the Tarzan Twins*.

It might be noted that doubt was cast on the authenticity of the 1936 Big Big Book. It is known that Burroughs did *not* personally adapt the many Big Little Book versions of his stories, and since the Big Big Book was an "original," i.e., not an adaptation from any known Burroughs story, many readers have suggested that it was not his work at all. Burroughs' working notebook clears up the matter, with an entry for the second "twins" story, started January 17, 1928, and completed February 20 of that year. The working title was the manageable *Jad-bal-ja and the Tarzan Twins*.

Immediately after the second twins story, Burroughs wrote *Tarzan and the Lost Empire*. Again the theme was a lost enclave of an earlier civilized incursion into primitive Africa; this time the enclave was Roman. Tarzan invades the lost country in search of Erich von Harben, Gretchen's older brother. In the story there is another liberal dose of atmospheric color, action, and romance, and again there are two perpetually warring cities, Castrum Mare and Castra Sanguinarius.

The plot emphasis is upon political intrigue in the lost "Roman Empire of the East," with wicked plotters seeking power and the satisfaction of their lustful whims. Tarzan and von Harben struggle desperately—and successfully—to defeat the wicked and to help justice to triumph.

Again, an excellent job by Burroughs, entertaining, atmospheric, and, if a bit too derivative of Burroughs' own earlier works, still standing fairly high in imaginative content.

Following *Tarzan and the Lost Empire* came *Tanar of Pellucidar* and then *Tarzan at the Earth's Core*. Because the latter book was discussed at length in conjunction with Burroughs' Pellucidarian series, I will pass over it now, except to note that the Harbenite used in the construction of the 0–220 was the discovery of the same Erich von Harben introduced in *Tarzan and the Lost Empire*.

Tarzan at the Earth's Core may be regarded as the last of the fine "middle group" of Tarzan stories. Although the Tarzan series went on for a good many more books, they tended to become increasingly—and excessively—derivative and formula-ridden, still entertaining reading in some cases and undoubtedly beloved of the true Burroughs devotee. But to the even slightly more objective reader, only a few of the later Tarzan books are of particular significance.

CHAPTER XVII

Last Tales of Tarzan

After the return of the Ape Man from Pellucidar at the end of *Tarzan at the Earth's Core*, the series began to run downhill very badly. Somehow Burroughs' store of inventions for the Ape Man seemed to have become exhausted and we are told by his son Hulbert that ERB did, indeed, grow tired of grinding out the vast volumes of Tarzan adventures that he had been producing for almost twenty years.

To this point I have largely avoided the psychological approach to criticism, except in the very general sense that Burroughs' fondness for superior men doing great deeds in exotic settings was a natural and obvious reaction to the general failures and frustrations of his own life prior to 1912. In the overall view, however, I have dealt with Burroughs' characters, settings and events as simple fictional characters, settings and events. I believe that this is the most valid view of them, and it was certainly Burroughs' own view of them.

Still, one might well speculate that the idea of carrying Tarzan back into the bowels of the Earth was symbolic of the author's wishes for his famous brainchild, and the fact that Burroughs had Tarzan become lost in Pellucidar may also be considered an expression of his inner wishes as well as a plot device.

But when Tarzan re-emerged from the inner world, his next adventure was recorded in a story written as *Tarzan and the Man-Things*, serialized as *Tarzan, Guard of the Jungle*, and published in book form under the previously discarded title *Tarzan the Invincible*. Again, the title itself may be regarded as symbolic of Burroughs' own feelings toward his most famous creation. The publisher for this new book, in 1931, was Edgar Rice Burroughs, Inc., and the new address was Tarzana, California, the location of the Tarzana ranch. Tarzana now had its own post office, serving a portion of the town of Reseda. *Tarzan the Invincible* was the first book published by the author's corporation, just as Burroughs, in 1923, had been the first author to incorporate himself. In a lengthy letter published in the May, 1937, issue of *Writer's Digest* and reprinted in full in the 1964 edition of the Heins bibliography, Burroughs explained his reasons for taking over the publication of his own books.

Publishing costs, like almost all others, were much lower in those days, and Burroughs' various publishers (for most of his books, A. C. McClurg, but for the last four prior to ERB's publishing his own, Metropolitan) normally brought his books out at a price of $2 for the new title. In those days before the paperback revolution hit American publishing, low-priced reprints in cloth binding followed first editions. Today, hardly a vestige remains of the low-price hardbound reprints, except in book-club editions.

Burroughs' reprints were handled, in the early days, by the A. L. Burt line. Later, Grosset & Dunlap took over the reprints. For many years the reprint editions were priced at 75¢, at one time (1920–21) going to $1.

In his *Writer's Digest* letter Burroughs wrote:

> Since I have been publishing my own books I have learned several things that I should like to pass on to young writers and to older ones too.
>
> I believe that my greed for higher royalties killed the very large sales of my $2 editions that I formerly had. I realize now the very small margin of profit in book publishing, and I can see that the very large royalty that I was finally getting left practically no margin of profit for the publisher so that he had to depend on the popular copyright sales for his profit. Naturally, he must have lost interest in exploiting the original editions. Had I been satisfied with half the royalty, he would have had plenty of money with which to advertise my books and still had enough for a substantial profit. This would have resulted in a much larger sale of original editions, probably a larger gross royalty to me, and a bigger popular copyright sale; for it is a fact that large sales of higher-priced editions of books stimulate the sale of reprints.
>
> It would have been better all around; and I wouldn't have had to publish my own books; but after all I don't know that I regret it, for it has been a lot of fun.

Burroughs did publish all his own new books from *Tarzan the Invincible* in 1931 and for the rest of his life. Reprints were divided between the author's operation and Grosset & Dunlap. (Two exceptions were the second Tarzan Twins book, published by Whitman, and a pamphlet published by the Tarzan Clans of America, a sort of captive Burroughs fan club owned by Burroughs himself, in 1939.)

The story of *Tarzan the Invincible* is little more than a replay of *Tarzan and the Golden Lion*. There is an international band of fortune-seekers (this time with a Communist conspiracy thrown in for good measure; the politics of the book are better than the story) attempting to steal the treasure of Opar. La of course reappears, and her romance with Tarzan bubbles over again, and of course the conspiracy fails.

Tarzan Triumphant (first book edition 1932) is a replay of the lost city story. This time the lost city contains a group of "Midianites," degenerate descendants of early Christians marooned in Africa and stewing there ever since.

Tarzan and the Leopard Men was written next, in 1931, although it was published out of sequence, the first book edition appearing in 1935. It represents nadir for the series. In it, Tarzan is knocked unconscious in a jungle storm, and awakens amnesic. The Leopard Men of the title are members of an animal cult and it is their custom to sacrifice human victims to their totem. For most of the book Tarzan wanders around the jungle not knowing who he is (this time Burroughs was repeating *Tarzan and the Jewels of Opar*) and the Ape Man and the Leopard Men and the Leopard Men's chosen victim, a beautiful white girl, spend chapter after boring chapter chasing one another up and down the river until the reader could scream. A better title for the book might have been *Tarzan the Interminable*.

And *Tarzan and the City of Gold* (book edition 1933) has yet another pair of warring cities, Cathne and Athne. In Athne an elephant totem is observed, with the elephant both a sacred beast and an "implement" of war. In Cathne the lion rules, and fights. For pure entertainment value *Tarzan and the City of Gold* was much better than the horrid *Tarzan and the Leopard Men*, but inventively the series was bankrupt.

Tarzan and the Lion Man was a slight departure in publishing for Burroughs, as it appeared in the general-interest *Liberty* magazine rather than one of the accustomed pulps, before its 1934 book publication. But the quality was not very good. Burroughs introduces a Hollywood crew shooting a jungle-adventure movie on location in Africa. The actors get into trouble, and some of them even get killed off, but Tarzan saves the rest. An amusing vignette is tacked onto the end of the book. In it, Tarzan travels to Hollywood and tries out for the part of Tarzan in a new movie. He is rejected as "not the type."

Tarzan's Quest (book edition 1936) goes all the way back to *The Beasts of Tarzan* and *Tarzan the Untamed* for its motivating device; Jane gets kidnapped. Of course Tarzan rescues her, and she and he come out of their peril with a large supply of immortality pills. Certainly Burroughs' works play a major part in the fictional treatment of life-extension themes, with various stories encompassing virtually every known variant on the idea: outright immortality, resurrection, reincarnation, time travel and suspended animation. But again, as a piece of fiction, *Tarzan's Quest* is at best run of the mill.

Tarzan and the Forbidden City (1938) goes underwater for a lost civilization story, and a cursory examination of the book leads one to hope that Burroughs had turned off the formula cooker and turned his imagination back on, but alas, he had not. Two submarine cities are found, endlessly at war; Tarzan and several others are made prisoner and exploit the combat situation to make good their escape. Next to *Tarzan and the Leopard Men* this is probably the worst of the Tarzan books.

In 1939 the *Official Guide of the Tarzan Clans of America* was published: it is a slim booklet and contains no fiction, but much Tarzan lore. It was written by Edgar Rice Burroughs. The Tarzan Clans were an attempt to promote Burroughs' books, even he by this time aiming his appeal at children. The club, which never really got off the ground, was a sort of combination Boy Scouts and Mickey Mouse Club, complete with tribal organization, elaborate rules, and club songs, games, and dances. A sample, the chorus of the *Tribal Hunting Song*:

> Oh, men of the jungle are we,
> The jungle far over the sea.
> Without any care and as free as the air
> We live with the apes in a tree.

Going back to fiction, *Tarzan the Magnificent* (book edition 1939) again has two warring tribes, this time of Amazonian mold. They are the Kaji and the Zuli, and a treasure in gems is at stake.

The final book in this period of Tarzan's existence was *Tarzan and the Madman*, which Burroughs wrote in 1940 but which was not published in any form until the first book edition in 1964. It would be a pleasure to report that this posthumously published novel is at the top of the Tarzan list, or even in the middle.

Well, at least it is not at the bottom, standing well above *Leopard Men*, *Lion Man*, and *Forbidden City*. But there is still another false Tarzan in the book, (shades of *Golden Lion* and *Lion Man*), and another lost civilization (shades of half a dozen Tarzan books at least, starting with *The Return of Tarzan* in 1912), and a false religion (shades of *Tarzan Triumphant* and

Leopard Men). It was as if the author had taken a set of the Tarzan books published to date, cut them up and folded them in, and produced *Tarzan and the Madman*. It has bizarre characters, some of them human, outlandish settings and cliffhanging action galore, but nothing new.

All of this not to say that these later Tarzan novels, from *Tarzan the Invincible* through *Tarzan and the Madman*, are hopeless trash. On the contrary, of the nine volumes (omitting the Tarzan Twins and Tarzan Clans material) only a very few are hopelessly bad. I would nominate *Tarzan and the Leopard Men*, *Tarzan and the Lion Man*, and *Tarzan and the Forbidden City* for total oblivion, but even so the factor of personal taste cannot be overlooked and there will surely be readers who disagree—perhaps violently—with this assessment.

The point, however, is that the nine Tarzan novels from *Invincible* through *Madman* represent the mining out of a totally familiar vein. The reader can often predict plot developments chapters ahead, something which the earlier Burroughs would never have permitted. The plot devices are the same worn tricks: the lost empire, the eternally warring cities, the maddened queen who falls in love with Tarzan and/or the maddened king who lusts after an innocent girl protected by Tarzan, the noble warrior who befriends the Ape Man, the imprisonment and escape of Tarzan.

The music went round and round and for loyal Burroughs fans it may have come out pleasant listening, but we'd all heard that song before.

These nine derivative books, however, were not the end of the saga of Tarzan. In 1939 Burroughs wrote two shorter Tarzan stories in the fashion of the *Jungle Tales* if not quite in the same spirited style. Of these, *Tarzan and the Champion* which appeared in *Blue Book* is a somewhat heavy-handed satire of an imaginary confrontation between a world champion boxer and Tarzan. Of course we know who emerges victorious, and it is not "One-Punch" Mullargan, the fighter.

The other, *Tarzan and the Jungle Murders* which appeared in *Thrilling Adventures* magazine, is described by Anthony Boucher as "one of the rare adventures in which the King of the Jungle functions as a formal detective." Boucher does not care much for the story, and in truth it is neither a very good detective story nor a very good Tarzan adventure, but it is an interesting departure from the rut into which Tarzan had long since fallen.

In November and December, 1940, Burroughs wrote a short novel which he called *Tarzan and the Castaways*. It was serialized, in much altered form, in *Argosy* magazine. For some reason the title also was changed, to *The Quest of Tarzan*, causing endless confusion between this story and the earlier *Tarzan's Quest*. In the first book edition, 1964, both the original text and the original title were restored, along with illustrations by the brilliant Frank Frazetta, one of the finest illustration jobs ever done on a Burroughs book. (The two shorter stories, *Tarzan and the Champion* and *Tarzan and the Jungle Murders*, are included in this book.)

Tarzan and the Castaways opens on board the tramp steamer *Saigon*, upon the deck of which stands the helpless Tarzan, disarmed, imprisoned, and suffering from amnesia again. Tarzan's new captors, an Arab and a German, plan to exhibit him with other African beasts as a genuine wild man.

Through devious means the ship winds up lost in the Pacific, where its survivors discover a lost Mayan colony dating back to the year 1452. The color is vivid and the lost civilization is handled well, although I find myself wishing that Burroughs had given more attention to the civilization of the island of Uxmal, and less to rather routine beast fights and human sacrifices. Still, the book is a marked improvement over its predecessors of some years, and the shift of setting offered grand hope of a loosening, if not an abandonment, of the Tarzan formula.

And in *Tarzan and "The Foreign Legion"* Burroughs really did cut loose from his formula. This book was written in 1944 while Burroughs was serving as a war correspondent in the Pacific, and the setting again is the Pacific, specifically the island of Sumatra. The villains this time are Japanese occupation troops. The heroes, a motley crew of Americans, British, Dutch and Indonesians (hence "the Foreign Legion," no relation to the French Foreign Legion) struggle through the war in jungle retreats.

The story is unlike any other in the series. It crackles with a new brand of suspense and humor. For the first quarter of the book Colonel Clayton of the Royal Air Force goes unrecognized by his comrades. Then:

> Suddenly recognition lighted the eyes of Jerry Lucas. "John Clayton," he said, "Lord Greystoke—Tarzan of the Apes!"
> Shrimp's jaw dropped. "Is dat Johnny Weissmuller?" he demanded.

The characters in *Tarzan and "The Foreign Legion"* are such stereotypes as might have stepped from the screen of a 1944 war movie, but in style and attitude it is a marked departure from the Tarzan formula prior to *Tarzan and the Castaways*. It was the last new work published in Burroughs' lifetime, appearing in 1947. The following year *Llana of Gathol* appeared, but this was composed of magazine novelettes originally published almost a decade before.

Two minor Tarzan works remain unpublished. These are *Tarzan & Jane: A Jungleogue*, dated March 3, 1933, and *Tarzan's Good Deed Today*, an undated humorous playlet.

An untitled fragmentary Tarzan novel also exists. Unlike a very short Venus fragment also remaining, the Tarzan fragment is of substantial length, some 20,000 words. An average Burroughs novel ranged from 55,000 to 65,000 words, although modern requirements dictate a minimum length of 80,000 words. Thus the Tarzan fragment may be regarded as anywhere from one-quarter to one-half of a novel.

The author's two sons have mentioned an interest in completing the work themselves. If they do so, it will not be as complete tyros. Aside from John Coleman Burroughs' work on *John Carter and the Giant of Mars*, and considerable experience scripting as well as drawing John Carter and David Innes comic strips, he and Hulbert Burroughs collaborated on three science-fiction stories which appeared in pulp magazines in 1939, 1940, and 1941.

The first two, *The Man without a World* and *The Lightning Men*, appeared in *Thrilling Wonder Stories*. They share a common rationale and the hero of the latter story is Mal Mandarck II, the son of the hero of the first. In the Mandarck stories a great space ark makes its way from Earth to a distant planet which is colonized as Nova Terra. In the latter story the colonists face and defeat a menace from indigenous beings.

The third John Coleman Burroughs—Hulbert Burroughs story, *The Bottom of the World*, appeared in *Startling Stories* for September, 1941. It involves a plot by one Fritz Megler, a scientist who lives in California, and Megler's opposite number Ola, a scientist of "Aqualia," Mu, to join forces and enslave both the surface and the Aqualian peoples in order to extract a serum of youth from them.

John Coleman Burroughs collaborated with his then wife, Jane Ralston Burroughs, on *Hybrid of Horror*, which appeared in *Thrilling Mystery* magazine for July, 1940. The story involves a living, carnivorous statue in an ancient New England manor, and is a routine horror story except for the statute itself, which, from the description given, is a fairly faithful image of a Martian green man.

Finally, early in 1967 Ballantine Books issued *Treasure of the Black Falcon*, a science-fiction novel by John Coleman Burroughs, perhaps distantly related to the much earlier *Bottom of the World* in theme. The later book involves an alien race surviving for centuries deep beneath the waters of the Atlantic Ocean, discovered in 1947 by a crew of treasure-hunting submariners. The book was met with enthusiasm by a small core of Burroughs loyalists, but otherwise aroused little interest or approval.

If John Coleman Burroughs and Hulbert Burroughs do not complete the Tarzan fragment themselves, there is sure to be a wealth of applicants for the job.[1]

As for Edgar Rice Burroughs' feelings as he wrote the last few Tarzan stories, I can only believe that *Tarzan and the Castaways* and *Tarzan and "The Foreign Legion"* were a liberation for the author. It is only guesswork of course, but I think that after years of unhappily reworking routine African plots, Burroughs made friends all over again with his famous creation by getting him away from the continent where both author and character had grown so restless.

When they went off to the Pacific—as Burroughs did in reality at about the same time that Tarzan did in fiction—Burroughs was happier than he had been for some time. To get Tarzan to the Pacific it was necessary to wipe his memory clean and put him in a cage, but it was worth it.

All of this may be sentimental fantasy, wholly detached from the facts of the matter, but I think that Burroughs really did have such feelings, and if he did, then there is a reality to it, of a very meaningful sort.

---

1. This fragment was ultimately completed by Joe Lansdale. See Chapter XXI, "Forty More Years of Adventure" for details.

CHAPTER XVIII

Descendants of Tarzan

One of the major points of this book has been to show that Edgar Rice Burroughs was not a "primitive" author, working in isolation from his predecessors and contemporaries, but that his works occupy a clear (and perfectly legitimate) place in the stream of imaginative literature. It is equally true that, as Burroughs had sources and inspirations for his various characters and themes, so also he served as a source and inspiration for many authors who have followed him.

As Rudyard Kipling, Edwin Lester Arnold, Dean Swift and perhaps others were to Burroughs, so Burroughs was to whole generations of authors of science fiction and jungle adventure tales who have come after. An exhaustive list of Burroughs imitators is probably impossible to make, and it is certainly not my intention to try. I will, however, in the next few pages, offer a quick survey of some of the descendants of Tarzan and of Burroughs' other creations.

Probably the most prolific of Burroughs' imitators was, ironically, "Roy Rockwood" (various authors working under the Edward Stratemeyer house name), whose piracies from Jules Verne, particularly *Five Thousand Miles Underground*, were a likely source of inspiration to Burroughs in the years before the first World War. Decades later, Stratemeyer/Rockwood conceived *Bomba the Jungle Boy*, a sort of junior Tarzan who operated in the Amazon jungle. (A majority of the Bomba books were written by John Duffield.) Bomba was quite a success, and after the initial book of the series appeared in 1926 it was followed by *Bomba at the Moving Mountain, Bomba at the Giant Cataract, Bomba at Jaguar Island, Bomba in the Abandoned City*, and so on and on.

Not only are the Bomba books poorly written, they reek of the most blatant racism:

To be white meant not only to look different, but to act differently, to think differently, to live differently. What inner thing was it that made those who wore white skin for a covering, like himself and Casson and Gillis and Dorn, different from the brown or copper-skinned natives?

. . . Why did [the Indians] feel so differently than he? Was it because they did not have souls? He dismissed this thought as improbable. But perhaps their souls were asleep. Ah, that must be it! They were asleep!

But his was awake. At least it was waking. Perhaps that was because he was white. The thought gave him a thrill. Now he was sure that he had found the truth. The natives' souls were asleep. The white men's souls were awake. And he was white!

But as bad as they are, the Bomba books sold well, as indicated by the length of the series, the fact that the books were frequently reprinted, and the motion-picture adaptations based upon them, and the still more recent comic magazines.

Five years after the first Bomba book literary jungle-lovers met C. T. Stoneham's Kaspa, hero of *The Lion's Way* (1931) and a sequel, *Kaspa, the Lion Man* (1933). Kaspa, as you would guess, was a feral child raised by lions. He was also the lost heir to a Canadian fortune. Discovered and returned to North America, Kaspa would periodically throw off the shackles of civilization and go racing through the Canadian forests, getting back to nature.

Perhaps to avoid the criticism heaped upon Burroughs for the nudism in his stories, Stoneham had Kaspa keep on a suitably modest bathing suit during his atavistic spells, which does tend to spoil the atmosphere of the otherwise rather well done pastiches.

A decade after Bomba made his debut, along came *Bantan—God-Like Islander*, by Maurice B. Gardner. Bantan operates from a Pacific island where he was cast ashore by the same storm that killed both his parents and destroyed their yacht. Gardner's plotting is fairly competent pseudo-Burroughsian, but he has a little trouble with sentence construction:

The suspicion had been nursed ever since Wanya had come into the stage of life when her faculties were supposed to have matured and her understanding was quite complete as far as to whom her heart prompted her whole being to feel she could love in the manner a maiden would love a warrior.

Still Bantan did well enough to be reissued as *Bantan of the Islands*, and was followed by a long series of sequels including *Bantan Defiant*, *Bantan Valiant*, *Bantan's Island Peril*, *Bantan Incredible*, and several more. The Bantan books never made the transition to paperback; however, the hardbacks turn up regularly at modest prices.

Several whole magazines have been published devoted to imitations of Tarzan, although for obvious legal reasons they could never openly acknowledge their debt. A *Jungle Stories* magazine appeared briefly in 1931 and then disappeared again. A second series of the same title (but with a different publisher) ran from 1938 to 1954.

The main attraction of this latter *Jungle Stories* was Ki-Gor, a blond pseudo-Tarzan whose adventures were chronicled by the pseudonymous "John Peter Drummond." The magazine also featured a sort of she-Tarzan, not at all a Jane figure but an independent jungle heroine, named Sheena. Sheena, whose adventures bore the by-line "James Alderson Buck," was so popular that she wound up in a magazine all her own in 1951, and later on television.

Ka-Zar by "Bob Byrd" was also featured in a magazine bearing his name, for several issues starting in 1937. Ka-Zar, like the earlier Kaspa, was raised by lions; like the earlier Kioga, his real family name was Rand; like Tarzan, he fought with apes, befriended elephants, and generally ruled a jungle domain.

Many pseudo-Tarzans were adapted to comic magazine format but few have survived to the present time. Ka-Zar turned up on the comic page as early as 1939, disappeared for decades, and reappeared in 1965 as the ruler of a sort of Antarctic Pellucidar!

I have already referred to Otis Adelbert Kline. His *Call of the Savage* was published in book form in 1937, and *Tam, Son of the Tiger* was finally issued in book form in 1962, thirty-one years after it was serialized in *Weird Tales*. The book combines elements of Tarzan and Pellucidar with just a touch of Barsoom thrown in for good measure.

Tam Evans is raised by Leang, a white tigress, discovers a lost underground world beneath Burma, and fights Thark-like monsters there. The four-armed monsters are identified with Hindu deities rather than the green men of Mars, but as so often is the case, the reader is free to draw a different conclusion if he wishes.

In October, 1940, *Fantastic Adventures* under the editorship of Raymond A. Palmer carried the novelette *Jongor of Lost Island* by Robert Moore Williams. Jongor—John Gordon—is the son of parents who crash-land in a sort of Lost World or Caspak surrounded by an all but impassable mountain range in the middle of the Great Australian Desert. Their radio is knocked out, and so they settle down to stay. After the death of both parents the little John Gordon almost forgets his name and it winds up slurred into Jongor.

Any resemblance between the name John Gordon and either John Carter or John Clayton is not necessarily coincidental.

In his Australian stronghold, the heroic Jongor rides on tame dinosaurs controlled by ancient superscientific means, fights centaurs, meets the members of an Opar-like colony of Muvian miners, and generally behaves in accepted Tarzan fashion. In 1944 *Fantastic Adventures* ran William's *The Return of Jongor*, and in 1951 *Jongor Fights Back*.

The first two of the Jongor stories were accompanied by cover paintings by J. Allen St. John, an artist associated with Burroughs for most of the latter's career, just in case any reader should fail to identify Jongor's source. The John Gordon stories total to the length of an average size book; they were reprinted by Popular Library in 1970 as three slim volumes á la *The Land that Time Forgot*, with suitably muscular Frank Frazetta cover art.

The best of all imitation Tarzans was William L. Chester's Kioga, *Hawk of the Wilderness*. The locale for Kioga's adventures was an unknown island north of the Bering Straits, where, warmed by ocean currents, an undiscovered Indian tribe survive. Kioga's parents were white explorers, Dr. and Mrs. Lincoln Rand, and after their death the boy was raised by Indians and animals in the strange northern land. The first Kioga novel was published by Harper in 1936, after running serially in *Blue Book*. DAW Books issued the sequels *Kioga of the Wilderness* in 1976, *One Against the Wilderness* in 1977, and *Kioga of the Unknown Land* in 1978.

Another rather good Tarzan pastiche is *Tharn, Warrior of the Dawn*, by Howard Browne. This novel was serialized in *Amazing Stories* starting in December, 1942, and its sequel, *The Return of Tharn*, ran there in 1948. Book editions of the two stories were published by Reilly & Lee in 1943 and Grandon in 1956, respectively.

Tharn (pronounced Tar'n, and if the reader wishes to substitute a *za* for the apostrophe, who is to stop him?) is a Cro-Magnon operating in a vaguely Mediterranean setting some 20,000 or more years ago. Browne postulates a rather higher level of civilization among these early people than is generally held to have been the case, and it is easy to read the Tharn stories as just two more adventures of Tarzan in lost African cities.

I hesitate to call Robert E. Howard's Conan the Cimmerian an imitation of Tarzan; the influence of Burroughs on Howard was great but Howard's imagination was so powerful that any Tarzan in Conan tends to be submerged in the latter's roaring, brawling, drinking, wenching personality. Yet the influence is there.

Conan, like Tharn, operates in an ancient world. His adventures appeared in *Weird Tales* between 1933 and 1936. A number of them were reprinted in *Skull-Face and Others*, a Howard collection issued by Arkham House in 1946, and six books of Conan material, starting with *Conan the Conquerer* in 1950, were issued by Gnome Press. In 1965 Lancer Books announced a new version of the Conan books in paperback, with the material re-edited and resequenced by L. Sprague de Camp.

The Lancer—and later Ace—series topped out at a dozen "official" Conan volumes, variously edited, annotated, and added to by de Camp, Lin Carter, and Bjorn Nyberg. Through the 1980s and 1990s a seemingly endless series of pastiches were published by authors too numerous to mention, as Conan became a franchised character like the Executioner or the Destroyer. An additional volume of Solomon Kane stories (see below) was produced by Donald Grant, a discerning publisher of limited editions in the science fiction and fantasy fields.

Fritz Leiber, obviously encouraged by the adventure series revival, brought back his own heroic pair, Fafhrd and the Gray Mouser, in a new series of paperbacks beginning with *The Swords of Lankhmar* and *Swords Against Wizardry*. Again, these stories are far from being pure Burroughs pastiche. The spirit of Howard, too, is present, as is Leiber's original talent. The point is that the influence of Burroughs is present in the creation, and the Burroughs-inspired revival in the whole epic-heroic field is an obvious factor in the creation of a market for works of the type.

Conan is a barbarian warrior who fights his way from mercenary to monarch in an ancient world of sorcery and combat. Like Tarzan he is periodically imprisoned, makes good escape, defies cruel monarchs, is a demon fighter. Unlike Tarzan, when a wench throws herself at him he is not reluctant to respond with enthusiasm.

Howard created a number of barbarian heroes not unlike Conan, but his one series of African adventures (see also *Skull-Face and Others*) feature Solomon Kane, a "dour Puritan" whose encounters with African magic, Wieroo-like vampire men, and other menaces make him a character of utter fascination.

As the works of one author may serve as an inspiration for a second, those works in turn may be a link to yet a third, and on for any number of generations of creativity. We can trace a line from Galazi to Mowgli to Tarzan to Conan to Michael Moorcock's Elric of Melnibone. Elric first appeared in the British *Science Fantasy* magazine in 1961; his early adventures were collected into two books, *The Stealer of Souls* (Spearman, 1963) and *Stormbringer* (Herbert Jenkins, 1965). In the decades since, the character has proven so popular that Moorcock continues adding to a seemingly inexhaustible saga.

Elric is a sort of melancholy Conan. Himself a weakling, he owns (if that is the right word) an enchanted sword which brings him victory in combat but which, in a sinister way, also brings him to new tragedy every time he uses it.

Writing as Edward P. Bradbury (take a quick look at the initials and see if you can fool yourself), Moorcock produced his own version of the first John Carter trilogy, featuring one Michael Kane in *Warriors of Mars, Blades of Mars*, and *Barbarians of Mars* (1965). The books have their advocates—most surprisingly, to me, the outstanding imaginative writer Samuel R. Delany— but for my own taste they smack too closely of the originals. There is a point at which emulation becomes mere imitation, and for me, the "Kane" books are beyond this point. Even so, this has proven to be one of Moorcock's most durable series, the books having been reissued many times (under the author's name) with the new titles *City of the Beast, Lord of the Spiders*, and *Masters of the Pit*.

Far more successful are Moorcock's tales of Dorian Hawkmoon, servant of the Runestaff. These books—*The Jewel in the Skull, Mad God's Amulet, The Sword of the Dawn, The Runestaff*—are set in a neo-feudalistic Europe of the future. The setting is reminiscent of Burroughs' *Beyond Thirty*, as the Dark Empire of Granbretan (remember Grabritin) attempts to conquer the petty dukedoms of Europe before turning to Asia and America in a planned world conquest. The characters are vibrant, the setting vivid, and the series is altogether a pleasure to read.

And Lin Carter's Thongor the Barbarian partakes of both Tarzan and Conan (with some Barsoom thrown in) in his initial appearance in *The Wizard of Lemuria* (Ace, 1965; revised as *Thongor and the Wizard of Lemuria*, 1970). Thongor fights his way across the ancient continent, encountering both sorcery and an ancient science capable of producing aircraft powered by perpetual motion:

> In the original model, when these springs had uncoiled, the floater was without motive power until they could be rewound by hand. Sharajsha had re-installed them in such a manner that the action of one spring-coil unwinding automatically unwound the second, and vice-versa.

Carter also revives the elder gods and unnamed horrors of the late H. P. Lovecraft, making *The Wizard of Lemuria* a three-ring circus.

And at least commercial, if not artistic, success is reflected by further volumes of the saga of Thongor: *Thongor of Lemuria*, *Thongor against the Gods*, and *Thongor in the City of the Magicians*.

In enumerating these descendants of Tarzan I have, to this point, omitted those cases in which self-appointed successor authors have taken it upon themselves not "to pastiche" the Ape Man with heroes of their own (however closely patterned upon the original), but to take over and continue the Tarzan series itself, using Tarzan and other Burroughs characters without disguise.

Perhaps the first company to pirate Lord Greystoke in this fashion was a company in Argentina which issued no fewer than *thirty* spurious Tarzan novels beginning in 1933. As reported by Darrell C. Richardson in 1947, these books were small paperbacks, listing J. C. Boviro as editor. They were all in Spanish, and included such titles as *Tarzan and the Sphinx*, *Tarzan and the Silver Buddha*, *The Death of Tarzan*, *The Resurrection of Tarzan*, and even *The Grandson of Tarzan*.

In the June, 1956, issue of *Other Worlds* magazine, Ray Palmer (who had left *Amazing* and *Fantastic Adventures* some years before) announced his intention of publishing a novel called *Tarzan on Mars* by "John Bloodstone" (Stuart J. Byrne). Forbidden by Edgar Rice Burroughs, Inc., to publish the story, Palmer announced that he would simply change the names of the key characters and publish anyway; the reader would know who was meant. He did not publish, although *Tarzan on Mars* has appeared as an amateur publication and as a serial in the pulp fanzine *Aces*.

In 1964 the New International Library of Derby, Connecticut, issued a paperback titled *Tarzan and the Silver Globe* by "Barton Werper." This book is a most outrageous piracy of *Tarzan and the Jewels of Opar*, with whole paragraphs and sections lifted bodily from the 1915 Burroughs work and inserted in the new book. Even the byline is taken from the name of the villain of the original.

Tarzan and the Silver Globe has been followed by *Tarzan and the Cave City*, *Tarzan and the Snake People*, *Tarzan and the Abominable Snowmen*, and *Tarzan and the Winged Invaders*, all of them very bad, all of them lifted, in varying degrees, from legitimate Tarzan stories.

These illegitimate descendants of Tarzan do raise a serious question concerning the matter of successor authors. After having read a number of stories of various sorts by successor authors, over a period of years, I had prior to the past few months concluded that their products were universally inferior to the original. To the extent that a successor author maintained fidelity to the original his work was superfluous. To the extent that it varied from the original, it tended to fracture the structure of imagination created by the original author. Either way, the successor's work would suffer.

I have come across one exception to this principle. It is *Skull-Face*, the title of the 1946 collection of Howard stories. *Skull-Face* was serialized in *Weird Tales* in 1929 and 1930, and it is a pastiche of the Fu Manchu stories of Sax Rohmer. Skull-Face is Dr. Fu just as clearly as he can be, portrayed as well as Rohmer ever portrayed him. Howard's hero, the American Stephen Costigan, is far superior in conception and presentation to any of the men Rohmer ever put up against Fu. To the extent that Howard maintains fidelity to the original, his work is superior.

To the extent that Howard does not rely upon Rohmer, he goes beyond Rohmer, extending rather than destroying the structure of the original author's work. Rohmer had never fully explained the origin of Fu, although he often hinted an Egyptian identity of incredible antiquity. Howard carries back beyond Egypt, makes Skull-Face a survivor of sunken Atlantis, and brings the whole audacious thing off perfectly!

Unfortunately, Howard was an unstable type who killed himself in 1936 when his mother died. He was only thirty. Without him, it may be possible to think of a few present-day authors who might do a creditable job of continuing the famous characters, but with the possible exception of completing the 20,000 word Tarzan fragment, I would think it best to leave the canon as it stands. Authors who admire Burroughs and wish to produce works in the same tradition have endless opportunities to do so with creations of their own.

Finally, there are of course the *authorized* pastiche Tarzan tales—various comic strip and comic magazine scripts, motion pictures and television scripts, and the texts of Big Little Books over the years representing most if not all of this particular breed. And, removed yet another generation, the already-mentioned *Tarzan and the Valley of Gold* by Fritz Leiber, based on the screenplay by Clair Huffaker. Leiber is a fine writer of science fiction, fantasy, and heroic adventures himself, and *his* Tarzan book is quite a good book. It does not, however, succeed in capturing the feeling and verve of the original Tarzan.

Imitations of Tarzan are the most numerous class of works directly inspired by the works of Edgar Rice Burroughs, but in the area of the interplanetary adventure tale he was responsible for vast numbers of stories only indirectly traceable to John Carter and the Virginian's later confreres. Perhaps the earliest pseudo-Barsoomian adventure was serialized in *All-Story* beginning in July, 1918.

Consider this very slim outline: an earthly adventurer, expert with the sword, is transported astrally to a distant planet where he falls in love with a beautiful princess, becomes involved in a series of wars and political intrigues, rises swiftly to the supreme leadership of a newly reunited empire, and becomes the husband of the beautiful princess. The hero's initials also happen to be J. C.

But he is not John Carter and the story is not *A Princess of Mars*, nor is the author Edgar Rice Burroughs. The hero is Jason Croft, the story is *Palos of the Dog Star Pack*, and the author is J. U. Giesy. The only major difference between the Giesy story and its Burroughs prototype is that when Jason Croft arrives upon Palos he finds that his astral self is incorporeal, a problem which he overcomes by displacing the spirit of a handsome and muscular Palosian youth just as the latter expires out of sheer despondency over his own stupidity.

Although *Palos* appeared in magazine form in 1918, its first book edition did not appear until 1965, issued by Avalon. Two sequels, *The Mouthpiece of Zitu* and *Jason, Son of Jason*, have little to recommend them.

In the May, 1923, issue of *Weird Tales* Vincent Starrett spoofed the astral-interplanetary theme with his very funny short story *Penelope*. Penelope is a distant star to which the protagonist of the story, Raymond, is strongly drawn whenever the star is in perihelion. When this occurs, Raymond locks himself in his room, and when he is pulled irresistibly to Penelope he just lets himself go and sits on the ceiling until perihelion is past.

He finally settles his strange urge for the star Penelope by instead marrying a girl named Penelope Pollard. (The story appears as lagniappe in *The Moon Terror* by A. G. Birch, Popular Fiction Publishing Company, 1927.)

It is not necessary to discuss the works of Otis Adelbert Kline at this point, except to mention that in addition to his three Venusian and two Martian novels, he also wrote a book called *Maza of the Moon* (McClurg, 1930) which bears a slight—but only very slight—resemblance to Burroughs' *The Moon Maid*.

"Ralph Milne Farley" (Roger Sherman Hoar), a friend of Burroughs, created a hero named Myles Cabot, whom he transported electronically to Venus in *The Radio Man*, serialized by Munsey in 1924. Arriving on Venus Cabot finds the planet inhabited by a humanoid race totally devoid of ears, who communicate by "natural radio." Fortunately, Cabot just happens to be a radio engineer, so he rigs himself up a portable artificial gear and passes as a Venusian.

The planet is also inhabited by races of intelligent ants and bees, both of gigantic size, and the story is devoted to Cabot's exploits on behalf of the humanoids in combating the tyranny of the ants. Of course he succeeds, and marries a Venusian princess as his reward.

In a sequel, *The Radio Beasts*, a second war is fought with the giant ants, this time to annihilation, with the giant intelligent bees of Venus in partnership with the humanoids. And in a third Myles Cabot adventure, *The Radio Planet*, the alliance of humanoids and bees breaks down and there is yet another insect war to fight. And, as usual, the Princess Lilla to rescue, again and again.

The Radio Man was published in book form by the Fantasy Publishing Company in 1948. The two sequels lay unreprinted in the pages of *Argosy All-Story Weekly* and later magazines until 1964, when they appeared in book form as paperback originals.

Edmond Hamilton's *Kaldar, World of Antares*, appeared in *The Magic Carpet* magazine for April, 1933. This magazine was a short-lived companion to *Weird Tales*. Hamilton's hero Stuart Merrick is transported to Kaldar by an experimental machine. On Kaldar he experiences the standard adventure. The princess' name is Narna and monsters are giant spiders called Cosps.

The story appeared in the 1964 paperback anthology *Swordsmen in the Sky*. The sequels *Snake Men of Kaldar* and *Great Brain of Kaldar* were reprinted by two small pulp reprint houses; all three stories were collected by Haffner Press into one volume, a book that commands quite a high price today.

When Robert E. Howard reacted to his mother's death in 1936 by "blowing his silly head off" (the quote is from L. Sprague de Camp) he left a draft for a novel called *Almuric*. Although he never got to polish the story, it was published in 1939 in *Weird Tales* and reprinted as a paperback book in 1964. Howard's "John Carter" is a muscular malcontent named Esau Cairn who is sent across space by a device known as the Great Secret.

Esau Cairn fights against intelligent apelike beings and against Wieroolike flying men as he struggles upward through the barbaric social strata of Almuric to win the hand of *his* princess, Altha. The book is severely flawed, but it shows the great vigor and drive of all Howard's work, and it is most regrettable that he did not live to revise the manuscript.

Undoubtedly the mouldering pages of pulp magazines contain many more stories more or less indebted to *A Princess of Mars* for their content. Just one curious sample—the Don Hargreaves stories of Festus Pragnell. Nine of these stories appeared in *Amazing Stories* between 1938 and 1943. They are rather heavy-handed but still enjoyable spoofs of Barsoom, featuring a hero, Hargreaves, who discovers that the Martians are huge creatures weighing thousands of pounds apiece, but he marries the princess anyway. The stories carry such titles as *Warlords of Mars*, *Outlaw of Mars*, *Twisted Giant of Mars*, and finally *Madcap of Mars*.

Leigh Brackett (Mrs. Edmond Hamilton) wrote many fine pastiches of the Burroughs canon, adding considerable of her own talent to produce excellent stories. Most of these appeared in *Planet Stories* over a long period of time from the early 1940s on into the 1950s. Two excellent tales of this series, *People of the Talisman* and *The Secret of Sinharat* were reprinted as a "double" paperback in 1964.

Miss Brackett's hero, Eric John Stark, is a combination of John Carter and Tarzan, raised by wild apes on the planet Mercury and known as N'Chaka, the Man Without a Tribe. Other of her Martian tales were gathered in the Ace paperback *The Coming of the Terrans* in 1967. The Burroughs connection is limited but the book stands well in its own right.

Leigh Brackett's contribution to the Venusian canon, *The Moon that Vanished* (*Thrilling Wonder Stories*, October 1948; included in *Swordsmen in the Sky*, 1964) is probably better than anything by Burroughs, Kline, or Farley and set on that planet.

Lorelei of the Red Mist, a novelette by the unlikely team of Leigh Brackett and Ray Bradbury, first appeared in *Planet Stories* for Summer, 1946. Or perhaps the team is not so unlikely. Miss Brackett is an admirer of Burroughs, and Bradbury has been repeatedly quoted concerning Burroughs. In the December, 1964, issue of *Show* magazine he said, "When I was 12, I decided to become a writer. It was inevitable that my first 'book' should be a sequel to a Mars volume by Burroughs."

The story itself is a strange combination of Burroughs-type swordplay and gore, and misty, moody fantasy, and is well worth reading. It was included in the paperback anthologies *Three Times Infinity* (1958) and *The Best of Planet Stories* (1975). The hero of *Lorelei of the Red Mist* is named Conan!

With the recent revival of interest in Burroughs and Burroughs-type adventure, contemporary authors are beginning again to produce new material in the Burroughs vein. I have already mentioned Lin Carter's *The Wizard of Lemuria*. Another example is *Warrior of Llarn* by Gardner F. Fox, a paperback original, 1964. Alan Morgan, Earthman, is transported to Llarn in the classic manner. There he fights the customary odds and enemies, and wins the traditional princess, Tuarra. The book is neither remarkably good nor remarkably bad, but succeeded sufficiently to rate a sequel, *Thief of Llarn*.

And still the march of pseudo–John Carters continues unabated. Michael Resnick's Adam Thane (in *Goddess of Ganymede*) reaches that satellite by spaceship rather than astral projection, but his adventures upon arriving are much in the tradition of John Carter. Similarly, John Norman's (pseudonym of John Frederick Lange) Tarl Cabot reaches Gor, or counter-Earth, only to plunge into very familiar sequences with warring royal cities, captured princesses, assorted fates-worse-than-death, and necessary plot ingredients provided by gratuitous stupidity on the hero's part. Cabot's adventures began with *Tarnsman of Gor* (1966) and *Outlaw of Gor* (1967) and continued for many years thereafter. The series was (and still is, in some circles) quite popular, but also highly controversial; the author's liberal use of sex of a distinctly misogynistic bent rendered both himself and his books pariahs in the mainstream science fiction community. See Chaper XXI, "Forty More Years of Adventure" for further details.

Jack Vance in 1968 started *his* John Carter, Adam Reith, on still another odyssey, this one across Tschai, the *Planet of Adventure*. Beginning with *City of the Chasch* Vance gives the reader an enthralling grand tour of his colorful and decadent world, populated by multiple alien races and exotic human societies. As protagonist Reith is, for once, a man of some intelligence and sensitivity, and his adventures are a pleasant change from the stereotyped idiocies of so many pseudo–John Carters. All the books in this series (including *Servants of the Wankh*, *The Dirdir*, and *The Pnume*) have appeared in multiple editions, most recently in an omnibus volume.

An unfortunate example of stereotyped idiocy is Robert Moore William's John Zanthar, subject of a series of paperback originals beginning with *Zanthar of the Many Worlds* (1967) and *Zanthar at the Edge of Never* (1968). For a new thrill, try reversing the syllables of this fellow's name—shades of Howard Browne's Tharn!

Anne McCaffrey, in *Restoree* (1967), finally added a female "John Carter" to the long roster. Her heroine Sara is snatched out of New York's Central Park by a UFO and transported to the distant planet Lothar, where her adventures are largely in the standard Carterian pattern, varied only by the feminine viewpoint.

Because the inner world tradition is so much older and so much better established than the interplanetary romance, it is far more difficult to ascribe works to the Pellucidar series for their inspiration than it is to Barsoom.

The Pellucidar theme is after all a fusion of existing themes, that of the world underground, that of the inhabited inner-shell of the Earth, and that of the surviving primitive country. Works that reflect any one or any combination of these ideas *might* be connected with Burroughs' work, but I know of none that can at all definitely be considered offspring.

Frank R. Stockton's *The Great Stone of Sardis*, for instance, bears certain resemblances to *At the Earth's Core*. Stockton's Roland Clewe invents an "automatic shell" which:

> . . . the moment it encountered a solid surface or obstruction of any kind, its propelling power became increased. The rings which formed the cone on its forward end were pressed together, the electric motive power was increased in proportion to the pressure, and thus the greater the resistance to this projectile, the greater became its velocity and power of progression, and its onward course continued until its self-contained force had been exhausted.

Clewe intends to use his shell for such purposes as drilling railroad tunnels, but as was the case with Perry's mechanical prospector, the automatic shell goes wrong. It plunges straight down into the Earth for mile after mile. Clewe follows toward the center of the Earth, but instead of finding a lost world he finds a gigantic diamond, eight thousand miles in diameter, and from here on the story bears no further resemblance to any of Burroughs' inner world novels.

A case might be made for Stockton's having been inspired by Burroughs, except that *The Great Stone of Sardis* was published first in 1898; a decade and a half *before* the first Pellucidar story was written. If there was any influence of one author upon the other, it would have been exercised by Stockton upon Burroughs. Actually, I do not think this was the case. *The Great Stone of Sardis* is a warning that, as Professor Altrocchi wrote in 1944, "similarity does not necessarily imply derivation." With this principle in mind, then, here are a few of the stories published since *At the Earth's Core* that do resemble the Burroughs work, some of them suspiciously so.

Plutonia by Vladimir Obruchev is a Russian novel that was first published in 1924; it did not appear in English until 1957, when an edition was produced by Lawrence & Wishart. Plutonia is an inner world discovered by explorers from our own surface world. It is replete with mastodons and other prehistoric beasts, and it might well be attributed to *At the Earth's Core*. It might just as easily be attributed to *A Journey to the Center of the Earth*. Or, for that matter, *Five Thousand Miles Underground*. Obruchev, in a note appended to his novel, credits Verne as his inspiration. But . . . it is known that Burroughs was out of favor with the Soviet government in its early years (as indeed he remains to this day anathema to Communists), but well *in* favor with the Russian people. A bit of protective misdirection on Comrade Obruchev's part is understandable.

Drome by John Martin Leahy ran serially in *Weird Tales* in 1927 and was published in book form by Fantasy Publishing Company Inc., in 1952. Leahy's adventurers, Bill Carter and Milton Rhodes, find their way into Drome, a Pellucidar-like inner world, by following a crack in Mt. Rainier. After a long and difficult journey and a number of experiences with hideous monsters, they find a country suffering from the expected tyranny and intrigue.

The wicked priest Brendaldoombro is defeated and Rhodes marries the beautiful princess (of course!) Dorathusa, and "off went the happy pair in the queen's barge for Lella Nuramanistherom, a lovely royal seat some thirty miles down river."

Drome is a strong contestant for the title of worst imitation Burroughs story ever published (if, indeed, it was intended as imitation Burroughs), but the prize itself is carried off by *The Inner World* by A. Hyatt Verrill, a three-part serial that appeared in *Amazing Stories* (then under the editorship of T. O'Conner Sloan) in 1935. *The Inner World* has been left mercifully forgotten in the back-issue files for thirty years, and it seems a cruelty to dust it off however briefly, but in the interest of scholarship some pain must be borne.

Verrill's protagonist, Henry Marshall Thurlow, travels to *his* Inner World by means never revealed. In his own words:

> How I came here—is of little importance. In fact I can scarcely say myself—it was all too chaotic, too nightmarish an experience to describe lucidly, and, besides, I lost consciousness for a considerable period—I do not know for how long—so I actually do not know myself exactly what transpired. The all-important fact is that the interior of the Earth is hollow, that I am writing this within that vast cavity, and it *is* inhabited. But such inhabitants!

Thurlow never does very much inside the Earth except wander around exclaiming in wonderment at odd life-forms and enigmatic machinery; there is not a word of dialogue in his "manuscript," and the reader is likely to find himself losing consciousness for a considerable period, at the sheer boredom of the narration.

Stanton A. Coblentz's *Hidden World* (Bouregy, 1957; originally published as *In Caverns Below* in *Wonder Stories*, 1935) is a different matter. Two friends,

David Innes faces a labyrinthodon in Pellucidar

Comstock and Clay, wind up in an inner world as the result of a mine cave-in. They become separated, are captured by the forces of traditionally warring nations, Wu and Zu, and each rises to the absolute dictatorship of the country in which he finds himself.

For once the book is not an adventure story, but a multifaceted satire in which Coblentz takes on everything from militarism to cosmetic crazes, sometimes entertainingly but all too often with an all too heavy hand.

A curious variant on exploitation is the 1964 Lancer Books paperback edition of *The Secret People* by John Beynon Harris, who is better known under his pseudonym John Wyndham. *The Secret People* first appeared in the English magazine *The Passing Show* in 1935; it reached the North American continent the following year when it was reprinted in *The Toronto Weekly Star*, and was reprinted again in *Famous Fantastic Mysteries* magazines in the United States, in 1950.

On all three occasions the story was treated as a new story in its own right. Its theme is one of a lost race, this time a race of albino Negro dwarfs (!) living in a complex of great caverns beneath the Sahara Desert. Mark Sunnet and Margaret Lawn wander into this lost world and have to get out before the caves are inundated by the new sea which is being created in the Sahara.

Now let us look at the 1964 edition. First of all, the cover painting is by Frank Frazetta, an artist selected because of his association with recent Burroughs books. Second, the back cover bears a large red headline, *Rocket to the Earth's Core*. Third, the blurb writer describes the book as "Worthy of a place on the shelf beside the works of Edgar Rice Burroughs." If such deliberate slanting of sales appeal is not illegitimate (I do not think it is), it tells us considerable about the power of Burroughs on the science-fiction market.

Tales of a hollow Earth are almost unknown today, except for reprints of tales from the 1930s or older. Of all science-fictional themes the hollow, inhabited Earth is one most thoroughly rendered impossible by modern scientific thought. Oddly, while scientific impossibility has discouraged the use of the theme in fiction, it still has some appeal to "fact" writers of an extremely far-out variety.

Still in print, and only one example of pseudo-scientific cult books stretching back to Marshall B. Gardner's hoary *A Journey to the Earth's Interior*, is Dr. Raymond Bernard's *The Hollow Earth* (Fieldcrest). The general stripe of Dr. Bernard's pursuits is indicated by P. Schuyler Miller's brief description of "Dr. Bernard's complete works, forty-one volumes on geriatrics, fluoridation, sex control, yoga, the Dead Sea Scrolls, the 'real' Christ, theosophy, flying saucers, and what you will."

The closest thing to a new inner world novel I have come across in recent years is Philip José Farmer's *Inside Outside* (1964). This is a strange, almost surrealistic novel with overtones of fantasy as well as science fiction. The book is constructed in a single non-stop sequence, without chapters or other breaks. It is not a satisfying work, but is a fascinating experimental treatment of an old theme.

Except for Vincent Starrett's *Penelope* and Festus Pragnell's Don Hargreaves stories I have omitted reference to parodies of Burroughs. Humorous variations on Tarzan are innumerable, but most have been visual rather than textual—motion pictures, television spoofs, and cartoons. Two science-fiction parodies have been *The Blonde from Barsoom* by Robert F. Young (*Amazing Stories*, July, 1962) and *The Yes Men of Venus* by Ron Goulart (*Amazing Stories*, July, 1963). Of the two, the Young story is far the better, deftly and lightly handled. The Goulart, unfortunately, is bitter instead of wry, vicious instead of entertaining, and generally in bad taste. It is hard to imagine why it was published.

Not a parody but a curious variation on Burroughs is found in Alfred Coppel's *The Hills of Home* (*Future Science Fiction* magazine, 1956). Coppel's protagonist, Kimball, a future space explorer, loses his grasp of reality when he travels to Mars and thinks he has reached Barsoom. The story is delicately handled, and generally successful.

Similar references to Burroughs (oddly, always to Barsoom) are found in Frederic Brown's *The Lights in the Sky are Stars* (1953), Robert A. Heinlein's *Glory Road* (1963), and Fritz Leiber's *The Wanderer* (1964). Heinlein's hero "Scar" Gordon in particular comments as *his* beautiful princess (who turns out to be an empress) sleeps in her tent and Gordon sleeps on the ground outside:

> So I crawled back into my sleeping silks, like a proper hero (all muscles and no gonads, usually), and they sacked in too. She didn't put the light back on, so I had nothing to look at but the hurtling moons of Barsoom. I had fallen into a book.

An amusingly imaginative switch on Barsoom is A. Bertram Chandler's *The Alternate Martians* (Ace Books, 1965). Chandler postulates an alternate universe in which Mars is populated by both Burroughs' Barsoomian Tharks and H. G. Wells' slithering monsters. A spaceship from "our" future is warped into this alternate universe, and then the fun begins!

A final possible descendant of John Carter, suggested by Roger Lancelyn Green in *Into Other Worlds*, appears in *The Two Towers* by J. R. R. Tolkien. *The Two Towers* is part of Professor Tolkien's great trilogy *The Lord of the Rings* (George Allen and Unwin, 1954, 1955, 1956). Green suggests that "Shelob in *The Lord of the Rings* is so like the Siths of the Barsoomian caves that an unconscious borrowing seems probable."

I personally find Shelob, a huge anthropophagous spider who guards a tunnel, more closely analogous to the *apts* which guard the carrion caves of Okar in *The Warlord of Mars*. Queried as to the possible attribution, Professor Tolkien offers this gracious but not very helpful reply:

Source hunting is a great entertainment but I do not myself think it is particularly useful. I did read many of Edgar Rice Burroughs' earlier works, but I developed a dislike for his Tarzan even greater than my distaste for spiders. Spiders I had met long before Burroughs began to write, and I do not think he is in any way responsible for Shelob. At any rate I retain no memory of the Siths or the Apt.

CHAPTER XIX

A Basic Burroughs Library

As hitherto intimated, a curious aspect of the entire Burroughs phenomenon is the fact that literally millions of men and women are quite convinced that they know all about Burroughs when they know little or nothing about him. They "know" his works as the result of seeing Tarzan motion pictures, comic strips and comic books, or they know him through his reputation which is in turn based upon the adaptations of his works to various media.

Without actually having conducted a survey on the subject, it appears that many librarians and teachers actually ban Burroughs from their shelves and classrooms . . . purely on the basis of reputation or adaptations. At least some of these persons, hopefully, should be sufficiently open-minded to investigate an author whose works have sold well over one hundred million copies and nearly a century after their first publication. Certainly Burroughs' popularity cannot be passed off as a mere fad. Many an author has come and gone, having achieved either critical acceptance or public popularity, or both, only to pass from the scene in a few years, seldom to be read again.

More often than not, this season's best seller is forgotten by next season, and the "book of the year" gathers dust when another year brings another book. Why have Burroughs' works lasted as they have? Why do his characters, absurdly overblown as they are, still bring a thrill of identification to the reader? I hope that this book on Burroughs has done at least something to illuminate these questions, and to suggest answers. But it is a truism that reading ponies or reviews is no substitute for reading books, and the only way to gain a real grasp of what an author attempted, what he achieved and what he failed to achieve, is to read his works.

Like that of any prolific author, Burroughs' output is of uneven quality. Several of his books have already attained the status of classics, as serious literary commentators are beginning to acknowledge, having been beaten to the realization by the reading public by some four or five decades. Other Burroughs books make good, solid entertainment reading, a classification not to be sneered at, while still others range downward through only marginal value to a few complete fiascoes.

In this chapter I will offer a recommended reading list, or rather four recommended reading lists, collectively constituting a basic Burroughs library. The knowledgeable Burroughs devotee will undoubtedly have his own favorites which will very likely vary somewhat from my lists. I can only say in advance to any such protester that my recommendations are based upon my best judgment, and that what differences exist are inevitably due to variations in our respective reactions to the books. It is hardly a matter of anyone's being definitively right or wrong.

Certainly the *basic* basic Burroughs library must be a small one; I make it just one book, and there seems little question that that book must be *Tarzan of the Apes*. Far and away Burroughs' most famous and influential book, *Tarzan of the Apes* is the definitive volume concerning the Ape Man. It is the book that made Tarzan a household word around the world, that started the entire fantastic Tarzan syndrome.

It is a good book, portraying the character of Tarzan in his development from infancy to the melancholy creature, part man, part beast, that he was through his best fictional years. The book shows Burroughs' strong points and his failings, and this in itself is for the best, for the purpose of this reading list is not merely to show off Burroughs at his best, but to show off the most representative selection of his works possible in a limited number of books.

The strong points of *Tarzan of the Apes* are its sense of reader identification, the strong and effective characterization of the central figure, the strangely believable exotic setting, the great suspense and the surprisingly intricate plot. The weak points: the shallowness of many of the secondary characters, the unconvincing depiction of the non-exotic settings, an embarrassing over-reliance on coincidence to make the plot work, and an unfortunate touch of racism.

Tarzan of the Apes is a surprisingly literate work stylistically (despite the "several various sources" of the framing sequence), and although the elaborate grammatical constructions to which Burroughs was addicted are out of fashion today, any strangeness caused by the style of the book is quickly assimilated as the reader becomes absorbed in the fast-moving plot. To the

reader whose notion of Burroughs is based upon preconception and stereotype, *Tarzan of the Apes* is an astonishing book. It is the basic Burroughs
library.

If the reader investigating Burroughs is willing to carry his research to
two books, I would suggest that *Tarzan of the Apes* be supplemented by a
science-fiction book and, as Burroughs' Martian series is his most important
contribution to this field, the one science-fiction novel chosen should come
from this series.

It is difficult to recommend a single book from the Martian series. Most
of them are well done, full of color and exotic detail; it seems reasonable
that the one book selected should feature John Carter rather than one of
the secondary Barsoomian heroes, and not without hesitation I would again
pick the first book of the series, *A Princess of Mars*. This is the book in which
Burroughs introduces John Carter and fills in his remarkable, if enigmatic,
earthly background. It is also the book in which the history and geography
of Barsoom are first revealed.

The book is strong when it comes to the characterization of John Carter,
and for the establishment of an exotic environment. Unfortunately, as Burroughs' first work, it is often weak in that area where Burroughs was most
often at his strongest: pacing. The framing sequence, although it holds the
reader's interest, is likely a bit too long; John Carter, upon his arrival on
Barsoom, sits around with the Tharks for an excessive period of time before
very much happens. During this time expository material is presented in a
fashion too static to be completely acceptable in a work of the type of *A
Princess of Mars*.

Finally, the book does not contain a complete story, but is merely the
opening section of a single long story that also fills *The Gods of Mars* (probably the best single volume in the series) and *The Warlord of Mars*.

Still, within a limitation of two books, a basic Burroughs library ought
probably to consist of *Tarzan of the Apes* and *A Princess of Mars*.

To step to a third, and really much fuller representation of Burroughs'
works, let us look at a selection of six books. Again, the titles previously
selected are retained. The remaining four are chosen to provide a broader
sampling of the author's works.

For the third book in the set I would suggest the best of Burroughs'
westerns, *The War Chief*. Again a book of character above all else, *The War
Chief* is also strong in setting and atmosphere, high in suspense and excellent
in action. Its faults are those common to Burroughs' works, a certain sense

of the story's having been contrived rather than naturally developed, and a sentimentalism which is overdone by modern standards.

Fourth is *The Mucker*, particularly the first half of this book. In Billy Byrne it offers a fine hero. In its head-spinning pace it might stand as the archetype of the pulp adventure story. But most important to the reader seeking a broad view of Burroughs' works, it provides glimpses of a full spectrum of settings and themes. In a single book it is virtually a catalog of the pulps.

The second portion of *The Mucker* does not hold up to the level of the first, settling down for too many chapters into the pattern of a routine western, but the first part *can* stand alone, and alone it warrants a place in the basic Burroughs library.

Fifth, to return to science fiction, the best of Burroughs' non-series scientific romances is *The Moon Maid*. The pseudo-science of the opening portion coupled with the audacious narrative premise of Admiral Julian's pre-memory of future incarnations, make for a "sense of wonder" reaction dear to the science-fictionist's heart. The social extrapolation of the second and third parts of the books, the portrayal of the feudal and then the nomadic societies of the conquered Earth show new facets of Burroughs' skill. The book hardly has a flaw; if there is one it is the contrivance of the plot to keep the Julian and Orthis bloodlines pure, and the continued encounters of the two families throughout the book.

To complete the six-volume library, we return to the Tarzan series, for a later book. The best candidate is *Tarzan and the Ant Men*. In this novel Burroughs' powers of imagination were at their peak. The insights into the character of Tarzan (as a grandfather!), the fantastic societies which the Ape Man encounters, the satire that peppers the book, make *Tarzan and the Ant Men* the outstanding volume of the later Tarzan series.

Its pro-war philosophizing adds another dimension to the high adventure tale, much as we may abhor the sanguinary inclinations of the author at that particular point in his life, while the two visits of the Ape Man to the feminist society of the Alali provide another view of the social attitudes of Edgar Rice Burroughs.

A fourth, and larger, Burroughs library would consist of the six books previously named, plus another half dozen. For the seventh through twelfth volumes of the twelve-book Burroughs library, my nominations are the following:

At the Earth's Core. The first book of the Pellucidar series introduces the reader to Burroughs' Inner World adventures, and to David Innes, Abner Perry, Dian the Beautiful, that fine villain Hooja the Sly One, the sagoths and the mahars. It is probably the best of the Pellucidar books, although a strong case might be made for the second of the series, *Pellucidar*, as the best of the group. Still, for introductory purposes, it seems mandatory to stick with the first volume of the set, with a strong recommendation of *Pellucidar* if the reader finds *At the Earth's Core* worth following up.

Tales of Three Planets. This book offers a marvelous variety of Burroughs' science fiction. Its lead novel, *Beyond the Farthest Star*, brings us to his final interplanetary (and only extrasolar) setting, Poloda, where, through Tangor, Burroughs clearly exposes his revised attitude toward war: a mature and realistic comprehension of the grinding horror of war, replacing the schoolboy romanticism of earlier days. The second tale, *The Resurrection of Jimber-Jaw*, shows a very different, flippant, slick Burroughs. And the final tale, *The Wizard of Venus*, can serve as an introduction to the Amtorian series. It gives a good picture of the character of Carson Napier, and a typical exploit on Amtor.

The Girl from Hollywood. Actually one of Burroughs' poorest novels, this is still worth reading as an example of his rare and unsuccessful attempts at contemporary realism. He should have stuck to romance, and he usually did. *The Girl from Hollywood* does offer an interesting view of life on the Tarzana Ranch, and a curiously out-of-focus view of Burroughs himself in the fantasized role of Colonel Custer Pennington.

The Land that Time Forgot. I suspect that if any really violent protest is raised against my listing of recommended Burroughs reading, it will be that *The Land that Time Forgot* deserves a higher place than tenth. The virtues of the book are undeniable: driving narrative pace and power, startling scientific speculation, and a magnificently imaginative setting. But the book contains no really memorable characters, and there is an occasional lapse in even the necessarily strained believability of so outlandish a tale as to make acceptance of the book's premises more difficult than necessary. Really, Fort Dinosaur!

The Gods of Mars and *The Warlord of Mars* complete the dozen. A reader who has enjoyed *A Princess of Mars* will unquestionably wish to complete reading the trilogy. The latter books continue John Carter's odyssey as he ascends the steps of Barsoomian leadership to their very summit. The books are full of startling concepts and thrilling action.

The races and societies portrayed, the fauna, flora, history, geography, sociology, science, religion and all other details of the Barsoomian setting are filled in with magnificent strokes.

The basic Burroughs library, then, at levels of one, two, six and twelve books, consists of the following:

1. *Tarzan of the Apes*

2. *A Princess of Mars*

3. *The War Chief*
4. *The Mucker*
5. *The Moon Maid*
6. *Tarzan and the Ant Men*

7. *At the Earth's Core*
8. *Tales of Three Planets*
9. *The Girl from Hollywood*
10. *The Land that Time Forgot*
11. *The Gods of Mars*
12. *The Warlord of Mars*

Beyond these dozen books it is still possible to draw certain guidelines as to what is worth the time of a reader whose dedication to Burroughs is less pronounced than that which calls for reading all—or at least all available—works of the author in question. I offer a general recommended reading list of Burroughs stories beyond the top dozen; again, this is no list based upon authority, it is my personal recommendation.

In the Tarzan series, in addition to *Tarzan of the Apes* and *Tarzan and the Ant Men*, a number of others are worth reading. Certainly *The Return of Tarzan* provides an interesting contrast of the Ape Man in civilized and savage settings. In Paris he is utterly out of place, unbelievable and even ludicrous; as he returns closer and closer to his jungle home he becomes increasingly capable and increasingly credible.

The Eternal Lover is a fascinating book, although the appearance of Tarzan is a minor one. *Beasts* and *The Son of Tarzan* hold up well and the *Jungle Tales* are still delightful.

Of the later books, in which Tarzan visits lost city after lost city in one strange land after another, almost all are readable. The fault lies in their repetitiousness. *Tarzan the Untamed* is the best of these and its direct sequel, *Tarzan the Terrible*, is nearly as good. The final three Tarzan books are also of interest: *Castaways* and *Foreign Legion* in particular for their evidence of a new period in Burroughs' writing about Tarzan. *Tarzan and the Madman*, on the other hand, is the ultimate and could very well be taken as the archetypal tale of Tarzan in an African lost city.

In the Martian series, almost everything is good except that which is excellent. The first three books of this series are listed in the basic Burroughs library; the next five are all distinctly worthwhile. Only *Synthetic Men of Mars* is a thoroughly bad book.

The tenth book in the series, *Llana of Gathol*, is actually a collection of novelettes, all of them entertaining albeit trivial, and of particular interest because of the face-to-face interview between John Carter and Edgar Rice Burroughs. Finally, *John Carter of Mars* offers a curious contrast between ersatz (*Giant of Mars*) and genuine (*Skeleton Men*) Burroughs.

The Pellucidar series starts off tremendously and runs downhill for the next five books, recovering only partially in the seventh and final volume of the series. *At the Earth's Core* and *Pellucidar* are excellent novels, *Tanar* and *Tarzan at the Earth's Core* both have their good moments but do not hold up to their predecessors. *Back to the Stone Age* and *Land of Terror* are, unfortunately, simply bad and worse. And *Savage Pellucidar*, although a bit better, is of extremely spotty quality.

In the Venus series, I will have to admit that for all the virtues that can be found in the books, they just do not reach *me* as an individual reader. Whether it is the cloddish and incompetent Carson Napier as hero, so weak by contrast with Burroughs' other protagonists, or perhaps the fact that in the Venus books Burroughs was following another's lead instead of leading as was his more usual performance, the Amtor books lack the immense appeal of Burroughs' other three series.

As far as a recommendation is concerned, if the reader enjoys *The Wizard of Venus*, which is in the basic Burroughs library (in *Tales of Three Planets*), the obvious course is to go back to the beginning of the series, *Pirates of Venus*, and penetrate as far into it and the three succeeding volumes as his interest carries him.

Of the miscellaneous works not included in the basic library, I think at least three are of more than minimal interest.

The Monster Men is not really a good book at all, but it is a charming old creaker. Its combination of the Frankenstein and Tarzan motifs is, to my knowledge, unique, not only in Burroughs' works but in those of all Burroughs' predecessors and his imitators as well.

Apache Devil is a magnificent sequel to *The War Chief*. Its depiction of the last days of the Apaches is highly effective, and its ending of tragedy submerged beneath seeming happiness shows a subtlety in Burroughs not often suspected.

Finally, *Beyond Thirty*, while not strong as a story, shows Burroughs in a predictive mood which can only astound those of us who read it two World Wars after its creation (and an apparently total world change).

David Innes, a hydrophidian, Ja the Mezop

Of interest beyond the works of Burroughs are those books which served as inspirations and sources for Burroughs. Again, the only one for which evidence exists in Burroughs' own words is Mowgli; the others must remain a matter of inference. All the more reason, then, for anyone interested in Burroughs from a scholarly or historical viewpoint, to examine these books. A recommended selection are:

For *Tarzan of the Apes*   *The Jungle Books*, Rudyard Kipling
                           Captured by Apes, Harry Prentice

For *A Princess of Mars,*   *Lieut. Gullivar Jones: His Vacation,*
    The Gods of Mars,   *The Wonderful Adventures of Phra*
    The Warlord of Mars   *the Phoenician,* Edwin Lester Arnold

For *At the Earth's Core,*   *A Journey to the Centre of the Earth,*
    Tarzan at the Earth's   Jules Verne. *Five Thousand Miles*
    Core   *Underground,* Roy Rockwood

For *Tarzan and the Ant Men* *Gulliver's Travels,* Jonathan Swift

For *Pirates of Venus*   *The Planet of Peril,* Otis Adelbert Kline

Other possible sources are suggested in the two chapters of this book devoted to precursors of Burroughs' various works, and scattered elsewhere throughout the book. The works listed above include the most significant and the most likely sources.

Reference to Burroughs and his works is fairly common and has often been made by critics of considerable stature in similarly prestigious journals.[1] Men such as Edmund Fuller, Gore Vidal, and R. V. Cassill have commented at length on Burroughs. Their remarks and others have been carried by the *Manchester Guardian, Esquire* magazine, *The Wall Street Journal* (!), and the Sunday *Book Week* supplement carried by the *San Francisco Examiner* and *New York Herald-Tribune* among other papers.

Antiquarian Bookman, a highly respected specialty magazine, devoted its entire issue for November 25, 1963, to Burroughs. The issue was sold out, was reprinted (minus most of its advertising contents), and sold out again. Several of the science-fiction magazines (*Galaxy, Amazing Stories, Analog, The Magazine of Fantasy and Science Fiction*) have covered the Burroughs revival of the 1960s at some length.

Perhaps the oddest bit of Burroughsiana is William Brinkley's 1956 novel *Don't Go Near the Water.* The first chapter of the book is devoted to a visit (imaginary) by Edgar Rice Burroughs to the Pacific islands of Tulara and Gug-Gug (imaginary), and the efforts of naval public relations officers to wring publicity from this visit.

George P. Elliott's 1964 collection of essays *A Piece of Lettuce* contains *Getting Away from the Chickens,* an ingenious piece comparing Burroughs and (of all people!) Henry James.

Both *The Reader's Encyclopedia* and *The Reader's Encyclopedia of American*

---

1. See Chapter XXI, "Forty More Years of Adventure" for more information.

Literature devote space to Burroughs and to Tarzan. Both comment favorably, the latter adjudging Tarzan "one of the most popular folk heroes of the mid-20th century."

At least three other books have indicated a growing acceptance of Burroughs on the part of the academic community. The first was published in 1940, *The Magic of Literature* compiled by Robert H. Cowley. Subtitled "A Miscellany for Boys and Girls" this volume contains excerpts from the works of many authors, and includes slightly over one full chapter from *Tarzan of the Apes*.

In 1962 Oxford University Press issued an edition of *A Princess of Mars* in its "Stories Told and Retold" series. (The book is "retold"—mostly shortened—by A. M. Hadfield.) The "Stories Told and Retold" series is intended for classroom use, and includes such titles as *The Tale of the Bounty*, *Robinson Crusoe*, *David Copperfield*, *The Hound of the Baskervilles*, *Treasure Island*, *Stories from Shakespeare*, *The War of the Worlds*, *Beau Geste*, *Kenilworth*, *Scaramouche*, and *The Prisoner of Zenda*.

The Oxford *Princess* even contains a section of student "Exercises": *What was strange about Captain Carter when the author met him again after fifteen years? How many limbs had the green Martian? Did the army of Tharks find it easy to defeat the Zodangans outside Helium?* One can readily imagine school children, berated for years for wasting their time on trash like Burroughs, berated now for failing to do their reading assignment in Burroughs!

Most recently, James R. Kreuzer and Lee Cogan produced their *Literature for Composition*, a textbook for use in composition courses. The opening pages of *Tarzan of the Apes* are reprinted and an analysis of Burroughs is included as a student assignment.

Specialist publications devoted entirely to Burroughs have been fairly numerous, by far the outstanding item being Henry Heins' *A Golden Anniversary Bibliography of Edgar Rice Burroughs*. Issued in 1962 as a mimeographed, loose-leaf booklet, the Heins promptly went out of print. In 1964 a second edition, grown now to 418 pages, professionally printed and clothbound, appeared. The edition was limited to 1000 copies and again, promptly went out of print. Several Burroughs bibliographies have appeared both before Heins and after (most notably Dr. Robert Zeuschner's 1996 *Edgar Rice Burroughs: The Exhaustive Scholar's and Collector's Descriptive Bibliography*), but the *Golden Anniversary Bibliography* remains the definitive work of its type. It is indispensable to the serious Burroughs researcher. Donald Grant released a third edition in 2001 but priced such that it would only be available to the well-heeled collector.

In a number of places I have referred to fan publications, or "fanzines." Perhaps a little explanation of these is in order. Since the 1930s (if not before) a literary cult devoted to science fiction and associated fantasy has existed. The science-fiction fans are organized into innumerable clubs, local, regional and international in size, often overlapping and sometimes competing in function. They hold club meetings and regional conclaves frequently, and annually, under the auspices of the amorphous World Science Fiction Society, hold a "world" convention.

Aside from meetings and conventions, the major activity of science-fiction fandom is centered on the publication of innumerable magazines and a small but not inconsiderable number of books. Their magazines, "fanzines," range in quality from poorly written and crudely duplicated pamphlets to some journals written and illustrated at a very high level and reproduced by elaborate processes. The circulation of these publications is generally on the order of a few hundred; some have a circulation so small as to approach invisibility, others have reached a peak of somewhat over one thousand. The rise of the Internet ushered in the era of the webzine, which in theory can reach anyone with a computer and Internet access. Rather than killing off the print fanzine the Internet seems to have inspired aspiring editors to take up the old ways; even some defunct fanzines have been resurrected for a new generation.

Within the science-fiction cult a number of smaller special-interest groups have developed, devoted to such authors as H. P. Lovecraft, J. R. R. Tolkien, Robert E. Howard and, of immediate concern, Edgar Rice Burroughs. The "Burroughs Bibliophiles" have existed for several decades now. Stimulated by the boom in Burroughs publications since 1962 the membership of the organization mushroomed from a few hundred to well over a thousand; today the membership has subsided to more modest levels. The organization, as is typical of the broader science-fiction fandom of which it is an offspring, devotes itself to an annual meeting and an ambitious publishing program.

The main publication of the group is *The Burroughs Bulletin*, which began as an infrequent but elaborate journal edited by Vernell Coriell of Kansas City, Missouri. The contents of the *Bulletin*, typical of Burroughs fan publications, is devoted to such matters as scholarly research into Burroughs' works, scientific analyses of the pseudo-scientific content of Burroughs' stories, critical and historical treatment of Tarzan motion pictures, reprints of rare items of Burroughsiana, and amateur attempts at Burroughs illustration. Coriell passed away in 1987; George McWhorter of Louisville,

Kentucky, picked up the editorial mantle, transforming the *Bulletin* into a glossy quarterly publication.

A number of independent Burroughs journals have come and gone over the years, with such names as *The Jasoomian*, *ERBivore*, and *Burroughsiana*. The most prominent was the Hugo-Award-winning *ERB-dom*, edited by Camille Cazedessus, Jr. *ERB-dom* ceased publication in 1976, although "Caz" is now publishing *Pulp-dom*, which incorporates elements of his old fanzine. A list of current (2004) fanzines is appended to this book, for those who wish to take their Burroughs involvement to the next level.

CHAPTER XX

The Surprise in the Safe

In the years following Edgar Rice Burroughs' death, it was generally believed that there were no unpublished manuscripts in existence. As late as 1962 Heins stated unequivocally in the first edition of his bibliography that Burroughs had "left no backlog of completed manuscripts to be published posthumously."

The discovery of further manuscripts took place in 1963, when Hulbert Burroughs, John Coleman Burroughs, and Joan Burroughs Pierce assumed active direction of Edgar Rice Burroughs, Inc., upon the retirement of Burroughs' longtime general manager, Cyril Ralph Rothmund. Taking inventory of the contents of the office safe, believed to contain only those manuscripts returned by publishers after they had been typeset, the three surviving members of the family were astonished to find, mixed in with these, a large number of unfamiliar manuscripts.

These manuscripts, representing over 500,000 words in unpublished Burroughs material, had lain forgotten for thirteen years since their author's death. A number of them have since been published. These are the novelette *Savage Pellucidar* (the final portion of the novel bearing the same name), *Tangor Returns* (the second half of *Beyond the Farthest Star* in *Tales of Three Planets*), *The Wizard of Venus* (also in *Tales of Three Planets*), and *Tarzan and the Madman*. Also, the original manuscript version of *Skeleton Men of Jupiter*, containing a foreword omitted from the *Amazing Stories* version, was used in the book edition, *John Carter of Mars*, and the radically different manuscript version of *Tarzan and the Castaways* appears in the book of that title, in lieu of the *Argosy* magazine version published as *The Quest of Tarzan*.

As editor for Canaveral Press during the years when its Burroughs first editions appeared, it was my privilege to examine these manuscripts prior to their publication, and to assemble the two collections of Burroughs' shorter science-fiction works, *John Carter of Mars* and *Tales of Three Planets*, as well as *Tarzan and the Castaways*. In all cases of varying texts, most particularly that of *Tarzan and the Castaways* and *The Quest of Tarzan*, the manuscript version rather than the magazine version was used.

During the same period I had the opportunity to examine many, although not all, of the remaining unpublished manuscripts. Some are obviously experiments on Burroughs' part, and some of these are obviously unsuccessful. Except for the reasons of scholarly interest it would probably be best for these to remain unpublished. One *The Scientists Revolt* is enough blot on an author's record.

A fervent wish of mine was fulfilled in 1967 with the publication of Burroughs' 1941 manuscript *I Am a Barbarian*. This lightly fictionalized biography of the emperor Caligula, as told by the slave Britannicus, is a radical departure in style and attitude from any other work of Burroughs. In my opinion it is an excellent work, one of his best, and deserving of wide attention.

Unfortunately it was published only in a high-priced, limited edition by Edgar Rice Burroughs, Inc. (their first book in nearly twenty years). To all available information it was not promoted at all. Reviews or other notices have been non-existent. It is most unfortunate; Ace Books eventually released a paperback edition, although that too created little stir beyond the devoted.

A survey of some of Edgar Rice Burroughs' unpublished manuscripts follows. I will restrict this list to those stories which I have personally read in manuscript form, omitting those, such as Burroughs' early autobiography and *Marcia of the Doorstep* (a novel), concerning which I lack first-hand information. The date following each title is that indicated in Burroughs' working notebook as the year in which the story was written:

Pirate Blood (1932). This curious novelette consists of an introduction and two distinct sequences of adventure. In the introduction the hero, Johnny Lafitte, is introduced as a high school athlete, the second best quarterback on the Glenora team. After graduation he becomes a motorcycle policeman instead of going on to college.

The first half of the main adventure arises from Johnny's duties as a policeman. A boyhood chum of his, Billy Perry, has embezzled "nearly a million in negotiable securities, gold and currency" from the bank where he works, and Lafitte is ordered to arrest him. Perry tries to escape in a "tiny little blimp," and in the scuffle he and Lafitte wind up floating across the Pacific in the craft. They suffer terribly as their supplies run short; Perry goes mad and leaps into the sea. Lafitte survives until the blimp comes to rest in the western Pacific, where he is picked up by a crew of modern-day pirates.

The remainder of the tale is given over to Lafitte's adventures with the pirates of the region, playing off two rival leaders, The Portuguese and the Vulture, against each other and to his, Johnny's, benefit. The story is a lurid one, full of Burroughs' typical action and bloodshed:

> A bullet whizzed by my ear as I ran aft. It came from the rifle of the fellow behind the foremast, and before he could duck back out of sight I dropped him. Now, the others fell back. It was a mixed crew: a Negro, a Chinaman, a couple of half-breeds, and two Malays, as nearly as I could judge; these were what was left.
>
> The Negro was the first to throw down his gun. As he did so he shoved his hands above his head; then the others followed his example. It didn't help them any. The only result was to save us a little ammunition. Those sweet babies behind me just shoved their guns into their belts and drew their krises; the rest was merely butchery. When they were through the deck was a shambles. Then I ordered them to search the schooner.

By no means one of Burroughs' top works, *Pirate Blood* does hold up fairly well; Ace Books issued the story in 1970, coupled with *Wizard of Venus*.

Murder: A Collection of Short Murder Mystery Puzzles (1932–1935). These stories are actually more puzzle than narrative, as Inspector Muldoon and the narrator visit the scenes of various crimes, question witnesses, and invariably come up with the correct identification of the guilty party. Regarding Muldoon we are told that:

> His technique in solving crimes is usually based on his ability to carry a complicated array of figures in his mind and to correlate them instantly and accurately, but he is equally adept in sifting other evidence.
>
> His questioning of suspects is such as to throw them entirely off their guard, as they cannot dream that a question concerning the age of Aunt Matilda when little Junior was born could possibly have any bearing on the guilt or innocence of the suspect . . .

Unfortunately, neither can the reader. The puzzles must be placed in the "unsuccessful experiment" category, although several of them were published in *Rob Wagner's Script*, a West Coast magazine of the mid-1930s.

Mr. Doak Flies South (1937–1938). Although still interesting reading for the dedicated Burroughs fan or the scholar, this novelette has been passed by the times. The general theme is the Grand Hotel—a varied group of characters brought together under stress, to interact for the exposure of their characters. The mechanism is the hijacking of a transcontinental airliner, a "Douglas Skysleeper."

The hero, Jerry Hudson, and the heroine, Larry Maxton, find themselves prisoners of a group of gangsters hiding out in an isolated area in Mexico, to which the airliner has been diverted. In addition to escaping from the criminals and bringing the latter to justice, the two young people must work out a romantic problem. Their respective fathers are trying to marry them off to each other, and the couple must somehow balance their automatic resistance to the contrived match against the fact that they are attracted strongly to each other.

Angel's Serenade (1939). Although not completed until 1939, this novelette is based on material Burroughs wrote as early as 1921, and the earlier date is more in keeping with the general feeling and tone of the story than is the later one. *Angel's Serenade* is the story of "Dickie-darling" Crode, an unfortunate orphan of the Chicago slums, who goes from the streets to an orphanage to the underworld. All his life Dick yearns for respectability, but all his success as a gang lord fails to bring him what he wants, and he ends his own life.

The Strange Adventure of Mr. Dinnwiddie (1940). This is an innocuous little tale of Mr. Abner Dinnwiddie of Utropolis, Kansas. All his life Abner was a little nobody; when his domineering wife Sarah died Abner booked passage for a Pacific cruise on the *Lusonia*.

On the same cruise Admiral Arnold Dinnwoodie was booked, but cancelled at the last minute. A Mata Hari type spy assigned to ferret secrets from the admiral mistakes Mr. Dinnwiddie for her prey, and the resulting comedy is fairly obvious.

Uncle Miner and Other Relatives. Although this manuscript is undated, references in it mark it clearly as of World War II vintage. It is the biggest surprise of the group, a disconnected, even surrealistic comic montage. Again, the manuscript has been read by a number of persons, and repeatedly their reaction was to compare it with Joseph Heller's *Catch-22*.

The manuscript is full of topical references: Wendell Wilkie, the Los Angeles subway, the O.P.A., Salvador Dali. The characters in the manuscript are the members of the mad Peaberry family, and the lunatic goings-on are totally indescribable.

Uncle Bill (1944). A very short story of murder and mystery, with a "surprise" ending that is telegraphed far in advance. Very bad.

The Avenger. Also undated, this is definitely one of Burroughs' earliest works, bearing a Chicago address for the author. (He moved his family to California in 1919). *The Avenger* of the title is a jealous husband who commits murder in the mistaken belief that he is attacking the secret lover of his wife who, of course, has no secret lover. Again, a very bad work.

Night of Terror. Also undated, this novelette can be placed in time by its references to Hitler, Eleanor (Roosevelt), the Greater Southeast Asia Co-Prosperity Sphere, and "this war," as no earlier than 1939. The story is cast in classic mold as two young lovers, Bill Loveridge and Shandy Mason, caught by a March thunderstorm near Duluth, Minnesota, seek shelter in an apparently abandoned mansion.

They find the inevitable corpse, but before the mystery of the death of the old man whose body it is can be unraveled, the plot is complicated by the arrival of a busload of patients from a nearby madhouse. Out for an airing, they too had been caught in the storm when their bus broke down, and now they seek shelter in the mansion. Soon a steady flow of corpses begins as the patients meet with violent death, one by one. "Ten little Indians" fashion, the murders continue until only Bill and Shandy remain, leading to a surprise denouement. As long as any possibility whatever exists of the publication of *Night of Terror* it would be grossly improper to reveal the outcome of the story.

There are few other major items among the known unpublished Burroughs works. The longest is *Marcia of the Doorstep*, a 125,000 word realistic novel. *More Fun! More People Killed!* is a 20,000 word parody of the hardboiled detective story.

Perhaps the most intriguing title is *Minidoka 937th Earl of One Mile Series M*. Although not yet released by the Burroughs family, this holograph is believed to antedate *A Princess of Mars*. Hulbert Burroughs indicates doubt that his father was the author of *Minidoka*, suggesting that ERB had heard the story, possibly from another member of the Burroughs family, and had written it down.

The story is reported to be of poor quality, but from a scholarly viewpoint, it will make fascinating reading, if and when it is released.[1]

Other known manuscripts are for the most part minor in nature. The existence of a second cache of unpublished material is doubtful but not

---

1. The story was finally published in 1998; see Chapter XXI, "Forty More Years of Adventure" for further details.

wholly inconceivable. The 1963 discovery was a distinct surprise, and a sequel would be no greater surprise than was the first discovery.

It seems unlikely that the publication of further Burroughs manuscripts will materially alter his standing. The first editions of recent years, *Beyond Thirty* and *The Man-Eater, Savage Pellucidar, Tarzan and the Madman, Tarzan and the Castaways, Tales of Three Planets, John Carter of Mars, The Girl from Farris', The Efficiency Expert,* and *I Am A Barbarian,* have neither shaken the faithful nor converted the heathen. Such autobiographical material as exists may well provide further insights into the man's character. But the available Burroughs canon is quite extensive and varied enough to provide the basis for understanding and judgment of the man.

The Burroughs "explosion" of 1962 through 1968 has seen almost 100 different hardbound and paperback editions of Burroughs books appear in United States, Canadian, and British editions. The huge press runs of the paperback houses in particular have totaled to roughly *fifty million* copies, more than all copies of all editions of Burroughs' works in the entire preceding forty-eight years since the first book edition of *Tarzan of the Apes.*

But this sort of popularity is hardly to be regarded as permanent. As Sam Moskowitz pointed out at a science-fiction symposium in the spring of 1963, the Burroughs "explosion" of the 1960s was an unnatural phenomenon, the outgrowth of a similarly unnatural, *de facto* suppression of Burroughs' works in the preceding decade or more.

The last major reprinting of Burroughs books had been done by Edgar Rice Burroughs, Inc., in the late 1940s. Following ERB's death in 1950 the Burroughs editions became more and more difficult to obtain. A warehouse fire in 1958 further depleted the remaining stock of books, and after this it was all but impossible to obtain Burroughs editions. A few Tarzan titles were maintained by Grosset & Dunlap, but, beyond these, Burroughs books were strictly a matter for the out-of-print and rare-book dealers. Paperbacks were all but unknown.

During this period the demand for Burroughs material became unnaturally pent up. Prices for out-of-print ERB material soared. Such titles as *Land of Terror, The Lad and the Lion, The Deputy Sheriff of Comanche County,* and the Tarzan twins books were quoted at prices up to $65 per copy.[2]

Once the floodgates were opened in 1962, editions poured forth at a furious pace. In the United States, Ace, Ballantine, Canaveral and Dover published simultaneously; Grosset maintained its titles. In Britain Four

---

2. Obviously 2005 prices will be substantially higher.

Square paperbacks issued dozens of Tarzan, Mars and Venus books. The demand for Burroughs has now largely been met, and the huge flow of editions has already slacked off. It may be hoped, however, that the tens of millions of books now in circulation, plus a smaller but continuing trickle of reprints in future years will keep Burroughs available, and that the famine of the 50s will not recur.

Certainly as the increased availability of Burroughs material has brought new readers in recent years, the ancillary activities which result will continue in the future. One example is the increase in scholarly and critical material dealing with Burroughs: articles in the general press, the Heins bibliography, the Burroughs fan press, etc.

In 1967 Prentice-Hall published *The Big Swingers* by Robert W. Fenton. An attempted biography of Burroughs (coupled with a review of the "career" of Tarzan in print and on screen), the Fenton book proved a major disappointment. Not so much inaccurate as it is shallow and incomplete, the book offers few facts if any which were not already thoroughly familiar and readily available from such sources as the fan-written biographical pamphlet *The Master of Adventure* by John Harwood. Burroughs is not made by Fenton to live, to breathe, to assume any dimension of sympathy or reality.

Regarding the "business" side of the Burroughs phenomenon, Fenton's treatment of the long-simmering "out-of-print" and "out-of-copyright" situation smacks of such caution, such pussyfooting around the real issues, that one must conclude that he yielded to extreme pressure from Edgar Rice Burroughs, Inc., to produce only an "official" version of the affair.

Why the long Burroughs drought? Why the sudden rush of the 1960s? Why the mishandling of the release of reprint rights, so that several editions of the same title were in print simultaneously from different publishers to the detriment of all? Why the worse botching of the release of first edition material?

These are the real issues of the Burroughs revival, and of these, Fenton says nothing.

The tragedy of the matter is that there is likely room for only one book of the type of *The Big Swingers*, and the Fenton book neatly co-opts that space. The existence of this very bad book may well preclude the publication of the *good* one that is needed for many years to come.

Scholarly inquiries into Burroughs' life and works continue. In the area of sources, while all of those cited or suggested in the present volume may not have served as direct inspiration for ERB, many of them seem to have influenced him, and more remain to be found. H. Rider Haggard and Andrew Lang's 1890 *The World's Desire*, for instance, contains two incidents suspiciously resembling occurrences in *Tarzan the Untamed*. Much work remains to be done in the works of Haggard, Kipling and other authors of their period.

Meanwhile a resident of Idaho Falls, Mr. Dale R. Broadhurst, has taken a different tack in his Burroughs research. Going beyond ERB's works, Broadhurst has retraced Burroughs' steps, back to the days of 1898 when Burroughs was a storekeeper in Pocatello, Idaho. Scrutinizing the microfilm records of the present-day *Idaho State Journal*, then the *Pocatello Tribune*, Broadhurst found a series of advertisements placed by Burroughs and presumably written by him. According to Broadhurst, "Burroughs advertised in August of 1898 that he could supply readers in Pocatello with any periodical from America or elsewhere." Broadhurst quotes another of Burroughs' *Pocatello Tribune* ads:

. . . new novels and magazines every day at Burroughs' . . .

Of Edwin Lester Arnold's books, for instance, 1898 would have been too early for *Lepidus* or *Gullivar Jones* but would have been in plenty of time for *Phra* or *The Constable* or *Ulla*, the reading of which might have whetted ERB's appetite for later books by the same author. By 1898 Burroughs might have stocked—and read—Haggard, Kipling, Swift, Verne, Wells, Harry Prentice, Helena Blavatsky. . . . Much sleuthing has been done since *Master of Adventure* was first printed, and much remains to be done. I for one look forward to further digging by the likes of Dale Broadhurst as well as those who pick up the baton from the previous generation of Burroughs scholars like Heins, Coriell and Cazedessus.

Regarding the final standing of Edgar Rice Burroughs in American letters, the obvious closing remark for this book would be, "Only time will tell." But more than ninety years have passed since the publication of *A Princess of Mars* and *Tarzan of the Apes* in *The All-Story*, and time is already beginning to tell. Burroughs' popularity with the reading public remains high. His science-fiction stories continue to be read in their own right, and to influence the works of today's authors. The fact that Pellucidar was a known absurdity when ERB "created" it, that the astronauts and cosmonauts of the coming decades will almost certainly show ERB's versions of Vanah, Barsoom and Amtor to be similar absurdities, will not destroy the appeal of the tales set there, for Burroughs' Mars is no more the real, astronomical Mars than is Tarzan's Africa the real Africa of Ian Smith, Jomo Kenyatta and Gamal Abdel Nasser.

The fantastic worlds of Edgar Rice Burroughs are never-never lands, dream worlds where virtue and courage win honor and beauty, where evil can be identified and confronted, and despite all odds defeated. If the worlds of Burroughs provide mere adolescent wish-fulfillment, perhaps we can use a little less sophistication and a little more of the virtue and courage ERB espoused.

In the broader view of imaginative fiction—science fiction, fantasy, "sword and sorcery," and so on—one asks whether the total influence of Burroughs will ultimately prove to be beneficial, or the opposite. Surely there are many thousands, perhaps millions of readers who are attracted by the color and pace of adventure literature. That these readers, many of them young, are amused and gratified by their contact with Burroughs and the myriad others both within and beyond the "Burroughs school" is probably a good thing, or at least innocuous. To read Burroughs, Edmond Hamilton, Edward E. Smith, John Norman, Robert E. Howard, Fritz Leiber (in his light moods), Michael Moorcock (in *his* light moods), and the endless others, is certainly no worse and probably much better than spending endless hours before a flickering television screen.

All the better if the Burroughs reader grows to an appreciation of science fiction and fantasy writers of more serious intent, of Heinlein, Bradbury, Clarke, Blish, Asimov, Bester, and the many others who have led their field over the years, of C. S. Lewis, of Tolkien, and of the glowing talents of Delany, Zelazny, Thomas M. Disch.[3] The waste is seen in the stunted mentalities who see Burroughs and the "Burroughs school" as the be-all and end-all, the pinnacle of development of imaginative fiction. Imagine otherwise normally intelligent persons regarding Tarzan as great literature—it is an absurdity at which Edgar Rice Burroughs would have been the first to laugh! This phenomenon, more than any chance of Burroughs' works being forgotten, is the potential tragedy of the case.

And in the end it is the appeal of Burroughs' heroes, most obviously of Tarzan, that will endure. Only three fictional heroes of the past have so gripped the English-speaking world: Conan Doyle's Sherlock Holmes, Edgar Rice Burroughs' Tarzan, and Siegel and Shuster's Superman.

All are supermen, each in his own way. Each possesses an immense appeal, this appeal very likely accounting for their popularity and durability. Each has a chance for immortality of a sort.

But Siegel and Shuster's Kryptonian refugee, "Clark Kent," the tight-suited and monogrammed Superman of the comics, will likely fall victim to McLuhan's now-famous dictum, "The medium is the message." The

3. In the twenty-first century new and exciting talents should be added such as Nancy Kress, China Miéville, William Gibson, Andy Duncan, Paul di Filippo, James Patrick Kelly, and Kage Baker. The field shows continuing vigor and the current crop of leading authors is an outstanding one.

medium in this case is the comic magazine, and the message is "This is kid stuff." So it must be, so it is ordained by publishers and editors, and so Superman seems consigned to juvenile readership and juvenile quality forever. A second problem here: with the removal of the original creators very early in the game, Superman has ever since been a committee production, with the inevitable vitiating effects of committee control over the creative act.

Sherlock Holmes is another matter. Beneath the seeming cold and remote *persona* of the great detective there is a charmingly real and appealing personality, a fact recognized by millions of *devotees* over the decades. The appeal of Conan Doyle's creation overpowered the author himself, it has survived translation, adaptation, and years of mismanagement by the author's survivors remarkably paralleling the Burroughs case.

But there is yet one major element in the Holmes mythos, a factor contributing both the appeal of the stories, and to the limitation of that same appeal. For in the Sherlock Holmes stories there is a focusing of time and space. The reader comes to feel at home in Victorian London although he has never passed within thousands of miles of the Thames. Speaking of Holmes and Watson, Vincent Starrett has written " . . . they still live for all that love them well: in a romantic chamber of the heart, in a nostalgic country of the mind, where it is always 1895."

And so it is—always 1895. Starrett, incidentally, knew and liked Burroughs during the latter's Chicago years. A number of amusing Burroughsian anecdotes appear in Starrett's 1965 autobiography, *Born in a Bookshop*.

Starrett would not say that for Tarzan it was always 1888—or 1915—or 1944—for all that internal evidence in the Tarzan books makes it possible to assign these or many other dates to various occurrences that appear in the canon. On the contrary, a major point of the appeal of much of Burroughs' work is the timelessness of the narration, the sense that the events described could be taking place any time, now, or better yet in some never-never world where time is not a relevant consideration.

This sense of timelessness raises Tarzan above the clutches of time. Of the three great supermen of modern fiction, perhaps he has the best chance of all to live forever.

CHAPTER XXI

Forty More Years of Adventure

Phillip R. Burger

Dyed-in-the-wool Edgar Rice Burroughs fans still drag the name of poor Edwin Lester Arnold through the mud.

Richard Lupoff's theory of a possible Arnold-Burroughs connection still provokes discussion, if not downright antagonism, within the Burroughs fan community forty years after it was first proposed. Come to think of it, Lupoff's name gets dragged through the mud almost as often as Arnold's because of the sheer audacity of the idea. Burroughs inspired by an obscure Victorian scribbler? Unthinkable! That fans continue to argue over the merits of this theory only highlights the value of Richard Lupoff's book four decades after it first saw print. Either that or those dyed-in-the-wool Burroughs fans can really hold a grudge. Maybe it's a little of both.

I was offered the rather daunting task of filling in those four decades as an addendum to Mr. Lupoff's now-classic study. I first found this book in 1973 when I was thirteen years old, not too long after I had stumbled across Burroughs' works in recent paperback reprints. I'm happy to say that for any thirteen-year-old discovering Burroughs today, Lupoff's study still serves as a marvelous guide to all the wonderful (and the few not-so-wonderful) outpourings of Burroughs' fertile mind. Lupoff claimed that he sought to trace "a middle ground between uncritical admiration and unfair condemnation of Burroughs," a path I will try to follow too. If the "dedicated Burroughs idolator" does not agree with Lupoff's approach, then he or she won't agree with mine. But that's OK, as there is room in the Burroughs doghouse for us both.

Before continuing, I feel I must step up to the plate for the much-maligned Edwin Lester Arnold. In his introduction to the old Ace Books reissue of *Lieut. Gullivar Jones* (inaccurately retitled *Gulliver of Mars*), Lupoff wondered "how a copy of *Gullivar Jones* found its way from England to America. . . . The book never had an American edition before now." That may be true, but as for a mysterious British book turning up in America, there are a couple likely explanations. The Chicago Public Library is one obvious source. When the main library was built following the Great Fire of 1871, it was stocked with books donated from England. The English continued to donate books for many years, as British fiction was popular with Chicago readers.

Another possible source was Chicago's famed Booksellers Row, the merchants of which stocked British imports. One of these shops was McClurg's, whose publishing arm would in time issue Burroughs' stories in hardcovers. If Burroughs' career was inspired by a book he had picked up from the shop of the publisher that would publish *his* books, we would have a coincidence dear to the Burroughs reader's heart.[1]

Now, this in no way constitutes "proof" that Burroughs had read *Gullivar Jones*; it merely shows that the novel was likely available in the Chicago of Burroughs' time. Many in the anti-Arnold camp have offered alternative sources, one of which, Gustavus W. Pope's *Journey to Mars* (1894), involves multicolored, sword-swinging Martians battling across a dying landscape. But the "proof" of influence is identical to Lupoff's claims for Arnold, hence neither better nor worse. Besides, this anti-Arnold theory still suggests that Burroughs borrowed ideas from others, the heretical notion for which Lupoff continues to be vilified.[2]

Barring the discovery of a long-lost letter or diary wherein Burroughs reveals his early reading habits, we must regretfully realize that source hunting like this is just an entertaining pastime, albeit one that keeps the antiquarian book dealers happy. By the way, Burroughs *did* own a copy of Arnold's *Phra the Phoenician* (this according to an inventory list of Burroughs' personal library), but the book itself is nowhere to be found. Perhaps it is sitting in a storage locker somewhere near Tarzana in California's San Fernando Valley, along with many of Burroughs' papers, all slowly being consumed by heat, rats, and termites.[3] Danton Burroughs, son of John Coleman Burroughs and grandson of Edgar, has been heroically trying to preserve the vast accumulation of the family legacy, but as the elder Burroughses were world-class packrats both, the amount of material is overwhelming. Despite Danton's best efforts, history is being lost to the balmy climate of paradise.

But Edgar Rice Burroughs still lives! Richard Lupoff predicted "from the vantage point of 1965" that Burroughs would achieve some form of literary permanence. From our vantage point we can say that he has, although of a diminished nature. Burroughs is no longer the ubiquitous presence on bookstore shelves that he once was, and slapping the Tarzan name on a product no longer guarantees good sales. But the reissue of Lupoff's book indicates that the old boy has not passed into literary oblivion just yet. The task at hand is to chart the up-and-down history of Burroughs and his readers over the last four decades. This will not be an exhaustive survey, by any means, and I will probably miss a lot. Plenty of Burroughs fans will inform me of my oversights and how wrong I am with my conclusions. With luck I have forty years of mud-dragging to look forward to.

The year 1975 represented a good time to be a Burroughs reader. This was the year of Burroughs' centenary, and the world press was paying appropriate attention. Ace Books had reissued its Burroughs titles a couple years previous, many with stunning new Frank Frazetta art, while also reprinting some of Burroughs' scarcest novels. (Ballantine would reissue the Tarzan books with Neal Adams and Boris Vallejo covers in just a few years, appealing to a new generation of readers.) Fans were merrily producing fanzines and attending conventions. Irwin Porges published his massive eight-hundred-page Burroughs biography. A British film adaptation of *The Land that Time Forgot* was released stateside that year. (While hardly the greatest cinematic triumph, it had the virtue of being produced by people who realized that since they could afford only bad special effects, they should then have *lots* of them.) Rumors abounded that Hollywood would produce a big-budget Tarzan movie. (It was not until 1984 that the resultant film, *Greystoke: The Legend of Tarzan, Lord of the Apes,* finally hit the theatres.) Any kid with a little spending cash could buy several cheap paperbacks at the local bookstore or newsstand; one could amass a sizeable Burroughs collection for very little money.

We are now in a new century, and the bookstore and newsstand are decidedly different places. Now one can find only a few Mars and Tarzan titles in mass-market paperback format in the better-stocked bookstores. (Forget the newsstand and the drugstore paperback rack, which is where I first found Burroughs.) Burroughs fanzines continue to be produced, but the number of fans moved to write about their favorite author—or moved even to subscribe—is shrinking. Burroughs conventions continue to be held, but many of the participants—and the number of participants is small—are of an increasingly advanced age. New Burroughs titles continue to be produced but mainly for the narrow collector's market. The great "Burroughs Boom" has long since passed, a casualty of changing tastes of both readers and editors as well as a reflection of a sea change in the publishing field as a whole. The science fiction genre has matured greatly since Burroughs' day, and what with charges of racism, sexism, and any other *-ism* you can think of, Burroughs would seem hopelessly outdated.

Of course, similar assessments were made of Burroughs in the early 1960s, and then along came the Burroughs Boom. Rasputin-like, Burroughs hangs on for dear life. His books do still appear in one format or another, and Hollywood continues to show an interest in Burroughs' properties, with (at the time of writing) big-budget adaptations of *A Princess of Mars* and *Tarzan of the Apes* in the works. Hollywood has probably dished out more bad Burroughs than good, but even so Burroughs the author continues to attract new readers. The Internet has added a new and still developing chapter to the ongoing saga. Best then to see what has come out under the Burroughs name since last Richard Lupoff assessed the field.

On the attractive letterhead of Edgar Rice Burroughs, Inc., beneath Roy Krenkel's sketch of Tarzan and the Golden Lion, are listed ninety-five works by the company's founder. Most of these have appeared in one form or another over the years, and with four decades of paperback reprints stuffing the nation's used bookstores there is a lot of Burroughs to be had. (Prepare yourself for sticker shock on a few titles though: back in the 1950s a hardcover copy of *Deputy Sheriff of Commanche County* would set you back sixty-five dollars, whereas today you might have to pay that much for a *paperback*.) The truly serious Burroughs fan can even find "Beware!" and "The Scientists Revolt," both salvaged by *The Burroughs Bulletin*. I don't recommend anyone making the effort unless you really must read *everything* written by Burroughs.

When Ace Books issued "Pirate Blood" (coupled with "Wizard of Venus") as a paperback original in 1970, the book represented the last of what we could call Burroughs' commercial fiction. That left twenty-four items on the letterhead unpublished. As detailed by Lupoff in chapter 20, many of the remaining items in the safe at Edgar Rice Burroughs, Inc., consisted of experiments and esoterica, stories that would appeal to the serious Burroughs devotee but no one else. Perhaps surprisingly then, the past few years have seen a smattering of new Burroughs titles appear, as some daring publishers have persuaded Edgar Rice Burroughs, Inc., to raid the safe and whittle down the list of unpublished items. Even some works not noted on the letterhead might see the light of day before too long. This activity hardly constitutes a new "Burroughs Boom"; nonetheless, there is enough being published that Edgar Rice Burroughs, Inc., may be forced to amend its letterhead.

The awkwardly titled *Minidoka 937th Earl of One Mile Series M* (1998) is supposedly Burroughs' earliest lengthy work, written during his sojourn on his brothers' gold dredge in Idaho sometime between the years 1901 and

1904. Burroughs had entertained his nieces and nephews (and later his own children) with fantastic bedtime stories; *Minidoka* may have arisen out of this family ritual. During that time Burroughs had also written and illustrated small books of poetry for his brothers' children, the first efforts of a creative mind trying to find its way. Being an expression of a family storytelling tradition, *Minidoka* has been presented to a modern audience as a children's book: an oversized, slender hardback with whimsical illustrations and the admonition "This book is meant to be read aloud." I do not know of any Burroughs fans who have read this story aloud to their children, but I would like to see their reaction. One can get a sense of an earlier generation's educational level when a phrase like "the crowd yelled itself into pulmonic solidification" is found in a book geared for the younger set.

Minidoka is set millions of years ago in the region of the Burroughs Idaho ranch, and it details the adventures of the titular earl as he duels with monsters, rescues the lovely (is there any other kind?) princess Bodine, battles the forces of Bodine's father, and travels to the topsy-turvy animal heaven, where the residents get their revenge on abusive humans. Burroughs' budding talent for name creation and wordplay is evident throughout, such as when Minidoka seeks out the fearsome Rhinogazarium in his Castle in the Air in order to steal the Power of Ab:

> Minidoka crept stealthily toward the Edge of the World. Gaining a good strategic point behind a parallel of longitude and bracing one foot firmly against a meridian, he gazed over into space. Lying a little distance from the Earth he saw the Castle in the Air builded by Ab, and taking out his pocket projector for wireless telegraphy, he signaled a challenge to the Rhinogazarium. Scarcely had he finished this daring and original act when lo and behold, forth came the Rhinogazarium first. Bellowing and tearing out huge chunks of space with his massive, horned snout, he lumbered down the ether path bordered by wild atmosphere, kicking up great clouds of ozone and weather. When within about three hops of Minidoka and Earth, he ground his feet into the climate and came to a sudden stop.

Burroughs' coining of new words recalls both Lewis Carroll and Edward Lear. His explanations of how Minidoka's antics created the modern Idaho landscape echo elements of Kipling's *Just So Stories*. And his crazy quilt of kingdoms is similar to L. Frank Baum's *Wonderful Wizard of Oz* which, as Robert Barrett points out in the introduction to *Minidoka*, was published only a short time before Burroughs wrote this tale and so may have inspired him to put pen to paper.

Should *Minidoka* have been dragged from the vault? The story is charming, and a major delight for Burroughs readers is to see their favorite author utilize his stock elements for the first time. But the story was written for children growing up in an Idaho gold mining camp a century ago; one would need a time machine to go back and find out what all of Burroughs' references mean. (Minidoka, by the way, is a small Idaho town, which became the site of a Japanese-American internment camp during World War II.)

Burroughs' longest novel, *Marcia of the Doorstep* (1924), and his lone serious attempt at playwriting, *You Lucky Girl!* (1927), were released simultaneously in 1999 by specialty publisher Donald Grant in deluxe limited editions. I have a soft spot for Burroughs' "realistic" novels—not for any literary value they may have but because they serve as windows into the Chicago or the Los Angeles of nearly a century ago. (Burroughs also relied on his stock plot devices and outlandish coincidences, elements that add a quirkiness to stories set in a contemporary urban setting.) Henry Hardy Heins had been a champion of *Marcia* since 1966, when he assessed the manuscript for possible publication at Hulbert Burroughs' request. (The poor showing of Edgar Rice Burroughs, Inc.'s 1967 printing of *I Am a Barbarian* pretty much squelched any further publishing plans by the company.)

That said, *Marcia* is not top-shelf Burroughs and will be a tough nut to crack for any reader who likes his Burroughs of the fantastic variety. In contrast, *You Lucky Girl!* is a breezy little tale of stage-struck girls and the men in their lives, quite advanced in its positive portrayal of female independence, although containing the standard Burroughs romantic denouement. *You Lucky Girl!* finally hit the stage in 1997 in Palmdale, California, fulfilling Heins' belief that the play was of sufficient quality for a small regional theatrical company.

Forgotten Tales of Love and Murder (2001) collects many of Burroughs' shorter pieces, most notably "Misogynists Preferred," "The Little Door," the Inspector Muldoon mystery puzzles, and the original version of "Resurrection of Jimber Jaw," among others. I will not contradict Lupoff's already expressed opinion on any of the stories included. The book was produced by two longtime fans, John Guidry and Patrick Adkins, and is packaged to resemble the original A. C. McClurg editions of Burroughs' novels. A follow-up volume or two are anticipated, which will round up the remainder of the items listed on the letterhead of Edgar Rice Burroughs, Inc.

Even so, it appears that the infamous safe is not the only place Burroughs tucked away unsold items. A story unknown to Lupoff back in 1965, "Jonathan's Patience," was included in *Forgotten Tales*; in addition, Danton

Burroughs has uncovered in some of his grandfather's miscellaneous papers a fragment of a Tarzan short story. I am involved in preparing Burroughs' writing notebooks for publication, which will include all plot synopses, drafts, character lists, maps, and sketches that he created for each story. It seems as if there will be no rest for the true Burroughs devotee; the man keeps pulling rabbits out of his hat more than a half century after his death.

Ever since Ray Palmer tried to whip up interest in "John Bloodstone" as the official Burroughs successor, fans have debated who, if anyone, should be allowed to write further adventures of Tarzan or John Carter. Repeating what Lupoff said earlier, "to the extent that a successor author maintained fidelity to the original his work was superfluous. To the extent that it varied from the original, it tended to fracture the structure of imagination created by the original author. Either way, the successor's work would suffer." Point taken, but the vast majority of Burroughs' own output consists of sequels which, by following Lupoff's line of reasoning, are superfluous and suffer in comparison to the original novels. (They do.) Burroughs decided to write series and his readers approved; the damage has been done. Why not (for the sake of an argument) a new series of Tarzan or Mars adventures?

When Ballantine Books published Fritz Leiber's *Tarzan and the Valley of Gold* (1966), the publisher numbered it as the twenty-fifth book in the official Tarzan canon, suggesting that future volumes might be added to the series. The momentum seemed to be there. Tarzan paperbacks were still selling well, Tarzan movies were still popular, and a Tarzan television series was in the works. In addition, John Coleman Burroughs' science fiction novel, *Treasure of the Black Falcon*, was released in 1967 by Ballantine, which trumpeted young Burroughs as "a new name in fantastic adventure— a name that perpetuates the best traditions of the creator of the Tarzan and Mars books." With an incomplete Tarzan novel still sitting in the safe at Edgar Rice Burroughs, Inc., one would think that Tarzan and John Coleman would get together. But weak sales of both *Valley of Gold* and *Treasure of the Black Falcon*, coupled with John Coleman's failing health, put the brakes on any hopes for a continuation of the Tarzan series. (Of course, Ballantine gracing *Valley of Gold* with the cover painting from its edition of *Tarzan and the Golden Lion* may have had something to do with the novel's poor performance; perhaps readers thought they already had the book.)

Edgar Rice Burroughs, Inc., did give official blessing in one form or another to a handful of books, and these must be described before detailing the fate of the unfinished Tarzan novel. The importance of these stories is less in their literary quality and more in how their existence altered the way Edgar Rice Burroughs, Inc., conducted its business. Whether for good or ill is a point of contention within the Burroughs fan community to this day.

None of these miscellaneous stories involves Burroughs' characters, although the Burroughs inspiration was something stressed mightily by the publishers. Philip José Farmer's *Hadon of Ancient Opar* (1974) is, as its title suggests, set in an earlier era of La's hometown. ("In Tarzan's Africa—12,000 years ago!" proclaims the cover blurb.) The youthful Hadon participates in the bloody arena games of Khokarsa with the intent of winning the princess and an empire. The Burroughs connection is fairly tenuous, and Farmer can't accept the idea of an Atlantean continent. Instead he postulates an island empire within an African inland sea from which colonies like Opar sprang. Farmer had planned on a series of novels, but only one sequel, *Flight to Opar*, was published.

Prolific British writer of American westerns J. T. Edson gave Tarzan an adopted son and set him through his jungle paces in *Bunduki* (1975), the first of several novels and stories. Bunduki—or James Allenvale Gunn—is an African game warden (and "blonde giant," as we are repeatedly reminded) who is kidnapped and taken to a jungle planet. Here he has some appropriately Tarzanic adventures before his kidnappers reveal that they want him to carry on with his old job in this new setting. The love interest is provided by Tarzan's adopted *granddaughter*, which complicates the family tree a bit.

John Eric Holmes' *Mahars of Pellucidar* (1976) began life as a fan pastiche. Wanting to read more Pellucidar adventures Holmes decided to write one. After first submitting it to Don Wollheim at DAW Books, who said he wouldn't touch it with a ten-foot pole for fear of what Edgar Rice Burroughs, Inc., would do, Holmes sent his novel along to Tarzana. (Fan writers still do this; all efforts are returned unread with a cordial note.) John Coleman Burroughs enjoyed the story and so authorized Ace Books to publish it. Holmes deliberately avoided any mention of Burroughs' original characters or locales, which can be a bit disconcerting (I don't think even the name Pellucidar is mentioned). A sequel titled *Red Axe of Pellucidar* exists but has been published only as a Burroughs convention souvenir.

All these novels cluster around the year of Burroughs' centenary and attest to his popularity at the time. But a short time after this the management changed at Edgar Rice Burroughs, Inc., and brought in a new philosophy. Marion Burroughs, former wife of Hulbert Burroughs, took control with a very pragmatic approach: protect the company's trademarks. Paramount to her was that Edgar Rice Burroughs be recognized as the creator of Tarzan and that Edgar Rice Burroughs, Inc., be recognized as the owner of the

Tarzan trademark, among others. As a result all these spin-offs lost their seal of approval and were shut down. (Edson came out the best by simply eliminating all Burroughs references in his later Bunduki novels, referring the reader to the early tales for background information.)

Fans who had enjoyed a chummy relationship with Hulbert and John Coleman were less than thrilled with Marion Burroughs' hardheaded business strategy. Why would Edgar Rice Burroughs, Inc., turn up its nose at the free publicity these spin-offs could generate? In truth Marion's policy was not all that unusual; if confusion is sown as to who created Tarzan or other characters, or who owns the rights to those characters, then the exclusive rights that Edgar Rice Burroughs, Inc., holds are potentially weakened. In the entertainment field it is quite common for the owners of high-profile trademarks to exert a little legal persuasion upon infringers, whether they be major corporations or fans writing stories about their favorite characters.

And so Edgar Rice Burroughs, Inc., has sought legal action against, for example, *Vogue* magazine for running a Tarzan-and-Jane pictorial without seeking permission, and against the producers of the erotic film *Jungle Heat* for denigrating the characters. (Although it is fun to see a gaggle of elderly fans at a Burroughs convention debating whether or not they should buy a porno film—because it is also a collectible.) A similar sense of ire was raised (and a lawsuit launched) with a remake of *Tarzan the Ape Man* (1981) that was little more than a vehicle for actress Bo Derek to display her feminine charms. Burroughs, Inc., has also exerted legal pressure on writers who have posted fan-written pastiches on the Internet. Such fans who thought they were simply sharing stories with fellow aficionados quickly learned that this modern technology was now at the forefront of the war in defining copyright and trademark law.

The wisdom of Marion's company policy is still being played out. Such lawsuits are oftentimes a necessary evil but are no substitute for marketing and promotion. However, Edgar Rice Burroughs, Inc., being a very small company, simply lacks the people and ability to marshal big publicity efforts. The irony is that people unknowingly infringe upon the rights of Burroughs, Inc., when Burroughs, Inc., does not promote itself as the owner of the Tarzan trademark. (In all fairness I must mention that Burroughs, Inc., has a brisk international business with franchising the Tarzan name; it's the American market where Tarzan seems to be diminished.)

With the release of the Walt Disney Company's animated Tarzan film in 1999 (along with a direct-to-video sequel and animated television series), nearly all new Tarzan products have been geared squarely at the children's market. The mighty ape-man with an eighty-five-year history is now associated in the public's mind with Disney rather than Burroughs. The ultimate result of this association is yet to be determined.

Before Disney came along, Edgar Rice Burroughs, Inc., did try to break out of its restrictive business plan with a new sequence of Tarzan book adventures, but this attempt at creating a continuing "franchise" met the same fate as the earlier effort. In a market dominated by higher-profile franchises, such as *Star Trek*, *Star Wars*, and a dozen or so other brand names, Tarzan is simply lost. Other products, like new comics and two syndicated television series, were approved of during this time, but the comics received spotty distribution, and the television shows were broadcast at the whim of the station that purchased the shows, and so did little to introduce the Burroughs name to a wider audience.

When Dark Horse Comics obtained the rights to produce new Tarzan comics in the 1990s, it launched its publishing program with, of all things, a novel. Horror and mystery writer Joe Lansdale was picked to complete Burroughs' unfinished Tarzan tale. The resulting *Tarzan: The Lost Adventure* (1995) was cleverly presented, being published first as a four-part, pulp-style serial, followed by hardback and paperback editions. Burroughs purists have pretty much rejected Lansdale's efforts outright (although that's hardly a surprise; it's the nature of a purist to approve only of the Real Thing). His writing style is not at all like Burroughs' (they said); he completely rewrote Burroughs' original fragment (they complained). In defense of Lansdale, the original fragment was little more than a plotless collection of standard jungle incidents; a lot of work was needed to make it a coherent and interesting story.

By the 1940s Burroughs' writing style had become stripped down in contrast to his early "lush" prose; Lansdale's clipped style, while occasionally jarring (would Burroughs have ever made Tarzan battle a "croc"?), is an appropriate extension in the evolution of Burroughs' prose. Lansdale also brought back the vicious "throw the decapitated head into the enemy's camp" ape-man, the Tarzan as an elemental force, which I found—perhaps perversely—refreshing. Like Leiber's *Valley of Gold*, Lansdale's effort represents a departure from the rut Burroughs had Tarzan in during much of the ape-man's later adventures; your reaction to both books will depend on how much you enjoyed being in the rut yourself.

Fan reaction aside, *Tarzan: The Lost Adventure* received respectable reviews in the mainstream press. But any positive effect on the Tarzan franchise was pretty much deep-sixed by *Tarzan: The Epic Adventures* (1996). Based on the pilot episode of the similarly titled syndicated television series, *Epic Adventures* represents that ultimate literary bastardization, an adaptation of an adaptation—in this case, the script borrowed elements from *Return of Tarzan* and *Tarzan at the Earth's Core*. How exactly this mishmash was to fit in with Burroughs' chronology is anyone's guess.

In hopes of making a big splash, Del Rey Books (the successor to Ballantine Books' science fiction line) hired Big Name fantasy author R. A. Salvatore to write the novel. Unfortunately Salvatore had never read a Tarzan novel in his life, and the script he was given to work with was written by someone who apparently hadn't either. The show's poor quality probably repelled any potential readers who might otherwise have given Burroughs a try. Even idle curiosity is not sufficient reason to seek out this misguided effort—unless, of course, you think changing Burroughs' implacable reptilian overlords of Pellucidar into a bunch of bikini-clad babes is actually an improvement over the source material. (A post-Disney, live-action Tarzan television series appeared in 2003 with an underwear model in the title role, set in modern Manhattan, and geared apparently toward thirteen-year-old girls who didn't mind that Tarzan was prettier than Jane. Alas, no one else tuned in. Thankfully there were no literary spin-offs.)

Philip José Farmer's Tarzan novel *Dark Heart of Time* (1999) marks the end of efforts to reestablish Tarzan in the adult market, even though it was meant to be the launching pad for further novels. Del Rey had planned to treat the book as a major release, issuing it as an oversized trade paperback and making the appropriate publicity announcements. Farmer had a long history with Tarzan, had won numerous awards, and was popular with both the Burroughs fans and science fiction readers. But *Epic Adventures* had proven a major fiasco and reissues of Burroughs' original Tarzan novels to coincide with the television series had performed poorly, so Del Rey became gun shy. *Dark Heart of Time* was finally released as a standard paperback with a nondescript cover and an easily overlooked blurb identifying the book as a Tarzan novel. Was the Tarzan name now considered a liability? For forty years Ballantine/Del Rey had been the authorized publisher of Tarzan novels, but the honeymoon was over.

Hindsight is a wonderful thing, and one can now identify obvious flaws in the way the franchise has more recently been handled. The books varied widely in appearance, with no uniformity in illustration or cover design (the paperback release of *Lost Adventure* has perhaps the most inappropriate cover since the days of Mahlon Blaine at Canaveral). The reader who stumbled across one of these titles would not have been drawn to the others—if they could be found—or to Burroughs' original novels which, to complicate matters further, had yet another cover design.

Even more egregiously, Burroughs' name was missing from the covers of both *Epic Adventures* and *Dark Heart of Time*. While that may be a blessing in the former case, one would think that Edgar Rice Burroughs, Inc., would require this to emphasize Burroughs as the creator of Tarzan. Burroughs himself required his name to be placed above the title of every Tarzan movie; he knew having his name before the public eye meant he had it before the eye of business as well, which would have led to more lucrative licensing deals.[4]

Ignoring the error of *Epic Adventures*, the four-year gap separating the release of *Lost Adventure* and *Dark Heart of Time* was far too long to maintain reader interest in the franchise. Die-hard fans, who would have bought the books regardless, represent only a small fraction of the potential readership. The predominant desire in spinning out the franchise is to lasso new readers, who would then seek out Burroughs' original works, thus maintaining the continuation of the franchise. Apparently this did not happen.

Another popular parlor game among Burroughs fans is debating how best Edgar Rice Burroughs, Inc., should run its business. I seem to have fallen into that inevitable groove, but I don't have any alternative business strategies that would point the way to a new Burroughs revival. Publishing is a cyclical business, and many an author experiences periods of popularity and obscurity, as Burroughs' history attests. Even if properly packaged and pitched, could the modern book market have supported an attempt at continuing the Tarzan franchise? The malaise in the Burroughs paperback market may be not so much a lack of interested or potential readers as a lack of interested publishers and editors. Even a successful franchise like Doc Savage ran up against the stone wall of a changing publishing world.

Bantam Books began reissuing these old hero pulps in 1964, about the time Burroughs was experiencing his revival, and it eventually republished all 181 of the original Doc novels, ending in 1990. Doc scholar Will Murray was contracted to write new adventures and he chose (God bless 'im!) to write under the old Street and Smith house name of Kenneth Robeson. Murray described his involvement in a recent letter:

> In 1990, I signed a contract with Bantam Books to write three new Doc Savage novels based on [head Doc writer] Lester Dent outlines and unused material. Philip José Farmer was contacted to write one. Bantam intended to publish four Docs a year. . . . I was told at that point or soon after, the schedule would be scaled down to three per year, because Bantam was experiencing list cutbacks. This despite the fact that my first Doc, *Python Isle*, and Farmer's *Escape From Loki*, were the first Docs to go to a second printing since 1969.

I turned in my seventh Doc, *The Forgotten Realm*, in December, 1992, and was asked for the plots for three more Docs. . . . But a week after negotiations started, I received a letter from my editor saying the series was being suspended . . . the result of another list cut, a severe one.[5]

Bear in mind, the new Doc adventures were selling well—"comfortably midlist" according to Murray—so a willing audience existed for such old-fashioned adventure tales. But Bantam Books was now one imprint among many in a larger publishing conglomerate; maintaining a small "boutique" line like Doc Savage—with the attendant editorial, design, and marketing duties—had become a luxury. The comfortably midlist authors—those whose books sell at a steady pace rather than in a bloom, as a bestseller does—were being squeezed out of publishers' catalogs and off the bookstore shelves. Such an author is Edgar Rice Burroughs.

But Burroughs may get the last laugh. The Burroughs fan in me pines for the days when his paperbacks were available wherever you looked. Those days are gone, but there are indications that Burroughs might get another day in the sun. The publishing world has changed since the Burroughs Boom, and Burroughs has managed to change along with it, albeit a trifle slowly. Still, there is enough evidence of renewed interest in Burroughs that I will be able to give this book a happy ending.

The appearance of any new Burroughs titles will neither add to nor diminish the man's standing in the world of American letters. With popular culture now a recognized (if grudgingly accepted) field of academic study, it is no surprise that Burroughs' works have undergone a fair amount of scholarly scrutiny during the last four decades. By running through academic journal indexes and databases one can find articles with such titles as "The Tarzan Myth and Jung's Genesis of the Self," "An American Demagogue on Barsoom," and "Tarzan and Columbo: Heroic Mediators." In these and many other studies Burroughs' literary qualities—or lack thereof—are often of secondary importance; that his work unashamedly reflects the era in which it first appeared, warts and all, is where the interest lies. By studying Burroughs' fiction one can better understand the times in which he wrote and the culture that produced the author.

That Burroughs gets such attention is both pleasing and perplexing. By way of example, Burroughs' efforts at Tarzana are utilized by Kevin Starr to highlight the growth of the Los Angeles area and the development of the California dream in his *Material Dreams: Southern California Through the 1920s* (1990). Burroughs might feel vindicated that Starr considers *Girl from Hollywood* "among the most powerful of the chorus of anti-Hollywood jeremiads to appear just before and in the aftermath of the murder of Desmond Taylor, the Fatty Arbuckle case, and the death of Wallace Reid from drug addiction." But then he might have been mystified by Starr's assessment that "Burroughs' dope-crazed lesbian film star Gaza De Lure is a tour de force of high camp." Likewise the identification of John Carter as "an inventive investor and efficiency expert given to interplanetary adventures." Well, in a study of this scope there are bound to be mistakes . . .

More Burroughs-specific than Starr's work, Erling B. Holtsmark's *Tarzan and Tradition* (1981) is well regarded by the Edwin Arnold (and Lupoff!) bashers of the die-hard set. A professor of classics at the University of Iowa, Holtsmark sees Burroughs' classical education as the dominant influence upon the Tarzan saga. (Pronouncing that Burroughs was inspired by Homer and Virgil sounds better than saying he got his ideas from Edwin Arnold and H. Rider Haggard.) Holtsmark's theory is intriguing but, like Lupoff's study (or even many fan studies) based on the perceived internal evidence of Burroughs' stories, it merely adds to the speculation of where Burroughs got his ideas rather than proving anything definitive.

Sarkis Atamian feels he has the last word on *The Origin of Tarzan: The Mystery of Tarzan's Creation Solved* (1997). A former professor of sociology at the University of Alaska, Atamian speculates that Burroughs drew much of his African background and lore from the writings of explorers Paul du Chaillu and J. W. Buel, the former being the sole source of information on gorillas—much of it laughed at during his day—until the early twentieth century. Atamian's research is an interesting addition to that tiny shelf labeled "Burroughs Scholarship," particularly with his rundown of all the African tiger references in the popular press of Burroughs' day. The book, however, seems never to have passed before an editor's eye and is marred by an egregious number of typos, misspellings, and an almost complete lack of structure. The amateurish presentation threatens to overwhelm what Atamian is trying to say.

I am hesitant to identify Philip José Farmer's *Tarzan Alive* (1972) as nonfiction. Under that label Farmer provides a wealth of information on possible sources of Africana for the Tarzan novels, including du Chaillu as well as the historical backdrop against which the Tarzan novels are set. He also places Tarzan within the classical literary tradition. In such ways he beat both Atamian and Holtsmark to their respective punches.

Farmer's conceit is that he purports to be writing the biography of the man "whom we shall call John Clayton, Lord Greystoke," the true-life story of the feral man upon which Burroughs based his stories and whom he claims to have interviewed. Farmer has related this tale, eyes misting, in a couple of television documentaries. You can be either amused or disturbed by this sincerity, depending on your mood. Is Farmer just playing into the Burroughsian notion that all his tales were true, or has Farmer come to believe that he actually interviewed the real-life Tarzan?

Either way, in order to make this biography work Farmer must hack Burroughs' novels to bits so that all the pieces fit. All the lost cities Tarzan visits? Gone. A trip to Pellucidar? Impossible. Give the heave-ho to Pal-ul-don as well. Such an approach might work for biographies of other fictional characters like Nero Wolfe or Sherlock Holmes (who become Tarzan's relatives in Farmer's detailed family tree) because those characters operated in something approaching the real world. But Tarzan's Africa is more fantasy than reality, so Farmer's book, at least for me, is useful only after I hack it to bits as well and extract what relevant information remains.

Richard Lupoff had few charitable things to say about Robert Fenton's 1967 Burroughs biography, *The Big Swingers*. (With a title like that, who can blame him? The book has since been reissued as *Edgar Rice Burroughs and Tarzan*.) Only a few years later this flawed study was superseded by something more substantial, Irwin Porges' ambitious and heavily illustrated *Edgar Rice Burroughs: The Man Who Created Tarzan* (1975). Consider the book's dimensions: 820 pages in an 8½-by-11½-inch format, two inches thick, the weight of a small bowling ball. You do not want this book dropped on you from a great height.

Porges was given unprecedented access to all of Burroughs' personal and business papers, and the resulting biography represents a treasure trove of primary source material for Burroughs scholars. Cherry picking from such goodies, though, can be a challenge. Porges' book is saddled with one of the most maddeningly vague indexes you are ever likely to see; it doesn't even cover the extensive notes or appendixes and seems to list almost everything under "Burroughs, Edgar Rice." Some fans have allegedly been working on a better index, but like many fan projects it seems to exist only "out there somewhere."

The amount of material Porges was given to work with would overwhelm most scholars. Burroughs' endless finagling over payments, real estate wheeling and dealing, negotiations over secondary rights, and endless disputes over motion picture rights—Porges covers every business transaction in which Burroughs was engaged. Such details are manna to the Burroughs fan who wants to see how Burroughs built his empire, but to the mainstream reader of biographies this is pretty leaden stuff.

Moreover, Porges is not strong in placing Burroughs in his context, historical or literary. This is because Porges sticks to Burroughs' primary source material, using almost no secondary sources to add some understanding to Burroughs as a man of his time. Burroughs' death is covered on the final page, leaving the impression that he had no impact on his society or the world of fiction. Other than his covering the Altrocchi letters and Kipling's comments (both of which are covered by Lupoff in this book), Burroughs' writing exists outside the field of American literature for Porges. Despite these flaws, fans consider Porges' effort as the "definitive" Burroughs biography. Ultimately the best thing about *Edgar Rice Burroughs: The Man Who Created Tarzan* is that Porges digested a massive amount of Burroughsiana and made it available for the scholars who have followed.

One recipient of Porges' largesse is John Taliaferro, whose *Tarzan Forever* (1999) is a more manageable biography. Taliaferro further distills the source material, leading some fans to deride the effort as "Porges lite." While distilling, quite a few errors crept in (causing yet more fan derision), although Taliaferro provides a smoother read than Porges. Taliaferro was attracted to the job because of Burroughs' pioneering marketing and promotion efforts. Unfortunately, he displays little sympathy for his subject or the era that shaped him, leaving the reader with a clearer sense of Taliaferro's opinions than of Burroughs'.

As Burroughs was stuck with cultural blinders of which he was unaware, so too is Taliaferro. He is quite unforgiving when it comes to Burroughs' perceived racial views and often sets Burroughs up just to knock him down. "Except for the black cavalrymen Burroughs met—and praised, though somewhat patronizingly—during his days at Fort Grant, he was resistant to knowing blacks as individuals and especially as equals." Now there is no proof to back up this statement; Burroughs' use of African stereotypes is apparently enough. (Taliaferro is himself patronizing in assuming that opportunities for "knowing blacks as individuals and especially as equals" were common in Burroughs' time. They weren't.) Taliaferro does a disservice to both Burroughs and himself by making such simplistic assessments on such a multilayered topic. Even so, Taliaferro is only one voice among many in damning Burroughs and his world for not being as enlightened as we like to think we are, so I will be visiting the subject of racism again.

Would-be Burroughs scholars need no longer feel completely shunned by the intelligentsia, as they now have a legitimate research facility where they can studiously scrutinize the works of the Master and his disciples without fear of disapprobation. At the University of Louisville (Kentucky, that is), deep in the bowels of Ekstrom Library, sits the special collections department. Therein lies the Edgar Rice Burroughs Memorial Collection, presided over by George T. McWhorter (current editor of *The Burroughs Bulletin*), an Oparian vault of some one hundred thousand pieces (and growing), representing most everything under the Burroughsian sun: first editions, pulp magazine editions, foreign language editions, comics by the drawerful, the gew-gaws and doo-dads of collectibles, Issus only knows how many fanzines, and Johnny Weissmuller's knife. (You'll find my master's thesis on Burroughs tucked away there as well, gathering dust on a back shelf.)

In addition to its value for research, the collection is the closest we will probably ever come to a true Burroughs museum. A remnant of the original Tarzana ranch, along with a few of its buildings, survived into the twenty-first century, where it was hoped a museum could be placed. Unfortunately that property has been sold to developers, who I am sure will build a slew of McMansions of identical size and shape, slap exorbitant price tags on them, and call it all progress. Such things make you understand Tarzan's low opinion of civilization. Those pilgrims traveling out west can at least visit the Tarzana Cultural Center, founded and run by Helen Baker, who is doing what she can to keep the Burroughs history alive in the town he put on the map.

On July 11, 2003, Edgar Rice Burroughs was inducted into the Science Fiction and Fantasy Hall of Fame, sponsored by the Center for the Study of Science Fiction at the University of Kansas in Lawrence. Burroughs has often been treated as the bad boy of the science fiction field, particularly by those writers and critics who disliked the genre's reputation as pulp entertainment, so his induction is a form of vindication.

In his *Under the Moons of Mars: A History and Anthology of "The Scientific Romance" in the Munsey Magazines, 1912–1920* (1970), science fiction historian Sam Moskowitz said that with *A Princess of Mars* "Burroughs turned the entire direction of science fiction from prophesy and sociology to romantic adventure, making the major market for such work the all-fiction pulp magazines, and became *the* major influence on the field through to 1934." If Moskowitz is right, Burroughs single-handedly ghettoized an emerging literary genre, relegated it to lowbrow pulp magazines for decades, and gave it the reputation of being escapist twaddle with no redeeming value whatsoever, all with just his first book. And Moskowitz was being appreciative!

Perhaps Moskowitz overstates his case, perhaps not. More succinctly, in his *Billion Year Spree: The True History of Science Fiction* (1973), Brian Aldiss complains that Burroughs' "influence has been immense, and often deadening." At one time the number of Burroughs knockoffs stuffing bookstore shelves was almost overwhelming and probably kept more serious science fiction writers (like Aldiss) from finding a place on publishers' lists. This influence may be generational: some of those kids who read Burroughs in the 1930s and 1940s became editors in the 1960s and 1970s, and they published authors who grew up with the same sordid background.

This "Burroughsian" literary trend has run its course, at least as a publishing phenomenon, but that still leaves dozens of Burroughs knockoffs not covered by Richard Lupoff in his chapter "Descendants of Tarzan." Even so, my efforts to highlight some of these works will represent only a fraction of what was produced. Some titles, such as the blatantly obvious *Azan the Ape Man*, I know of through reputation only, and likewise the products of innumerable small (and short-lived) paperback houses of the 1960s and 1970s. I have never seen a copy of Charles Nuetzel's *Swordsmen of Vistar* (1969), released by Powell Sci-Fi. I suspect I am now too old and jaded to appreciate such a book should I ever stumble across it.

When Ace Books reissued Otis Adelbert Kline's interplanetary romances back in the early 1960s editor Don Wollheim played up the Burroughs connection for all it was worth, even soliciting endorsements from Burroughs fanzine editors to entice the faithful. "Otis Adelbert Kline is your meat!" proclaimed Vernell Coriell in *Planet of Peril*, hoping a gastronomical allusion would whet the potential reader's appetite. "The only author to be compared with Edgar Rice Burroughs, but whose work is as original as Burroughs' own!" While one may quibble with such a literary assessment, there is no doubt that the Burroughs name sold books, and did so through the early 1980s.

Don Wollheim was instrumental in promoting what he termed "sword and planet" adventures through both Ace Books and his later DAW Books imprint. Place the action on a distant planet, throw in some sword fighting and a feudal society, mix with some high-tech trappings (oh, and a princess or two, I guess) and *voila!* "what you get is a terrific science-fiction adventure of the Burroughs type." Thus Wollheim described *The Sword of Lankor* (1966) by Howard L. Cory (pseudonym of Jack and Julie Anne Jardine). Actually, the adventures of the tawny-eyed barbarian Thuron of Ulmekoor on the planet Lankor read more like Lin Carter imitating Burroughs and Robert E. Howard, but as it was an entertaining read, I won't complain about Wollheim's liberal promotional practices.

Carter, a stalwart member of Wollheim's stable, was described by one of his publishers as "the modern Edgar Rice Burroughs." I have a sneaking suspicion Carter made such a proclamation long before his publisher did. Beyond the Thongor novels mentioned by Lupoff, Carter embraced the full-blooded Burroughs model for three separate series, providing plenty of meat for those wanting an alternative to Otis Adelbert Kline.

Jandar of Callisto (1972) launches the saga of one John Dark and his escapades on the Jovian satellite. Dark, a medevac pilot during the Vietnam War, crashes near a lost city deep in the Cambodian jungle and then quite literally stumbles into an ancient matter transporter that whisks him off to Callisto. Once there Carter hammers away at the standard Burroughsian tropes: capture by towering emotionless warriors (in this case the insectoid Yathoon); the development of friendship between Dark—now rendered Jandar—and a Yathoon chieftain; the introduction of a haughty princess in peril (the unfortunately named Darloona); and Jandar's involvement in the struggle between Darloona's people and the cruel sky pirates of Zanadar, who fly about in gigantic papier-mâché ornithopters.

While the action may be standard fare, the setting is colorfully presented. After the initial trilogy (completed by *Black Legion of Callisto* and *Sky Pirates of Callisto*), Carter continued to spin out sequels for a total of eight volumes, but the quality dropped steeply as the series progressed. Only with *Lankar of Callisto* did Carter play any variation on the theme, where he gets himself transported to Callisto's surface!

For Wollheim's fledgling DAW Books, Carter produced another pseudo-Burroughs series, beginning with *Under the Green Star* (1972) and continuing for four more books. Carter's anonymous narrator is a bedridden cripple who learns the secrets of astral projection. Traveling about the universe with the speed of thought, he eventually comes across a nameless planet beneath a green star and is pulled into the preserved body of a legendary hero, Chong the Mighty. Mighty convenient, that!

The World of the Green Star boasts mile-high trees that house entire cities, as on Amtor; giant insects, as on Amtor; and a nubile princess—not an Amtor exclusive—named Niamh. Like the Callisto books, Carter starts off with a colorful adventure, but the novels slide in quality as we go along. Still, the setting is picturesque, and the action suitably bloodthirsty for those who find such characteristics of paramount importance.

And with *Journey to the Underground World* (1979) Carter launched yet another Burroughs-style series, this time a Pellucidar variation. Rather than a hollow earth we have the cave world of Zanthodon beneath North Africa. Here there be dinosaurs and saber-toothed tigers, pseudo-Korsars, and buxom cave girls in fur bikinis. Carter rambled along in this series for five books, none of which seemed to have a plot—which puts this series more in the tradition of *Land of Terror* than *At the Earth's Core*.

Carter may have been no Burroughs, but compared to other imitators he came much closer. Take Mike Sirota, who cranked out two Barsoom-style series beginning with *Prisoner of Reglathium* (1978) and *Master of Boranga* (1980). Eric Wayne wakes up in Reglathium after dying in a mundane motorcycle accident and is immediately made captive by the ubiquitous nomad tribe. Roland Summers is shipwrecked on Boranga after passing through one of those rifts in the space-time continuum that science fiction writers like to think are dotting the planet. He immediately teams up with a barbarian warrior who gets to utter that classic Burroughs-styled line: "I could almost believe that you are not of Boranga, as you claim, to speak the words you just did." The protagonists of both books then proceed to spend endless chapters asking questions and talking, talking, talking, while Sirota pours on the background information to compensate for the lack of an interesting story. The passivity of the narration is well summed up in the last paragraph of *Prisoner*: "On the first night of my arrival upon this bleak world I was a captive of the Red Tuels. Since that time I have spent the majority of mygs [days] in captivity in one form or another. Now, within the reeking walls of the Johva Fortress, I once again found myself a prisoner of Reglathium."

Sure, Burroughs heroes are captured and imprisoned on a routine basis. But they are men of action, not perpetual navel gazers. Sirota's characters wouldn't last a day on Barsoom. I'm sure Eric Wayne escaped from the reeking walls of the Johva Fortress; I just have no interest in finding out how.

Wherever Don Wollheim went, Burroughs imitators were sure to follow. British writer Kenneth Bulmer was one of Wollheim's workhorses at Ace, churning out paperback originals by the bucketful. For DAW Books, Bulmer, under the pseudonym Alan Burt Akers, proved equally reliable, chronicling the adventures of one Dray Prescot on the planet Kregen in the constellation Scorpio to the tune of four novels a year (for a few years, anyway).

Prescot is an eighteenth-century sailor who finds himself transported to Kregen by the immortal Savanti to perform sundry deeds in *Transit to Scorpio* (1972). Apparently he is a hot property, as the even more powerful Star Lords utilize him to perform *their* deeds, which primarily consist of stamping out slavery in all its forms (something Burroughs turned a blind eye to on Barsoom). Kregen boasts several sentient races and innumerable cultures, allowing Bulmer to run through multiple variations of the standard sword-and-planet situations. Bulmer's writing style is a bit awkward, but as these are supposed to be the memoirs of an eighteenth-century sailor, I guess the style isn't all that out of place.

The Prescot series eventually stretched to thirty-seven volumes before low sales caused DAW to drop the series (even though it was purported to be Wollheim's favorite). Bulmer did, however, find a new market in Germany, where he produced some fifteen or more adventures. Thus serious Dray Prescot fans must learn German to find out what other events befell their hero.

Burroughs always maintained that his "inspiration" for writing fantastic literature was the rottenness of similar stories he read in the pulps—he could do it just as well or better. It should then be no surprise to find authors who responded in a similar way to Burroughs' perceived literary shortcomings. Lin Carter's frequent Conan collaborator, L. Sprague de Camp, was one such writer who felt that his inability to create a fully functional society and a logically constructed biosphere were among Burroughs' greater failings. What exactly is the basis of the Barsoomian economy? How does John Carter support such an enormous navy? Where do those ubiquitous sleeping silks and furs come from? And do the hordes of banths infesting the dead sea bottoms have any food source other than lost princesses?

De Camp's response was a series of fey novels set on the planet Krishna, beginning with *The Queen of Zamba* (1949). Krishna is a pseudo-medieval world under a technological blockade by the Terran authorities in the hopes that it stays that way. In this and subsequent novels, such as *The Hand of Zei* and *The Hostage of Zir*, de Camp sends a series of unlikely heroes to infiltrate Krishnan society and perform Burroughsian deeds, all the while keeping their Terran origins secret. As one of de Camp's prime characteristics is his sense of humor, these adventures never do run smoothly. An unintentional bit of humor, by the way, shows that it is sometimes better for a science fiction writer to be vague rather than specific: one character is introduced as being slumped over his typewriter. Hard enough to find one of those today; imagine how readers will be puzzled in a few hundred years.

Despite de Camp's strengths as a writer, historian, and armchair archaeologist, his tongue-in-cheek style renders his stories more light in weight than they might otherwise be. His efforts to create a cultural backdrop to his alien societies are both forced and artificial. (Characters constantly reference nameless works of Krishnan literature: "I can show you your way about here, as Sivandi showed Lord Zerré through the maze in the story"— "like Qabuz in the story who was trying to climb the tree for the fruit and always slipped back just afore he reached it.") Certainly Burroughs' world building may seem simplistic compared to much in modern science fiction, yet Barsoom remains a more appealing creation than what more critically praised writers have come up with. I would like to think that Burroughs was innovative in rendering Barsoomian society more nuanced by giving the natives their own profanity.

In his *Science Fiction Handbook* de Camp concludes that Burroughs, while a sloppy writer, is nonetheless harmless to children because sex is absent from his books. The same cannot be said for the already-mentioned Gor novels of John Norman (pseudonym of John Frederick Lange Jr.). When Ballantine Books sprang *Tarnsman of Gor* upon an unsuspecting world in 1966 it predicted that "one day the name of John Norman will be counted among the top writers of sword and sorcery." The readership liked the combination of Barsoom-style action and a more open sexual outlook, and so a new Gor novel dutifully appeared every year until there were eventually twenty-five volumes.

But only a few volumes into the series, it became apparent that the Gorean society Norman created was built upon an unsavory foundation. As summed up by John Clute and Peter Nicholls in their *Encyclopedia of Science Fiction* (1993), "the plots begin to revolve around a singularly invariant sexual fantasy in which a proud woman—often abducted for the purpose from Earth—is humiliated, stripped, bound, beaten, raped, branded, and enslaved, invariably discovering in the process that she enjoys total submission to a dominant male and can derive proper sexual satisfaction only from this regime." Not only did Norman sabotage an adventure series by indulging in rape fantasies but . . . it's the same rape fantasy, over and over again. No wonder Betty Ballantine dropped the series after seven books (which Don Wollheim—savvy businessman he—picked right up).

But long before the Gor books became either titillating or offensive, they became out-and-out dull. For Norman is a writer who must describe *everything*, regardless of what is happening in the story. As an example, in *Assassin of Gor* (1970) Norman presents an extended Roman-style arena action sequence. Hero Tarl Cabot has engaged in numerous thrilling combat contests. Then he is handed a bow:

> It is small, double-curved, about four feet in length, built up of layers of bosk horn, bound and reinforced with metal and leather; it is banded with metal at seven points, including the grip, metal obtained from Turia in half-inch rolled strips; the leather is applied diagonally, in two-inch strips except that, horizontally, it covers the entire grip; the bow lacks the range of both the longbow and the crossbow, but, at close range, firing rapidly, it can be a devastating weapon.

And on and on, for two entire pages—and in the middle of what was otherwise a pretty good action scene. Was Norman breaking up the action sequences to give the reader a breather? Was he just being a meticulous world builder? Who cares? Norman leaves nothing to the reader's imagination, and using your imagination is where most of the pleasure in reading lies. If this is how Norman handles action scenes, you can glean some idea of how he describes his sexual situations.

Perhaps emboldened by John Norman's commercial success in the sword-sex-and-sorcery field, Andrew J. Offutt produced another modern variation on the Barsoom theme in *Ardor on Aros* (1973). Hank Ardor finds himself plunked down on a distant planet with the inevitable giant nomads and threatened princess. But while John Carter was able to protect Dejah Thoris from the lustful advances of Lorquas Ptomel, Hank Ardor is not swift enough to prevent the fate worse than death. Make that *fates*.

Much to Ardor's surprise, the ravaged princess decides to get a little pleasure out of the pain she is forced to endure. Luckily Offutt is interested in more than detailing another rape fantasy (was Norman's approach really more mature than Burroughs' supposedly asexual characters?) and uses the situation as a springboard to highlight the Aros social structure. Offutt is well versed in the sword-and-planet school of literature and peppers his tale with references throughout (Ardor even meets a woman named Dejah Thoris). The story reads easily, though Offutt indulges too much in a casual, slang-laden narration. The book is so 1973, I can't comprehend some of Offutt's references—and I grew up during the era!

Leigh Brackett revived her *Planet Stories* hero Eric John Stark for a trilogy of adventures beginning with *The Ginger Star* (1974). Brackett bowed to the pressure of modern science, transplanting Stark from the dead sea bottoms of Mars to the frontier world of Skaith beyond the Orion Spur, a setting science won't invalidate for a few more years. The setting is colorful and the action suitably packed—in short, Brackett's usual good job. Still, one wishes Brackett hadn't abandoned her Mars, as that was as much an integral part of the early Stark novels as Stark himself. Brackett provided a non-Stark Martian adventure with the oft-reprinted *Sword of Rhiannon* (1954) for those who don't wish to abandon the Red Planet. And Lin Carter—of course!—produced a series of Brackett pastiches with such titles as *The Man Who Loved Mars* (1973) and *The Valley Where Time Stood Still* (1974).

André Norton's *Witch World* (1963) may seem an odd choice for inclusion in the "Burroughs School" of science fiction. Like Brackett before her, Norton turned her childhood love of Burroughs into a writing career, becoming a popular author of what were originally packaged as juvenile science fiction adventures. *Witch World* was a departure in both style and appeal. Norton sets up a classic Burroughs situation: Simon Tregarth is hunted by sinister forces and, like Robert E. Howard's Esau Cairn, is given a chance to escape—in this case via an esoteric gate into a parallel universe. There Tregarth immediately runs into a fleeing damsel (although hardly helpless), allies himself with the witches and warriors of Estcarp in their battle against invaders from beyond another dimensional gate, and engages in suitably swashbuckling action while Norton gives us the grand tour of her world.

Prior to this time science fiction was primarily marketed to a young male audience. *Witch World* stood out by having strong female characters and a more adult tone. *Web of the Witch World* continues Tregarth's adventures, but with *Three Against the Witch World* Norton shifts her tone even further, downplaying the science fiction elements and moving the women to center stage. Like Marion Zimmer Bradley's Darkover books, the Witch World series started out as male-oriented science fiction but morphed into female-centered fantasy. Not only did women read science fiction, they wanted to read about women as well.

Norton had a profound impact on the field in much the same way Burroughs did before her. Under Don Wollheim's control DAW Books published copious Burroughs knockoffs. Now under Betsy Wollheim, DAW is known for its roster of female writers—Mercedes Lackey, C. J. Cherryh, and Tanith Lee, to name a few. The sword-and-planet school of writing has run its course. Or perhaps it is better to say that it has evolved into more mature and diverse forms. So, Burroughs deserves to be in that Hall of Fame after all.

A surprisingly large number of white jungle lords populated the pulp jungles of the 1930s and 1940s, providing Tarzanic thrills to readers who couldn't get enough of the mighty ape-man. In addition to Kazar and Ki-gor, there was Sangroo the Sun God in *Jungle Stories*, Ozar the Aztec in *Top Notch*, Morgo the Mighty in *The Popular Magazine*, Kwa of the Jungle in *Thrilling Adventure*, and Matalaa the White Savage in *Red Star Adventures*. Modern Tarzan variations have been fairly rare; Tarzan has been such a strong presence in American culture that any feral child story would be seen to owe its existence to Burroughs. Philip José Farmer wrote several such tales, and he makes it quite clear that his jungle lords owe their existence to Tarzan. Perhaps too much so!

Farmer may not care for the comparison, but he is to Tarzan as John Norman is to John Carter. *A Feast Unknown* (1969) is the earliest and most notorious of Farmer's explorations of the Tarzan mythos. Like his later *Tarzan Alive*, Farmer is purportedly writing about the "real" Lord Greystoke, here rendered as Grandrith. *A Feast Unknown* was originally commissioned by a small publisher of adult books and Farmer took up the challenge to write an "exercise in respectable pornography" (according to one critic, anyway).[6] Burroughs' asexual ape-man is transformed into a sexual warrior. This Tarzan has a penis, and he's not afraid to use it!

Lord G. does battle with Doc Caliban (Farmer's version of Doc Savage), who turns out to be Grandrith's half-brother by way of Jack the Ripper (if I have my Farmer genealogy straight). The two engage in a most graphic sibling rivalry, using weapons both physical and Freudian, to determine who is the alpha male of the jungle, all the while dealing with the machinations of a group of immortal Blavatskian mahatmas known as the Nine. Clute and Nicholls consider *A Feast Unknown* "a brilliant exploration of the sado-masochistic fantasies latent in much heroic fiction" and "a narrative *tour de force*." However, if this pseudo-sexual slugfest is too much for you to handle, Farmer conveniently synopsizes the events in his more approachable Lord Grandrith adventure *Lord of the Trees* (1970).

Now, I must confess that I just don't *get* Farmer. I've tried over the years to find the appeal in this popular author and he just doesn't reach me. (Of course, many say the same thing about Burroughs.) Still, many Burroughs readers love the guy. But the following passage from the opening page of *Dark Heart of Time*, in which Tarzan is chased by some mysterious trackers, illustrates my dissatisfaction:

> The first spear thrown at him nicked the inside of his left ankle. Its steel head rammed into the tree trunk with a loud thunking sound.
>
> The second spear slammed into the liana. Though the parasitical plant was thick and tough, it was severed by the keen-edged blade.
>
> By then, the ape-man had climbed above the cut end of the liana. He had speeded up his ascent a fraction of a second after the first spear had thudded into the thick bark. His fingers gripping the sides of the great vine, his body bent and leaning out almost horizontally, his soles against the trunk, he swarmed upwards.

This is not an action scene; this is a clinical description of a man climbing a tree. Like John Norman, Farmer indulges in the details, sabotaging the story's momentum by including extraneous information. Perhaps Burroughs ruined me for more subtle authors and more nuanced explorations of his themes. Then again, Farmer wishes very much to be like Burroughs but is unable to create the narrative drive that made Burroughs so appealing.

Farmer's Ras Tyger in *Lord Tyger* (1970) is another babe raised in the African jungle by loving ape parents. As much of his simian education consists of classes in Swahili, Arabic, and English, apparently these apes are not all they appear to be. Ras' more earthy education occurs via the boys and girls of the nearby village. Farmer runs through the entire sexual catalog as Tyger grows from groping initiate into a libidinous demon, terrorizing the villagers in a way that Burroughs was unable to address. To give Farmer his due, Clute and Nicholls consider *Lord Tyger* "possibly the best written of PJF's novels."

A final Farmer offering is *The Adventure of the Peerless Peer* (1974), which has Holmes and Watson traveling to Africa and teaming up with Tarzan on a case. This pastiche had *not* been authorized by Edgar Rice Burroughs, Inc., and so was hounded off the shelves. I have not seen a copy since it first appeared, although I am told it is quite good. If you like Farmer. Probably time for me to try him once again.

How's this for a scenario: Weldon and Katherine Rice are aboard Ares Probe One bound for Mars. Their infant son, along for the ride, is in protective stasis. An unexplained phenomenon—a rift in the space-time continuum, perhaps?—whips their ship across the galaxy, where it crashes on a distant planet. Both parents are killed, but the child is found by a race of intelligent felines, who raise the human as one of their own. His name—*Balzan of the Cat People*!

Balzan clawed his way through only three novels, starting with *The Blood Stones* (1975), which was attributed to Wallace Moore (pseudonym for Gerard F. Conway). Balzan receives the standard feral upbringing, although a Tarzan-style education is jettisoned in favor of the tutelage of the spaceship's onboard computer (from which Balzan presumably learns Terran colloquialisms like "Dammit to hell"). I find it impossible to criticize stories of this type; if you are drawn to a book upon which is emblazoned "Balzan of the Cat People" then you will get pretty much what you expect. There is nothing exceptional about these books; they are the literary equivalent of the potato chip, meant to be consumed with a minimum of fuss and bother. Still, the cover design makes these my choice for the most embarrassing books to be caught with in public.

Hyperprolific British author John Russell Fearn produced for the emerging English postwar paperback market his Tarzan variation Anjani in the hastily written *The Gold of Akada* (1951). Anjani suffers the standard traumatizing childhood experience of murdered parents and abandonment in the African jungle. The twist here is that Anjani has a twin brother. Each is raised by a different tribe; each becomes the lord of his own jungle. Anjani is the noble twin; Tocoto is the less pleasant personality. When they meet they become mortal enemies. (Boy, this beats Phil Farmer by a quarter century!) *Gold of Akada* (and its sequel *Anjani the Mighty*) received its first American publication through Gary Lovisi's one-man press Gryphon Books, along with Fearn's Martian quartet, featuring Clayton Drew in the role of John Carter.

Let it not be said that women have never responded to the call of the wild. In Pat Murphy's *Wild Angel* (2000), Sarah McKensie is orphaned in the California gold rush country and adopted by a she-wolf that has just lost her pup. The parallel between Kala and the she-wolf Wauna is deliberate: Murphy borrows many plot points from *Tarzan of the Apes* in the story of her feral child. Sarah isn't the vicious trickster that Tarzan could sometimes be, but she still disports herself well as a mighty hunter and fighter. One element of Burroughs' writing that Murphy wished to emulate was his streamlined, straight-ahead plotting. Given the number of bloated fantasy epics taking up shelf space these days I wish more authors would follow Murphy's lead.

Alan Dean Foster's *Luana* (1974) is another of those resilient babies that survives an airplane crash and grows up to be queen of the jungle. At least, I think that's what the book is about. I haven't seen a copy of this epic in thirty years and the fog of time has removed any memory of my having actually read it. The only thing I recall is Frank Frazetta's luscious cover illustration, which was about as Burroughs-like as one could wish.

Not wanting to speak about *Luana* in complete ignorance, I asked Mr. Foster if he could jog my memory and he graciously complied. *Luana*, as it turns out, was the novelization of a bargain-basement Italian adventure film. The American distributors gave the movie a bigger push than it deserved, hiring Frazetta to do the promotional art and convincing Ballantine to issue a novel to sow yet more interest. As explained by Foster:

> The actual film was so hopeless that what I did . . . was end up "nov-elizing" the Frazetta cover. . . . More of my inspiration came from memories of Irish McCalla on TV, as Sheena, Queen of the Jungle. Irish was the first member of the opposite sex whom I, in my burgeon-ing adolescent haze, realized might be good for something besides serving as a subject for new and inventive insults.

> The capper to the whole *Luana* business was that after the book came out, a representative from Disney Studios contacted Judy-Lynn del Rey to inquire if the film rights to the book might be available. He hadn't noticed that it was a novelization of an existing release. Broke both our hearts.[7]

A perverse sense of curiosity will keep me searching for a video release of *Luana*. Oh, and a copy of the book too, I suppose. I'd hate to think Mr. Foster went to all that work, and all I or anyone remembers is the Frank Frazetta cover.

For the small-fry set there is Babette Cole's picture book *Tarzanna!* (1991), a story of a female you-know-who and her adventures in jungle and city. Tarzanna meets boy-explorer Gerald (why Gerald's parents allowed him to explore Africa alone is not explained), Gerald convinces Tarzanna to come to civilization, and hijinks ensue. The obvious source of Tarzanna's moniker makes one wonder why the Burroughs lawyers didn't descend like a herd of pachyderms upon the writer and the publisher of this otherwise innocuous tale.

It took the better part of a century for someone to address the fact that all the innumerable jungle lords swinging through the world's far places are of a uniformly pale complexion. Such is not the case with Charles Saunders' warrior-hero Imaro, who charged through a series of stories and novels beginning in 1974. Set in a fantastic prehistoric Africa akin to the mythical Hyborian Age of Robert E. Howard's Conan tales, Imaro was "specifically created as the brother who could kick Tarzan's ass."[8] Indeed, one of the drawbacks to the series is that the character is *too* powerful; Imaro can easily kick the ass of any man, god, or monster that crosses his path. Such is the fault with much heroic fantasy, but outweighing this is the vividness of Saunders' fantasy world. Culled from African history, culture, legend, and myth, the Imaro series is a unique and robust alternative to all the pseudo-medieval and pseudo-Nordic fantasy novels that glut the modern bookstore.

When DAW Books issued the first Imaro novel in 1981 (simply titled *Imaro*, a reworking of several previously published stories), it bore the cover blurb "The Epic Novel of a Black Tarzan." This was quickly changed to "The Epic Novel of a Jungle Hero," not as a result of sensitivity training classes at the publishing house but because Edgar Rice Burroughs, Inc., threatened to sue for trademark infringement. The resultant delay meant the book received spotty distribution, and while two more Imaro novels would appear (the last in 1985), the character never caught on except with a small coterie of devotees. But by this time the fantasy market had changed, with a shift away from the styles of Howard and Burroughs to one dominated by Tolkien clones. Two more Imaro novels remain unpublished.

Saunders' creative reaction to Burroughs was a positive response to the otherwise thorny issue of racism in the Tarzan books. "It is only natural," writes Catherine Jurca, "that Edgar Rice Burroughs' *Tarzan of the Apes*, a novel that so openly endorses imperialist assumptions and ideology, has become a bete noir of postcolonial studies."[9] Indeed, the number of studies that take on the racial assumptions behind the Tarzan stories is ever growing. Other critics have not been as restrained as Jurca. "Since 1912, one Racist medium after another has asserted 'white supremacy' and assaulted 'Black Counciousness' [sic] from Edgar Rice Burroughs [sic] (ERB) first Lord of the Apes story," N. Khalfani Mwamba passionately states. "[Tarzan] is Racist, Sexist, Adventurist, and Individualist. Thus, the massive Tarzan media march will thrive in America for exactly as long as Racism, Sexism, Adventurism and Greedy Individualism thrive in America."[10] So much for stories meant as mere entertainment. And so much for what Richard Lupoff identified as "an unfortunate touch of racism" in *Tarzan of the Apes*.

When attempting to draw from Burroughs' fiction his personal views on race, people either praise his tolerance or condemn his bigotry, often using the same examples. To Burroughs defenders, the Waziri are portrayed in a noble and heroic manner; they willingly accept a man of a different race into their tribe. To his detractors, the Waziri are a tribe of superstitious savages upon which Tarzan asserts his dominance. The racial problem is deeper than one of offensive words or stereotypes. Richard Lupoff noted that the 1963–64 Ballantine Tarzan reprints (and all subsequent printings) "are expurgated of racial slurs; in fact the editing goes to lengths to remove racial references other than slurs." So what is left to be offensive? The following is a sequence from chapter 5 of a Grosset & Dunlap reprint of *Tarzan, Lord of the Jungle* (available through the early 1960s), including wording that is anathema in modern discourse. The thoroughly unpleasant Stimbol explains to his young partner, Blake, how best to deal with the natives:

> "Now let me handle the niggers—that's more in my line—and I'll see that you get a square deal and a good, safe bunch, and I'll put the fear of God into 'em so they won't dare be anything but loyal to you" . . .
> "Don't be a fool, Stimbol," said Blake. . . . "These black men are human beings. In some respects they are extremely sensitive human beings, and in many ways they are like children. You strike them, you curse them, you insult them and they will fear you and hate you."

Burroughs is portraying Stimbol as a very bad man, who by the novel's denouement will achieve the grisly end he so richly deserves. However, such literary subtleties are no longer enough to justify keeping "the N-word" in what is supposed to be escapist fiction, and so Ballantine replaced it with "men" while leaving everything else intact. What remains, though, is an attitude not easily erased, where black Africans are recognized as human beings but condescendingly considered to be "like children." Chances are that Burroughs didn't even think about this blanket characterization as he was writing the book. But the underlying assumption, whether made consciously or not, is that the adult—that is, the white Western male—knows what is best for the simple African native, who lacks the brain power to decide for himself.

Through Tarzan, Burroughs is considered the poster child for Western ignorance of Africa, if not the source of that ignorance. Charles Saunders feels that Burroughs' "racially incorrect Tarzan novels defined Africa's place in the world for most of this century."[11] Actually, the image of the jungle-clad, cannibal-filled, unchanging, and unchangeable Dark Continent was a literary tradition of ancient lineage long before Burroughs took up a pen. A thorough exploration of this mythic Africa is provided by Dorothy Hammond and Alta Jablow in their 1970 study *The Africa That Never Was: Four Centuries of British Writing About Africa.* (The book is dedicated to Lord Greystoke, which is either a wonderful joke or wonderful coincidence.) Given that Burroughs' supposedly reliable sources on the "real" Africa, from Henry Morton Stanley to Theodore Roosevelt, likewise perpetuated the myth, it is unlikely Burroughs could have produced anything other than what he did. That defense, however, does not wash with those who consider Tarzan symbolic of white oppression of blacks worldwide.

The standard defensive line is that Burroughs utilized the stereotypes and language of his day and that we should not expect an author writing within a different worldview to meet the standards of our supposedly more enlightened era. Critics would say that the continuous reprinting of the Tarzan books only perpetuates these stereotypes upon new generations of readers, particularly upon the young who cannot be expected to understand the historical context of the Tarzan tales—and everything else Burroughs wrote, for that matter. Such a worldview (according to one) represents "the all-consuming nasty racism" that is part and parcel of the Tarzan mythos. The "gross misjudgment" of assuming black Africans as savages "was built into the Tarzan legend, as if he was some kind of wild-child caucasian Christ plunked down to save the people of 'darkest Africa.' . . . [T]hat's pathetic and nothing but an excuse for the perpetuation of colonization, economic rape and cultural genocide."[12]

So, do the Tarzan books reflect one individual's nurtured racist attitude, or is this the inevitable outlook of a white middle-class male born ten years after the Civil War? The various critics quoted throughout would say these are one and the same. But I am not convinced that Burroughs was being deliberately hateful. He would probably have been flabbergasted by the rape and genocide quote. Steven Barnes, one of the few (if only) male African American writers working regularly in the science fiction field today, feels that Burroughs probably never thought black people would read his books; why would he need to portray black Africans as anything other than props to be moved about to serve the plot? I suspect Burroughs' editors shared the same unenlightened viewpoint, and judging by letters that appeared in the pulp magazines praising Burroughs, his initial readership did as well. (In spite of feeling personally offended by such stereotyping, Barnes considers Burroughs a great writer; he even considers the Tarzan books his favorite series.[13])

One needn't stick to Tarzan to find passages that raise an eyebrow. Burroughs uses racial conflict and contrast in ways that are just not acceptable any more. Is *Gods of Mars* a critique of racial bigotry with its reversal of races, or is Burroughs cheaply playing upon the white American fear that a violent black underclass (represented by the subterranean-dwelling First Born) will one day rise up to prey upon the oppressive white ruling class? Was Burroughs being progressive or insulting when in *Land of Terror* David Innes describes the black Ru-Vans as "fully as intelligent as any of the white race of Pellucidar that I had seen" and thinks that enslavement by the Ru-Vans was "a lesson in true democracy"? In *The Eternal Lover* Nu of the Neocene feels an affinity for "the black and half-naked natives" of the Greystoke estate, "whom the whites looked upon as so much their inferiors that they would not even eat at the same table with them." Yet Nu experiences love "just as normal white men have always loved. . . . His passion was not of the brute type of the inferior races."

The language Burroughs used strikes us today as racist, the "rhetoric of empire" that "render[s] indigenous peoples as mere fixtures of that landscape . . . and denie[s] the import of their own languages, laws, customs, mores, intellects, histories, and world-views," or so summarizes Matthew Frye Jacobson in his study on the era's literature.[14] It was, however, the only language Burroughs had to work with. Such words as "race," "primitive," "savage," and "barbarism" had fluid definitions in Burroughs' time, and often have multiple meanings in any one of Burroughs' novels. Phrases like "lower races" or "Negroid features" were part of everyday language for Burroughs, now anathema to us. Language changes over time, as do our attitudes toward it.

So what then do we do with poor Mr. Burroughs? Is it possible to edit Burroughs so that he becomes inoffensive? Is such a thing even desirable?

I would say no. Changing a few words still leaves the racial underpinnings intact, while continual chopping will get us to the point where Burroughs is no longer Burroughs. John Hollow summed up this solutionless problem eloquently when he wrote, "If we now know that Burroughs has all the faults of the pulps, including racism he shares with Poe and Haggard, and a sexism he shares with all adventure writers, then we really have grown in wisdom as in age. But we were not hopelessly wrong-headed when we were young—Burroughs did have a powerful and coherent imagination."[15] Burroughs is constantly rediscovered by young readers who are intelligent enough to reject his outdated racial assumptions while enjoying the story. The subject of racism in Burroughs will be discussed for quite some time. Despite all his best intentions, Burroughs turns out to be an intellectual challenge.

"A curious thing happened to Edgar Rice Burroughs on the way to oblivion," an unsympathetic book reviewer observed back in 1964. An author whose works "were long out of print and far out of vogue" had staged a surprising comeback—the Burroughs Boom, selling ten million paperbacks a year.[16] The curious thing that happened to Edgar Rice Burroughs on the way to the twenty-first century is his disappearance as a paperback regular. Changes in publishing practices, reading tastes, and social mores makes Burroughs now seem a relic of a former time—again.

All is not gloom and doom, however. Edgar Rice Burroughs *still* lives, and he has survived nearly a century because every generation discovers a unique and entertaining voice speaking from beneath the crackpot science, the antique moral code, and even the ethnic stereotyping. The other curious thing about Burroughs is that when he fades from one market he pops up again in another. As the copyrights permanently lapse on his early books, enterprising publishers have been reprinting Burroughs' high-profile titles as literary classics. Not having to pay royalties to an author or his descendents makes such works appealing to publishers from a financial angle. Thus is revealed the secret to achieving literary immortality.

Tarzan of the Apes has naturally received the most attention, with at least half a dozen editions on the market, most in high-quality trade paperback format. The University of Nebraska Press was first to choose a non-Tarzan title, launching a science fiction reprint series with *The Land that Time Forgot* in 1999. Nine volumes in trade format have appeared so far, representing fourteen volumes of the old Ace and Ballantine paperbacks. The prestigious Modern Library has followed up their edition of *Tarzan of the Apes* with two science fiction titles; perhaps more will follow.

The print runs on these titles are negligible compared to those during the Burroughs Boom, perhaps reaching only 5 percent of the Ace and Ballantine runs. But these low numbers are balanced by several positives. Bookstores keep on hand trade editions far longer than the one or two months in which mass market paperbacks must prove themselves. Because they are more durable, trade editions appeal to libraries, exposing Burroughs to even more potential readers. Trades also appeal to the snob factor in readers who wish to rise above the crassness of the gaudy pocket-sized paperback. A side benefit for the science fiction and fantasy field is that the trade format has proven an easy and lucrative way for once-standard backlist authors to be given new life, with such stalwarts as Robert A. Heinlein, A. E. Van Vogt, and Edward E. "Doc" Smith being given the high-end treatment.

Are we seeing an echo of the Burroughs Boom? It is still too early to tell if this trend will continue or if further Burroughs titles will appear as more of his works slip into the public domain. A new generation of editors who grew up on Burroughs are introducing the Master of Adventure to a generation unfamiliar with him. We shall see how this plays out.

Despite multiple editions of *Tarzan of the Apes*, the remaining Tarzan novels have as yet to appeal to mainstream publishers as potential classics. Perhaps we are seeing an inevitable weeding out of a prolific author's work, as Burroughs' better-known titles are adopted into the mass of writing known as world literature. Jules Verne wrote as many titles as Burroughs; he is now best known for a half dozen. Rider Haggard's extensive output has been reduced to multiple editions of *She* and *King Solomon's Mines*. Booth Tarkington is now familiar only through *The Magnificent Ambersons* and *Penrod*, and P. C. Wren through *Beau Geste*. Burroughs should at least see *Return of Tarzan* and maybe a few more Tarzan titles given the classic treatment. The Burroughs fan in me laments the bulk of his output disappearing from popular editions; then again, no one's life will be diminished if *Tarzan and the Forbidden City* is not readily available.

This does not mean that all Burroughs besides half a dozen classics will disappear. Beyond the traditional publishing venues, print-on-demand technology has allowed other publishers to dip into the Burroughs well and issue small print runs at minimal cost. Such publishers as Wildside Press, Quiet Vision, and the Burroughs-specific ERBville Press will keep the lesser titles around (as they are doing for Haggard and Verne as well). Their lower overhead costs make it feasible for them to turn a profit on works that have less demand. Audio and electronic editions are growing in number, and a burgeoning supply of titles is available for free on the Internet. A large chunk of Burroughs' work is more widely available in a wider variety of formats than at any time in history—in everything but the mass market paperback, the form that fueled the first Burroughs Boom. The current boom is more like a gentle swell than the prior tsunami, but presently more Burroughs titles are in print than have been in a decade.

I have not devoted much space to the Internet, except in passing, because of its ephemeral nature (a Web page there one day can be gone the next) and because it is still unclear what effect this technology will have on Burroughs' popularity. (The Web did not bring about the death of the book, for example, as many predicted.) A cursory Internet search reveals innumerable Web pages devoted to Burroughs. (The biggest is "ERB-zine" run by Canadian fan Bill Hillman at www.erbzine.com.) One can download novels, fan written pastiches, and articles of both a fannish and scholarly nature; join discussion lists involving people from all over the world; invade chat rooms; and view every cover of every edition of every Burroughs book ever printed. Furthermore, one can find more pulp art, book art, and comic art than could possibly fit in even the most diligent collector's collection. A quick search revealed that I could even order an electronic version of Charles Nuetzel's *Swordsmen of Vistar*. Imagine my surprise.

But are new readers stumbling across Burroughs via the Internet or on-line bookstores and giving his stories a go? Judging by the reader reviews on the largest such retailer, amazon.com, some are finding Burroughs without the aid of traditional "bricks and mortar" stores, and new Burroughs readers do pop up on the two main Burroughs Internet mailing lists from time to time. (Jim Thompson runs the Edgar Rice Burroughs Chain of Friendship List—or ERBCOF-L for short—while Bruce Bozarth maintains the ERBlist. Addresses change on some of the Internet sites listed; a search on the key words should get you to the ones that are in operation.) This chapter in Burroughs' ongoing tale is still being written, and an analysis will have to wait until the *next* revision of Richard Lupoff's book.

Two or three generations ago, long before television or video games, boys (and not a few girls) were falling out of trees trying to imitate Tarzan. In 1999 the Disney animated film reintroduced the character and his distinctive yell to a new generation, although these young moviegoers expressed little interest in seeking out the original books. It has often been lamented that as the number of entertainment diversions have increased, fewer young people look to reading for pleasure. But everything old is new again (thank goodness!), as J. K. Rowling's phenomenally successful children's novels detailing the adventures of boy wizard Harry Potter have been credited with reintroducing untold millions to the low-tech pleasures of reading.

Cynical wags say that Pottermania is being fueled by adults, and while it seems as if every adult commuter on my morning ferry is reading a Harry Potter novel, it is only because their children lent them the books. Gosh, children and their parents sharing books. Imagine the possibilities if those kids should ask "What did you read when you were my age?" It is not too much of a jump from the world of Harry Potter to Burroughs' fantastic worlds, particularly for young boys who might feel that Harry Potter is beneath them. At least one publisher, the venerable Dover Books, has issued *Tarzan of the Apes* and *At the Earth's Core* as "juvenile classics" (perhaps not the best choice of words) to entice children of the Potter generation—or their parents. The appeal of the exotic and the marvelous has not diminished over the years. Plus, both Harry Potter and Tarzan sport similar forehead scars, which is a good selling point.

What it is that children, let alone adults, will take up and read is one of the world's great mysteries. Hordes of psychologists have been trundled out to explain Harry Potter's popularity, just as they were to explain Tarzan's. A great deal of ink has recently been spilt over the revival of another dead white male, imperialist G. A. Henty (1832–1902). Dutiful-son-of-the-empire Henty cranked out dozens of tales of teenage boys proving their bravery in distant corners of the empire in such titles as *With Clive in India* and *With Kitchener at Khartoum*. With World War II and the effective end of the British Empire, Henty and his worldview were relegated to the dustbin of history. Yet a modest Henty revival has been fueled by the home-school movement, its members seeing in Henty an antidote to the dumbing down of school textbooks and the preachy moral relativism that suffuses modern children's literature. With his meticulous historical scenes and stalwart teenage protagonists, Henty has proven invaluable in getting boys, always the least willing to crack open a book, interested in both reading and history.

Like Burroughs, Henty carries with him into the twenty-first century some excess cultural baggage, a "literary treatment of the exotic locale that was patronizing at best and appallingly racist at worst," as one chronicler of the revival observed.[17] One hopes home schoolers use such shortcomings as a springboard for further discussion. (But then, the publisher Preston/Speed posted this comment on its readers review webpage: "The fate of populations abandoned by civilized overlords is one that our previous generation might have considered before pressing the Atlantic nations of Europe out of black Africa.") But most are willing to see beyond these shortcomings, viewing Henty as a writer who promotes (in the words of Preston/Speed) "lessons of honesty, pluck, strength of character and religious tolerance."

Now one can argue the last point (and I'm not sure if any Burroughs hero can be described as "plucky"), but the underlying lessons seen in Henty are those that Richard Lupoff has praised as being present in the fiction of Edgar Rice Burroughs, a moral underpinning that seems fated to be lost and discovered again through the generations. And while you may not get a lesson in the facts of science or history from reading Burroughs, you might receive the inspiration to seek the facts for yourself, as such Burroughs readers as astronomer Carl Sagan, paleontologist Philip Currie, and primatologist Jane Goodall have done. An education can be found in the most unlikely of places. Henty inspired a number of statesmen and historians during his initial reign of popularity. It will be interesting to see who Harry Potter will inspire.

So, if G. A. Henty—or muttonchops or bell-bottom pants, for that matter—can come back into style, I hold out high hopes that Edgar Rice Burroughs will experience repeated bouts of popularity and condemnation. Then someone will be called upon to revise this book yet again, to track down more authors inspired by Burroughs and those who may have inspired him as well.

For instance, rifling through a used bookstore I came across a copy of *The Silver Fang* (1930) by George F. Worts (once famous for his "Peter the Brazen" adventure stories). Malabar MacKenzie is the bored son of a Wall Street pirate who discovers that his grandfather was the real deal in the South China Seas and was known as the Silver Fang. Disgusted by his father's piratical ways, the younger MacKenzie travels to the Orient in response to his ancestor's "pirate blood." While I can't say that Burroughs read this novel, it is well positioned in time to have provided the inspiration, even if only through that one phrase, for Burroughs' story "Pirate Blood." And the publisher of *The Silver Fang*? Why, A. C. McClurg, of course. Ah, coincidence, coincidence . . .

Even though Burroughs-inspired sword-and-planet novels are no longer being written, many a science fiction author makes passing (and often affectionate) references to Burroughs. The lengthy list of nods and winks includes Robert Heinlein's *Number of the Beast* (1980), Terry Bisson's *Voyage to the Red Planet* (1990), Kevin Anderson's self-explanatory anthology *War of the Worlds: Global Dispatches* (1996), and Robert Charles Wilson's *Darwinia* (1998). Max Allan Collins even got Burroughs into the thick of things in *The Pearl Harbor Murders* (2001), wherein our intrepid author turns detective in the shadow of the Japanese attack. My wife, Heather, discovered multiple references to Tarzan books and the then-new Elmo Lincoln movie in Christopher Morley's *Haunted Bookshop* (1919). Alas, Morley is anything but affectionate. But this shows that Burroughs hides in some interesting corners of literature. Happy hunting!

If you ever get to a Burroughs convention and you see a gathering of silver-haired fans sitting about the hotel lobby, toss out a comment on the Burroughs-Kline feud. Then sit back and watch the fireworks. To fans, old arguments never die, nor do they fade away. Eventually the conversation will turn to Edwin Lester Arnold. Poor Edwin. But at least he has achieved a level of literary immortality, with *Phra the Phoenician* and *Lieut. Gullivar Jones* being revived whenever Burroughs gets reprinted. And you can bet that during the argument Richard Lupoff will be dragged in for another round. After forty years he can hold his own. Not only does Burroughs still live, but Lupoff does as well. Prepare yourself for forty more years of adventure . . .

NOTES

1. See Bessie Louise Pierce, *A History of Chicago*, vol. 3, *The Rise of the Modern City, 1871–1893* (New York: Alfred A. Knopf, 1957), 169, and Helen Lefkowitz Horowitz, *Culture and the City: Cultural Philanthropy in Chicago from the 1880s to 1917* (Lexington: University Press of Kentucky, 1976), 32, 121–22. I uncovered this information while researching my master's thesis, "Glimpses of a World Past: Edgar Rice Burroughs, the West and the Birth of an American Writer," Utah State University, 1987. (Yes, my thesis advisers took me seriously.)

2. As if on cue, just as I was completing this chapter, fan writer Dale Broadhurst reappeared with an Internet article detailing the original Lupoffian brouhaha, the fan response, and attitudes toward Edwin Lester Arnold today. See "Lupoff of Mars," www.erbzine.com/mag11/1108.html.

3. This inventory list is part of the Burroughs Memorial Collection at the University of Louisville library. A personal search of Burroughs' library (or the scattered remnants thereof) did not turn up the copy of poor *Phra*. Like many another fanzine writer, I was unable to resist the allure of commenting upon Lupoff's Theory; see "Theories Come and Theories Go—Literary Theories," *Burroughs Bulletin*, n.s., 32 (Fall 1997): 10–14. Oh, the University of Nebraska Press has reissued *Lieut. Gullivar Jones* with yet *another* introduction by Lupoff. Arnold still lives!

4. The argument against letting other authors write new Tarzan tales is the worry that Burroughs' originals will disappear, as happened with Robert E. Howard's Conan stories. The effect of L. Sprague de Camp's

efforts on expanding the Conan franchise is now much debated, as Howard became a victim of Conan's success. Dozens of Conan novels by diverse hands appeared in the 1980s and 1990s with nary a reference to Howard as the character's creator, while the original stories fell into limbo. Luckily the early years of the twenty-first century have witnessed a concerted effort to bring Howard back into print and reestablish him as the creator of Conan.

5. Will Murray, e-mail message to the author, May 8, 2003.

6. Thomas L. Wymer, "Philip José Farmer," in *Dictionary of Literary Biography*, vol. 8, *Twentieth-Century American Science Fiction Writers*, ed. David Cowart and Thomas L. Wymer (Detroit: Gale Research Company, 1981), 169–82.

7. Alan Dean Foster, e-mail message to the author, May 2, 2003.

8. This is according to a webzine interview with Charles Saunders at *www.scifidimensions.com*.May01/charlessaunders.htm.

9. Catherine Jurca, "Tarzan, Lord of the Suburbs," *Modern Language Quarterly* 57.3 (Sept. 1996): 479.

10. N. Khalfani Mwamba, "Why Do Tarzan Keep Tarzanin' Agin, an' Agin', an' Agin?" http:www.nbufront.org/html/X-PressYourself/TARZAN IN.html.

11. Charles R. Saunders, "Why Blacks Should Read (and Write) Science Fiction," in *Dark Matter: A Century of Speculative Fiction From the African Diaspora*, ed. Sheree R. Thomas (New York: Warner Books, 2000), 402.

12. Bruce Kirkland, "This Tarzan could get lost in his own jungle," review of the motion picture *Tarzan and the Lost City*, *Toronto Sun*, 27 April 1998, http://www.canoe.ca/JamMoviesReviewsT/tarzan_kirkland.html.

13. "Steven Barnes: White & Black," *Locus* 50 (March 2003), 84–86. Also a telephone interview with Mr. Barnes, 8 July 2003.

14. Matthew Frye Jacobson, *Barbarian Virtues: The United States Encounters Foreign Peoples at Home and Abroad, 1876–1917* (New York: Hill and Wang, 2000), 110.

15. John Hollow, "Rereading *Tarzan of the Apes*; Or, 'What Is It,' Lady Alice Whispered, 'A Man?'" *Dalhousie Review* 56 (Spring 1976), 92.

16. "Claptrap Classics," review of *A Princess of Mars* and *Fighting Man of Mars*, *Time*, 21 Aug. 1964, 88.

17. David Frum, "When Boys Were Boys," *The Weekly Standard*, 20 Oct. 1997, http://www.csus.edu/indiv/f/friedman/spring02/govt112/reading% 5Ch4%5Cboys.html.

A Checklist of Edgar Rice Burroughs' Books

(This list contains seventy-five books published through 2001. Alternate, partial, or omnibus titles are omitted.)

1. *Tarzan of the Apes*, 1914, McClurg.
2. *The Return of Tarzan*, 1915, McClurg.
3. *The Beasts of Tarzan*, 1916, McClurg.
4. *The Son of Tarzan*, 1917, McClurg.
5. *A Princess of Mars*, 1917, McClurg.
6. *Tarzan and the Jewels of Opar*, 1918, McClurg.
7. *The Gods of Mars*, 1918, McClurg.
8. *Jungle Tales of Tarzan*, 1919, McClurg.
9. *The Warlord of Mars*, 1919, McClurg.
10. *Tarzan the Untamed*, 1920, McClurg.
11. *Thuvia, Maid of Mars*, 1920, McClurg.
12. *Tarzan the Terrible*, 1921, McClurg.
13. *The Mucker*, 1921, McClurg.
14. *At the Earth's Core*, 1922, McClurg.
15. *The Chessmen of Mars*, 1922, McClurg.
16. *Tarzan and the Golden Lion*, 1923, McClurg.
17. *Pellucidar*, 1923, McClurg.
18. *The Girl from Hollywood*, 1923, Macaulay.
19. *The Land that Time Forgot*, 1924, McClurg.
20. *Tarzan and the Ant Men*, 1924, McClurg.
21. *The Cave Girl*, 1925, McClurg.
22. *The Bandit of Hell's Bend*, 1925, McClurg.
23. *The Eternal Lover*, 1925, McClurg.
24. *The Moon Maid*, 1926, McClurg.
25. *The Mad King*, 1926, McClurg.

26. *The Outlaw of Torn*, 1927, McClurg

27. *The War Chief*, 1927, McClurg.

28. *The Tarzan Twins*, 1927, Volland.

29. *The Master Mind of Mars*, 1928, McClurg.

30. *Tarzan, Lord of the Jungle*, 1928, McClurg.

31. *The Monster Men*, 1929, McClurg.

32. *Tarzan and the Lost Empire*, 1929, Metropolitan.

33. *Tanar of Pellucidar*, 1929, Metropolitan.

34. *Tarzan at the Earth's Core*, 1930, Metropolitan.

35. *A Fighting Man of Mars*, 1931, Metropolitan.

36. *Tarzan the Invincible*, 1931, Burroughs.

37. *Jungle Girl*, 1932, Burroughs.

38. *Tarzan Triumphant*, 1932, Burroughs.

39. *Apache Devil*, 1933, Burroughs.

40. *Tarzan and the City of Gold*, 1933, Burroughs.

41. *Pirates of Venus*, 1934, Burroughs.

42. *Tarzan and the Lion Man*, 1934, Burroughs.

43. *Lost on Venus*, 1935, Burroughs.

44. *Tarzan and the Leopard Men*, 1935, Burroughs.

45. *Swords of Mars*, 1936, Burroughs.

46. *Tarzan and the Tarzan Twins with Jad-bal-ja the Golden Lion*, 1936, Whitman.

47. *Tarzan's Quest*, 1936, Burroughs.

48. *The Oakdale Affair and the Rider*, 1937, Burroughs.

49. *Back to the Stone Age*, 1937, Burroughs.

50. *The Lad and the Lion*, 1938, Burroughs.

51. *Tarzan and the Forbidden City*, 1938, Burroughs.

52. *Carson of Venus*, 1939, Burroughs.

53. *Official Guide of the Tarzan Clans of America*, 1939, Tarzan Clans of America.

54. *Tarzan the Magnificent*, 1939, Burroughs.

55. *Synthetic Men of Mars*, 1940, Burroughs.

56. *The Deputy Sheriff of Comanche County*, 1940, Burroughs.

57. *Land of Terror*, 1944, Burroughs.

58. *Escape on Venus*, 1946, Burroughs.

59. *Tarzan and "The Foreign Legion,"* 1947, Burroughs.

60. *Llana of Gathol*, 1948, Burroughs.

61. *Beyond Thirty and The Maneater*, 1957, Science-Fiction & Fantasy Publications.

62. *The Girl from Farris's*, 1959, the Wilma Company.

63. *Savage Pellucidar*, 1963, Canaveral Press.
64. *Tales of Three Planets*, 1964, Canaveral Press.
65. *Tarzan and the Madman*, 1964, Canaveral Press.
66. *John Carter of Mars*, 1964, Canaveral Press.
67. *Tarzan and the Castaways*, 1965, Canaveral Press.
68. *The Efficiency Expert*, 1965, House of Greystoke.
69. *I Am a Barbarian*, 1967, Burroughs.
70. *The Wizard of Venus and Pirate Blood*, 1970, Ace Books.
71. *Tarzan: The Lost Adventure* (with Joe Lansdale), 1995, Dark Horse Comics.
72. *Minidoka 937th Earl of One Mile Series M*, 1998, Dark Horse Comics.
73. *Marcia of the Doorstep*, 1999, Donald M. Grant.
74. *You Lucky Girl!* 1999, Donald M. Grant.
75. *Forgotten Tales of Love and Murder*, 2001, Guidry & Adkins.

A List of Burroughs' Fanzines

The Burroughs Bulletin
The Gridley Wave
George T. McWhorter, editor
Rare Book Room; Ekstrom Library
University of Louisville
Louisville KY 40292

The Burroughs Newsbeat
James Van Hise, editor
57754 Onaga Trail
Yucca Valley CA 92284

Edgar Rice Burroughs News Dateline
Mike Conran, editor
1990 Pine Grove Drive
Jenison MI 49428

ERBania
D. Peter Ogden, editor
8410 Lopez Drive
Tampa FL 33615

ERB Collector
Bill Ross, editor
7315 Livingston Road
Oxon Hill MD 20745

ERBzine
Bill Hillman, editor
www.erbzine.com

Pulp-Dom
Camille Cazedessus, editor
P.O. Box 2340
Pagosa Springs CO 81147

Fantastic Worlds of ERB
Frank Westwood, editor
77 Pembroke Road
Seven Kings, Ilford, Essex
IG3 8PQ
England

Acknowledgments

The author wishes to express his appreciation of the many persons whose efforts helped make possible the present volume. These include:

Messrs. Camille Cazedessus, Jr., Vernell Coriell, John Harwood, and David G. Van Arnam, Burroughs fans and scholars all, whose prior researches have been used shamelessly throughout.

Mr. Hulbert Burroughs and Edgar Rice Burroughs, Inc., for whose hospitality, assistance in locating Burroughs documents, access to and permission to publish the correspondence and other hitherto unpublished material in both the introduction and main text of this book, especial gratitude is due.

The Rev. Henry Hardy Heins, bibliographer, scholar, and friend, whose kindness and patience exceed even his almost unbelievable knowledge.

Messrs. Alfonso Williamson, Reed Crandall, and Frank Frazetta, for the Burroughs illustrations in this book.

Finally, a question: If the editor edits everyone else's books, who edits the editor's book? And an answer: David Garfinkel. Thank you, Dave.

Richard A. Lupoff

The "with an essay by" author would like to thank the following individuals (in impersonal alphabetical order) for providing assistance, needed information, or simply serving as a sounding board: Steven Barnes, Frank X. Blisard, Danton Burroughs, Alan Dean Foster, Scott Tracy Griffin, Scotty Henderson, John Eric Holmes, J. G. Huckenpöhler, Will Murray, and James Van Hise.

Oh, and Richard Lupoff for asking.

And whoever stocked the book section of Towers Department Store in Mississauga, Ontario, back in June of 1973.

Phillip R. Burger

Bibliography

Akers, Alan Burt [Kenneth Bulmer]. *Transit to Scorpio*. New York: DAW Books, 1972.

Aldiss, Brian W. *Billion Year Spree: The True History of Science Fiction*. New York: Schocken Books, 1974.

Altrocchi, Rudolph. *Sleuthing in the Stacks*. Cambridge: Harvard University Press, 1944.

Anderson, Kevin J., ed. *War of the Worlds: Global Dispatches*. New York: Bantam Books, 1996.

Arnold, Edwin Lester. *Lepidus the Centurion*. New York: T. Y. Crowell, 1901.

———. *Lieut. Gullivar Jones: His Vacation*. London: S. C. Brown, Langham, 1905.

———. *The Story of Ulla*. London: Longmans, Green, 1895.

———. *The Wonderful Adventures of Phra the Phoenician*. New York: Harper and Brothers, 1890.

Arnold, Sir Edwin. *The Book of Good Counsels*. London: Smith, Elder and Co., 1893.

———. *The Voyage of Ithobal*. London: G. W. Dillingham Company, 1901.

Ash, Fenton. *A Trip to Mars*. London: W. and R. Chambers, 1909.

Astor, John Jacob. *A Journey in Other Worlds; A Romance of the Future*. New York: D. Appleton and Company, 1894.

Atamian, Sarkis. *The Origin of Tarzan*. Anchorage: Publication Consultants, 1997.

Atheling, William, Jr. [James Blish] *The Issue at Hand; Studies in Contemporary Magazine Science Fiction*. Chicago: Advent Publishers, 1964.

Auel, Jean. *Clan of the Cave Bear*. New York: Crown, 1980.

Bailey, J. O. *Pilgrims through Space and Time: Trends and Patterns in Scientific and Utopian Fiction*. New York: Argus Books, Inc., 1947.

Bangs, John Kendrick. *The Enchanted Typewriter*. New York: Harper and Brothers, 1899.

————. *A Houseboat on the Styx; Being Some Account of the Diverse Doings of the Associated Shades*. New York: Harper and Brothers, 1895.

————. *Mr. Munchausen, Being a True Account of Some of the Recent Adventures beyond the Styx*. Boston: Noyes, Platt and Company, 1901.

Baum, L. Frank. *The Wonderful Wizard of Oz*. Chicago: George M. Hill, 1900.

Bayliss, A. E. M., and J. C. Bayliss, eds. *Science in Fiction*. London: University of London, 1957.

Beale, Charles Willing. *The Secret of the Earth*. London: F. T. Neely, 1899.

Benet, William Rose. *The Reader's Encyclopedia*. New York: T. Y. Crowell Company, 1965.

Benoit, Pierre. *Atlantida*. London: Hutchinson, 1920.

Bernard, Raymond. *The Hollow Earth*. New York: Fieldcrest Publishing Company, 1964.

Birch, A. G. *The Moon Terror*. Indianapolis: Popular Fiction Publishing Company, 1927

Bisson, Terry. *Voyage to the Red Planet*. New York: Morrow, 1990.

Bleiler, Everett F. *The Checklist of Fantastic Literature*. Chicago: Shasta Publishers, 1948.

Blodgett, Mabel Fuller. *At the Queen's Mercy*. Boston: Lamson, Wolffe and Company, 1897.

Brackett, Leigh, ed. *The Best of Planet Stories*. New York: Ballantine Books, 1975.

————. *The Ginger Star*. New York: Ballantine Books, 1974.

————. *People of the Talisman and the Secret of Sinharat*. New York: Ace Books, 1964.

————. *The Sword of Rhiannon*. New York: Ace Books, 1953.

Bradshaw, William R. *Goddess of Atvatabar*. New York: J. F. Douthitt, 1891.

Bretnor, Reginald, ed. *Modern Science Fiction*. New York: Coward-McCann, 1953.

Brinkley, William. *Don't Go near the Water*. New York: New American Library, 1956.

Brown, Frederic. *The Lights in the Sky Are Stars*. New York: Dutton, 1953.

Browne, Howard. *Return of Tharn*. Providence RI: Grandon Company, 1956.

————. *Warrior of the Dawn*. Chicago: Reilly and Lee, 1943.

Burroughs, John Coleman. *Treasure of the Black Falcon*. New York: Ballantine Books, 1967.

Carter, Lin. *Black Legion of Callisto*. New York: Dell Books, 1972.

———. *Jandar of Callisto*. New York: Dell Books, 1972.

———. *Journey to the Underground World*. New York: DAW Books, 1979.

———. *Lankar of Callisto*. New York: Dell Books, 1975.

———. *The Man Who Loved Mars*. New York: Fawcett Publications, 1973.

———. *Sky Pirates of Callisto*. New York: Dell Books, 1973.

———. *Thongor of Lemuria*. New York: Ace Books, 1966.

———. *Tolkien: A Look Behind "The Lord of the Rings"*. New York: Ballantine Books, 1969.

———. *The Valley Where Time Stood Still*. New York: Doubleday Books, 1974.

———. *Under the Green Star*. New York: DAW Books, 1972.

———. *The Wizard of Lemuria*. New York: Ace Books, 1965.

Chandler, A. Bertram. *The Alternate Martians*. New York: Ace Books, 1965.

Chester, William L. *Hawk of the Wilderness*. New York: Harper and Brothers, 1936.

———. *Kioga of the Unknown Land*. New York: DAW Books, 1978.

———. *Kioga of the Wilderness*. New York: DAW Books, 1976.

———. *One Against the Wilderness*. New York: DAW Books, 1977.

Clute, John, and Peter Nicholls. *Encyclopedia of Science Fiction*. New York: St. Martin's Press, 1993.

Coblentz, Stanton A. *Hidden World*. New York: Thomas Bouregy and Co., 1959.

Cohen, Morton N. *Rider Haggard*. London: Hutchinson, 1960.

Cole, Babette. *Tarzanna!* New York: G. P. Putnam's Sons, 1991.

Collins, Max Allan. *The Pearl Harbor Murders*. New York: Berkley Books, 2001.

Cory, Howard L. [Jack Jardine and Julie Anne Jardine]. *The Sword of Lankor*. New York: Ace Books, 1966.

Cottrell, Leonard. *Lost Cities*. New York: Rinehart, 1957.

Cowley, Robert H. *The Magic of Literature*. London: Blackie, 1947.

Crawford, Joseph H., James J. Donahue, and Donald M. Grant. *333: A Bibliography of the Science-Fantasy Novel*. Providence RI: Grandon Company, 1953.

Cromie, Robert. *A Plunge into Space*. London: F. Warne, 1891.

Davenport, Basil. *Inquiry into Science Fiction*. New York: Longmans, Green, 1955.

Day, Bradford M. *The Supplemental Checklist of Fantastic Literature*. Denver NY: Science-Fiction and Fantasy Publications, 1963.

de Camp, L. Sprague. *Lost Continents*. New York: Gnome Press, 1954.

———. *The Queen of Zamba*. New York: Ace Books, 1982.

———. *Science-Fiction Handbook*. New York: McGraw-Hill, 1953.

———. *The Search for Zei and the Hand of Zei*. New York: Ace Books, 1963.

Douglass, Ellsworth. *Pharoah's Broker*. London: C. Pearson, 1899.

Doyle, Arthur Conan. *The Lost World*. London: Hodder and Stoughton, 1912.

Edson, J. T. *Bunduki*. New York: DAW Books, 1975.

Elliot, George P. *A Piece of Lettuce*. New York: Random House, 1964.

Emerson, Willis George. *The Smoky God*. New York: Fieldcrest Publishing Company, 1964.

Eney, Dick, ed. *The Proceedings; Discon*. Chicago: Advent Publishers, 1965.

England, George Allan. *Cursed*. Boston: Small, Maynard and Company, 1919.

———. *Darkness and Dawn*. Boston: Small, Maynard and Company, 1914.

———. *The Flying Legion*. Chicago: A. C. McClurg and Company, 1920.

Eshbach, Lloyd Arthur, ed. *Of Worlds Beyond*. Reading PA: Fantasy Press, 1947.

Farley, Ralph Milne [Roger Sherman Hoar]. *The Hidden Universe*. Los Angeles: Fantasy Publishing Company, 1950.

———. *The Radio Beasts*. New York: Ace Books, 1964.

———. *The Radio Man*. Los Angeles: Fantasy Publishing Company, 1948.

———. *The Radio Planet*. New York: Ace Books, 1964.

Farmer, Philip José. *Adventures of the Peerless Peer*. Boulder CO: Aspen Press, 1974.

———. *Dark Heart of Time*. New York: Del Rey Books, 1999.

———. *A Feast Unknown*. North Hollywood CA: Essex House, 1969.

———. *Flight to Opar*. New York: DAW Books, 1976.

———. *The Green Odyssey*. New York: Ballantine Books, 1957.

———. *Hadon of Ancient Opar*. New York: DAW Books, 1974.

———. *Lord of the Trees*. New York: Ace Books, 1970.

———. *Lord Tyger*. New York: Doubleday and Company, Inc., 1970.

———. *Tarzan Alive*. New York: Doubleday and Company, 1972.

Fearn, John Russell. *Anjani the Mighty*. New York: Gryphon Books, 1998.

———. *Emperor of Mars*. New York: Gryphon Books, 1995.

———. *Gold of Akada*. New York: Gryphon Books, 1998.

Fenton, Robert W. *The Big Swingers*. Englewood Cliffs NJ: Prentice-Hall, Inc., 1967.

Foster, Alan Dean. *Luana*. New York: Ballantine Books, 1974.

Fox, Gardner F. *Thief of Llarn*. New York: Ace Books, 1966.

———. *Warrior of Llarn*. New York: Ace Books, 1964.

Gardner, Brian. *On to Kilimanjaro*. Philadelphia: Macrae Smith Company, 1963.

Gardner, Martin. *Fads and Fallacies in the Name of Science*. New York: Dover Publications, Inc., 1957.

Gardner, Maurice B. *Bantan of the Islands*. Boston: Meador, 1964.

Giesy, J. U. *Palos of the Dog Star Pack*. New York: Avalon Books, 1965.

Golding, William. *The Inheritors*. London: Faber and Faber, 1955.

Green, Roger Lancelyn. *Into Other Worlds; Space-flight in Fiction, from Lucian to Lewis*. London: Abelard-Schuman, 1958.

Greg, Percy. *Across the Zodiac: The Story of a Wrecked Record*. London: Trubner, 1880.

Haggard, H. Rider. *King Solomon's Mines*. London: Cassell and Company, 1885.

———. *Nada the Lily*. London: Longmans, Green, 1892.

———. *She; A History of Adventure*. London: Longmans, Green, 1886.

Haggard, H. Rider, and Andrew Lang. *The World's Desire*. London: Longmans, Green, 1890.

Hamilton, Edmond. *Kaldar, World of Antares*. Royal Oak MI: Haffner Press, 1998.

Hammond, Dorothy, and Alta Jablow, *The Africa That Never Was: Four Centuries of British Writing About Africa*. New York: Twayne Publishers, 1970.

Harris, John Beynon. *The Secret People*. New York: Lancer Books, 1964.

Harwood, John. *The Literature of Burroughsiana*. Baton Rouge LA: Camille Cazedessus Jr., 1963.

Heinlein, Robert A. *Glory Road*. New York: Putnam, 1963.

———. *Number of the Beast*. New York: Fawcett Colombine, 1980.

———. *Orphans of the Sky*. New York: New American Libary, 1964.

Heins, Henry Hardy. *A Golden Anniversary Bibliography of Edgar Rice Burroughs*. West Kingston RI: Donald M. Grant, Publisher, 2001.

Herzberg, Max J. *The Reader's Encyclopedia of American Literature*. New York: Crowell, 1962.

Holberg, Ludvig [Baron von Ludwig Lewis]. *Nils Klim's Journey under the Ground*. Boston, 1845.

Holmes, John Eric. *Mahars of Pellucidar*. New York: Ace Books, 1976.

Holtsmark, Erling B. *Tarzan and Tradition: Classical Myth in Popular Culture*. Westport CT: Greenwood Press, 1981.

Hope, Anthony [Hawkins, A. H.]. *The Prisoner of Zenda*. London: J. W. Arrowsmith, 1894.

———. *Rupert of Hentzau*. London: J. W. Arrowsmith, 1898.

Horowitz, Helen Lefkowitz. *Culture and the City: Cultural Philanthropy in Chicago from the 1880s to 1917*. Lexington: University Press of Kentucky, 1976.

Howard, Robert E. *Almuric*. New York: Ace Books, 1964.

———. *Conan the Conqueror*. New York: Gnome Press, 1950.

———. *Red Shadows*. West Kingston RI: Donald M. Grant, Publisher, 1968.

———. *Skull Face and Others*. Sauk City WI: Arkham House, 1946.

Jacobson, Matthew Frye. *Barbarian Virtues: The United States Encounters Foreign Peoples at Home and Abroad, 1876–1917*. New York: Hill and Wang, 2000.

Kipling, Rudyard. *The Jungle Book*. London: Macmillan, 1894.

———. *Something of Myself*. Garden City NY: Doubleday, Doran and Company, 1937.

Kline, Otis Adelbert. *The Call of the Savage*. New York: Edward J. Clode, 1937.

———. *Maza of the Moon*. Chicago: A. C. McClurg and Company, 1930.

———. *Tam, Son of the Tiger*. New York: Avalon Books, 1962.

———. *The Outlaws of Mars*. New York: Avalon Books, 1961.

———. *The Planet of Peril*. Chicago: A. C. McClurg and Co., 1929.

———. *Port of Peril*. Providence RI: Grandon Company, 1949.

———. *The Prince of Peril*. Chicago: A. C. McClurg and Co., 1930.

Knight, Damon. *In Search of Wonder*. Chicago: Advent Publishers, 1956.

Kreuzer, James R., and Lee Cogan. *Literature for Composition*. New York: Holt, Rinehart and Winston, 1976.

Leahy, John Martin. *Drome*. Los Angeles: Fantasy Publishing Company, 1952.

Leiber, Fritz. *The Wanderer*. New York: Ballantine Books, 1964.

———. *Swords Against Wizardry*. New York: Ace Books, 1968.

———. *Swords of Lankhmar*. New York: Ace Books, 1968.

———. *Tarzan and the Valley of Gold*. New York: Ballantine Books, 1966.

Leighton, Peter. *Moon Travellers*. London: Oldbourne, 1960.

Lloyd, John Uri. *Etidorhpa*. Cincinnati: Robert Clarke Company, 1895.

London, Jack. *The Star Rover*. New York: The Macmillan Company, 1915.

Lucian (of Samosata). *Selected Works*. Translated with an introduction and notes by Bryan P. Reardon. Indianapolis: Bobbs-Merrill, 1965.

Lupoff, Richard A. *Barsoom: Edgar Rice Burroughs and the Martian Vision*. Baltimore: Mirage Press, 1976.

Margolies, Leo, ed. *Three Times Infinity*. New York: Fawcett Books, 1958.

Marquis, Don. *Archy and Mehitabel*. New York: Doubleday, Page, 1927.

Martinson, Harry. *Aniara*. New York: Alfred A. Knopf, 1963.

McCaffrey, Anne. *Restoree*. New York: Ballantine Books, 1967.

Merritt, Abraham. *The Face in the Abyss*. New York: H. Liveright, Inc., 1931.

Moorcock, Michael. *The Jewel in the Skull*. New York: Lancer Books, 1967.

———. *Secret of the Runestaff (The Runestaff)*. New York: Lancer Books, 1969.

———. *The Sorcerer's Amulet (The Mad God's Amulet)*. New York: Lancer Books, 1968.

———. *The Stealer of Souls*. London: Neville Spearman, 1963.

———. *Stormbringer*. London: Herbert Jenkins, 1965.

———. *Sword of the Dawn*. New York: Lancer Books, 1968.

Moorcock, Michael [Edward P. Bradbury, pseud.]. *Barbarians of Mars (Masters of the Pit)*. New York: Lancer Books, 1965.

———. *Blades of Mars (Lord of the Spiders)*. New York: Lancer Books, 1965.

———. *Warriors of Mars (City of the Beast)*. New York: Lancer Books, 1965.

Moore, Wallace [Gerard F. Conway]. *The Blood Stones*. New York: Pyramid Books, 1975.

Morley, Christopher. *The Haunted Bookshop*. Garden City NY: Doubleday, Page, 1919.

Moskowitz, Sam. *Explorers of the Infinite*. Cleveland: World Publishing Company, 1963.

———. *Under the Moons of Mars: A History and Anthology of "The Scientific Romance" in the Munsey Magazines, 1912–1920*. New York: Holt, Rinehart and Winston, 1970.

Murphy, Pat. *Wild Angel*. New York: Tor Books, 2000.

Nicolson, Marjory Hope. *Voyages to the Moon*. New York: The Macmillan Company, 1948.

Norman, John [John Frederick Lange]. *Assassin of Gor*. New York: Ballantine Books, 1970.

———. *Outlaw of Gor*. New York: Ballantine Books, 1967.

———. *Tarnsman of Gor*. New York: Ballantine Books, 1966.

Norton, Andre. *Three Against the Witch World*. New York: Ace Books, 1965.

———. *Web of the Witch World*. New York: Ace Books, 1964.

———. *Witch World*. New York: Ace Books, 1963.

Obruchev, Vladimer. *Plutonia*. London: Lawrence and Wishart, 1957.

Offutt, Andrew J. *Ardor on Aros*. New York: Dell Books, 1973.

Orwell, George [Eric Blair]. *1984*. New York: New American Library, 1949.

Osbourne, Lloyd. *The Adventurer*. New York: D. Appleton and Co., 1907.

Pierce, Bessie Louise. *The Rise of the Modern City, 1871–1893*. Vol. 3, *A History of Chicago*. New York: Alfred A. Knopf, 1957.

Poe, Edgar Allan. *The Narrative of Arthur Gordon Pym*. New York: Harper and Brothers, 1838.

Poe, Edgar Allan, and Jules Verne. *The Mystery of Arthur Gordon Pym*. Westport CT: Associated Booksellers, 1960.

Pope, Gustavus W. *Journey to Mars*. New York: G. W. Dillingham, 1894.

Porges, Irwin. *Edgar Rice Burroughs: The Man Who Created Tarzan*. Provo UT: Brigham Young University Press, 1975.

Prentice, Harry. *Captured by Apes*. New York: A. L. Burt, Publishers, 1888.

———. *Captured by Zulus*. New York: A. L. Burt, Publishers, 1890.

Raspe, R. E. *Baron Munchausen*. Holicong PA: Wildside Press, 2003.

Resnick, Michael D. *Goddess of Ganymede*. New York: Paperback Library, Inc., 1968.

Rockwood, Roy [Edward Stratemeyer]. *Bomba the Jungle Boy*. New York: McLoughlin Brothers, 1926.

———. *Five Thousand Miles Underground*. New York: Cupples and Leon Company, 1908.

Roy, John Flint. *A Guide to Barsoom*. New York: Ballantine Books, 1976.

St. John, J. Allen. *The Face in the Pool, A Faerie Tale*. Chicago: A. C. McClurg and Co., 1905.

Salvatore, R. A. *Tarzan: The Epic Adventures*. New York: Del Rey Books, 1996.

Saunders, Charles R. *Imaro*. New York: DAW Books, 1981.

Schreiber, Herman, and Georg Schreiber. *Vanished Cities*. New York: Alfred A. Knopf, 1957.

Seaborn, Adam [John C. Symmes, attributed]. *Symzonia; a Voyage of Discovery*. New York: J. Seymour, 1820.

Shelley, Mary W. *Frankenstein; or The Modern Prometheus*. London: Printed for Lackington, Hughes, Harding, Mavor, and Jones, 1818.

Sirota, Mike. *Master of Boranga*. New York: Zebra Books, 1980.

———. *The Prisoner of Reglathium*. New York: Manor Books, Inc., 1978.

Starr, Kevin. *Material Dreams: Southern California through the 1920s*. New York: Oxford University Press, 1990.

Starrett, Vincent. *Born in a Bookshop*. Norman: University of Oklahoma Press, 1965.

Stilson, Arthur B. *Polaris of the Snows*. New York: Avalon Books, 1965.

Stockton, Frank R. *The Great Stone of Sardis*. New York: Harper and Brothers, 1898.

Stoneham, C. T. *Kaspa, the Lion Man*. London: Methuen and Co., 1933.

———. *The Lion's Way*. London: Hutchinson and Co., 1931.

Sue, Eugene. *The Wandering Jew*. New York: Harper and Brothers, 1846.

Swift, Jonathan. *Gulliver's Travels*. New York: J. W. Lovell, 1883.

Taliaferro, John. *Tarzan Forever: The Life of Edgar Rice Burroughs, Creator of Tarzan*. New York: Scribner, 1999.

Thomas, Sheree R., ed. *Dark Matter: A Century of Speculative Fiction from the African Diaspora*. New York: Warner Books, 2000.

Tolkien, J. R. R. *The Lord of the Rings*. London: George Allen and Unwin, 1956.

Van Arnam, David G. *The Reader's Guide to Barsoom and Amtor*. New York: Richard A. Lupoff, 1963.

Vance, Jack. *Big Planet*. New York: Ace Books, 1957.

———. *City of the Chasch*. New York: Ace Books, 1968.

———. *The Dirdir*. New York: Ace Books, 1969.

———. *The Pnume*. New York: Ace Books, 1970.

———. *Servants of the Wankh*. New York: Ace Books, 1969.

Verne, Jules. *An Antarctic Mystery*. Philadelphia: Lippincott, 1899.

———. *A Journey to the Center of the Earth*. New York: G. Routledge, 1887.

———. *Mysterious Island*. New York: Scribner, Armstrong and Co., 1875.

Wells, H. G. *The First Men in the Moon*. London: G. Newnes, 1901.

———. *The Island of Dr. Moreau*. London: W. Heinemann, 1896.

———. *The Time Machine*. London: W. Heinemann, 1895.

———. *The War of the Worlds*. London: Harper and Brothers, 1898.

Wells, Lester G. *Fictional Accounts of Trips to the Moon*. Syracuse NY: Syracuse University Library, 1962.

Werper, Barton [Peter T. Scott and Peggy O. Scott]. *Tarzan and the Abominable Snowmen*. Derby CT: New International Library, 1965.

———. *Tarzan and the Cave City*. Derby CT: New International Library, 1964.

———. *Tarzan and the Silver Globe*. Derby CT: New International Library, 1964.

———. *Tarzan and the Snake People*. Derby CT: New International Library, 1965.

———. *Tarzan and the Winged Invaders*. Derby CT: New International Library, 1965.

White, E. B., and Katherine S. White, eds. *A Subtreasury of American Humor*. New York: Coward-McCann, Inc., 1941.

Williams, Robert Moore. *Jongor Fights Back*. New York: Popular Library, 1970.

———. *Jongor of Lost Land*. New York: Popular Library, 1970.

———. *The Return of Jongor*. New York: Popular Library, 1970.

———. *Zanthar at the Edge of Never*. New York: Lancer Books, 1968.

————. *Zanthar of the Many Worlds*. New York: Lancer Books, 1967.

Wilson, Robert Charles. *Darwinia*. New York: Tor Books, 1998.

Wollheim, Donald A., ed. *Swordsmen in the Sky*. New York: Ace Books, 1964.

Worts, George F. *The Silver Fang*. Chicago: A. C. McClurg and Co., 1930.

Zeuschner, Robert. *Edgar Rice Burroughs: The Exhaustive Scholar's and Collector's Descriptive Bibliography of American Periodical, Hardcover, Paperback, and Reprint Editions*. Jefferson NC: McFarland and Company, Inc., 1996.

Index

Faust, Frederick, xxxix
Fearn, John Russell, 249–50
A Feast Unknown (Farmer), 247–48
The Feline Light and Power Company is Organized (Morgan), 84
Fenton, Robert W., 220, 238
feralism in literature and legend, 126–27, 145, 151, 247, 249–50
Fieldcrest (publisher), 199
The Fight for Balu (ERB), 148
A Fighting Man of Mars (ERB), 94–95
Filippo, Paul di, 222n3
first editions: Ekstrom Library archive of, 239–40; identifying, xix; posthumous, 3, 91–93; publishing sequence for, 177. *See also* publishing; reprint editions
The First Men in the Moon (Wells), 74
Five Thousand Miles Underground (Rockwood), 30–31, 184, 196, 210
Fleming, Ian, 172
foreign language translations, xix, 240
Forester, C. S., 164
Forgotten Tales of Love and Murder (ERB), 148n1, 229–30
"For the Fool's Mother" (ERB), 148n1
Foster, Alan Dean, 250–51
Foster, Hal, 147
Four Square (publisher), 219, 219–20
Fox, Gardner F., 194
framing techniques, story, 31–32, 55, 102, 138, 203–4. *See also* Burroughs (as book narrator/character)
Frazetta, Frank, 181, 187, 199, 226, 250
Freemasonry, 158, 173
Fuller, Edmund, 210
Future Science Fiction (magazine), 200

Gardner, Brian, 164
Gardner, Marshall B., 199
Gardner, Martin, 28–29
Gardner, Maurice B., 185–86
Gardner, Thomas S., 130
Garfinkel, David, xviii
Garis, Howard, 30
Gernsback, Hugo, 67, 83–84
The Ghostly Script (ERB), 115, 163
Gibney, Albert J., 109
Gibson, William, 222n3
Giesy, J.U., 192
The Girl from Farris's (ERB), 46, 65, 117, 145
The Girl from Hollywood (ERB), 56, 65–66, 117, 168, 206–7, 237
Girl of Pellucidar (ERB), 92
Gnome Press, 188
The Goddess of Atvatabar (Bradshaw), 30, 59
The God of Tarzan (ERB), 148
The Gods of Mars (ERB), 85; *All-Story* publication of, 13–14, 122; completion of, 27–28, 137; racism and, 254; on ERB recommended reading list, 206–7; story framing for, 8, 49–51
Godwin, Tom, 17
Golden Anniversary Bibliography (Heins), xxiiin1
A Golden Anniversary Bibliography of Edgar Rice Burroughs (Heins), xxix, 211
Golding, William, 46
The Gold of Akada (Fearn), 249–50
Goldsmith, Cele, 91
Goodall, Jane, 259
Gor series (Norman), 245–46
Goulart, Ron, 200
Grandon (publisher), 187
Grant, Donald (publisher), 188, 211, 229
Grant, Douglas, 172
The Great American Paperback (Lupoff), xviii

In the Bison Frontiers of Imagination series